PRAISE FOR JONATHAN WHITELAW

'Jonathan Whitelaw is a terrific writer'
Spain

'Furious, diabolical and delightful'
Anthony O'Neill

'A brilliant, sharply funny read'
Dan Hall

'A lot of devilish fun is in store for readers'
Stephen Booth

THE BINGO HALL DETECTIVES

JONATHAN WHITELAW

Harper
North

HarperNorth
Windmill Green,
Mount Street,
Manchester, M2 3NX

A division of
HarperCollins*Publishers*
1 London Bridge Street
London SE1 9GF

www.harpercollins.co.uk

HarperCollinsPublishers
1st Floor, Watermarque Building, Ringsend Road
Dublin 4, Ireland

First published by HarperNorth in 2022

1 3 5 7 9 10 8 6 4 2

Copyright © Jonathan Whitelaw 2022

Jonathan Whitelaw asserts the moral right to
be identified as the author of this work

A catalogue record for this book
is available from the British Library

PB ISBN: 978-0-00-851370-2

Printed and bound in the UK using 100%
renewable electricity at CPI Group (UK) Ltd

All rights reserved. No part of this publication may be
reproduced, stored in a retrieval system, or transmitted,
in any form or by any means, electronic, mechanical,
photocopying, recording or otherwise, without the prior
permission of the publishers.

MIX
Paper from
responsible sources
FSC™ C007454

This book is produced from independently certified FSC™ paper
to ensure responsible forest management.

For more information visit: www.harpercollins.co.uk/green

For Margaret, without whom there would be no mystery

Chapter 1

KELLY'S EYE

"We're not Starsky and Hutch. Would you *please* slow down!"

Jason gritted his teeth. His mother-in-law was a notorious backseat driver. Too fast, too slow, too close to the curb, watch out for that cyclist, wasn't that the turning there, are we there yet? She had mentioned them all. It should have been a scenic drive through the lakes to the peaceful town of Penrith – not the Cannonball Run.

His grip on the steering wheel tightened. "I'm going at the limit, Amita," he said, trying to keep his voice light.

"I don't care what that thing says, you're going too fast," she fired back. "I'd like to be able to see my grandchildren at least once more, if that's alright with you? Which reminds me, do you drive like a maniac with them in the car and I'm not here? Does your wife know about your lead foot?"

"I know where I'd like to put my lead foot," he muttered.

"What?"

"Nothing," he sighed.

Silence descended in the car. Jason had been spending a lot of time with his mother-in-law recently. And it wasn't through choice. It wasn't that he disliked her – Amita Khatri could be very warm and generous when she chose to be. It was when she chose *not* to be that he had a problem. With everything that had been going on, he had enough problems to worry about.

"Bugger, did I bring my glasses?" she said, reaching for her handbag.

"They're on your head," said Jason, concentrating on the road.

"So they are," she tutted. "Rats, have I brought my pen?"

"Front pocket of your bag."

"Yes, so it is," she said, finding her bingo blotter. "Now I can't remember if I have the money to pay Georgie for that magazine subscription –"

"You've rolled up a tenner and put it in the pocket of your cardigan."

Amita patted her tummy where the pocket was. She cocked an eyebrow at Jason.

"Anyone would think you were spying on me."

He thought about answering her back. He thought about saying how she'd spent the last hour before leaving the house going through a very vocal checklist, as if she was packing for an attempt on Everest rather than an evening with Penrith Bingo Club. He thought about telling her that he'd missed most of the news and all of the weather because of the racket she'd been making. Jason thought about lots of things before deciding it wasn't worth the argument.

"Just looking out for my favourite mother-in-law," he said with a forced chirpiness.

"And if I believe that, I'll believe anything," she snorted, a hint of a smile behind her frown.

Jason smiled. He let his grip on the wheel loosen and reached down to the radio.

"You're not putting that on, are you?" asked Amita. "I can't listen to *anything* before the bingo," she said sharply. "It's one of my superstitions. You know this, Jason. You know that I've got to be absolutely in the zone, completely focussed, ready to pounce when those balls come out of the machine."

"Isn't it all electronic now?" he asked. "Don't they have a big screen with a random number generator doing all the hard work?"

"You don't know what it takes to play the numbers," she said. "No radio."

To make sure he had understood, she slapped his hand. He gritted his teeth.

"Fine," he huffed, adjusting himself. "But I want it put on the record that I think you take this bingo far too seriously. It's not the World Cup, you know. It's a load of old folk gathered in a church hall, gossiping about the neighbours."

"How dare you," Amita gasped. "We do *not* gossip. We're there to win."

"Oh, come off it, Amita," he laughed. "You go in there, every week, and talk about everyone who hasn't turned up for half an hour. You play a bit, then you stop for free tea and a Digestive biscuit before kicking off the second half for a right proper bitching session. The clock strikes nine and you all shuffle back out, ready to gather up as much gossip as you can in the week. Cutthroat competition is not the name of the game."

"It is more competitive than you'll ever know," Amita huffed. "Just last week Margaret Cullin won fifty pounds on a full house."

"I'm sure the *Financial Times* was relieved to get a front page that night."

"And then there was last month, when Madeleine Frobisher went home with the rollover jackpot."

"How much was that then?" asked Jason.

"Seventy-five pounds and forty-six new pence."

Jason rolled his eyes. "The excitement never stops," he said. "Look, I never said you didn't play *any* bingo. Obviously you do. All I *am* saying is that you spend an awful lot of time talking about people behind their backs. Is that or is that not the case?"

Amita considered her words carefully. She chewed them over, thinking about the accusations levelled at her. She always did when Jason was the one pointing the finger. She hated to give him an inch. He always took the mile and then some.

"No comment," she finally said.

That made Jason laugh. "No comment?" he said. "No comment? What's that supposed to mean?"

"It means no comment, that's what it means. You're supposed to be a journalist Jason, you should know what 'no comment' means by now."

"I *am* a journalist," he fired back.

"Oh yes, sorry, I had forgotten," Amita folded her arms. "I'd forgotten that watching daytime television in your pyjamas and the latest from the frontline of vacuuming the stairs were cutting-edge reporting these days. How silly of me."

There was a noticeable chill to the air between them now. While Jason knew he'd probably gone too far with his criticism of the bingo club, he thought she was being more than cruel now.

The Musgrave Monument in Market Square loomed through the darkness. Jason felt its clock face was watching him as they drove beneath its glare, almost egging him on to say something. The nineteenth century tower was the focal point of the town; every road seemed to lead to it in the end. If Penrith had a skyline, the Monument's pyramidal peak and bunting would be the highlight.

"No need to kick a man when he's down," he said, his voice like muted thunder. "I'm out of work, you know."

"I know it all too well, Jason," said Amita in that snippy, condescending manner he hated with a vengeance. "I know that, while my daughter is out breaking her back to keep your family afloat, you're messing around on that computer of yours, playing games and watching football highlights."

"I'm trying to find a new job," he said, teeth clamping together, jaw tight. "I was made redundant, Amita, you know this. I'm trying my hardest to get another reporter gig, but it's a very tough market."

"I've told you a million times, Jason," she sniffed. "You should go freelance and make your own work."

Jason had heard this all before – from Amita, from his family, from everyone who cared to have an opinion. The only thing worse than being out of work was being told how to get another job. It made his blood boil.

He was about to launch into a furious tirade when Amita screamed.

"Look out!" she yelled, slamming her hands onto the dashboard.

Jason panicked. He fumbled with the steering wheel as the headlights flashed across the street. A gathered pack of anoraks, corduroy trousers and sensible walking shoes appeared then vanished into the darkness as he wrestled the car out of the way. He slammed on the brakes and they came to a halt – no harm done.

"Bloody hell," he breathed. "They came out of nowhere."

"You weren't concentrating," said Amita, unclipping her seatbelt. "And you were going too fast, like I said!"

He started to plead his case but she was gone, out of the car door, before he got the chance. He caught his breath, pinching the bridge of his nose.

"The Sheriff of Penrith is off to greet her citizens," he said to himself.

But just then he noticed Amita had left her handbag. She was not a woman usually parted from her weapon of choice, and he thought he'd better deliver it to her before he got accused of rifling through its mysterious contents.

Mustering the energy, he got out of the car, stopping first to make sure he definitely hadn't run over any lagging members of the bingo club. The chilly autumn air made his face tingle and woke him up a little. He felt guilty for being so snippy with Amita – she'd hit a sore spot when it came to work. He had little to show for an afternoon of emails and job-hunting. He'd make it up to her with her bag by way of a peace offering.

The gathered group was making quite a noise outside the church hall. Even in the dim light of the evening he could make out Amita at the centre of the action. Something was clearly up.

He pressed the button to lock the car, and it bleeped with a satisfactory chirp as he walked casually over to the assembled gang of elderly Penrith locals.

"What's going on then?" he asked Amita, but before she could answer, a tall, broad-chested old man spoke to him without looking away from the centre of the crowd where Amita was holding court with another well-dressed septuagenarian, both of them vying for supremacy.

"Madeleine's dead," he said bluntly. "Broke her neck."

"Madeleine who?" asked Jason.

"Frobisher," said the old man.

"Is that her that won the monthly jackpot?" asked Jason.

"Aye," said the old man, his moustache twitching as he sneered at him. "That's her."

"Guess she didn't have time to spend it then, eh?" Jason elbowed the pensioner in the ribs, egging him on for a laugh.

The crowd fell silent. Suddenly every pair of bespectacled or laser-surgically-enhanced eyes was on Jason. He could almost taste the contempt hanging in the air as he tried to back away. But Amita pushed her way out to the edge from the centre of the group, grabbed her bag, and locked eyes with him.

"And you are going to write the story?' she said in a voice that Jason knew would lead to trouble.

Chapter 2

ONE LITTLE DUCK

"Awful. I mean, it's just awful. You don't think something like this would happen to somebody you know, do you? Especially not to someone like Madeleine."

Amita dunked her Digestive into her tea. She pulled it out quickly, checking to make sure the integrity of the biscuit was still intact. After a breathless second to see if it still held up, she took a bite, already preparing for the next dunk.

The church hall was more muted than usual. As a mark of respect to Madeleine, bingo had been cancelled for the night. The organisers, the local vicar and the hall's janitor, however, had let the crowd in to get their tea. Jason suspected they feared a riot would break out if they didn't. He sat at the end of a long, foldable table not far from Amita and her cronies, wishing he hadn't got out of the car.

"I really can't believe it," said Amita, as if she hadn't already expressed her shock.

There was a round of muffled grunts of agreement from the other pensioners.

"And Madeleine, of all people," said the well-dressed OAP from outside. "Awful business."

"Yes, I said that already, Georgie," Amita tutted.

The two pensioners darted dirty looks at each other. The rest of the group could only watch in silence as the titans clashed over their cups of Earl Grey.

"Glad she had such concerned friends," Jason said, puffing out his cheeks.

"Quiet, Jason," said Amita. "You know you're really not supposed to be in here unless you've paid your annual membership. That tea is meant for bingo attendees only."

"I'll gladly return it then if we can go home."

"In a minute," she waved him away. "Does anyone know who found Madeleine? Was it a member of her family?"

"Madeleine Frobisher is dead!" boomed a lady in a wheelchair. The whistle of her hearing aids was almost as piercing as her voice.

"We know, Ethel," tutted Georgie. "That's what we're talking about."

"Somebody found her next to that big bloody house of hers," Ethel added.

"It was the postman, that's what I heard," said Sandy, the broad-chested old man who had snorted at Jason.

"Oh no, not Geoff," said Georgie. "He's a lovely chap. What a terrible thing to find when you're at your work."

"Geoff?" asked Amita. "Don't think I know him. Is he new?"

"No," Georgie said with a half-laugh. "He's been doing that delivery route – the posh bit – for *years*. Amita, where have you been?"

A ripple of muted scoffs from those who sided with Georgie and her immaculate blouse and matching neckerchief. The others remained silent, engrossed in their tea. Until Sandy spoke up. He was a man of few words, and Amita had heard more from him tonight than she normally did in a month. There was always a table of men of a certain age who didn't say much and, she suspected, came more for the biscuits than the bingo. "I've never heard of the fella. I have a lovely lady postie who does our patch," Sandy announced.

"I don't live anywhere near Madeleine," said Amita, grabbing the chance. "We're on the other side of town. We wouldn't be on the same delivery route as the road heading towards the lakes. Although, now I think about it, if he does the big houses, you wouldn't be on that route either, Georgie, not where you live. Would you?"

It was a commendable come-back, even Jason had to admit that. When his mother-in-law wanted to turn on the venom she still could. And she was clearly sparring with one of the best here.

Georgie said nothing, her mouth a thin line across her made-up face. She busied herself with a long gulp of tea before smoothing out imaginary creases in her blouse.

"Broke her neck, by all accounts," said Sandy, with an uncharacteristic wobble in his voice. "That's what the chat in the town is, anyway. Seems she was up a ladder cleaning the windows of that big house of hers and, wallop, off she fell. Real bloody shame."

More muted agreements from the table.

"Did you know her well, Sandy?" asked Amita.

The old man sat up a little straighter. He dusted crumbs from his silver moustache, the middle dark with tobacco stains, and shook his head. "Not any more than the rest of you. You'd see her about the town. You'd always know when Madeleine was about, wouldn't you? She beamed a big smile every time she stepped into a room."

Slightly louder agreements from the group around the table.

"Always helpful, too," Sandy continued. "She always volunteered the old stables up at her place if we needed to store tools or compost from the allotments over winter. Very kind. Think she was part of the Women's Institute, too, if I'm not mistaken."

"She was," Georgie piped up. "And very generous with her time she was too. A lovely woman, full of great ideas. She also made a lovely upside-down cake, usually for one of the summer fetes. You don't get a lot of upside-down cakes anymore, do you?"

This time the chorus of agreements was almost deafening. The conversation, Jason concluded, had finally proved that even if they couldn't agree who knew the most about Madeleine's demise, cake was one topic they could agree on.

"Madeleine Forster is dead!" Ethel yelled again.

"Yes, we *know*, Ethel," said Georgie, getting more than a little irate. "It's all any of us has been talking about for the last twenty minutes. Try to keep up."

"Imagine trying to clean windows at her age," the eldest of the group remarked. "It's no wonder she slipped."

The words seemed to linger in the stale air of the church hall.

"No word of when the funeral will be?" asked Amita, sneaking another biscuit.

"She was only found this morning, Amita," said Georgie. "Give the woman a chance to get cold first, would you?"

"I know, I was just . . . well, it's normally quite quick, isn't it, with these sorts of things? Unless, you know, there's something fishy."

"Fishy?" Georgie leaned forward, her eyes sharpening like a hawk that had spied its dinner. "What do you mean by fishy?"

Amita was midway to taking a bite from her biscuit, but stopped. She sensed the group was looking at her. Even Jason had leaned forward a little.

"Fishy, you know, suspicious," she said.

"Suspicious? What could possibly be suspicious? It was a terrible accident, Amita. Poor Madeleine fell and broke her neck. Absolutely awful. Only mercy is it would have been quick."

"I'm not *saying* it's suspicious," Amita said. "I'm merely pointing out that these sorts of things normally have the police involved, don't they? Don't they, Jason? You'd be familiar with this type of thing, wouldn't you. You know, inquests . . ."

The group shifted to stare at *him* now. He cleared his throat. "Yeah, sometimes," he shrugged. "Depends on the circumstances."

"And does what happened to Madeleine Frobisher sound like it has 'circumstances'?" asked Georgie pointedly.

To his surprise, Jason felt a little under pressure. Georgie, it seemed, could be quite intimidating when she turned her glare on him. He found himself stumbling over his words, his hands sweaty. "Well, it's hard to say without all the relevant information," he said weakly. "I don't have contact with the police anymore."

"He's out of work at the moment," said Amita, in a sort of stage whisper. "Has been for six months now."

"Yes, thanks Amita," he said.

"Madeleine Frobisher is dead!" Ethel shouted.

Jason wasn't sure if he was supposed to acknowledge her or not.

"So you think there might be grounds for an inquest?" Georgie's questions continued.

"I didn't say that," said Jason.

"What *are* you saying then? Out with it, man!"

Jason felt very hot suddenly. He tugged at the collar of his jumper, desperate for air. "I'm saying that if the police think there's a reasonable doubt that it wasn't some horrible accident, which it sounds like it was by the way, then they'll investigate. I don't know, I'm not a copper. I don't know how they think with these things."

None of the faces staring at him looked very convinced.

"If I had to guess, they'll take a look at the area where she was found, outside her house, right? If it all looks like it adds up then I guess that's that, a simple but awful accident."

"But what if it *doesn't* look like that, eh?" Amita goaded him. "Then I would be right, wouldn't I?"

Jason held his breathe to stop himself saying something he'd regret. All of this just to prove a point, to score one over her rival, Georgie. He despaired.

"Yes, Amita," he said with a long sigh. "You would be right."

"There'll be one more star in the heaven tonight! Madeleine is dead!"

"We know, Ethel!" Amita and Georgie and some of the others said in unison.

A bell broke up the conversation. At the door, the vicar stood holding the little bell apologetically. The hall janitor was standing beside him, mop and bucket in his hands, a look of disinterest on his face.

"Good evening, ladies and gentlemen," said the pastor timidly. "Just to let you know that we have to vacate the hall now. It's a pity as I think we all could be doing with a little company after hearing of what happened to Ms Frobisher. I'm sure our thoughts and prayers go out to her family and I'll gladly pass on any messages of goodwill and remembrance to them."

The hall erupted in a cacophony of scraping chair legs and creaking bones. The members of the bingo club slowly filtered out of the hall, wishing their best to the vicar, Mr Jones and one another. Amita and Jason were at the back of the procession.

"That bloody Georgie," said Amita, keeping her voice down. "She's always out to get me. Always looking for a chance to cut me down to size."

"She's quite formidable," agreed Jason. "I wonder who sharpens her claws at night."

"She's a widow."

"Lucky bugger got out early then."

"Jason, please," said Amita disapprovingly. "Although I shouldn't have expected any help from you."

"What does that mean?"

They bade farewell to the vicar and walked down the main road towards the car.

"It means when I ask you to back me up I expect a little more than I don't knows and ifs, buts and maybes," said Amita, blowing into her hands.

"Oh, come on," he said. "You can't expect me to say I think this Madeleine woman was killed. I don't even know who she is . . . was!"

"All I'm saying is that it's open-ended."

"You would say that, you're the Sheriff of Penrith, Amita. Any time there's a sniff of trouble you are all over it like a rash."

They climbed into the car.

"And how do you know it's open-ended?" he asked. "You've got as much information as I have. And I know diddly-squat."

"You never know with these things," she said. "A woman found dead outside her home, suffers a broken neck after a fall. These things don't happen in Penrith."

"Maybe not often," said Jason. "But you don't even know if it was a broken neck that killed her."

"Everyone at the bingo club seemed to think it was."

"Ah yes, the bingo club," he laughed. "A bunch of nosy folk with too much time on their hands. Very reliable sources."

"Sounds rather like you, now you mention it, Jason. And anyway, they can be *very* reliable when it comes to the local community," she said. "They have ears everywhere. We take pride in the civic goings-on of our hometown. Something you should take onboard."

"Come off it. I've just seen some of your so-called reliable pals," said Jason, turning the car around. "There are a few in there as old as the ark. You're trying to tell me they have their marbles intact? I've heard of an unreliable narrator but that takes the biscuit."

"That is a very rude appraisal of the elderly community, Jason. I don't approve of it."

Jason shook his head. He could feel his heartbeat getting faster. Another full-on argument was brewing between the two of them. Maybe he had been a bit quick to dismiss Amita's friends. After all, he wasn't in a position to throw stones. He thought better of stoking the fire and reached for the radio instead.

"Don't put on that radio," sniped Amita.

"Why? You're not playing bingo. No more playing the numbers tonight."

"I know. But something doesn't add up. I need peace to think."

Jason nodded. He drummed his hands on the steering wheel as they continued on the road home.

"None of what happened seems suspicious to you, Jason?" she asked.

He took a deep breath, his nose whistling. "Look, bad things happen to people all the time," he said. "It's just the way of things, I'm afraid. We don't live in a wonderful, magical world where we're all wrapped in cotton wool."

"Yes, I'm aware of that," she said. "But you don't know for certain. You don't know, absolutely, that there isn't a sinister side to Madeleine's death. It's not like you've ever done anything like this before."

"Yes I have," he said solemnly.

"What?"

"Years ago, when I was a cub reporter in Manchester, before I moved up here," he said. "Thrown in at the deep end with a pretty awful murder of a young lad who was only twenty or so."

"You've kept that quiet," she said.

"Don't believe everything you see on TV about journalists, Amita," he said, watching the road. "We don't all like to go shouting about the worst and most horrible stories we've covered. Usually, it's a case of getting in and out as quickly and cleanly as possible and trying to forget that it ever crossed your desk."

"I'll bet," she said. "Mind the road."

"I was sent out on what looked like a run-of-the-mill death, or as run-of-the-mill as something like that can be. I had to do a dreaded door knock, to speak to the family of this young guy. His dad and stepmum answered the door. They let me in, spoke to me for hours about how they were utterly heartbroken, gave me some lovely memories, all of that. I was devastated by their words, of course, but delighted to be able to include such a moving tribute. This was a great story. I headed back to the offices, near Piccadilly, and started typing up my notes. Next thing I know, the whole newsroom is in uproar."

"Why?" asked Amita, hooked.

"Between me leaving their house and getting back to my desk, the stepmum had been arrested *and* charged with the young lad's murder."

"What?" she blurted. "She killed him?"

"Yup," Jason nodded, concentrating on the road ahead. "A matter of hours before I'd been sat there, in the front room, chatting away."

"And she didn't show anything? Any guilt? Any remorse?"

"Absolutely not," he said. "She was as calm, collected and outwardly heartbroken as anyone would be when their stepson had been discovered dead. It all came out at the trial, of course. The lad had found out she was ruining his dad financially, dodgy investments, shopping, holidays, running all over town with other men and all of that, proper juicy stuff. The young man had threatened to expose the whole thing and she bashed him around the head with a lead pipe and dumped his body. But she hadn't been too clever covering her tracks. The police caught her on CCTV.

Apparently she'd run a whole load of red lights on the way to and from the train tracks where she dumped him. So maybe you're right – I really should watch my driving."

"Blimey," said Amita. "I had no idea."

"It was a long time ago," he said. "My point is, you're right, you can never tell who or what is going on. Not just behind closed doors, but even behind someone's eyes. I was sat not two feet from a woman who had murdered someone a matter of hours previous and I couldn't tell. But she was caught, pretty easily in the end, because she hadn't thought it out, hadn't planned ahead. You can't go about murdering people willy-nilly, Amita. Not if you want to get away with it."

Chapter 3

CUP OF TEA

The sound of the kids screaming wasn't how Jason imagined his daily wake-up calls. He pictured in his mind something much more subdued. Like birdsong or the gentle lapping of waves from a sprawling, golden-sand beach. He would get out of bed, glide over to the balcony of his Malibu mansion overlooking the Pacific and take in nature's splendid glory.

That was how to start the day. Not with the umpteenth rendition of *Row Row Row Your Boat*, the lyrics changed to every word being 'fart'. Or worse. He thought about pulling the duvet back over his head. He thought about pretending to be dead. Then he heard his wife calling.

"Jason Brazel, I swear to god, if you're not down here getting your bairns their cereal in ten seconds, I'm leaving you."

He rolled over onto his back and stared up at the ceiling. It was still dark outside, that's how early it was. While he was unemployed, time had lost all meaning. It was a shapeless, amorphous space punctuated only by the school runs and being Amita's taxi service to the bingo once a week. The thought of his mother-in-law made his head hurt and he covered his face with his hands.

"Jason!"

"Coming, my darling," he said, his throat sore.

Maybe he was coming down with something. He'd spent an hour in the company of fifty pensioners last night. They were always carrying something. Maybe it would be serious and he'd be laid up for a while. Right now, that didn't sound so bad.

He threw back the duvet and kicked his feet out the side. There was something wet down there. He didn't want to look. 'Get up, get out, don't look back.' An old reporter had told him that when he'd first started as a journalist. 'Don't look down alleyways and never, ever turn around if you hear somebody screaming. It's more trouble than it's worth.' Pretty sage if totally counterproductive advice, Jason had thought.

He hurried downstairs, weaving between the dirty washing, mostly his, strewn across the landing. Thundering into the kitchen, he corralled his children before another verse could start. They were plonked on stools, bowls filled to the brim, and munching away in under three minutes. Just in time for Radha to come in fixing her hair.

"You look nice," he said, pouring her coffee.

"Thanks," she said, untangling a knot. "We've got a Zoom call with the London marketing team this morning. I have to look presentable."

"You mean the hoodie and jogging bottoms look isn't presentable anymore? Damn. I thought I'd cornered the market with that one."

"Shut up," she said, smiling. "You know what the London team is like. It's all Armani suits and no knickers. We can't appear to look like the poor northern cousins."

"But that's what you are."

"We are *not* poor northern cousins, Jason," said Radha, hurrying around the kitchen like a tidying tornado. "We're a respectable, very profitable branch of the firm. And we're getting a big marketing push, hence the call."

Jason ignored her. "Doesn't Mummy look pretty? Look, she's combed her hair and everything."

"Brushed," said Radha, scooping the kids' bowls from under them and dumping them in the sink. "Mummy brushes her hair. Daddy combs his, sometimes."

"Ouch," he grabbed his chest, feigning a broken heart.

"You look lovely," said Clara, their youngest.

"Like a princess," agreed Josh, older by two years.

"Aww, bless your cotton socks, the pair of you. Now come on, time for school."

"Do we need anything from the shops while I'm on the school run?"

"I told you last night, *I'm* dropping the kids off this morning," said Radha, the pile of toys, bags, dirty washing and plates building up in her arms.

"Did you?"

"Yes. Means you can get the whole morning for job-hunting."

Jason's stomach sank. He felt a shudder start at the base of his spine and work its way up until it made his head hurt. Logging on to the laptop and staring blankly at his CV was about the last thing he had any stomach for.

"Yeah, I suppose so," he shrugged.

"You've been out of work for six months, Jason. The paper closed down, it's gone. I drove past the offices yesterday. They've started taking all the desks and filing cabinets out. It's a shame."

Jason didn't say anything. He stared off into the middle of the kitchen, his mind a million miles away. Almost twenty years he'd worked at the *Penrith Standard*. It was as local as local newspapers got. He'd covered everything from ring road proposals to proposals on the ring road. Village fetes, ugly duckling competitions, even three prime-ministerial visits trying to drum up votes – he'd been there. Two decades was a long time in local news. When it was announced the paper was closing he had been devastated. So devastated, it seemed, he was *still* out of work.

"Time waits for no man," he said sadly.

"And no woman either. I've got to go."

Radha kissed him quickly on the cheek and rounded up their children. They were out of the door in less than thirty seconds, leaving Jason alone with the washing-up.

Only there was something wrong. Something wasn't quite right. He looked around the kitchen. Then he poked his head into the living room. For a brief, all too short moment, he was alone, completely alone. Amita was nowhere to be seen.

With more than a hop in his step, he reboiled the kettle. Spreading a thick layer of marmalade on his toast, he whistled his way into the living room. Settling into the middle of the couch, he turned on the TV with an almost ceremonial grace. Flying down the channels he sought out the football highlights and settled in. With his pinkie raised, he lifted the top-most slice of toast towards his mouth.

The marmalade glistened, dripping off the edges of the perfectly-toasted bread. He was just about to sink his teeth in when the front door clicked open.

"Hello! Did I miss you? Anyone still here?"

The toast dropped from his grip and landed on his chest, face down. Jason scrambled around trying to save it, but it was useless. He had been defeated. Amita caught him mid-salvage operation and tutted loudly.

"You're not even dressed yet," she said. "It's gone eight and you're still in your pyjamas."

Sticky fingers, sticky top, crumbs everywhere, Jason slammed the plate down beside him and tried not to scream.

"Good morning, Amita," he said, knowing his marmalade-covered top looked even worse in comparison to his mother-in-law's perfectly colour-coordinated tracksuit. "So lovely to see you up and about at this time. Tell me, do you do it deliberately?"

"I don't know what you're talking about, you silly man," she said. "I went out for my morning run, recorded a very good time as it happens, thanks for asking, and now I'm back home, my house, where I live, with you and my family. Is that answer enough for you?"

She buzzed about him like a fly until the whole sofa, cushions and all, had been rearranged around him. All Jason could do was sit there and let it happen. The football highlights were switched off before her backside had touched her chair by the window. The rolling news now dominated the screen.

"Why don't you apply for one of these channels?" she asked, finger pointing at the TV.

"Excuse me?" he just about managed.

"The news, on the television. You see some right states on there. You could do that. Why don't you apply?"

"I'm not a broadcast journalist, Amita. It's a different skill-set."

"You mean you *have* a skill-set?" she smiled.

Jason didn't return the gesture. Instead he sat there, watching more successful journalists than he was read the same news over and over again.

"Oh, I meant to tell you," said Amita, turning down a report about wind farms. "When I was out I ran into Bill Fee."

"I have absolutely no idea who that is," said Jason.

"Bill Fee, you do know who he is," said Amita. "He used to work in the butcher's. Has a lazy eye. You never quite know if he's looking at you or if he's watching out for the next bus to come up the road. He had a bit of a drinking problem a few years ago. Wife left him."

Jason felt the tendons in his neck tighten. He desperately wished to be on a beach somewhere. Or at the bottom of an active volcano. Anywhere but his living room.

"Anyway, Bill says that Madeleine's funeral probably won't be until next week," Amita went on. "Seems that there's going to be a delay as the police want to carry out a post-mortem." She paused for breath and a little dramatic effect. "Did you hear what I said, Jason? There's going to be a post-mortem. Isn't that interesting?"

"No, it's not," he said. "I told you and your cronies last night, it's fairly standard procedure in unexpected deaths like hers. It doesn't mean there's a killer on the loose or anything like that."

"Still interesting though, isn't it?"

"No, Amita, it's not. It's bloody morbid that you're so fascinated by the death of somebody you knew. And anyway, how does this Bill character know about the post-mortem?"

Amita fished out her phone from the pocket of her shell suit. She waved it at him before tossing it over.

"The police put out a statement on Facebook late last night," she said.

"Wait . . . how . . .?" Jason stuttered. "You're on Facebook? *I'm* not on Facebook. Since when did you get on Facebook?"

Amita smiled at him smugly. She leaned back in her chair, the lower part kicking upwards to lift her legs.

"Get with the times, Jason," she said. "All of us are on Facebook. It's how you find out what's going on around here. The Sheriff of Penrith, that's what you call me, isn't it? Well, a sheriff needs to know what's going on in her town. And people just *love* to put everything on there."

Jason was defeated. This was a new low, even by his pretty poor standards. He tossed Amita's phone back to her and got up, shoulders slumped, head bowed.

"Where are you going?" she asked him.

"To my grave," he said.

"Okay," she said, scrolling through her phone. "Do you want to make me a cup of tea on your way?"

Chapter 4

KNOCK AT THE DOOR

Amita sat perfectly still. She didn't want to wake Jason. Her son-in-law was back in bed. She knew what she thought about that. But she wasn't going to let it get her angry. Not just now, anyway. She had five minutes to herself.

The light from the hall drifted up through the loft hatch. A long, stretched rectangle lifted high into the rafters of the house. Old cobwebs, stringy and loose, swung lazily back and forth as the central heating brought some warmth to the attic. Amita gave the hatch a quick look to make sure Jason hadn't found her. Satisfied, she licked the rolling paper on her little cigarette and popped it into her mouth.

She patted her pockets for a lighter and eased her way over to the small vent in the side of the roof. She delicately weaved between the boxes of Christmas decorations and suitcases filled with old clothes and memories. Flipping the shutters open, she could see the terraced roofs stretching down the road. From up here she could spy on the neighbourhood as much as she liked. And, more importantly, she could see Radha coming.

Amita didn't smoke much anymore. There had been a time where a cigarette was never far from her mouth. Forty a day from turning fourteen had left its mark on her lungs. But she'd quit, just like that, when she turned fifty. A little secret puff now and again from one she'd rolled herself wasn't going to hurt her, she told herself. She also told herself that it was still bad for her and that she really should learn. That's why she came up to the attic when nobody was looking.

At that thought she lit the end. Taking a long drag, she puffed the smoke out of the vent and watched it drift away into the brightening, pale grey sky. Her eyes fell on the rolling hills and countryside peeking out between the other houses of the street. Out there, among the hills and meadows, and the glinting surface of Ullswater, fiercely bright in the sun, was Madeleine Frobisher's house.

Amita had never been to it; nobody she knew had ever been invited. She hadn't told the others but she'd always thought of Madeleine to be a little otherworldly. Not snooty or snobbish, she was quite friendly, or at least always had been to Amita. No, it was something else about her, something distant and unattainable. As much as Amita was a pillar of the community, she had never felt like she could get close to Madeleine. She always had a barrier up, a block that kept her safely hidden from the others.

Georgie Littlejohn had tried, of course. The thought of that woman made Amita sneer to herself. Georgie was always putting her nose in where it didn't belong, always trying to be everyone's best friend and talking about them as soon as they were out of earshot.

"More faces than Musgrave Monument," she said aloud, forgetting where she was.

She darted a quick glance at the hatch. No noise from below. She was safe. She turned back towards the vent and stared out again towards Ullswater. It was a big, old, crumbling house Madeleine lived in – she had seen it on Google Maps. Set back from the main road, separated from it by a flat, wide field, it had been surely rather grand in its day. Although that day was long ago now.

Amita couldn't help but feel a little numb thinking about Madeleine. Death had a strange way of creeping up and shaking you by the shoulders, rattling you to your bones. It was happening more and more, of course. None of her friends were getting any younger. Every winter there would be another spate of deaths, another list of faces she'd learn to miss and long for. She tried to not let it get her down. What was the use in lamenting something that was inevitable? She wondered whether anyone outside these four walls would miss her very much when it was her turn.

Poor Madeleine, though – to fall and break her neck like that. What kind of way was that to die? Why the hell had she been up a set of ladders in the first place? She must have had enough money to pay for window cleaners. Why take the risk?

The thought had been eating away at the back of her mind. She took another drag from the cigarette, the short shaft now burned down almost to her fingertips.

"Bugger," she said, pinging it out through a slit in the shutter.

"Amita!"

Jason's voice came from behind her. She was startled and jumped, bashing her head against the sloping beam of the roof.

"Bugger," she said, grabbing at her crown. "Bugger, bugger, bugger."

"Amita! Are you up in the loft?"

"Yes!" she shouted, wincing in pain.

She stumbled her way back to the hatch, bumping into boxes and toppling over stacks of old VHS films and DVDs. Her slippers slapped loudly on the creaking boards of the attic until she reached the lip of the hatch. Jason's head appeared from below.

"What the hell are you doing up here?" he asked, hair poking out in untidy clumps.

"I thought you were asleep . . . again," she said, towering over him.

"I was. I woke up," he said.

Looking beyond her, he tried to find some evidence. Then he sniffed the air.

"Can you smell smoke?" he asked.

"No, get out of the way."

She kicked him gently. He wobbled, grabbing hold of the ladder.

"Watch it!"

"I'm freezing here. Let me down, move," she ordered him.

He did as he was told. Amita clambered down the ladder after him, pulling the hatch closed as she went and locking in the scent of smoke. She folded up the ladders and put them back in the cupboard.

"What were you doing up there?" he asked, scratching his stubbly cheek.

"I was looking for something," she lied.

"What?"

"None of your business, that's what."

29

"Charming," he said. "Seriously. What were you looking for? Maybe I can help find it."

"You? Help me? Pull the other one, Jason, I think you're still asleep."

"I'm offering to help, Amita. No need to be an arsehole about it."

She thought she'd maybe been too harsh on him. She had felt that a lot recently. It wasn't that she didn't like her son-in-law. He was fine. To a degree. But she hated laziness. And Jason Brazel was borderline bone idle.

"No, you've got a job to find," she said, subtly checking her pockets for her tobacco and lighter. "Have you found one yet?"

"No," he said sullenly. "And I'm not going to find one locally, am I? The *Standard* was the only local paper in the area. I'll have to go somewhere bigger and that means a commute."

"I've told you that you should go freelance," she followed him. "How hard can it be to be your own boss, eh?"

"That's not how it works, Amita."

"How what works?"

"Journalism."

"What's so hard about finding a story and writing it up? You know how to do that, don't you?"

"Yes."

"Well, just go and find some stories," she was pressing him now.

They reached the kitchen and he retreated to the fridge.

"You have to have your ear to the ground, like I showed you on social media."

She waggled her phone at him. He looked suspiciously up at her as he made a fresh pot of tea.

"And I gave you the hottest story in town last night. Madeleine Frobisher. Breaking news – it's a scoop." She snapped her fingers.

"There are no stories about Madeleine Frobisher, Amita, you're barking up the wrong tree," he said.

"But you don't know that."

"I know that you can't go about inventing murder plots or whatever it is you want out of thin air," he said sternly. "That's called making stuff up and it's very, very bad when you're a reporter."

"What about her family and friends? Wouldn't people like to read about the nice things we have to say about her?"

"Yes, probably," he said. "When we had a local paper. But, in case it's escaped your notice, we don't and aren't likely to get one back anytime soon. You can thank big business and centralised newsrooms for that one, Amita."

"I don't know what any of that means," she said. "You could surely do *something*."

Her phone beeped.

"There we go, something already," she said.

She unlocked the screen. Jason peered over when he knew she wasn't watching him. The phone was full of notifications. He was a little jealous. He couldn't remember the last time somebody other than Radha messaged him or sent him a meme. He was just thankful the network reminded him of how little credit he had left.

"We're getting somewhere," she said, showing him the screen. "Georgie has put in our group chat that Madeleine's funeral is on Monday. There's going to be a procession from St Andrew's in town. We're invited."

"We?" asked Jason, slurping loudly from his mug.

"Yes, we," she said, reading the message. "Me, the WI, the gang from bingo, anyone and everyone who knew her. I wonder what happened with the post-mortem. They can't have found anything or they'd be delaying the funeral."

"How delightfully morbid of you, Amita."

Her fingers danced across the screen. That was another thing she was better at than Jason. He didn't have the thumbs for it. A ping went off.

"Seems the police have ruled it an accident after all," said Amita.

"You sound almost disappointed," he said.

"Her body was released to her family, a distant cousin by all accounts, who's making the arrangements. The funeral directors have put out a notice online. Oh, I do hope it's Maguire's. They have such lovely cars."

"Now I know what to get you for Christmas," he smirked.

That drew a disapproving glare from his mother-in-law.

"How do you know all of this anyway?" he asked, quickly changing the subject. "The woman was only found yesterday morning, wasn't she?"

"Contacts," Amita winked. "Seems that Brenda, you know Brenda, don't you? She's the one with the terrible gout in both of her feet. Which is ironic as she used to be an amateur gymnast."

"How is that ironic?" Jason was confused.

"I think she drinks too much. You never see her without a glass of red wine in her hand."

Jason thought he liked the sound of Brenda.

"Anyway, yes, Brenda's sister's youngest is an officer with Cumbria Police. And she has the inside line on what's happened to poor Madeleine. See, it pays to have contacts in high places."

"I'm a journalist," said Jason. "All of my contacts are in low places. It works better that way."

Amita locked her phone. "So there you have it, a funeral on Monday. I imagine it'll be a big affair, a lot of people. Madeleine was very well liked. A lot of people found her to be a little . . . eccentric, not me though. I thought she was lovely. Such a shame."

"Yes, so everyone keeps telling me."

The pair stood in silence for a moment. Jason yawned before Amita started tidying up.

"Are you going to start looking for a job then?" she asked. "Probably enough time before lunch, eh?"

"Yes," Jason rolled his eyes.

He was about to fetch his laptop from beneath a pile of toys when the doorbell went. It gave him a little jolt of excitement and he abandoned the computer.

"I'll get it," he said, trying not to sound too giddy.

He grabbed the door handle and felt the icy chill of the wind from outside. When he saw who was standing on his doorstep, he felt a little colder.

"Bloody hell," he said, taking in the two uniformed officers.

"What's the matter?" Amita trailed off when she saw the cops.

"Mr Brazel?" one of them said to him, breath smoking. "Mr Jason Brazel?"

"Yes," Jason just about squeaked out. "Yes, that's me."

"Could you get your coat please, sir? We'd like to have a word with you down the station, if that's alright."

"Why? What's he done?" asked Amita, surging forward. "Look I know he drives a bit too fast now and then, but he's never hit anyone. Well, not anyone I know about."

"Amita!" Jason said through gritted teeth.

"Would you come with us Mr Brazel, please."

"What's this about?" he asked. "Am I under arrest?"

The cop shifted from one foot to another. Then he took a step back, arm outstretched and gesturing to a waiting patrol car parked up on the pavement.

"We're a bit pushed for time, sir," said the officer. "If you don't mind, I can explain on the way to the station."

Jason took a gulp of cold air. He looked at Amita, almost wanting her to rescue him. Taking his anorak from the peg near the door, he threw it over his shoulders and stepped out onto the porch. The officers led him amicably down the path towards their car and he was guided into the backseat. As the car pulled off he watched Amita stand at the door, her thumb already tapping out a text on her phone. The Sheriff of Penrith had another scoop.

Chapter 5

MAN ALIVE

Jason had never been in a police station before. Contrary to popular belief, journalists weren't regularly thrown in cells for the night for raking through bins and dishing dirt. In his career he had managed to avoid any direct brushes with the law. He liked to keep his relationship with Her Majesty's Constabulary limited to pleasantries with the local press office on the phone.

So far the experience wasn't living up to expectations. Jason wasn't quite sure what he was supposed to expect. Twitching lights, bars on the windows, a tape recorder on the table. None of that was here. Instead he'd been led through the front door by the two officers who had picked him up, and put in a warm, comfortable room with a long sofa and coffee table. He'd even been offered a cup of tea – which he refused. Somewhere in the back of his mind he remembered a TV show or movie telling him never to accept anything the police offered. It was a test. He wasn't sure if he'd passed or not.

With the adrenaline still pumping through him, his thoughts turned to why. He couldn't think of anything he might have done wrong. Even Amita's pleas that he drove too fast wouldn't warrant this sort of treatment from the police. He let his mind wander a little, drifting all the way back to his late teenage years when he'd once smoked a joint with Terry O'Brien in the ruins of Penrith Castle. That was a long time ago now. Surely there were more serious crimes than that needing to be investigated.

He hadn't been arrested. He clung onto that thought. If he was in trouble, he would have had the handcuffs slapped on him and been huckled into the police car. He'd come of his own volition. That had to count for something.

Then he thought of Amita. It was probably just as well he hadn't been nicked. It didn't take much for his mother-in-law to hold a grudge. Being arrested, on his own doorstep, in front of her – that was grounds for a lifetime of torment over and above the norm.

The door opened suddenly, breaking his train of thought. A short man with a bad comb-over pasted to his head came strutting in. His suit was poorly fitting and shiny, folds gathering on his over-polished shoes. He walked with a purpose and confidence that seemed at odds with his appearance. Sitting himself down with force on a chair across from Jason, and clearly more used to having these conversations in interview rooms, he slapped a folder down on low the table between them, then sinking back into the too-soft chair

"You Brazel?" he asked bluntly.

"Yes," said Jason, fascinated by the seventies haircut on this man.

"DI Alby," he said. "I've got the *delightful* task of speaking to you."

"Lovely to meet you, too," he fired back.

Alby sneered a little. His big round eyes, that poked out from his flushed face, closed over until they were slits of dark.

"Don't get funny with me, son," said the detective inspector. "I've got a stack of paperwork so big it's getting my britches in a twist. The last thing I need before I collect my pension is to deal with one of you lot."

Jason thought about this for a moment.

"What lot?" he asked, unsure if he should be offended.

"A hack," said Alby. "A reporter, a journalist, you know. Amateurs who make things up and then wonder why us hard-working coppers come down hard on them."

"Er . . ." Jason didn't know where to begin. "I'm not sure you've got the right journalist here, Detective Inspector. I'm out of work at the moment and –"

"Enough!"

Alby's voice was surprisingly loud. Jason didn't think something so commanding could come from such an odd-looking man. He found himself sitting a little more upright on the sofa.

"I'm not here to mess about, Brazel. I don't have the time or the patience," said the detective. "I need all the information you have on your old work."

The confusion continued. Jason wasn't sure if he could risk infuriating this clearly very angry man further. He decided against a flippant response and played it straight.

"My old work?" he asked. "What about it?"

Alby measured him a little. After a moment of consideration, he reached down for the folder and flipped through the pages. He stopped at one sheet and pulled it out. Turning it around to face Jason, he slid it across the table.

"Recognise that?" he asked suspiciously.

Jason focussed on the sheet. A black and white picture of a photocopier stared back at him. Before he could answer, Alby shoved another photo under his nose.

"What about this?"

Another black and white image, this time of a desk and ergonomic chair. Alby didn't hold back. He pushed another photo, this one showing an industrial shredding machine, followed by a photo of a microwave oven.

"And these?"

The pictures flooded in thick and fast. Cameras, computers, laptops, phones, keyboards, notepads, even filing cabinets. Everything you would need to stock a newspaper office, and then some.

"Well?" asked Alby expectantly.

"Well . . ." Jason looked at the scattered photos in front of him. "These are some lovely bits of kit, DI Alby. But I'm not sure why you're showing them to me. Unless you're looking to replenish your CID with a whole lot of equipment? I can't help you I'm afraid, I'm a journalist, not a stationery salesman."

Alby slammed his hands down on the table. The bang made Jason yelp louder than he wanted to. He blinked. Alby's face was turning a furious purple.

"I'm not looking to buy, Brazel! I'm trying to find the bugger who's stolen them!"

"Stolen them? From where?"

"From your office."

"My office? I told you, I'm out of work."

Alby straightened his hunched back. The purple was starting to fade from his cheeks and forehead. He licked his dry lips and cleared his throat. "I've been a police officer for thirty-two years, Brazel," he said angrily. "I've caught murderers, thieves, fraudsters, extortionists, arsonists, thugs, yobs, luddites and downright bad buggers in that time. I'm due to retire in three months, looking forward to me and the wife spending more time together, getting up at midday just in time to go fishing and then home for a lovely tea. A career well worked, my service to this community more than paid. And how do my superiors treat this end of an era for local law enforcement? They put me on a case of mass theft from a derelict newspaper office – chasing paperclips and filing cabinets that nobody in their right mind would want to steal. Does that sound like gratitude to you, Brazel?"

Jason was stunned. He shrugged cluelessly. "I don't know, Detective Inspector," he said. "I've never caught a mastermind photocopier thief before. Although you'd have thought, in this case, he'd have left some prints at the scene . . ."

Jason couldn't help himself. He braced for the explosion, but it was going to be worth it.

The outburst didn't arrive. Instead, Alby sat back and loosened off his tie, unfastening the top button of his creased shirt.

"Very good, Brazel. Very good, lad," he said.

"I try," Jason said. "So let me get this straight in my mind. You sent two uniformed officers around to my home and lifted me while I'm still in my pyjamas before lunchtime, all to ask me if I recognised some equipment from an office I haven't worked in for six months?"

Alby rubbed his temples. "You don't know anything about this stuff going missing, do you?" he asked, defeated.

"No," answered Jason, flatly.

"It's all worth about fifteen grand," Alby said. "Seems some smartarse realised there was a load of gear still kicking about the *Standard*'s offices before the repo men came to clear the place out. And like I said, this mug has been put in charge of trying to find it."

"Why me?" asked Jason. "What about the editors and the owners? Wouldn't they make more sense than me? I was just a beat reporter."

"You're the only one still left in the area, son," said Alby. "How about that? The last man standing. Sound familiar?"

Alby didn't wait around for the answer. He scooped up the pictures of the stolen office equipment and stuffed them back into the folder in one giant mess. He marched off towards the door.

"Hey!" Jason called after him, getting up. "Is that it?"

"That's it," said the cop, not bothering to look around. "You're free to go, Mr Brazel. Your help with this investigation has been invaluable and the eternal thanks of Cumbria Police goes with you."

He stormed out of the room with a pathetic flourish. A uniformed officer standing guard outside hopped to attention as Jason followed the DI.

"I can go home, then?" he asked.

"You can do what you like."

"But I've only been here for what? Twenty minutes? You dragged me all the way down here for less than half an hour. How am I supposed to get home?"

"You're a big boy, son, you'll work something out."

Alby marched through the reception area, Jason in close pursuit. The detective inspector swiped his ID badge on a scanner beside a door and slipped through before Jason could follow. The door shut with a heavy thump and the click of a lock, leaving him behind.

"Thank you!" he shouted, hoping Alby could hear. "Thank you very much."

He let out an exasperated sigh. A young policewoman was sitting behind the front desk, clacking furiously on her keyboard. She didn't look up at Jason, eyes locked on her screen. He was a little relieved at that, considering he was still in his pyjamas. He pulled his coat about him a little tighter and checked the pockets. There was nothing in them. No wallet, no phone, not even a token moth to flutter away when he emptied them.

"You've got to be kidding me," he groaned.

Letting the last of his dignity die in peace, he trudged over to the reception desk and the busy policewoman.

"Excuse me," he said, feeling bad about disturbing her. "I've just been given the hairdryer treatment by your Detective Inspector Alby."

A little smile made the officer's mouth curl.

"Go on," she said.

"You might have seen me when I came in. I was picked up by two of his finest goons and brought here before I could dress for the occasion. Is there any chance I could use a phone to arrange a lift? Do you guys even still have actual phones that plug into the wall?"

"Yes, we do," she said, pulling a dusty handset out from beneath the desk. "We're the police, not MI5. We're grateful we have the internet."

Jason laughed. He took the phone and started to dial the number he'd been sworn to remember in the event of an emergency. No emergencies had ever cropped up that he had ever needed to use it. As the line rang, he voiced his thanks to the cop and prepared to eat a huge slice of humble pie.

"Hello, Amita," he tried to sound upbeat. "It's Jason. Yes, Jason, your son-in-law. You know, the one you just watched be taken away by the police. Listen, before you start panicking, everything is fine," he said. "But I need you to do me a small favour . . ."

Chapter 6

HALF A DOZEN

"This is good funeral weather."

"Stop it," said Amita, tutting loudly as she fixed her lipstick in the visor mirror.

"No, I'm being serious," Jason looked up at the murky sky swirling like a giant, grey bowl of broth. "It's good weather for a funeral. Not too bright, none of this sun breaking the sky carry-on. It's raining, but not too heavily that people will have to huddle under umbrellas. A nice atmospheric drizzle that'll sit on the coffin but not make it too slippery. You don't want a corpse rolling around Market Square after all."

"Jason Brazel, watch your mouth. Show some respect to the dead," said his mother-in-law, finished with her adjustments. "What kind of thing is that to say? Eh? Absolutely awful."

"What's awful is the fact you've dragged me along to this to be little more than your taxi service. What's wrong with your own car?"

Amita stared forward, not wanting to answer him. Jason took the hint. He knew when he was beaten. And after a weekend of cold shoulders, frosty jibes and the embarrassment of being picked up from a police station in his pyjamas, he didn't have the energy to press harder.

Instead, he let out an easy sigh. He shifted uncomfortably in the driver's seat, fidgeting. He reached to loosen his black tie, but Amita cut him off at the pass.

"Don't even think about it," she said curtly. "I'm not having you going into this funeral with all of my friends watching on and you looking like a half-shut knife."

"I wasn't doing anything."

"Oh yes you were," she continued. "As if the embarrassment of you being taken away by the police wasn't shameful enough. I've got to live with these people, you know."

"Firstly, I didn't do anything wrong. Secondly I was *helping* with a police inquiry. Thirdly, who the hell is going to know about that? You've stayed locked up in the house all weekend, and I didn't see any of your spies at the station."

"They'll know," she nodded out of the windscreen. "They *always* know, that lot."

Some of the bingo regulars Jason had met were already milling around outside the gates of St Andrew's. Clad head-to-toe in black, they stood out in the gloom like pieces of a chess set. Sandy, the broad-chested gentleman, wore a heavy black mac and matching hat. He was pushing Ethel in her wheelchair. Nearby, Georgie Littlejohn was holding court, relishing the attention, tipping the brim of her wide, luxurious-looking hat back every time someone else filtered into the church.

Jason always hated funerals. There was a stagnant, almost hostile feel to most of them. People who hadn't seen one another for years suddenly thrown into the same room together – all under the banner of grief. He'd never been to a funeral where anyone had told the truth. If eulogies were to be believed, the world was populated with the most generous, loving, kind and patient people. And that clearly wasn't the case.

"Hold up," he said, leaning forward. "I think that's the team bus arriving."

"Team bus . . ." Amita trailed off.

A thoroughly modern hearse drew up into Market Square. It circled around the great clock tower at a ceremonially slow pace, shoppers and passers-by stopping to take in the spectacle. As it glided past Jason and Amita in the car, the tastefully discreet logo of Maguire & Daughter Funeral Directors was the only splash of colour among the black.

"No flowers?" asked Amita. "For the coffin."

"And no family car following behind, either," added Jason.

The hearse was alone. It pulled up at the pavement closest to St Andrew's and the chief mourner got out. She instructed the pallbearers to remove Madeleine's coffin just as the rain started to fall a little heavier. An impromptu guard of honour from the bingo club collective had formed on the path to the church. A couple of the locals stopped to pay their respects as the funeral procession took its short walk to the chapel.

"That's our cue, I think," said Jason.

Amita grabbed his arm.

"Wait until they're all in," she said quietly.

"Why? What's wrong?"

"We'll sit at the back, probably for the best."

"Don't be silly, you knew her just as well as the rest of them, Amita. You can sit where you like."

"Hold back for a minute."

Jason didn't understand the politics at play here – clearly it was very complicated. But finally, Amita gave him the nod and they got out of the car and stood a little way off from the small crowd. He shuffled his feet and watched the bingo mourners filter into the church behind Madeleine's coffin. Satisfied, Amita then walked quickly in behind them, Jason in tow.

The chapel was quiet. An organist out of sight near the altar was playing a quiet, dismal rendition of *Abide with Me*. Sandy pushed Ethel all the way down to the front, and the rest of the bingo club dispersed across the pews, careful to leave plenty of respectful room for one another.

"In there," whispered Amita.

They took their seats on the last row of pews. Jason's back was beginning to stiffen; he'd been sitting for too long already. The hard, well-worn wood of the pews wasn't helping his already bad posture. He tried to stretch his leg and bashed his shin on the seats in front.

"Would you behave yourself," Amita whispered angrily. "You're worse than the bairns."

"Sorry," he said.

"Would you like an order of service?" A washed-out-looking member of the parish handed them each a single sheet. Jason thanked him and turned the order of service over.

"Pretty plain, isn't it," he said. "No picture of her. No touching family message or thanks."

"Or where the meal will be held afterwards."

"Ah yes, the all-important free lunch, how could I forget?"

"No, I'm not being flippant, Jason," said Amita, forensically scanning the order of service. "There's no afterwards because I don't think there is any family."

"So? Maybe they're all abroad. Or dead."

"Maybe," she sighed. "Very sad. She was always quite a private person, I suppose. I don't think I remember her ever talking about children or brothers and sisters, but she was always very polite asking about my grandchildren – she cared about family even if she didn't have much of her own. Still, nobody but a bunch of neighbours and nosy parkers like Georgie Littlejohn, it's rather sad."

Jason let the nosy parkers jibe slide. He looked about the congregation again. Amita was right, it was all locals – mostly fellow pensioners.

"Who's that down there?" he said, pointing over to the far side of the church.

Amita craned her neck. Jason thought she might fall forward if she strained any further. A man was sitting alone. His suit was neatly cut around his strong shoulders. A bald patch was visible beneath the wisps of his dirty blonde hair. He was staring at the coffin close to the altar, eyes glassy.

"No idea," said Amita. "There are a few faces I don't recognise. Not many, mind you."

"Funny that. Imagine Madeleine having a life outside of the circles you know."

"Jason, please," she said. "We're in a church."

He was silent after that. Jason wasn't much for pestering gods.

Father Ford, the vicar who ran the bingo on Wednesday nights, stepped up to the altar. He cleared his throat, his polite and timid way of asking the congregation to be quiet. They duly did and all eyes fell on the altar.

"Good morning, ladies and gentlemen," he started. "Thank you all for coming to this, a funeral service for our beloved, dearly departed sister, Madeleine Frobisher."

Jason rolled his eyes. He leaned in close to Amita. "Do you reckon he practises this sort of thing in the bathroom mirror?" he asked.

"What did I just tell you?" Amita snapped. "Show some respect."

Jason reclined as much as the pews would allow.

"Madeleine was a pillar of our community. Indeed, looking around here today, I can see a lot of familiar faces from this community. That you've turned out to pay your respects to Madeleine is very touching and I'm sure she would appreciate this show of love and support."

A murmur of agreement went around the congregation. Amita spied Georgie leading the mourning, a tactful dabbing of fake tears from her immaculate make-up adding to the effect. She swallowed some of her bitterness.

"Madeleine was a very private person. It's often the case with a rural community like Penrith that you find people have lots of space and room to live on their own," Father Ford continued. "And indeed, while many of you knew her from various events and clubs around the town, she always carried herself with a quiet, gentle dignity. In fact I remember the first time I met Madeleine. She was at one of my first Sunday sermons when I moved here from Liverpool. She came up to me at the end of the service and shook my hand. And I always remember she said that I really needed to polish my shoes as they were filthy. I felt very told off but she assured me I had done a very good job. I think we all probably have stories like that about Madeleine. She was an ever-present part of life here in the town and she will be greatly missed."

More agreement. A few louder sobs this time punctuated the draughty atmosphere of the church. Jason was trying his very best not to drift off. Amita, however, was leaning forward. She had a hold of the pews in front of her, knuckles almost white as she held on tightly.

"As Madeleine had no family or close relatives in the area, I've invited one of her closer friends from the local bingo club to say a few words."

Father Ford nodded in Amita's direction. For a brief moment the blood in her veins froze. She hadn't been expecting this. Then she panicked, thinking she had forgotten. She was about to stand up – an uncomfortable impatience growing – when Georgie, a few rows in front, stood up instead.

"What the . . .?" Amita whispered. "Close friend? It was Ethel she used to be pals with, when Ethel was more herself. Georgie never had anything nice to say about Madeleine."

"I have a feeling that's about to change."

Georgie strutted her way to the altar. She made a show of composing herself when she was up there, even going so far as to fan herself with a flopping hand. She adjusted her hat so she could read from a stack of papers she had prepared. Amita's shock turned to anger.

"Madeleine Frobisher", Georgie paused for effect, "Was a good woman. She was a beautiful woman. She was a friendly, all-round good egg sort of woman. She was the kind of woman you wanted in your team. She got things done. And I think everyone in this church will agree, she always looked utterly fabulous doing it."

Jason unfolded himself. He leaned in close to Amita again.

"This Georgie woman loves the sound of her own voice, doesn't she?" he whispered.

"There's nothing she enjoys more," she agreed. "She's a one-woman gossip hub. Can't bear not to be in the know. No wonder she's making out like she was a confidante of Madeleine."

"Madeleine was a doer," Georgie went on. "I like doers. Doers get things done. That's what Madeleine did. As you all know, she was on the bingo club committee, the summer and autumn fete committees. She was Treasurer of the Penrith Women's Institute for five years and, more recently, played a very notable part in campaigning to have the *Antiques Roadshow* filmed at Ullswater. She will be dearly and sorely missed by everyone in the town and beyond. And I will sorely, *sorely* miss my friend."

Georgie stepped down from the altar. She looked around quickly, almost expecting applause. When none was forthcoming, she kissed her fingers and touched Madeleine's coffin as she walked past, returning to her seat. Amita watched her the whole way but Georgie never looked up. She was too busy, lost in her pretend grief.

"Pathetic," Amita hissed. "This is the same woman who once deliberately spilled coffee over Madeleine's Chanel suit because it looked better on her than it did on Georgie. She denied the whole thing, of course. But I ask you, how many earthquakes do you think we get in Penrith?"

"I have no idea," said Jason sarcastically. "Aren't we known to be Europe's earthquake capital?"

That drew a smile from his mother-in-law. Father Ford took up his place at the altar again. He continued the ceremony, his voice cracking and confidence ebbing away the further he went on. Finally he was put out of his misery when the organist chimed up with a bum-note-riddled rendition of

All Things Bright and Beautiful. Jason winced, and it wasn't only because of the missed key changes.

"Bloody hell," he said. "That's hardly appropriate."

"Shut up and sing," said Amita between verses.

The pallbearers came back and collected Madeleine's coffin. Leading it out of the church, the occupants of the pews slowly filtered out behind the casket. Jason and Amita waited until the end again, the bingo regulars giving her a nod and smile as they walked past. Ethel was humming an old song, upbeat and catchy, as a stony-faced Sandy pushed her along. Georgie deliberately threw Amita a dirty look as she glided by. Bringing up the rear was the middle-aged, balding man. His flat face was bright red as tears streamed down his rounded, ruby cheeks. He snorted loudly as he passed Jason and Amita.

"Poor fella," said Jason. "He's the postman."

"He is?" asked Amita. "We should say something."

"Amita, wait, hold on. Is this the time or place?"

Jason was too late. She had ducked out of the aisle. Walking up to the man, she touched him on the arm.

"Geoff, isn't it?" she said quietly as the funeral procession headed outside. "My name is Amita. I was one of Madeleine's friends. This is my son-in-law, Jason."

He looked at them both. He sniffed again, wiping his nose with his hand.

"We just wanted to let you know that we're here for you if you need anything. Anything at all. It must have been awful to find her like that."

"It was," he said, his voice hoarse. "I keep seeing that moment over and over again. She was lying there, just lying there. Her neck was broken, I knew it. She was such an elegant woman – and there she was with all the life drained out. It was like something out of a bad dream."

"I know," Amita said sympathetically.

"The police, they've been great," Geoff said. "I had to give a statement, had to speak with them. They've offered me counselling and everything. I just wish I could wipe that image of her from my mind, you know? I keep seeing her there. It's awful."

He started to sob again. Amita patted him on the arm as Father Ford appeared and helped him away.

Outside, the traffic had been stopped by the chief mourner. The whole town centre was quiet. Only the rhythmic footsteps of the pallbearers, marching in time between the two banks and the bakery, broke the eerie stillness. They loaded Madeleine's coffin into the back of the hearse. As the door was closed, it was as if a valve was released and the whole town seemed to kick back into action. The crowd began to disperse and Amita felt a little better. Fewer prying eyes, fewer wagging tongues.

She sidled up to Ethel in her chair, Sandy watching the hearse pull away and disappear into the traffic.

"It was a nice service," said Amita.

"Lovely," said Ethel. "Although there should have been more music."

"After that excuse for a hymn?" asked Amita. "I don't think I could have coped."

But Ethel was lost in a daydream again, humming a golden oldie and tapping her foot.

Amita shook her head. Sandy seemed to wake from a trance when he noticed she was standing beside him.

"Sorry," he said. "Didn't see you there. Are you going to the cemetery?"

"No, I don't think so," said Amita. "We've got the bairns to pick up from school this afternoon. And it's not really for me to go."

"I'll be there to say a farewell on behalf of the bingo club. Otherwise it would only be the vicar and Madeleine's housekeeper. Oh, and I hear Georgie's going," he said.

"Yes, I'll bet she is."

"Damn shame, all of this," he said, looking down at the ground. "Damn shame. Madeleine was a lovely woman."

"She was," said Amita. "Still, it's a bloomin' shame what's happened to the postman, too. He's distraught."

Sandy looked up. Across the square, the postie was speaking with a few of the others from the bingo club. They were taking it in turns to give him a hug. He nodded and tried to smile at them, but he was utterly heartbroken, eyes glassy and red raw. Georgie Littlejohn strode over to offer her own support, her ankles wobbling in her high-heels as she navigated the cobbles of the pedestrian zone.

"Poor fellow," said Sandy. "But you would be, wouldn't you? You don't expect to find a body when you go to your work. Let alone somebody who's had a bloody terrible accident like . . . like Madeleine."

He stuttered a little. Short of breath, he took a big gulp of air. It was a fleeting moment of weakness Amita didn't recognise in him. She was about to ask if he was alright when he realised it was time for the interment.

"Got to go, Amita," he said, hurrying away from her, taking Ethel with him. "I'll see you at the bingo."

"Of course, eyes down," said Amita.

Sandy was too far away to hear her. Jason wandered over to her jangling the car keys in his pocket.

"Everything alright?" he asked her. "You're the colour of boiled –"

"Do not finish that sentence, Jason Brazel," she said strictly. "Absolutely disgusting language. And at a funeral, too. You should be ashamed of yourself. Absolutely ashamed."

"Phew, you *are* alright," he feigned panic. "I thought for a second you might have been having one of your turns."

Amita wasn't listening to her son-in-law. She was too busy thinking. She watched Sandy's tall, broad back vanish among the high street shoppers out early for bargains. Then she turned back as if looking for someone, but the square was empty of black-clad pensioners out to mourn one of their own.

"Bugger," she said, clicking her fingers. "I wanted to speak to her."

"Speak with who?"

"The housekeeper."

"What housekeeper?"

"The one who kept house for Madeleine."

"She was here?" asked Jason.

"Yes, Jason, she was here," she sighed, looking to the heavens. "Try to keep up, would you. You're supposed to be a journalist."

"I *am* a journalist," he said, heading for the car. "I don't have anywhere to do my journalism, that's all."

"Yes, I agree," said Amita, her mind racing. "Which I think might be the first time in our long history together. I must still be mourning."

"Clearly," Jason said.

"You know what they say when there's trouble afoot?" she said. "You don't usually have to look very far from home."

"Who says that exactly?" he asked. "Have you been reading your *Detectives for Dummies* book again?' Jason raised an eyebrow.

"And if Madeleine's accident wasn't an accident after all," said Amita, ignoring her son-in-law's dig. "Then we have to discover who has the most to gain from her death. I know you think I read too many serial killer thrillers, but I'm not looking for a psychopath around every corner. Love, money, revenge . . . that's what we need to think about. We're simple creatures at heart, Jason. I think maybe all of us could do something dreadful if the right reason came along."

Chapter 7

LUCKY SEVEN

Jason knew it was a bit cheeky of him to think it. But he really did enjoy being out of the house for the evening. The clink of beer glasses, the throbbing lights of the fruit machine. Even the stale, predictable, utterly monotonous chit-chat of the local loud-mouths putting the world straight seemed very welcoming.

In the six months since he'd been laid off, he'd not been out to the pub. At first he hadn't really wanted to. There was nothing to celebrate. And he'd seen far too many good men and women in his profession go the way of the drink. Wasted talent was one thing, losing it all for the sake of booze was a completely different matter. An avoidable matter, at that.

This trip to the local was, therefore, a little special. Not only was he getting out and away from Radha and the kids for the evening, he was catching up with an old colleague. He knew he was out of the loop when it came to the world of journalism. Out of the loop when it came to a lot of things, actually.

"Right, cards on the table, Brazel. When was the last time you read up on the latest search engine optimisation techniques?"

"You're a git," Jason said, laughing into the fourth pint glass of the evening. "I thought this was supposed to be a social, friendly catch-up. Not an inquisition."

"You're stalling for time, Brazel. I won't spare your blushes when you admit you don't know what SEO is."

Laura McCann was a bloody good journalist, Jason had always thought so. They'd been in the same year together at college in Carlisle. She'd even spent time working for the *Standard* before being snapped up by a proper local in Manchester. From there she'd fought, clawed and worked hard to get a place at a national broadcaster in London. She was flying high while he dwelled in the doldrums in the sticks.

And how different things could have been. When they graduated, it had been Jason who left Penrith for the bright lights of Manchester and a low-paying internship. But after a year he was back home, living with his parents and knocking on the door of the *Standard*, begging for a job. The big, bright lights of the city were appealing at first. Maybe they had been too appealing. For a lad from Penrith, who had thought Carlisle and its three nightclubs was the pinnacle of hedonism, Jason had been a little overwhelmed. And it had started to creep into his work.

So he had returned home to Penrith with his tail between his legs, his ego severely bruised and his savings all but spent. Thankfully the *Standard* had given him a chance.

Jason was grateful, of course. So grateful that he had stayed at the *Standard* long past his sell-by date, with no inclination to ever leave again, despite watching his colleague Laura's meteoric rise. He had never resented Laura's success. There had never been any bitterness for what might have been with both of them. If anything, he had been glad to see her get on. While she was chasing up leads on government corruption and police brutality, he had covered the Penrith finals of Cumbria's Cutest Dog. Woe betide anyone who tried to tell him that wasn't a great gig. That was the thing – he had genuinely loved local news – giving people a voice, getting their problems heard. It didn't matter if it was someone complaining that the temperature in the pasty oven in the bakery was set too high, or it was kids campaigning for safer roads, he had cared about all (okay, *most*) of the stories he had hammered out. Now he was self-*un*employed while Laura championed the fourth estate at the very highest level.

The worst part of it all was the fact she was so nice. Jason couldn't really hold anything against her. If she'd been some egomaniac, he wouldn't have had a problem hating her guts. As it was, Laura McCann was one of the nicest people he'd ever met in journalism. And she always had time for him.

"Okay, you've got me," he held up his hands. "I don't know what search engine optical illusion, or whatever it is you call it, is. But I maintain that, as a member of Her Majesty's unemployed, I shouldn't *have* to know about it."

"Ah, the great unwashed argument, nicely done," she smiled, draining her gin and tonic.

"I try," he said. "Have you enjoyed your trip back home? How are your parents?"

"They're fine, holding on in there," said Laura. "Which is a shame really because I'd quite like to retire to Rimini with the money from their house. But you can't have it every way, can you."

"No, you can't. Still, it's good that they're alright."

"Yeah, they're fine. They still worry about me being down in London, despite the fact I'm forty and have been out of the house longer than I was in it. Parents, eh?"

"Parents," Jason agreed.

She pointed at his half-drunk pint and gestured to the bar. Jason was feeling a little lightheaded. He had no idea what time of the night it was.

"I probably shouldn't," he said.

"I probably shouldn't, either. I've got a train back to London to catch at the disgustingly early time of six in the morning."

"Oh, alright then, you've twisted my arm."

"Thought so."

Laura hopped up from behind their table and took her empty with her. Jason sat back in his chair, drinking in the atmosphere of the pub. It was warm and comfortable, a fire crackling away in the corner. The lights were fuzzy around the edges, giving the whole place a sort of ethereal quality to his ever more inebriated eyes. He could have fallen asleep there and then.

"Best listen to that mother-in-law of yours," came a ghostly voice at his ear.

It was joined by a clammy, ashen-white hand resting on Jason's shoulder. He looked around, confused and a little frightened. The hand and voice belonged to an old man. His straggly hair hung down like tentacles from beneath his flat cap. It was almost as white as his skin. Two big, sunken, dark eyes stared out like marbles on either side of a pointed nose. His wax jacket seemed to hang off his shoulders like he was a coat hanger, spindly legs rattling around in wellies. A little dog sat stiffly to attention at his feet, looking up at Jason as if for inspiration.

"I beg your pardon?" he asked the old man.

"Your mother-in-law," he said again. "She's a clever woman. She's very clever. I'd listen to her if I were you. She talks a lot of truth does Amita Khatri. One of the few people who does."

He nodded slowly. The little dog did the same.

Jason looked at the pair of them and twisted in his chair. "I'm sorry, is this some sort of joke?" he asked. "Are you two supposed to be a double act or something? Who put you up to this? Was it Amita?"

"Just listen to her, lad," said the old man again.

He leaned in closer to Jason. The smell of stale whisky and pipe tobacco seemed to ooze out of his pores.

"Listen to what she's got to say about everything," he prodded Jason with a skeletal finger. "She's onto something, she always is. She's the cleverest woman I've ever met, your mother-in-law."

Laura came back with the drinks. She set them down and stared at the old man, his dog and Jason.

"Bloody hell Brazel, I go to the bar and already you're chatting up somebody else," she laughed.

"I'm not chatting up the Grim Reaper here, believe me. Or his dog."

The old man let out a grunt, his wafer-thin mouth smiling a little. He tipped his cap at Laura and clicked his fingers, the little dog following him as he headed for the door.

Jason blew out his cheeks. He shook his head as he reached for his fresh pint.

"A friend of yours?" asked Laura, sitting back down.

"Absolutely not," he said. "In fact, I've never seen that old geezer before in my life."

"Don't think you'll have long to catch up with him. He was white as a sheet."

"A lovely reanimated-corpse shade of white, I thought," laughed Jason. "You know it's a funny old thing, Laura. Since I lost my job I've been around the house a lot more, which means I've been dragged into the seedy, sleaze-filled world of the local pensioners by my mother-in-law. If you think you've got contacts, you've seen nothing compared to these guys. Nothing escapes their attention, absolutely *nothing*. And they all know each other, of course."

"You becoming one of the cool kids then, Brazel?" she smirked. "Never had you down for the popular crew."

"I'm the driver," he said, sighing with satisfaction at his lager. "And Amita, that's my mother-in-law, she's the queen bee. Or at least she's trying to be. The rivalries, Laura, honestly, it's worse than Westminster at that bingo club, I'm telling you."

"Oh, it can't be that bad," said Laura, lounging back in her chair. "You're going soft in your old, unemployable age."

"Am I?"

He plonked his glass down with dramatic flair. Wagging his finger at his old colleague, Jason prepared to go into full flight. "You won't think I'm mad when I tell you what the latest thing is," he said.

"I wouldn't hold your breath, but go on," she said.

"Right, here's the thing," he said. "Are you ready?"

"As ready as I'll ever be."

"Okay, get this," he rubbed his hands together. "Amita, my seventy-year-old mother-in-law, believes that one of the old dears who died recently might have been murdered."

Laura's face was blank. She sipped from her gin and tonic casually.

"What's wrong? Why aren't you laughing?"

"It's not very funny, is it, even by our profession's admittedly low standards of humour," she said.

"But it's ridiculous! The woman fell off her ladder when she was cleaning her windows. Open-and-shut case."

"I assume the local plods don't think there's anything fishy?"

"Absolutely nothing in it," said Jason. "A tragic accident. I was at the funeral this morning, hence the black tie."

He tugged at his tie, now sporting the addition of dinnertime stains. Laura smiled wryly.

"A death is a death I suppose. Local community shocked and all of that," she said. "It's a good local story. We used to fire out a hundred of these a month, remember."

"Oh I remember," he groaned.

"Good way to cut your teeth in this game. Who was the deceased?"

"You won't know her. I didn't," he said. "Unless you're big into the local WI scene . . ."

"My parents might know her. Name?"

"Frobisher, Madeleine Frobisher."

Jason had seen genuine shock on another human being's face. As a journalist, he had to know the difference between the genuine article and faux-indignation. It helped to weed out the genuine from the bogus who simply wanted to get into the local paper – or those who wanted to stay out of it, for that matter. It was as much to his surprise as Laura's when she was overcome with that look. Pure shock.

"Madeleine Frobisher," she said after a moment of recovery.

"That's right," he started to worry he'd done something wrong.

"*The* Madeleine Frobisher?"

"Madeleine Frobisher, that's what I said, McCann. You're starting to scare me. What's wrong?"

Laura put her drink down and pulled her phone out, all in one whirlwind motion. She started swiping away on the screen, shoulders hunched over as she concentrated hard.

"This her?" she shoved her phone in his face.

Jason recoiled. When his eyes could refocus, he looked at a series of pictures of a glamorous young woman trussed up in feathers and fancy frocks.

"What is this?" he asked.

"Is that the same woman?"

Jason wished he hadn't drunk so much. He took Laura's phone and scanned through the pictures. Some were in black and white, others in colour, but all of them old. He squinted, trying to make out the face of the young woman who was smiling, sometimes dancing, other times singing into a mic.

"I guess it could be," he said. "A long time ago. I don't know, I never really knew her, I just saw her kicking about town or at the bingo when I dropped Amita off."

"Do you reckon your mother-in-law could identify her as the woman in these pictures?" asked Laura, snatching back her phone.

"The Sheriff of Penrith? Probably. She has a photographic memory for faces, places, times, figures of speech, colours of socks and the number Pi . . . when it suits her."

"I'll send you these over right now," said Laura. "Can you promise me to show them to her when you get home, and to let me know?"

There was a sudden urgency about his old friend now. He wasn't sure what was going on but he could chase away the fuzziness just long enough to ask, "What's this about Laura? You look like you've seen a ghost."

She took a large gulp of her gin. Wiping her mouth, she set her phone down on the table and steepled her fingers. "If, and it's a big if, the Madeleine Frobisher whose funeral you were at this morning is the same one I've just shown you, then this country has lost one of its finest ever singing talents."

"You what?" he blurted. "The old woman in the Chanel suit was a singer?"

"Not just any singer, Brazel. A Eurovision singer. You've been looking at pictures of Maddy Forster, as she was known then."

Jason choked a little on his big gulp of beer. He composed himself and tried to retain some dignity.

"Cobblers," he said.

"It's not cobblers, Jason. You must have heard about Maddy Forster. Madeleine was a singer. A bloody *good* singer, too. And she represented her country in the 1968 competition. Came a disappointing tenth though, lost out to Spain by quite a bit of a margin, actually. Which is totally unfair in my view. *Love Me for One More Day* is about as classic a sixties pop tune as you can get. Robbed."

"Wait, just hold on a minute here," said Jason, waving his hands about. "Pause for breath, McCann, and rewind at least four or five steps. Madeleine Frobisher, the lovely old lady found with a broken neck last week, represented Great Britain at the Eurovision Song Contest? *The* Eurovision Song Contest?"

"It's a big if, Jason," Laura conceded.

"Well, I'm overwhelmed," he said. "Overwhelmed that we had a famous star in our midst and didn't know anything about her."

"In fairness, you probably wouldn't," she said. "She retired in the early seventies. There was a bit of a scandal, really quite awful actually, which I imagine is why she changed her name."

"So how come you know about her?"

Laura began to blush. She shook her head.

"Oh no, don't come over all shy with me, McCann," he said, drumming his fingers on the table. "I've known you long enough to know when you're only pretending to be embarrassed."

"You're such a git, you know that?" she said smiling. "Okay, fine, I admit it. I'm a Eurovision fan, okay? Is that such a terrible thing to be? And is it such a terrible thing to have gone to the last ten contests in a row? Is it so awful to run a few online forums and Facebook groups where we talk about entries and history and trivia? And is it unforgivable that you met your partner at a Eurovision-themed quiz night?"

"Oh no," said Jason, clapping his hands to his face. "Not Claire, too? Please, not Claire. She's meant to be the sensible one out of you two."

"Guilty as charged," she said, lifting her phone. "That website and those pictures I sent you, it's our little shared therapy. A comprehensive guide to everything and anything about the greatest and most viewed singing competition in the world. That's why I recognised the name right away. No one else would – but I run a forum where fans post who they've spotted, a sort of 'Where Are They Now?' page. Years ago, someone mentioned they'd seen Maddy at a WI event, going by a different name. But only a superfan would know that. And I guess I come under that category, for my sins. Come on, test me!"

"I'll take your word for it, thanks all the same," he groaned.

The bell for last orders went off from behind the bar. There was a sudden rush for everyone to get their final drinks. Jason drained his pint glass and offered Laura another one.

"No, I'm alright, thanks. I need to get back to the hotel and pack. I'm up in like three hours to get the train."

"Ouch," he said. "I'll think about you when I nestle down on the couch at two."

They collected their coats and headed out the door. It was much colder now, a crispness making everything that little bit sharper around the edges. Jason flipped up the collar of his coat and stamped some warmth into his feet.

"You okay to get back on your own?" he asked.

"That's very kind of you, Brazel," said Laura. "But it's you I'm more worried about."

"I'm only a fifteen-minute walk up the road, I'll be fine," he hiccupped.

They hugged closely, Laura patting him on the back.

"Just keep your chin up, mate, that's all you have to do," she said. "You're a good journalist, a great one. You need to remember that sometimes and keep going. You'll get a gig soon enough. Don't cut off your own nose to spite your face."

"Thanks Laura," he said, a lump starting in his throat. "I don't know. It's been tough, you know? Had me questioning why I'm even still bothering trying to be a reporter."

"Hey, come on, don't be like that," she rubbed his arm. "You're a good journalist, Jason. You always have been. Remember what you used to say to me when we were in college? Journalism is what we need to make democracy work."

"Walter Cronkite," Jason laughed. "I had a picture of him on my desk in digs, do you remember?"

"Oh yeah, I remember. I also remember thinking you must be some brilliant mind if you were quoting famous American journalists all of the time."

"See, it's just that easy to fool you," he said.

"Well, it's stuck with me all these years," Laura laughed.

"I've still got that picture," said Jason. "Pretty sure it's in the attic along with my copy of *1984* that was read to death. I wanted to be George Orwell so badly, or any journalist of note so badly. I wanted to see the world, take down dictators, uncover the tragedy and triumph of the human spirit from the frontline. I wanted to make a difference, Laura. Not to mention make a few quid and have people recognise me in the street for being 'that guy'. And now look at me. Here I am, out of work, out of ideas, out of pocket and out of touch. How'd that happen?"

"You're drunk, Brazel," she said kindly. "Go home to your beautiful wife and your adorable kids and get a good night's kip. I've got news for you, the world is still going to be a burning mess in the morning, and all those people you said you wanted to be will still be dead. You'll bounce back, I know you will."

He turned away from her and began walking up the road towards home.

"Hey!" she called after him.

"What?" he called back.

"Imagine if it *was* Madeleine the singer," she said. "And she *had* been murdered. I reckon every newspaper in the country would want a bit of that action."

Jason stopped. By the time he turned around Laura was already too far gone. The soggy, blunt drunkenness began to retreat. He fished his phone from his coat pocket and dialled Amita's number. It went straight to voicemail.

"Bloody hell, Amita! You're the only person in the world that actually turns their phone off when they go to bed. Nobody does that, you know!"

He pinched the bridge of his nose, squeezing his eyes tightly shut.

"Focus, sorry, focus. I'm sending you some pictures to your email account. I don't know which one it is, hopefully it's the one you can remember the password for. I want you to look at these pictures very carefully and tell me if they are a younger, much younger, version of Madeleine Forb . . . Forb . . . Frobisher."

His lips and tongue were starting to go numb with the cold. He picked up the pace until he was almost running along the pavement.

"Madeleine Frobisher. Look at the pics and tell me if you think it's her. I'll explain when I get in. No, hold on, it's too late. I'll explain in the morning. All I'll say is, you might be on to something. And if you are, it might, just might, be my ticket back into the big time. Or into the big time for the first time. Something like that, anyway. Okay, bye. Love you, bye."

He hung up. Then he stopped. He looked at his phone in horror.

"Love you?" he grimaced. "I'm going to pay for that in the morning."

Chapter 8

GARDEN GATE

The noise was unbearable. Jason's head felt like it was about to explode. He hid under the pillow, teeth clamped together in a vain attempt to make the agony go away. It was only Radha stepping around the bed to head to work.

"I told you last night, didn't I?" she said, her voice booming like a foghorn inside Jason's head. "A pint and a half and you're kaylied."

He managed to roll over onto his back. A cold sweat made his pyjamas stick to his chest, his arms and his back. He pulled the pillow away from his face, trying to breathe.

"Please stop," he begged his wife. "I can't handle it. I think my brain is melting."

"You're such a cry-baby," she said, sitting down beside him. "Do you remember the days when we would go out every night? Pub quizzes, dinner, the cinema, all to the tune of two or three or more drinks. Then we'd get up in the morning, go to work and do it all over again. Remember those days, Jason? You know, when we were young and in love?"

He lifted his head too quickly. The throbbing between his temples intensified but he didn't care. "You don't love me anymore?" he asked.

Radha laughed. She kissed him on the forehead and grabbed her jacket from the door handle.

"Of course I love you, you big lump," she said. "I'm even taking the kids to school for you. How's that for a dedicated wife?"

"Oh my god, I think I could cry with relief," he said, lying back down.

"Don't get too comfortable. My mother will be home from her run any minute. And you know how delicate a soul she can be when she knows you're hung over."

Jason wasn't in control of the noise that came out of him. He closed his eyes for a few blissful seconds. If he could stay there forever, he would. Somehow the stars had aligned, everything had just fallen into place perfectly. He was comfortable. Now he could rest.

"Jason!"

His hands gripped the duvet, the sheets, everything they could. He scrunched them into tiny little balls. He didn't open his eyes. He couldn't bear the punishment.

"Jason! Are you in?"

Amita came thumping up the stairs. Thump, thump, thump, thump. It was less a seventy-year-old pensioner in her running shoes and more a giant with an axe to grind.

He dearly loved his mother-in-law, deep down. Chiefly for all of Radha he saw in her, the strength she had raised her daughter with. And now he knew she was doing the same with her grandchildren. Plus he relied on her for so many things, from looking after the kids to constantly supporting him in his search for work. He had no real grounds to ever be mad with her, though he knew she loved winding him up. But he was in no fit shape to deal with her this morning. The Sheriff of Penrith had no off switch. And with her head filled with notions of murder and mayhem, he was bracing himself for a full-frontal assault.

"Jason, are you in . . ."

Amita trailed off as she opened the door. He could feel the satisfaction radiating off her like the roaring fire in the pub last night. The pub. It came flooding back to him. Not the fuzzy warmth or the comfort. The stale taste of booze on his tongue. The pounding headache that was a game of agonising tennis between his temples.

"I might have known," said Amita, tutting.

"Go away," he said feebly, pulling the pillow over his face. "Can't you see I'm in utter misery? Please Amita, show some mercy."

"Mercy?" she laughed. "You've had about as much mercy as you're ever going to get, laddie. Your wife has gone to work, *and* taken your children to school because you're still too sozzled."

"I'm not sozzled," he said, throwing the pillow away. "If I was sozzled, I wouldn't have a head that feels like it's been danced on by the local clogging society."

She sniffed the air. Through his bleary eyes he saw her waft away the air from her nose.

"It smells like a brewery in here."

"Another fine observation, Sherlock," he said, throat dry. "Where *do* you get your detective skills?"

"Right, last chance Jason, I'm losing my patience here," she said sternly.

"You have patience?"

That had torn it. Amita turned quickly and headed out of the bedroom. Jason lay still, wondering what his mother-in-law was doing. She came back in brandishing her water bottle from her run.

"Amita?" he asked.

She didn't answer him. She unscrewed the top and threw it over him. The water was ice cold and went up his nose. He shot bolt upright, flapping his arms, coughing, spluttering and generally making a scene.

"Bloody hell!" he shouted. "I can't . . . I can't breathe!"

He tumbled out of the bed. Landing hard on his knees, he coughed until he retched. The water dripped off his greasy, waxy skin and he stared down at his slippers, mashed under his hands.

"Are you finished?" Amita stood over him.

"Why did you do that?" he asked, sitting up and leaning against the bed.

"Because we have work to do."

Jason rubbed his eyes. His hands smelled of beer. Amita was right. The fusty warmth of the bedroom was making him sweat out last night's libations. He felt awful. Amita stepped into his eye line. She had her phone in her hand. He winced at the brightness of the screen in the dark.

"What are you doing?"

"Shut up and listen," she said, tapping the screen.

"Bloody hell, Amita! You're the only person in the world that actually turns their phone off when they go to bed. Nobody does that, you know!"

His voice sounded out from the speaker. It was like a light bulb going off above his head. He sat, face slack, as the message he'd left for Amita was played in full. When he said he loved her, he wanted to be swallowed up by the clothes scattered about him.

"Care to explain yourself?" she said, ending the call.

"Listen, it was a force of habit," he said. "I tell Radha and the kids that I love them all the time. It's second nature and –"

"No! Not that!" she shouted.

Jason just about managed not to throw up with the sudden audio bombardment. His stomach bubbled and gas crept up his throat.

"Madeleine," she said. "Madeleine Frobisher. That's her in those pictures you sent me."

"Pictures?" he rubbed the back of his head.

"Yes, photos that you sent across last night. The ones of the woman looking glamorous, on stage singing. I looked at them this morning. It's definitely Madeleine."

"Great, fantastic," he said, pulling himself back into bed. "I'm glad we solved that mystery."

"You also said I might be on to something," she said. "You also said you might be able to get back into journalism if I *was* right."

"Did I?" he was starting to drift off. "Doesn't sound like something I would say."

"Jason!"

Her voice was like a foghorn. He sat upright again, the cobwebs now fully blown away. His shoulders ached, his stomach hurt and his head was pounding. But he knew he wasn't going to get any more sleep.

"We've got work to do." She started tidying up around the bed. Pulling a T-shirt, jumper, his jeans from the laundry basket, and a fresh pair of pants and socks from a drawer, she threw them at him.

"What are you doing?" he said. "I just want to vegetate in bed today until Radha and the kids get home. Is that so much to ask?"

"Yes, it is. Come on, get dressed. We're going out."

"Out? Where?"

"Madeleine Frobisher's house."

She stopped and looked at him. Shaking her head, she pulled the curtains open, letting the first cracks of dawn into his pit.

"You're not fit to drive. I'll do it," she said.

"Why the hell are we going up to Ullswater?"

She stopped and sighed.

"You said last night in your message if the pictures you sent across were Madeleine then you might have a chance to get back into work. That's what you said, isn't it?"

He was silent.

"Do you want me to play the message again?"

"No, please, don't," he said, cheeks flushing with embarrassment. "Hearing me saying I love you once is more than enough for one lifetime, thanks."

"I've held up my end of the bargain," she said. "I'm telling you that Madeleine Frobisher is the woman in those pictures."

The rusted gears and levers of Jason's mind were very slowly starting to crank back up. He remembered Laura telling him about Madeleine's brush with fame in the sixties and seventies. He remembered the Eurovision revelations and what she had said about if Amita's suspicions were true.

"How sure are you?"

"One hundred per cent," she replied sharply.

"You remember her from back in the day?"

"No," said Amita. "Popular music's never been my thing. All that guitar and loud drum nonsense rots your brain."

"I might have known," he rolled his eyes and felt his head hurt more.

"But I knew Madeleine enough when she lived here to be able to identify her as a young woman. And that was her in those pictures."

Jason reached for his own phone. He brought up the photos Laura had sent him. A young, fresh-faced Madeleine Frobisher beamed back at him. He scrolled through them, each getting more and more dramatic. Life seemed to radiate from her as she stood centre-stage, mid-song, basking in the glory of the crowd. He felt his chest getting tight and his stomach churning. He needed fuel.

"There's nothing in this you know," he said. "She might have had a glamorous past she was keeping schtum about, but Madeleine Frobisher died from a tragic accident. You have to let it go."

"And what if she didn't?" asked Amita, pointing at him. "What if there's shady goings-on? She clearly was important to some people all those years ago. And more importantly now, there could be a killer on the loose."

"The Sheriff of Penrith," he said. "You can't help yourself but interfere, can you?"

"Do you want to go on living like some defunct relic from the past?" she asked him.

Jason blinked. He hadn't been expecting that. "What?"

"I see you, Jason, every day. You're sitting around here rotting away, willing away the hours between breakfast and dinner. You're dying, right in front of my eyes. And it's not just me who's noticing it. Your wife is too, and your children."

"There's nothing wrong with me," he said half-heartedly.

"Oh yes there is. You used to have such energy. Remember the skinny young man who first met me all those years ago? The one who used to make us all laugh and tell us stories from the glamorous world of journalism? Where did he go?"

Jason felt a lump forming in his throat. He couldn't really argue with his mother-in-law. She was right. But it still hurt to hear it.

"Surely if you had even a sniff of a chance to get some of that zest, some of that life about you again, you would take it with both hands," she said. "This is that chance, Jason."

He looked down at the photos again. A text message made his phone ping. It was Laura. She'd sent a picture of a half-eaten bagel and a coffee on the table of a train. *"Back to the Big Smoke and reality. Take care of yourself, mate."*

Nothing fancy, simply a friend's concern. His hangover hadn't cleared up any, but Jason felt something lifting him. The pain in his chest was gone and he got to his feet.

"Madeleine Frobisher's house," he said. "Where is it?"

Amita's eyes widened. She stifled a smile.

"On the road to Ullswater, about a fifteen-minute drive from here."

"Okay," he said, snatching up his pants and socks. "We go for a drive and a look around, that's all. Nothing dramatic, no heroics. You let me do the talking if we run into anyone, and absolutely no mention of murders or killers on the loose. It's just a man and his mother-in-law going for a drive in the country. What could go wrong?"

"What could go wrong indeed," she said.

Jason didn't like the sound of that and he wished he hadn't said it. If the fates had never been tempted before, they certainly had now.

Chapter 9

DOCTOR'S ORDERS

Amita leaned forward. She hated driving, always had done. The thought of speeding down a motorway at seventy miles an hour in a tin can terrified her. She couldn't understand why anyone would want to actively find reasons to do that. Sure, cars were practical. And over her lifetime she'd seen them become an indispensable piece of kit. None of that, however, made her like driving any more. She tried to avoid it as much as possible.

Jason sat beside her. He wasn't helping, of course, hands tightly gripped on the handle above the passenger door. He'd accused her countless times of being a backseat driver. It was all well and good when it wasn't her foot on the accelerator. But he was even *worse* than her.

"Could you speed up a bit, Amita?" he said. "The A66 has an expectation that there aren't queues forming behind cars."

"I'm trying to concentrate," she hissed.

"I appreciate that but the line is getting rather long," he said, looking in the mirror. "I really don't think thirty-five is an appropriate speed."

"We'll get there in one piece, that's all that matters."

"Try telling that to the furious lorry drivers and angry mob in our wake that actually have somewhere to go."

The exit appeared and she let out a sigh of relief. They pulled off the A66 to a chorus of beeps and horns from the traffic. Amita, in her own unique way, ignored them. As they turned off the major roads, the countryside blossomed into full view around them. Gone were the grey, drab buildings of industrial estates and towns; in their place, rolling fields and acres of forest, all resplendent in their autumn colours.

The traffic had disappeared, too. The tidy road that cut through the scenic Cumbrian landscape was empty. The sun was bright now; the clouds chased well away and out of sight. It made everything seem that little bit more alive as the frosts of winter were delayed for one more day at least.

"We don't come out here enough," she said, concentrating on the road. "It's so beautiful, one of the most beautiful parts of the country. And it's on our doorstep."

"It's always the same, Amita," said Jason, almost mournfully. "You always ignore what's right under your nose. And to be fair, it is a rather lovely morning. It's not so nice when the rain is belting down and everything is grey."

Amita had to agree. She continued along the road as Jason concentrated on the directions. His phone spoke and he switched off the maps.

"Just around this corner," he said.

Amita slowed down. They trundled through a narrow stretch of the country road protected from the sun by a thick canopy. The golden browns and burnt oranges of the leaves gave off a magical feel and, as they rounded the corner, pulled back like a curtain to reveal Madeleine Frobisher's estate.

"Blimey," said Jason. "Is that it?"

"Apparently so."

The house wasn't quite what they'd been expecting. A wide, open field of untidy grass, white and scorched from the summer sun, separated it from the road. Crumbling paintwork and cracks snaked up the outside of what had once been a proud, typical English country house. From what they could see, several windows were boarded up towards the rear of the huge, decaying building. Trees and bushes were overgrown and running wild, reaching out to try to swallow the main house and reclaim it for their own.

Amita turned the car into the long, winding path that led to the front door. Potholes and divots made them bounce around as they carried on up the driveway. Jason bumped his head off the roof and yelped in pain.

"Not exactly what I'd pictured," he said.

"No, nor me," Amita agreed. Despite her Googling, the house and grounds were shabbier than she'd imagined. Clearly once a grand country house, now it barely looked like *anyone* lived there, let alone Madeleine who was always so well turned out.

She navigated the broken pathway and pulled up at the open courtyard at the front of the mansion. Up close, Madeleine's home was no better. Thick weeds made for an unsightly ring around the base of the building. The tall windows were filthy with dust and dirt, the light of the day showing them in all their ugly glory. Inside was dark and foreboding, no sign of life anywhere at all. Jason and Amita climbed out of the car and looked around.

"It sort of makes sense and it sort of doesn't," he said.

"What's that supposed to mean?" she asked.

"It's a big house in the country, just what you would expect of a former pop star, no matter how long ago it was. But it's in a pretty shabby state."

"Near condemned is what I'd call it," she added. "It really wasn't what I was expecting of Madeleine Frobisher at all. She was always so well presented. She put the rest of us to shame."

"Even Georgie?"

"*Especially* Georgie Littlejohn," Amita couldn't help but twist the knife. "It was almost one of her trademarks. You'd never see her wear the same outfit twice. And to think that this is where she lived. It doesn't make any sense."

"Be fair, Amita. It's a lot easier to look after yourself than one of these old country estates. These things are protected by heritage orders and all kinds of paperwork. They're more trouble than they're worth. That's why all the old toff families open them up to the public – it's hard enough to break even with a lot of these places."

Amita couldn't argue, but she found it difficult to comprehend. Looking at the ramshackle building made her heart hurt a little. This was no place for anyone to live, let alone a woman of Madeleine's age.

"I imagine this is Grade I listed," said Jason, closing the car door with a thump. "There are a few of these places around here, although most of them are in much better nick. We used to get called up by the estate managers when they were holding craft fairs and tours of the gardens.

They loved a bit of free publicity and it was always a nice day out, to be fair. But I've never been out here, never even knew it existed, in fact."

"Clearly there was a lot about Madeleine Frobisher that none of us knew," said Amita thoughtfully.

They stood looking at the big, old house for a few minutes more, unsure what to expect from it.

Then Jason came to his senses. "Right, what's the plan?" he asked, clapping his hands together.

"Plan?" asked Amita innocently.

"Yes, the plan. The plan of action."

"I don't have a plan."

"What do you mean you don't have a plan? You've dragged us all the way out here and you don't have a plan? What were you expecting to happen when we got here?"

"I was *expecting* the family journalist to at least have *some* clue as to where to begin," she fired back. "Isn't this bread and butter to people in your profession? Door-knocking, I think you call it?"

Jason started to answer. Then he stopped. He looked at his mother-in-law. "This isn't exactly a door knock," he said. "And how do you know what that is, anyway?"

"I know how to use the internet, Jason, I'm not totally dense. Door-knocking, according to Google, is when you turn up at someone's door, quite literally, to ask them questions."

"Exactly," he said. "This isn't a door knock. There's nobody to answer. The owner is dead."

"So what are you going to do?"

Jason sniffed. He looked about the empty courtyard in front of Madeleine's mansion. Then he gave a quick glance down the driveway.

"Right, let's have a shufty around the back, seeing as nobody is looking," he said, hoisting up his trousers.

"Is that legal?" she asked. "Aren't there laws against trespassing?"

"You should have come up with a better plan, then."

They wandered around the side of the house. The shadows were long and dark as the trees and wild forest rose high above them. Dirty moss and lichens stuck to the side of the mansion like barnacles on the hull of a ship. The weeds were bigger around here and everything felt even more tired and disused.

A high wall extended out from the back of the house. In its centre was a battered old door hanging limply on rusted hinges, paint peeling off in great chunks. Jason peered through the gap.

"See anything?" asked Amita.

"It's the gardens," he said, pulling the door open a little more. "Let's have a quick peek."

"Jason, I really don't think we should."

"You were the one who wanted to find out what happened to Madeleine," he said. "If anything did. We're only looking around her garden, we're not breaking in or anything."

Amita didn't like it. But she followed her son-in-law as he stepped beyond the door. A wide, unruly garden stretched out in front of them, ringed by a high wall of grey stone laced with cracks. The remains of a greenhouse were all that broke up the mayhem of the overgrown grass and bushes. Jason let out a whistle.

"And you tell me our garden at home is bad," he said.

"Something doesn't add up here," said Amita, nudging a broken plant pot with the toe of her trainer. "The house, the garden, it's all such a mess. But Madeleine was a proper lady. I never saw her with a hair out of place. She was immaculate, all of the time."

"Like I said before, some people put up a good front," he said.

"No, I mean, yes, you're right. But this is different," she said. "This is *such* a contrast between the woman I knew and how she lived at home. And then there's the fact she was cleaning her own windows, you know, when she fell. Madeleine Frobisher was a lovely woman, Jason, truly she was. She would do anything for anyone. But she never struck me as the domestic type. And taking a look around this place hasn't convinced me otherwise."

Amita spotted something in a large clump of bleached white grass near her foot. She stooped down and picked it up.

"Police tape," said Jason.

The small length of blue and white tape fluttered in the chilling breeze. Amita swallowed, her throat suddenly dry.

"This must be where she was found," she looked up at the house. "She must have been cleaning some of those windows up there."

Jason peered up at the tall windows overlooking the gardens. They were high, too high, dangerously high. Then he looked down at the hard paving stones below them.

"Wouldn't fancy falling from up there," he said. "It must have been instant."

"What the hell was she doing up there?" said Amita.

Her voice began to crack a little. Jason sensed a change in her. His mother-in-law, the confident woman who liked to be in charge, was retreating. She seemed almost vulnerable as she rubbed her arms, still holding onto the shred of police tape.

"You okay?" he asked her.

"Yes," she said after a slight pause. "Yes, fine, it's just . . . I don't know. I'm not sure what I was expecting to find up here, Jason. And seeing the state of this place and where, you know, Madeleine met her match. It's all a little real."

"Yeah, I guess you're right," he said. "Maybe we should go."

"Yes, I think that's probably for the best."

He reached out and took Amita's arm. He led her through the garden door, and they headed back around the side of the estate and towards the car parked in the courtyard. But, as they were about to leave, a blood-curdling scream came from the bowels of the manor house. Jason and Amita looked wide-eyed at each other.

"What was that?" she whispered.

"I don't know," he replied. "It came from the house."

There was another scream followed by a desperately sad howl. Jason and Amita turned back to face the crumbling Frobisher mansion, unsure what to expect.

"What should we do?" she whispered.

"I'm not sure," he said. "The journalist in me says we should go and investigate. But the hangover says we turn and walk away like nothing has happened and never speak about it again."

"I don't think —"

Before Amita could reveal her decision, the front door of the mansion burst open. A little woman, bent over herself and pawing at the air to stay steady, came staggering out, bawling. She collapsed to her knees on the steps and looked directly at Jason and Amita.

"She's dead," she sobbed. "She's bloody dead."

Chapter 10

COCK 'N' HEN

The inside of Madeleine Frobisher's mansion wasn't much better than outside. The smell of damp and rotting wood hung in the air like a ghostly presence. In the short tour Amita and Jason had been given, there was very little that showed this was a home to anyone, let alone a former pop star.

The walls were mostly bare, layers of dust clung to almost every surface, including the floor. The weak autumn light shining in the windows only made the place seem sadder somehow, as if life was completely unwelcome here.

Amita and Jason had been led through the gloom to a small kitchen in the rear. At least here there was some heat. The dying embers of a fire in the corner seemed to beat away the deathly emptiness of the rest of the house.

Jason helped the crooked woman down onto a chair beside a big, gnarled worktable. She had stopped crying now but was ashen white.

"I'm sorry," she said over and over, her accent tinted with Scots. "I . . . I was so shocked when I found out."

"It's been a big shock for us all," said Amita, trying to comfort the woman. "I don't think any of us were expecting to hear this awful news."

"No . . . no," said the woman.

She rubbed her eyes and sniffed. Jason felt awkward. He shifted his weight from one foot to the other. Amita picked up on his fidgeting.

"Why don't you put the kettle on, Jason?" she said.

It was a relief to be given something to do. He hopped into action without question, seeking out the kettle, mugs and some tea bags. Amita pulled up a chair beside the woman and rubbed her back.

"It's just so sudden," the woman said. "I mean, you wake up every morning and you don't think about it, do you? You think you've got years and years left and suddenly, whoosh, it's all gone, forever."

"I know, I know," said Amita. "Like I said, it's been a terrible shock to us all. She'll be very sorely missed."

"Oh, she will that," the woman agreed. "There won't be a day that goes by where I won't think about her. I always say that to Stanley – he's my husband, been married for fifty years – I always say to him, you don't miss what you've got until it's gone."

"That's a song lyric, isn't it?" asked Jason.

The two women stared at him blankly. He shook his head and poured out the tea. "Philistines."

"It can all change in the blink of an eye. It's so shocking, isn't it?"

"It really is," Amita agreed. "You have to cherish every single moment with the people you love. Because they're not going to be around forever."

"That is so true," the other woman said, taking her tea from Jason.

"Did you know Madeleine well?" Amita asked.

The crooked woman's face dropped. She sat upright for the first time and looked at her, then at Jason.

"Madeleine?" she snorted. "Madeleine's been dead for a week."

Amita was silent. She looked at Jason for inspiration.

"But I thought . . . you came screaming out of the house saying she's dead, like you'd only just found out."

"Don't be daft," said the woman. "I'm her housekeeper, I think I'd know if she had kicked the bucket or not. And now I've got a double loss to mourn.'"

"So who's dead now?" asked Jason.

The housekeeper nodded towards a basket down by the door. Amita nodded at Jason, silently urging him to investigate. He put down his mug and edged over. Trying to stay at a safe distance, he pulled back a filthy blanket in the basket with his shoe.

"Bloody hell fire," he said.

Amita shot up from the kitchen table. "What is it?"

"It's a cat," he said. "Or it *was* a cat."

"A cat?" Amita turned to the housekeeper.

"It's Tumnus," she said, starting to cry again. "Poor Tumnus. We had her for ten years. I came in this morning and she wasn't moving. So I offered her some milk and she still didn't move. Then I saw she wasn't breathing and . . . well. She's gone."

She started to howl again. "Madeleine pretended she hated Tumnus. She was always giving me trouble for feeding her and keeping her around the house. She used to say 'Edna,

87

don't feed that bloody cat, it'll think this is its home and there are enough strays in here already'. I think she probably quite liked Tumnus really, she just couldn't admit it."

Jason replaced the blanket over the dead cat. 'I don't know what the drill is. How do we dispose of this?"

"Jason," Amita chided. "Don't be so insensitive. Edna here is clearly upset."

"I am, you know," Edna said, looking between them. "You don't think it's going to affect you as badly as this. It's only a cat, after all. But with everything that's happened in the last week or so, what with Madeleine passing and me being ill, it's been very stressful."

"I'll bet," said Amita, sitting back down. "You said you were Madeleine's housekeeper?"

"That's right," the colour was returning to Edna's cheeks. "Been here for years, I've lost count actually. It's like a second home, this place."

"A second home that could do with some TLC," said Jason.

"Yes, well, it's not what it used to be," said Edna, a little embarrassed. "But they cost so much to maintain, these old houses. Madeleine couldn't afford it and in the end I think she simply stopped bothering. She wasn't as young as she used to be. Who is?"

She nudged Amita's arm. Jason rolled his eyes.

Amita was a little more polite. "So you knew her well?"

"Yes, I'll say. We were like that," Edna knotted her fingers. "The good times and the bad, I was there for Madeleine. And she was there for me, too. A couple of years ago I had a bit of a scare, I found a lump you see. Had to go to the doctor's but the waiting times were like an execution. You know what they're like."

Again she nudged Amita who smiled back politely.

"Anyway, I told Madeleine I'd need a week off, just in case there was something sinister. Not only did she give me a *month*, she paid for me to go private. She was like that. It was – "

"Let me guess, an awful shame what happened to her," Jason interrupted her.

Edna nodded and sipped her tea. He ignored the dirty look coming from his mother-in-law and pressed ahead with his questions.

"Are you here every day, Edna?" he asked.

"Yes, five days a week," she answered. "I normally get here about nine and can stay all the way up until six or seven, depending on what needs to be done; shopping, cleaning, collecting things, everything really. I'm not as young as I used to be, getting up and down these stairs to dust isn't as easy as it used to be."

Amita looked about the place. It was hardly spick and span. She didn't rate Edna's dwindling skills as a housekeeper, especially given the state of the place. She began to wonder if Madeleine was being Madeleine, keeping her friend on from the kindness of her heart, even if it was costing her a small fortune. Amita had never had staff. She'd grown up in a two-room back-to-back in Sheffield with no running water and an outdoor toilet shared by the whole terrace. Jason running her around Penrith and to the bingo was as close as she had ever come to being waited on. But she could imagine a full-time wage wasn't something to take on lightly, especially in hard times.

"And what happened the day Madeleine was found?" asked Amita. "We heard it was the postman who, you know, made the discovery."

"Yes, poor chap," Edna sniffed. "Geoff, he's salt of the earth. Couldn't be more helpful."

"In what way?" asked Jason.

"He's always been very generous with his time. He's always happy to give me a lift into Penrith if it's on his way. We've had him here for about five years, I think. Nothing's too much bother for Geoff. He'd wait by the mailbox at the end of the drive and beep if he knew I needed a lift."

"You didn't see Madeleine, the day that she died?" asked Amita.

Edna put down her cup. She pulled a scrunched-up tissue from the sleeve of her cardigan and wiped her nose and cheeks. Twisting it between her hands, she bowed her head.

"I can't remember," she said.

"What do you mean?" asked Jason.

"I can't remember, isn't that awful of me?" she said. "I can't remember the last time I spoke with Madeleine. After all these years together, after everything she had done for me. I can't . . . I can't even remember the last time we spoke."

She started to cry again. Amita shifted over and gave her a hug. Jason was confused. He had been in positions like this before. Grieving relatives, friends, loved ones, it was hard to make sense of what they were saying sometimes. Grief made fools of everyone and everyone reacted differently. But this was his job. He had to get to the truth.

"I'm sorry to hear that," he said as warmly as he could. "But I don't understand, Edna. If you were here every day, all day, why can't you remember the last time you spoke with Madeleine?"

Edna sobbed for a moment more. When she pulled herself together, she looked blearily at Jason by the sink.

"I had a turn," she said.

"A turn? What happened?" he asked.

"Jason," Amita said. "That's personal. You don't have to say, Edna, if you don't want to."

"I'm only asking," he said.

"I was taken ill the night before Madeleine died," said the housekeeper. "I know I've not been in the best of health for a while – I'm on so many pills and I do get muddled about which ones I've taken – but I've never passed out before. A proper funny turn, it was. The doctors think I fainted and probably hit my head on the way down. I'm lucky I wasn't like Madeleine – I could have been a goner . . ."

"What exactly happened?" asked Jason.

"Oh, the doctors gave me a list as long as my arm – blood pressure, angina, dicky kidneys – I've got the lot. They always use such big words, don't they? I think they get enjoyment from it. But basically, I've got the lot. Although I can't complain, they looked after me properly, even organised a taxi for Stanley and me when they let me go the next day."

"What do they think caused you to faint?" Jason pressed.

"It could be all sorts, they said. Low blood pressure, stress, or just me being plain clumsy. Whatever it was, they said it explains why I can't remember a darned thing. Global Amnesia, they call it," said Edna. "It was horrible, absolutely horrible."

"How very convenient . . ." Jason muttered.

He was getting frustrated. Amita tutted loudly. She leaned over and took Edna's cup.

"Do you want a top-up?" she asked, stepping between them. "How about a biscuit? Do you have any biscuits in this big, draughty house?"

"There are some caramel logs in that cupboard over there."

"Oh I love a caramel log," said Amita happily, fetching the biscuits. "And a teacake, too. Just occasionally, they're very sweet. It's a nice treat, though."

"It is," Edna smiled. "Although do you know what I really love? A snowball."

"Now *there*'s a lovely treat now and then," Amita agreed. "Although have you seen them these days? They're half the size and flat like an oyster. Everything is changing, Edna. Soon we won't have anything left from the old days."

She refilled the housekeeper's mug as Jason started to pace back and forth around the kitchen. Taking long gulps of tea and bites from their caramel logs, the two women sat in happy silence. Amita gave a quick, knowing look to Jason who stopped his pacing.

"What's that condition the doctors said you had again, Edna?" Amita asked quietly.

"Global Amnesia," Edna cupped her mug between her hands.

"What's that then when it's at home? The doctors said it could be down to a number of things?"

"That's about the gist of it," Edna said. "The doctors said it was most likely brought on by extreme stress or a stressful situation."

"And are you stressed? Are you worried about anything?"

"Where do I start?" she said. "I was worried about this house, worried about Stanley. His back's gone again, you see. Worried about the grandkids, worried about not being able to get up and down the stairs here like I used to. Worried that if I lose my job here then who's going to pay the bills? We're already struggling, can't get by on Stanley's pension alone and mine's not due for another year. And I was worried about Madeleine."

"Madeleine?" Amita asked. "What about her?"

"I heard shouting," the housekeeper continued. "The day I had my turn. I remember that. Shouting from upstairs. It was Madeleine and another voice. I think it was a man. She'd sent me home early but I popped back to make sure Tumnus was fed. I heard the voices from upstairs and, the next thing I know, I've blacked out. I woke up again in the back of an ambulance, on my own with the paramedics. They were lovely, they told me where I was and where I was going. Madeleine had called the ambulance. She always looked out for me. But I was on my own when I came around."

Amita looked at Jason. He had a look of concern stretched across his face.

"And you don't know who the other voice belonged to? No visitors or anything?" she asked.

"No, I don't think so," said Edna. "Madeleine had insisted I take the rest of the afternoon off. I was a bit relieved to be honest. It meant I could go into town and pick up a few things for dinner. Stanley likes his corned beef but it's got to be a certain make. And they don't do it in all of the shops. It's always a faff but he likes what he likes."

"When was this, Edna?" asked Jason.

"Was two weeks ago, before all of this horrible business. First her funeral, then Tumnus going. I could be doing with some good news, I really could."

"I think we all could," said Amita.

"You never know, you might be in Madeleine's will," laughed Jason.

"Jason," said Amita.

"I should bloody hope so," said the housekeeper. "After everything I did for her. On my hands and knees every day for thirty years, scrubbing her toilets and emptying her bins. I bloody hope so."

Amita blinked. She gave a quick look over to Jason who was just as surprised.

"I'm sure you will be," she said. "You two must have been close, spending all of that time together."

"We were like sisters," said Edna. "Sisters love each other, they enjoy each other's company. But they also fight."

"Did you fight with Madeleine often?" asked Jason.

Edna's face went hard, her mouth stiff at the edges.

"In thirty years we only ever fought about one thing. Every time it was the same thing, the same subject. For three decades I could never get a straight answer from her. She was a kind and darling woman. But, my god, she could be stubborn when the mood suited her."

"What did you fight about?" asked Amita.

"This place," she looked about the kitchen. "The house."

"The house?" asked Jason. "What about it?"

"Look at it. It's much too big for a woman of Madeleine's age, god rest her. Even fifteen, twenty years ago it was starting to be a bit much. A beautiful big house like this with a garden and acres of land. She should have done something with it, put it to good use."

"And you told her this?"

"I was sick of telling her," sniffed Edna. "I told you. We only ever fought when the house came up. I told her she

94

should open it up to an animal charity, give it over to all the wee dogs and cats that get abandoned. It's awful, it breaks my heart, it really does. She should have turned this place into a refuge years ago instead of letting it fall into ruin and have me waxing and sweeping up dust that only came back the next week. She never did it though, never wanted to leave the house. She always said it was *her* refuge. I never understood that. How could she need a refuge? She could defend herself and look after herself. Not like those poor wee animals."

She shook her head.

"And you never fought about anything else?" asked Amita.

"Not a thing. Like I said, we were like sisters. Best pals. I sometimes used to wonder if there was anyone else in the world she knew as well as me. She was more than my boss, she was a pal, a soulmate. I miss her already."

Edna stared off into space after her little rant, eyes welling up. Amita fetched the mugs and dumped them in the sink. Jason subtly gestured to the door.

"We're off now, Edna," she said.

The housekeeper seemed to snap out of a trance. She smiled weakly, then her face dropped a little.

"Hold on," she said. "Who *are* you two?"

The question caught Amita off-guard. She started to stammer before Jason stepped in. "Jason Brazel, freelance reporter," he said confidently. "I'm doing a piece on the great country estates of Cumbria and we came across this place while out driving, isn't that right?"

"Yes . . . that's right," said Amita.

Edna didn't seem to care. Her eyes had fallen on the cat box near the door. She started to well up.

It was enough of a cue for Jason to make briskly for the kitchen door. "Thank you for your time," he said, almost dragging Amita with him. "We'll be in touch if we need anything else."

They hurried out of the kitchen and through the draughty mansion. Practically bursting out of the front door, they scrambled to the car. Amita started it up and pulled off down the driveway, not stopping to look back.

"Blimey," said Jason. "That was a near thing. I thought she might twig who we were."

"You shouldn't tell lies like that, Jason. You can get us into trouble."

"We came to find out more information, Amita, and that's what we've done," he rubbed at his temple. "But, bloody hell, it's made my head spin."

"Yes, mine too," she said. "Edna seems like a nice woman and all, but don't you think there was something a bit off about her?"

"What do you mean?" he asked, still wincing.

"I'm not sure," she said. "The whole ailing housekeeper act was as stale as that tea. For someone in charge of cleaning and tidying, the place was in a right old state. Clearly she's too old for the job."

"But Madeleine and her were like sisters, she said so herself," said Jason. "How would you feel about sacking your sister from a job you'd given her for thirty years?"

"Even the thought of working for my relatives makes my teeth itch, Jason."

"Thanks, Amita," he said.

"Blood relatives," she sighed. "You're different."

"So you've said, many times," he laughed.

"You know what I mean. No, Edna the housekeeper – it doesn't all add up, to my mind."

"She was in the hospital though. The woman isn't well, Amita," he said. "If anything, it makes what the police are saying even more watertight."

"What do you mean?"

"Well, Madeleine's housekeeper has taken ill with one of her funny turns," he said. "Who's going to wash the windows? Nobody else around here that we know about. She fills the bucket, climbs the ladder and –" he slapped his hands together "– Wallop! Goodnight Vienna."

Amita winced at the thought. "Jason, please."

"Sorry," he said. "You get the picture."

Amita chewed it over, watching the road twist and weave ahead of them.

"Just because Edna was in hospital doesn't mean she's not involved somehow," she said.

"How do you figure?"

"You heard her when we mentioned the will," she said. "That was venomous, bitter even. If she thought she had something to gain, money, or the house to turn it into an animal shelter or something like that, then she wouldn't stop, would she?"

"You mean she might have recruited someone else?" he asked.

"Possibly," she said. "It's not beyond belief that Edna had an accomplice. What was the name of her husband again? The one who liked corned beef?"

"Stanley, wasn't it?"

"That's right," she said. "Who's to say that Stanley isn't a big, strapping six-foot-plus former wrestler with hands that can crush apples and a powerful temper to match?"

"That sounds more like Sandy, if you ask me," Jason snorted. "This is all getting very complicated. And the more I think about it, the more my brain hurts."

"As much as it pains me to say it, I think you might be right and –"

She slammed on the brakes. It wasn't enough. The huge articulated lorry was going too fast. The driver frantically swirled the wheel but the cab was too close. A long, painful screech pierced Amita's and Jason's ears. They winced as both vehicles came to a complete stop.

Amita and Jason looked at each other. They stayed silent for a moment. Then both said the exact same thing at the same time.

"Bugger."

Chapter 11

LEGS ELEVEN

"Where did he come from?" asked Amita, her hands shaking.

"I don't know," said Jason. "But I didn't like the sound of that massive scrape up the side of the car. It sounded very aggressive and, more importantly, *very* expensive."

A rattle came from the window. A surly-looking workman in a hi-vis vest and hard hat was frothing at the mouth. Amita rolled the window down just a crack. He craned his head and barked through the gap.

"Why don't you watch where you're going, you stupid old bat!"

Amita blinked. She thought, for the briefest of moments, that the workie was speaking to somebody else. Then his words settled in her mind. And she realised that she *had* to be the target.

She was about to give back as good as she had been given, but her son-in-law jumped to her defence first.

"Hey!" Jason shouted. "You can't speak to her like that. You were the one speeding down a country road."

"She should have seen me coming! The truck is forty-four tonnes, for god's sake!"

"And you were driving it like a maniac!"

"I'll show you a maniac, mate!"

"Oh yeah?"

"Yeah!"

"Yeah?"

"Yeah, I will."

"Well, go on then."

"I will. You don't want me to mate, believe me!"

"Oh I'm sure I do."

"I will then."

"Go ahead."

"Alright then, I will."

Amita's neck started to hurt looking back and forth from Jason to the lorry driver. She was about to call time on this battle of wills when the worker slammed his hands on the roof of their car. He stormed off around the back of the car and headed for the passenger door.

"Oh god," said Jason. "I didn't think he would *actually* rise to it. Quick! Lock the door, Amita!"

She shot a finger to the lock button next to the radio. In her haste, she slipped and turned the radio on. The door opened as ABBA's *Waterloo* came blaring out of the speakers. A big, thick, ham-like hand grabbed Jason by the shoulder and pulled him sideways. If the music hadn't been so loud, Amita was certain she would have heard her son-in-law whimper. His eyes were as big as saucers as he was bundled out of the car by the surly workman.

"Bloody hell," she said, quickly getting out herself, the music still booming from the speakers.

Amita might have found it funny if she wasn't scared to death by what the workman was going to do with Jason. She hurried around the back of the car. The driver had Jason by the scruff of his jumper. He tossed him like a rag doll until Jason tumbled over the remains of a stone wall that lined the country road. He toppled over the edge, legs up in the air.

"Jason!" Amita shouted.

The lorry driver paid no heed. He started to climb over the wall, a mean grimace on his pock-marked and stubbly face. Amita thought about trying to stop him. She knew she couldn't *physically* do it – the man was a small giant with a gut to match. Instead, she scrambled for her phone. She was about to dial 999 when a voice called out from down the road behind them.

"What's going on here?"

The lorry driver stopped, a leg astride each side of the wall. His grimace instantly changed. The terrible anger vanished and he looked panicked. Amita turned to see a man in an immaculate suit walking down the country road towards them. He was also wearing a hard hat and he carried a hi-vis vest over his arm. He was pointing at the workman as he walked briskly towards the scene of the crash.

"What's happened to that man on the other side of the wall?" he asked as he neared them.

Jason's head popped up from behind the stones. He was grey, eyes still wide. He looked about like he'd been woken from a deep sleep.

"Well?" asked the man in the suit.

"Erm . . . nothing Mr Francis," said the workman. "Nothing at all."

"Nothing?" said Francis, his voice deep and smooth. "I come down here and see one of my lorries has been rubbed up against a car and one of my employees looking like he's about to tan a hide, and you say there's nothing going on?"

The workman slunk back over from the wall. He was still the same huge man, but now he looked like a scolded schoolboy. He bowed his head and took off his hard hat. Passing the rim around his hands, he tucked his chin into his sweaty chest.

"Is everyone alright here?" asked Mr Francis, turning his attention to Amita. "Nobody hurt, nobody injured?"

He rested his hand on Amita's shoulder and gave her a warm smile, his eyes a cool blue that sparkled in the dim light of the morning. There was a charm about him, not a hair out of place on his well-groomed head. And the smell, Amita noticed, was expensive cologne.

"Er . . . no," she said. "I mean, well, yes, there has been an accident. It was all a bit of a blur really."

"Are you okay, madam?" Francis took Amita's hands in his and warmed them. "You're not injured, are you?"

"No, no I'm fine, just a little shaken."

"Okay, that's okay. Would you like me to get you an ambulance? A doctor, perhaps?"

"It was only a bump, Mr Francis," the workman piped up.

"Are you a doctor?" he fired back at his employee. "Do you have a medical degree?"

"No, honestly I'm fine," said Amita. "Truly, I am. Nothing a good cup of tea won't sort out."

"That's it settled then," he said, offering his arm. "You're coming with me to the site office. We'll get you a nice cuppa and maybe rustle you up a biscuit or two."

"No . . . really, that's far too much."

"I insist," said Francis. "I'll get my men to sort out this mess and bring your car up to the site."

"Please, Mr Francis,"

"Call me Rory," he said. "And you are?"

"Rory, no sorry, *you're* Rory. I'm Amita. And I really couldn't," Amita tried to insist, but not very hard. "My son-in-law and I must be getting back to town."

"After. Come on, my car is just up here."

He led her up the road towards a long, sleek BMW that looked like it was still going a hundred miles per hour, even though it was parked up at the side of the road.

"Well, if you insist, Rory," said Amita, looking back over her shoulder.

Jason was clambering over the wall, the big workman still towering over him. He looked unsteady on his feet as he gave his nemesis a wary look. Rory Francis opened the back door and gestured for Amita to climb in. She did and immediately relaxed. The warmth of the heated seats instantly warmed her and she smelled the newness of the leather seats.

Francis got into the driver's seat. He adjusted the rearview mirror so he could see Amita. His cool eyes reflected back at her.

"Comfortable?" he asked.

"Yes, absolutely," she said. "Very."

"Right, we're just up the road here. We'll get you sorted quick as a flash."

"But what about Jason and –?"

"He'll be fine. My man will bring him up. And we'll sort your car out, no problem."

He pulled off. Driving past the crash, Amita watched as Jason nervously climbed into the cabin of the truck.

As they passed the huge lorry, she noticed the name on the cabin – Francis Construction.

"No coincidence, I take it?" she said.

Francis laughed. He watched her carefully in the mirror.

"Silver spoon firmly in mouth, I'm afraid," he said. "My father started the company in our back garden when I was a nipper. He built it up, built it up, built it up, so to speak. And now I have the dubious honour of following in his footsteps."

"And do you get your hands dirty, Mr Francis?" she asked.

"Silver spoon, but brickie's hands," he flashed them at her. "Dad had me on the site before I could walk. I went to a public school, but every summer I was out rain or shine helping with the lads."

He turned off the country road. Scaffolding was being erected all across the two fields either side of the track. Workmen were busy putting together the skeletons of a brand new housing estate. They passed a huge sign that showed an artist's impression of what some of the new homes would look like.

A small village of portacabins stood among the mud and chaos at the back of the field. A ramshackle old farmhouse was close by, chickens scattering as Francis pulled his car up close to them.

"We're here," he said. "Now won't you come in, Amita, and we can get this mess sorted out once and for all?"

"But Jason . . ."

"He's on his way. Look, they're going to collect your car already."

He pointed out of the back window. A flatbed lorry was trundling down the track they'd come up from the country road. Amita felt a little less guilty now that something was happening.

"Alright," she said. "Just one quick cuppa."

Francis led her up the metal steps of the nearest double-decker portacabin. When he opened the door there was a flurry of action as four workmen hopped about pretending to be busy. They quickly scattered as Francis led Amita to a table. He cleared off the empty crisp packets and scrunched-up newspapers and set about making her tea at the small kitchen area in the corner.

"Now, Amita, tell me," he said. "That's not a very Cumbrian name, if you don't mind me saying."

"I *do* mind you saying, actually," she said. "I've been Cumbrian since I was ten, as it happens. I've got a brother and two sisters who were born in Cumbria and my parents furnished the whole county with everything from televisions to light bulbs for the better part of thirty years. So what's a Cumbrian name when it's at home?"

Francis laughed. She didn't suppose anything fazed him. He was a businessman, a smooth talker, someone who believed entirely in his own press and felt he was right all of the time. She reckoned that sort of thing went along with the territory. When your name is on the side of lorries and above giant billboards, it must take a lot to shake your confidence.

"I'm second-generation Cumbrian," she said. "And proud of it, I might add."

"Okay, I believe you," he said, pouring hot water from the kettle. "I like to get personal pretty early. I call a spade a spade. And in my profession, there are plenty of those."

He brought the tea over and sat down beside her. She took a sip. It was awful, weak. He might as well have gathered puddle water and served her that instead.

"Listen, you have to be honest with me, Amita," said Francis, reaching out and touching her hand. "You are alright, aren't you? You're not injured in any way? No side effects from the crash? No headaches or blurred vision?"

"No, nothing, I told you," she said. "I was pretty much at a stop when your lorry scraped up the side of my car."

"Okay, good, thank god for that," he said. "Which brings me neatly on to my next subject. Your car. I know a very good man in Carlisle who'll be able to fix it for you no bother. And it won't cost you a penny. If you leave it with me, then we don't have to get the insurance people involved. And believe me, for a truck that size and a firm like mine, that's an almighty pain in the backside. Do you understand?"

Amita realised now why she was being given the golden treatment. Francis had been buttering her up, keeping her sweet so she wouldn't cause a fuss. That's why he was so concerned about her wellbeing. She was a little disappointed. He was undeniably charming. He smelled and looked good and he could charm the birds from the trees. Then she came back to her senses.

"That's why I'm here then," she said, using her faux anger to push the mug of horrid tea away. "I'm here so you can make sure I don't sue."

"Sue is such an ugly word, isn't it?" he laughed. "I don't want you to sue, of course I don't. This is one of the biggest housing developments that this area has ever seen. We've got permission to build a hundred new homes here for families of all sizes. And a lot more when the estate next door sells up."

"Next door?" Amita asked.

"Yeah, the one a field over," he pointed out of the window. "We're going to do the same with that place."

She followed his finger. He was pointing in the direction of Madeleine Frobisher's estate. Something twitched in the back of Amita's mind. She wasn't quite sure what it was. But it was something.

There was a toot from outside the door. Francis got up and peered out.

"Ah, there we go," he said. "Your chariot has arrived safely. And your son-in-law too, by the looks of things. Jason, was it?"

"That's right," she said.

Francis waved out of the window by the door. He turned back to Amita and clasped his hands.

"Now what do you say, Amita, darling?" he said. "Why don't you let me take care of the car personally? I'll have it good as new and delivered anywhere you want. No charge, no fuss, nobody needs to know. How does that sound? Too good to be true?"

"And we all know what that means, don't we?" she said.

The door opened as Francis laughed again. Jason came staggering in, muddy and covered in bits of grass and hay. The surly driver, who still looked ready to decapitate him, lingered by the door until Francis dismissed him.

"You must be Jason," he said, shaking his hand. "Rory Francis. I've been having a lovely chat with your mother-in-law about getting your car all fixed up free of charge. A bloody pain, all of this, but you're both okay so no harm done. Can't apologise enough, of course. These things happen though, don't they?"

Jason looked bewildered. He pointed at Amita, then to Francis. He shook his head.

"I can't believe you left me alone with that Neanderthal," he said.

"Who?" asked Francis.

"Your employee. He's spent the last fifteen minutes growling, swearing under his breath, and cracking his knuckles every time he looked at me. I felt like the last bit of fried chicken in the bucket at a cannibals' Christmas convention."

Francis laughed loudly and slapped Jason on the back. The force almost knocked him flat on his face. Thankfully, he steadied himself in time before he suffered another indignity.

A knock came at the door. Jason jumped. He spun around to look at it. He retreated behind Amita as Francis opened the door.

"What the bloody hell is that bloody heap doing in my bloody yard?" barked an old man, storming into the portacabin.

His boots squelched and dragged dirt behind him as he came. His face was purple like beetroot, his fuzzy mutton chops a brilliant white. He looked around at everyone in the room in turn and snarled.

"Well? Somebody want to explain why that pile of rust and rivets is parked up in my bloody yard?"

"Rust and rivets?" Jason asked. "What are you talking about?"

That drew the ire of angry Mutton Chops. He cocked his eye at Jason like it was a loaded pistol.

"Oh aye, it speaks, does it?" he said. "And who might you be? The Queen of Sheba?"

"Jason Brazel," he said, a little bemused. "I'm a journalist."

"A journalist!" Francis blurted. "You're a journalist?"

"That's right, a journalist. Is there a problem?"

"You never told me your son-in-law was a journalist," said Francis to Amita.

"I didn't think it was important," she shrugged. "Why? Is there a problem?"

"Aye, there's a problem," barked Mutton Chops. "A pretty big bloody problem in the shape of that battered old car that's parked up in my yard out there, blocking me in!"

"*Your* yard?" Amita asked.

"Is there an echo in here?" he snapped. "Aye, and don't let this fly-by-night in the Italian suit let you think otherwise. The name's Taylor, Mike Taylor. My family has owned this here farm, and the land, for one hundred and forty-two years and ten months. They can build what they like on it as long as the money is right. And the sooner they knock into next door, the better. I'll be off."

"You own this land?" asked Jason.

"Heavens to Murgatroyd, haven't you been listening, son? Aye, I do. And I'm looking to get away from all of this bloody noise from Francis and his conquistadors and get some bloody peace. But I can't do that with a lump of battered metal and four wheels blocking me in."

Amita cleared her throat. She was getting quite sick of all this. She nodded at Jason and bowed a little as she excused herself.

"Well, it was lovely to meet you both," she said. "But Jason and I have got a lot to be getting on with."

"Yes, of course," said Francis. He handed her his card as she was leaving. "Give me a call, any time Amita," he said. "We'll get that car of yours sorted out in a jiffy. Absolutely no need to speak with those insurance bozos, am I right?"

He smiled and patted Jason on the back again as they left the portacabin. Mike Taylor didn't say anything. Amita was a little miffed at that.

* * *

The car had been deposited close to the ramshackle farmhouse. A tractor was sitting in an open garage just beyond it, blocked in by their motor. Amita laughed at that and she thought about stalling a little longer. Then she noticed the side of the car where the lorry had scraped itself along.

"Good grief," she said, taking in the huge silver streaks and scratches where the paint had been destroyed. "The car's been through the wars."

"I tell you something right now," said Jason, getting in. "You'll have to come up with a better line to tell Radha than that. She's going to go ballistic. And I'm *so* glad I had nothing to do with it."

Amita climbed in. She shut the door, pulled her seatbelt on and went to turn the key. Then she stopped.

"Mike Taylor. I don't recognise that name," she said.

"So what?"

"He owns this land and has presumably sold it to Rory Francis to develop."

"That's what it looks like," said Jason, patting grass from his jumper.

"And they're expanding into Madeleine's estate, too. At least that's what Rory said before he realised you were a reporter."

"Rory, is it?" he smiled. "You two are quite chummy already, then?"

"Don't start," she said, shifting the car into gear. "We've had enough of a morning as it is without you getting any of *those* sorts of ideas in your head."

Jason giggled. Amita navigated their way down through the growing houses and back onto the country road, heading for Penrith.

"In fact, I think we've had such a morning of it, we're in need of a treat," she said.

"A treat?" Jason perked up. "What kind of a treat?"

Amita tapped the side of her nose knowingly.

"You'll see," she said.

Chapter 12

ONE DOZEN

The smell of the full English was about as welcome a scent as Jason had ever hoped for. He sat there for a moment breathing it all in. He even closed his eyes, the blind sniffing making it somehow that little bit better.

"Are you quite finished?" asked Amita.

He opened his eyes. She was staring at him from across the table, arms folded, her salmon and scrambled eggs untouched. Jason picked up his knife and fork and stabbed a thick, juicy, Cumberland sausage. Lifting the whole banger up as one, he raised it in front of his nose and looked at it like it was some great renaissance master's finest work.

"You know something, Amita," he said, peering at her beyond the sausage. "Sometimes, just sometimes, I actually think you might be the best mother-in-law in the world."

She blinked. He took a giant bite of the sausage and let his eyes roll back in his head as the flavour exploded on his tongue.

"Jason, this isn't feeding time at the zoo. Your bairns aren't as bloody silly as that, and you certainly shouldn't be, either."

After the initial euphoria of his first sausage, the flavour flood gates were open. He unleashed himself on the rest of the breakfast. Bacon, black pudding, a hash brown – not too burned around the edges – tomato, mushrooms, beans and an egg, ever so slightly runny but not enough to make everything else on the plate gooey. He demolished his meal, stopping only for large gulps of tea.

Murphy's had been a favourite haunt of the whole Brazel family for years. He'd brought Radha here many times when they were hung over. He had once interviewed the mayor of Penrith in the shop window during an election campaign, only to be attacked by local environmentalists with a grudge. And the place had hosted not one but two christening parties for the kids.

A step above the usual greasy spoon, it had undergone numerous changes over the years. From a quaint little tearoom to a sustainably and locally sourced produce deli with an added restaurant, Jason always relished a chance to sit down inside its hallowed walls. He enjoyed it even more when someone else was paying.

The breakfast was soon little more than a memory. Jason scooped up the last of the sauce with a piece of buttered toast and sat back, sighing with relief. He topped up his tea and picked at his teeth.

"Are you quite finished there?" asked Amita, still to begin her own meal.

"Yes, thank you," he said. "Much better. I'm starting to feel a bit like a human being again. Or as close to it as I can muster."

He lifted the hot water pot and smiled at a waitress who nodded in acknowledgement. Amita picked up her knife and fork and hovered over her breakfast. She was about to start when she thought better of it.

"What's wrong?" asked Jason. "I thought you liked it in here."

"I do," she said, pushing the plate away. "You know I do. But I can't stop thinking about this morning."

"The car? I'm sure Radha will understand." He didn't look convinced

"Not the car. It's Madeleine. That house. It wasn't right."

"Something didn't add up, I'll give you that."

"What?" She looked up.

"Nothing," he smiled. "Sometimes when I'm working on a story I need to decompress with all the information. That Edna woman couldn't shut up, even if she wanted to. There was a lot to digest. So what *exactly* is it about Madeleine that's got you bothered?"

"The windows," she said.

"The windows?" he leaned back. "I can see why she couldn't afford a window cleaner – they were vast."

"Yes, but did you see them? They were filthy, inside and out," said Amita. "When I was growing up in Sheffield my mother used to always say you could tell who cared about their homes by the state of their windows. The good houses, like ours, always had beautiful clean windows. The houses with filthy windows were usually filthy families."

"What's your point?" he asked.

"My point is taking pride in your home costs you nothing. My mother always taught me that. When my family moved here from India, we had nothing, so we had to make do. Little things like a tidy home, clean clothes, spotless windows

– they start to mean a lot to folk who can barely pay the bills, Jason. My mother's pride in her home, it always stuck with me, especially when I had my own house and family. I know a thing or two about cleaning windows and you saw the state of Madeleine's up at the house. If you were setting out to clean them, would you start with the outside ones at the top? And, more to the point, was Madeleine the kind of woman to do that, full stop? Madeleine Frobisher climbing a ladder doesn't make sense."

Jason scratched his chin. He should have put this together – in his cub reporter days he'd always been bursting with theories. But it was his mother-in-law who was on the trail here. She leaned on the table between them and kept her voice low.

"I told you back there, Madeleine was a lady," she said. "She wasn't the type of person you would think would clean *anything* herself, let alone windows fifteen, twenty feet up in the air."

"The whole house was filthy," said Jason. "I think old Edna might have been bordering on stealing a wage."

"This is another thing," Amita snapped her fingers. "Why would Madeleine clean the windows on her own if she had a housekeeper? A housekeeper who told us that she does everything in the house? Although there was precious little evidence of that, I might add. What on earth would possess someone like her to get the ladder and shammy out and go climbing up rickety ladders to start cleaning huge windows?"

"You don't know the ladder was rickety," he said. "Let's not start adding in facts we don't know are true."

She leaned back. The waitress appeared beside them and smiled warmly. She placed a fresh hot water urn and cleared away the empty plates. She left Amita's breakfast where it was.

"There's something not right about it, not right at all," she said. "What about that turn Edna she said she had?"

"Rather conveniently leading to Global Amnesia," said Jason.

"That's the one. Brought on by stress, was it? She heard a man's voice coming from somewhere in the house and that brought it on. So now she can't remember what happened or the last time she spoke with Madeleine. Doesn't that all sound a bit fishy to you?"

"It does and it doesn't," he said.

"What's *that* supposed to mean?"

"It means that she's clearly got a lot of pressures in her life," said Jason. "She said it herself – her husband, the work, all of that. And she's no spring chicken. I'm saying that maybe this little bout of amnesia *could* be genuine."

"Or it could be a cover," said Amita.

"Cover?" he asked, pouring them more tea. 'This is the tricky part. We can come up with as many madcap theories as we like – but if there's no motive, no proof, then we're just as bad as your gossiping bingo pals. So yes, it could be a cover . . . but for what?"

"Cover for her doing away with poor Madeleine."

Jason raised his eyebrows. "And why would she do that?"

"You heard her, at the end, before she started asking *us* questions," she kept her voice low. "She was hoping to be in the will. She was bitter about it, too, said it with real venom, I thought. Trust me, you don't get to my age without knowing that half the tears at a funeral are for the dear departed and the other half are for people who didn't get whatever inheritance they thought was coming to them.

And the more folk have, the more they have to fight over. I know people, Jason. I know when people are bitter. And that Edna woman is bitter. Bitter about something that goes beyond what we know. That wasn't only a dead cat she was wailing about. She said it herself that she only ever fought with Madeleine over the house and how it could have been put to a much better use."

"So you think she bumped Madeleine off in the hopes of getting a big payout in the will?"

"I don't know. Maybe. It's perfectly plausible. Set up her own refuge . . ."

"Like Noah," Jason snorted.

"I wouldn't laugh, Jason," said Amita. "People can be very passionate about animals. Cats, dogs, rabbits, gerbils, you name it. In fact, some folk care more for animals than they do for people."

"I can believe that," he said.

Amita ignored the barb and drummed her fingers on her chin.

"Or what about the lovely Mr Francis? He seemed rather keen to start building on Madeleine's land."

"A bit far-fetched though," Jason said. "In fact, it sounds like something from those bloody crime books you're always reading. I swear, Amita, every time you finish one, you've spent the next week thinking that Colonel Mustard has been bludgeoned to death with the candelabra in the dining room."

"I'm serious," she stared at him.

Jason felt his mother-in-law's glare. It wasn't the usual angry glare or the look of her constant disappointment. There was an earnest plea here, a plea to be believed. He shook his head, clearing his mind.

"Okay, let's look at what we've got," he said. "The police say Madeleine died in a tragic accident. We've heard through word-of-mouth that she had a broken neck from a fall. Her long-term housekeeper is wracked with guilt and bitterness about not remembering their last encounter, and hoping she's in her will. None of that points to foul play, not on its own, Amita. If there's one thing I learnt from my job, it's that usually the answer to most crimes is under your nose. Most people aren't the master criminals you think they are. And I'm not sure there's a story in it for me when it's already out there that she's dead."

"But she used to be famous," she said. "That comes with its own problems. You can't ever walk away from something like that. Especially if she was a Eurovision singer, or whatever you call it."

"True," he nodded. "But it was a long time ago. When did Laura say it was? The late sixties. That was decades ago. I'm sure you can't remember any of her songs. We didn't even know she'd been famous. Probably a one hit wonder. Can you name me one of her tunes?"

"I hate pop music," she said, crossing her arms. "All thump, thump, thumps."

Amita looked down at her breakfast. Her appetite had vanished.

"Hold on," Jason said.

He pulled out his phone. Tapping on the screen, he slid it over the table to her. She blinked and brought it close enough so she could see without her glasses. A huge stage in what looked like a theatre was on the screen. She pressed play and the camera pulled out to reveal the audience and a large orchestra. A round of applause went up as a woman in a long, glittering dress with a huge train came gliding out into the middle of the stage. She smiled and bowed and waited for the music to start.

The orchestra fizzed into action, playing a graceful, elegant encore. Then she started to sing. Her voice was powerful and measured, and she smiled all the way through the performance. When she was done, the whole auditorium stood in applause. She bowed and blew them kisses before the video ended. Beneath the clip was the title 'Maddy Forster, Royal Variety Performance, 1971'.

"That proof enough for you?" he asked, taking his phone back.

"Blimey, what a voice," said Amita. "I mean, I don't really like that sort of music. But she was a wonderful singer."

"Apparently so."

"So what happened to her?" she asked. "Why isn't she still famous? Why didn't she tell us?"

"Who knows? Maybe there was a scandal, maybe she just fizzled out," he said. "I haven't properly looked into it. This is one of about four hundred clips Laura has sent through to me since she's been on the train back to London. And when that breakfast starts shifting some of the alcohol from my bloodstream I'll be able to focus and do some proper research."

Amita nodded. She stared down at her salmon and scrambled eggs. Her mind was still racing. An uncomfortable thought had started to form and she was having difficulty shaking it.

"Jason," she said slowly.

"Hm?" he was looking at his phone.

"Have you thought about the consequences of our little investigation?" she asked him.

"The what?" he looked up. "What consequences? We haven't done anything wrong."

"No, that's not what I mean, not us," she said, her eyebrows pulling in, mouth tight, as if holding back what she was about to say. "I'm thinking more about our theory that Madeleine might not have died from a freak accident."

"It's your theory, Amita," he said. "I'm just sniffing around hoping for a story."

"That's what I mean," she said. "I mean, what if we're right? What if Madeleine *was* murdered? Don't you see what that means?"

Jason looked blank.

"It means that there's a murderer on the loose, right now, here in this area. Someone committed a killing only a few days ago. And now they're out there, walking round free as a bird. What's worse is they might get away with it. And if they get away with it, what's to stop them doing it again?"

She watched as what little colour had returned to her son-in-law's face begin to drain away again. She could pinpoint the exact moment when he realised what she was saying was true.

"Blimey," he said, sitting up straighter. "I hadn't thought about it like that."

"Exactly," she said.

They sat staring at each other for a long moment. Neither of them really knew what to say to follow that. Thankfully, or rather unthankfully, a familiar voice interrupted them.

"Fancy seeing you two here at this time," said Georgie Littlejohn.

She came marching up to the table, designer scarf draped about her shoulders. She was holding a perfectly manicured, yapping little Pekingese in her arms. It kept trying to lick her but she batted it away.

"Good morning, Georgie," said Amita, trying to refocus. "Yes, we come in here sometimes for a spot of breakfast, or lunch, or anything that takes our fancy."

"Yes, so I can see," she nodded down at Amita's untouched eggs and salmon. "How are you keeping? Dealing with the shock okay?"

"The shock?" Amita asked.

"Yes, the shock from the crash."

Amita had to rejig her thoughts a little. Jason wasn't quite so polite as to stay quiet.

"How the hell do you know about the crash?" he blurted. "It couldn't have been an hour ago."

"I beg your pardon?" Georgie sneered.

"The crash. Our crash. How can you know about that already? It was in the middle of nowhere and it only just happened, relatively speaking."

"I have my sources," said Georgie smugly. "You had a bit of a bump with a Francis lorry, I believe."

"How could you *possibly* know that?" said Jason, looking at Amita for support. There was none forthcoming. "Are you on some kind of supercharged neighbourhood watch?"

"Bless you," she said. "No, my grandson Rupert, he's on his work experience this week at the site over next to Madeleine Frobisher's estate. He wants to be an engineer and he's out there getting hairs on his chest, hopefully. He messaged me to say he recognised your mother-in-law being towed into the yard."

She looked mockingly at Amita who was silent with rage, her hands curled up into tight fists. Jason wasn't sure if she was about to explode or throw a punch. Neither was desirable.

"Yes, we're both fine," he said, trying to take the sting out of the situation. "And Mr Francis has very kindly offered to pay for the repairs."

"To avoid the insurance, no doubt," Georgie quipped. "Yes, he's a nice fellow. Although I can't say I approve of the company he keeps. That farmer, what's his name – Michael Taylor – is a bit of a brute."

"You think?" asked Amita, finally able to speak. "I actually thought he was quite charming. Didn't you, Jason?"

She cocked her eyebrow. Jason might have been dealing with a hangover but he wasn't so stupid as to ignore a blatant signal for silence from his mother-in-law.

"I've always found him to be a bit of a blunt instrument," said Georgie. "Always swearing, drags mud everywhere he goes. I'll be glad when he's gone."

"Gone?" asked Amita.

"Yes, he's moving. He's sold that farm of his to Francis. That's why they're building there. And, from what Rupert tells me, they'll be starting work in Madeleine's estate soon enough now that she's, well, gone. It was a lovely service, wasn't it? I thought the vicar did a wonderful job considering the circumstances. I was completely embarrassed to be asked to speak at it. But I thought, what would Madeleine do if she were in my shoes?"

Georgie tossed her hair back over her shoulder, feigning mild grief. Her dog barked in sympathy. Amita sneered and Jason stayed quiet.

"Oh, that reminds me," Georgie went on. "We're going to be holding a little vigil for Madeleine, on Wednesday night before the bingo, in Market Square. I thought it would be a good chance for us all to turn out and show some community support.

A ping went off from Georgie's handbag. She tutted and dug around, pulling out her phone. She tutted again.

"Marvellous, that's all I need," she said. "The piper for the Penrith Caledonian Society's monthly Highland Fling has pulled out, been diagnosed with a hernia. As if my schedule wasn't busy enough, I'm now going to have to find somebody else who plays the bagpipes."

"You've got enough hot air in you, why don't you give it a go?" said Amita quietly.

"What's that?" Georgie was too busy on her phone to hear her properly.

"Nothing."

Jason flashed a subdued smile at his mother-in-law.

"Anyway, I must go, these charity events and good causes don't plan themselves. See you at the vigil on Wednesday night then, Amita. Seven sharp, in Market Square. Bring a candle if you have any and some money for the collection."

"Collection? What for?" asked Jason.

"That poor postman who found her," she said. "Now I must dash. Toodles."

She made a scene of leaving, blowing between the tables and out through the door, thanking and smiling at the staff. When she was safely out of earshot, Jason puffed out his cheeks.

"Toodles?" he said. "I didn't think anyone actually spoke like that."

"Nobody does," said Amita. "Our Georgie is one in a million."

"One in seven billion is still too high if you ask me."

"Yes."

Jason reached over and pulled the salmon and scrambled eggs towards him. "If you're not hungry? Shame to let this go to waste." He tucked in. "So you'll be going to this vigil, then?" he asked.

"Yes, looks that way, doesn't it," said Amita.

"What a palaver. The woman is dead. Move on. No amount of memorials and moping around is going to bring her back. And as for this collection – what a crock. I didn't get a collection when I was made redundant. He's milking it."

"Now, now," said Amita. "He did look awful at the funeral, remember. What was his name again? Billings?"

"Geoff Billings," said Jason between gulps. "I only remember because he's a postie, who delivers bills. Seems like an appropriate name."

He expected a little laugh from that. But Amita was staring off out of the windows. She was deep in thought and, if she was honest, more than a little worried. She couldn't get over her realisation that there might be a killer on the run. Beyond the cars and the town, the hills and the countryside, someone who was capable of murdering Madeleine Frobisher was walking free. And it might just be down to Amita and Jason to catch them.

Chapter 13

UNLUCKY FOR SOME

One thing Jason didn't regret about being out of work was the time he got to spend with his children. In the six months he had been at home he'd come to realise how big they were getting. Not only physically, although he was struggling to lift Josh, he weighed like a sack of potatoes. His two kids were quickly becoming little people all of their own. They had their own personalities, knew what they liked and certainly what they didn't. Being there for them when they left for school and when they came home again in the afternoon had been a real privilege. He hadn't quite realised how much he had missed already in their short lives. Work, it seemed, was a cruel mistress that not only robbed him of time, but precious memories too.

Not that this afternoon's jaunt was going to be a golden memory he'd talk about on their wedding days. A draughty old warehouse, on the outskirts of Carlisle, converted into the saddest-looking soft play centre he had ever seen wasn't going straight into the family album – not that he ever got round to printing out the myriad photos on his phone. The floor was filthy, the play mats were threadbare and the stench coming from the ball pits would have knocked a lesser man on his back.

Jason didn't tend to speak with other parents when he took the kids out. He spoke to strangers all of the time for work, or at least he used to when he was *in* work. It wasn't that he was particularly socially anxious. The conversation was always predictable anyway. Which one is yours? How old are they? Isn't this place expensive? Did you see the game last night? What do you do for a living?

The last question in particular was one that he liked to avoid. Journalism didn't have quite the Clark Kent image it had once had. Everyone had the internet at the touch of a button these days. And invariably that meant they were exposed to some of the world's biggest lies paraded as truth. Jason wasn't pious enough to think that his own journalism was worthy of a Pulitzer. Far from it. In the illustrious history of the great prize, a gong had never been handed out for the best coverage of an oil stain that looked like Elvis. He knew his place in the grand scale of things. But telling people he was a journalist normally made them wary. Or worse still, preachy. If he'd been told that newspapers 'only print a load of lies' once then it had been a thousand times. People, he found, were naturally suspicious of a person who asked questions for a living. And they rarely thawed.

"Daddy! Daddy! Look over here!" Clara shouted, her voice louder even than the general din of the place.

"Look over here, Daddy! Look! Look!" Josh chimed in.

His kids were at the highest point of the jungle gym. They were waving frantically, chests pushed out with pride at conquering the multicoloured Everest.

"I see you, I see you," he said, waving back with a smile.

They vanished again, gobbled up by the apparatus that would over-stimulate them so much that later they'd either sleep for ten hours or not sleep for ten hours. Jason had to laugh at that thought. Since becoming a dad he'd realised why there were so many activities for children. Sure it helped with their development, brought their little brains on and gave them the social skills to function as a normal human being. But more importantly, it gave weary parents like him and the rest of the planet a chance of a good night's sleep.

"Is this seat taken?"

A voice interrupted his daydream. He sat up with a snort as a young woman stood over him. Jason instinctively felt a little uncomfortable. She was wearing an enormous quilted jacket and skinny jeans with wellies. He recognised the designer logo on the side of her sunglasses that were perched neatly on top of her head. She had a huge phone in one hand and a steaming coffee in the other.

Jason knew that gone were the days of ruddy-cheeked Cumbrian farmers' wives who never left the farmhouse kitchen toiling to feed the hungry workers. Instead, they had social media feeds to fill and plenty of gossip. Of course, there were also those who worked the farms themselves, building their own eco-empires. They had conquered the farmers' markets and kicked the old, outdated notions to the kerb. But there was still room for the city-dwellers who'd moved up from the smoke, who didn't like mud on their tyres or the latest designer wellies. It was all about as far removed from anything Jason did as was humanly possible.

"No," he said. "Go ahead."

She didn't thank him, and instead looked a little miffed it had taken him so long to answer her. She pulled out the only other chair at the table with a screech, and sat. Everything seemed like a chore for her. She was sighing and huffing every few seconds. He wasn't sure if she was trying to get his attention, or if it was simply a habit.

Jason tried not to stare, but he couldn't help it. He was instinctively drawn to everything that frightened him, like a moth to lamplight. He supposed she wasn't any older than thirty. She had a full face of make-up on. Her clothes were immaculate and seemed to ooze expense. He knew nothing of designer brands, only that he recognised something hugely expensive when he saw it. A Range Rover would no doubt be parked outside next to his scraped and battered dad-mobile. Everything about this woman screamed intimidation, with her scary 'look at me but don't dare look at me' attitude. He was safer behind his keyboard, locked away from society. This was all too much for him.

The Designer Mum finished whatever it was she was doing on her phone. She took the tiniest of sips from her coffee, and settled in to view the mayhem. Jason thought he should take a leaf out of her book and pretend to be doing something hugely important on his phone. Only then did he realise he'd left it in the car.

Expletives were generally not approved of in children's soft play centres. He managed to stifle his enough that only a muffled grunt that could easily have been wind came out. Unfortunately, it was enough to attract the attention of his table-mate. She looked over at him. He felt her eyes taking in everything about him – from his scruffy hair and stubble to that dried-up bit of porridge he hadn't realised he'd dropped onto his shirt until he sat down earlier.

"Which one is yours, then?" she asked.

He thought about pretending to be deaf. That was a risky tactic. How far would he need to go with the ruse? And what would happen if the kids started screaming or panicking? There was nothing else for it – he had to go in.

"I've got two of the little blighters," he said, trying to sound peppy. "They're in the bowels of that giant rainbow-coloured death maze."

He nodded at the jungle gym, all slides, climbing frames and swings. The mum smiled. She raised her eyebrows a little and he decided to tone down the language a little.

"What about yourself?" he sounded almost conversational.

"Oh, my little lass is in there, too. She's the one with the sequin T-Shirt and pigtails, you can't miss her."

Jason didn't have the heart to tell her that's what *all* the little girls were wearing – including Clara. He nodded and smiled.

"Do you come here often?" he asked. He instantly felt his cheeks flush. "I mean, you know, the soft play centre, do you come here, with your children, often? To, you know, let them play."

"Yes, I do," she laughed, revealing two rows of perfectly white teeth. "Although it's been a few years since I heard that chat-up line."

Jason panicked. He felt his chest tightening. This was going disastrously. He should have kept his stupid mouth shut and just sat there like a mute weirdo. At least then he couldn't ever be accused of flirting. What would Radha think? Or Amita?

"Oh no, sorry, I wasn't . . . I wasn't trying to chat you up," he was tripping over his words now. "I mean, that's not to say that you're not worth chatting up. Of course you are. You're a very attractive young woman. But that's not what I was doing, honestly, I was only trying to make conversation and —"

"It's fine," she said, holding up her hands. "I was just messing with you."

Jason should have felt more relieved. The giant knot that now took up most of his chest didn't release at all. He had a sudden urge to grab Josh and Clara by the earlobes and hurry them into the car and back home as quickly as possible. Then he thought better of it. That would look like he'd done something wrong. He sat perfectly still.

"I'm Stacey," she said.

"Jason," he replied.

"They're good these places, aren't they?"

He scanned that question forensically. It seemed genuine enough so he carried on.

"Yes I suppose so," he said. "If you like paying for the privilege of sitting in a warehouse while your kids pick up all kinds of fun bugs from the equipment."

"I see your point," she said, rattling the table. "Plus this coffee tastes like dirty bath water."

"I doubt the owners have ever seen a bath, let alone run one," he twitched his head over to the cafe bar behind them. "There's a distinct air of hygiene aversion about this whole place."

He inwardly cringed. Hygiene aversion, giant rainbow death maze – what was *wrong* with him this afternoon? The echoes of a thousand sub-editors berating him for flowery language made the hairs on the back of his neck stand on end.

"Still," said Stacey. "Gets the little ones out of the house for an hour and tires them out."

He smiled at that. Parenting, it seemed, was a universal language.

"So what do you do?" she asked. "When you're not being dragged to these bloody places."

"I'm a journalist," he said. "Technically."

"Technically? What does that mean?"

"It means that while I am a journalist, I'm not actually doing any journalism at the moment."

"Why not?" She seemed interested.

"It's a long story. But the short of it is I was made redundant when they closed my local paper. And I'm too stubborn, too proud and probably too lazy to go out and get another job at a bigger, better place."

"I see," she said. "You're right, by the way."

"Right? Am I? About what?" he asked.

"You really aren't chatting me up, are you?"

Jason felt like a valve had been released, letting all the hot air out of him. He instantly relaxed and laughed.

"No, I don't think my wife would approve," he said.

"Being a journalist must be good fun though," said Stacey. "You must get to meet loads of interesting people and see the world."

"Not for the *Penrith Standard*, sadly," he said.

"Have you ever interviewed anyone famous?" her eyes widened.

"Not really," he shrugged. "Politicians and local weirdos, for the most part. Which is fine as there's not much of a difference between them, it turns out."

"Oh," her disappointment was clear to see. "I thought you might talk to film stars and folk off the telly."

"I did once interview the late, great Bob Holness," he said.

"Who?"

"Bob Holness," Jason said again. "The TV presenter. You remember, *Blockbusters*."

He started humming the theme tune. Stacey looked blank.

"Oh come on, it was on every day, or it felt like it. School kids competing for protractors and dictionaries and things like that. He was the presenter, old Bob. Did you know he was the first person to ever play James Bond in an adaptation from the books?"

"I didn't know that," said Stacey. "Because I don't know who Bob Holness is. But I'll look him up."

"You should," said Jason. "A teatime quiz institution. Anyway, that's my claim to fame. He was up here doing a book tour or something. A lovely man, he bought me an Empire biscuit."

"Sounds like a superstar."

"Happier times." Jason smiled.

He made a mental note to look up old *Blockbuster* episodes online when he got home. That would cheer him up.

"What about you?" he asked. "What do you do with yourself when you're not stuck in here?"

"I'm a full-time mum," said Stacey.

"Bloody hell."

"What?" she laughed. "What's wrong with that?"

"Absolutely nothing. I've been out of work for six months and tried being a full-time dad. Let me tell you, it's not as fun or as easy as people make out."

"Exactly," she said. "This is the thing. I tell people that I'm a full-time mum and they automatically think that we get up at noon and watch Netflix. But I'm more of a skivvy than a lady of leisure. Running the house, dirty washing, stains of every kind, and that's usually just my wake-up call at six."

They both laughed at that.

"I do a blog, too," said Stacey. "Well, it's more on Instagram. I'm trying to be one of these influencer types."

"You've lost me," he said.

"You've never heard of influencers?"

"You had never heard of Bob Holness. That might make us even."

"Seriously," she smiled. "But you're a journalist and you don't know what an influencer is? How is that even possible?"

"I'm living proof," he shrugged.

"I thought you guys were never *off* social media. I thought that's how you all got your stories – you know, viral videos, people doing daft stuff, cute dog and cat clips."

"I'm not on social media," he said. "Mostly because all of that stuff scares me."

"Scares you?" she laughed. "What's scary about influencers?"

"You speak a different language on there," he said. "One false move and you're toast, from what I understand. One joke, one comment in the wrong place, one misinterpreted little moment and there's a pile on – you're 'cancelled', is it?"

"Yeah," she nodded.

"It's the court of public opinion and there's no jury, no judge. I don't trust myself to not make mischief, purely accidentally. That's why I stay away from it all. I don't even like using a computer. But I acknowledge I have to be a part of the digital revolution. So I keep it all to a minimum."

Stacey shifted her chair around so she was closer to Jason. Her expensive perfume made him nervous. How could a scent be expensive? It was remarkable.

"Here, this is my account," she offered him her phone.

Stacey scrolled through picture after picture of her with her little girl. There was a focus on meals and products, advice on potty training and when best to take kids out for playtime, and such.

"I know I'm completely out of touch with the digital age," said Jason. "But you can make a living out of this?"

"Oh yeah, definitely," said Stacey. "Some of the celebs can make millions from being influencers. In fact, some of the celebs are only famous because they *are* doing it."

"But . . . how? If that's not a silly question. Spot the journalist."

"Ads and sponsorship mostly," she said. "They get paid by Instagram if they have enough followers. And companies will send them stuff to advertise on their feeds."

"And you do that?" Jason asked.

"I try to," she said. "But I don't have the sort of following that lets me go to Chanel and ask them for their latest clobber. Although there are a few local companies that have been happy to send me stuff for Mia – clothes, toys, that kind of thing. It's hard, though. I'm like super-old compared to some of the big influencers."

"And how old are you? If you don't mind me asking?"

"Twenty-five."

"Twenty-five!" Jason shouted. "That, Stacey, is not old. Never in the history of the human race has that even been considered to be old."

"It is, though," she said. "In this world. There are kids doing this stuff. So it makes it harder for me to build a following."

"I see," he said. He didn't see.

"You can make money from it in other ways too," she leaned in conspiratorially. "There's a bit of a scam you can run, with the stuff that you're sent. You get it for free. Do a post on social media, then you're free to sell it on."

"Free to sell it on?"

"You know what I mean," she winked. "Like this jacket. I've still got the labels on it."

She twisted around and showed that the tags were still attached to the back of the giant hood.

"I'll sell this and pocket the cash."

"Oh," nodded Jason. "And that's not allowed is it?"

"It depends on who you ask," she said. "My grandad is a policeman. I wouldn't tell him in a hurry."

"But you'd tell a random stranger like me?" he asked.

"You're not a stranger, you've got kids."

Jason rolled his eyes. He scrolled through her Instagram feed again. He still didn't quite understand what was going on. And he'd never felt quite so old. The world was completely different from how it was only a few years ago. There were new opportunities for people, new jobs that he hadn't even thought of. A pang of guilt ran through him like a lightning bolt. He really needed to try harder.

"Brazel!"

A booming voice echoed all about the huge warehouse. Jason jumped, Stacey's phone spilling out of his hands and clattering onto the sticky table. He looked about, trying to bring himself back to his senses.

DI Frank Alby came marching towards them, his face creased with anger. He was out of his suit but still looked like a detective, all bluster and casual disregard for the rest of the world.

"What the hell do you think you're doing?" he barked at Jason.

"What?" was all he managed.

"What are you doing looking at my granddaughter's phone?"

"Granddaughter?" Jason gulped.

"Grandad! Stop it!" Stacey protested.

"Alby is your granddad?" Jason asked.

"You know him?"

"Yes," said Jason and Alby in unison.

The furious detective inspector paced around the table. He was flexing his hands, readying them for what Jason feared would be a punch. He didn't take his eyes from him, just in case.

"What's going on here?" brayed the cop.

"Nothing, absolutely nothing, DI Alby," said Jason. "I'm here with my kids. And Stacey . . ."

"I sat down beside him with my coffee. Mia is over in the gym thing."

"I don't believe it," said Alby. "You do know who this character is, Stacey? He's a *journalist*. Not only is he a journalist, he's not a very good one. And I reckon he's been stealing from his old place of work."

"Oi!" Jason felt justifiably angry. "That's a misrepresentation, not to mention an assassination of my character. I could have you for that."

"I'll assassinate my boot right up your arse if you don't stop sniffing around my granddaughter, Brazel!"

He lunged forward. Jason flinched so badly he ended up on his feet. He felt two sets of arms wrap themselves around his legs.

"What's going on, Daddy?" asked Josh.

"Who's the man with the red face?" asked Clara.

Alby immediately backed off. His face was still scarlet but he seemed less intimidating.

"Come on guys, I think playtime is over," Jason said, picking Clara up.

He slowly made his way around the table.

"It was lovely to chat to you, Stacey," he said. "And the very best of luck in your influencer career. I wouldn't let your angry granddad get in the way of you building your online empire."

That drew a hiss from Alby who was stalking him around the table. Jason made for the door. Maybe it was the confidence of knowing he had his kids as protection. Or perhaps it was a rush of blood to the head – but he wasn't for leaving quietly.

"I think you should consider an even earlier retirement, Detective Inspector Alby," he said, making sure he had a clear line to the door. "I don't think your policing skills are as sharp as they used to be if you still think I'm stealing photocopiers and printers from the old office. And as for that temper, you might want to calm down. For your great-granddaughter if nothing else. You might live a bit longer."

He slipped out the door before Alby could retaliate. Hurrying out to the car park, he fumbled with the keys, not daring to look back for fear of a frothing DI charging after him. He bundled the kids into the car and quickly took off. As he checked the rear-view mirror, he spotted the Range Rover in the space beside his.

Chapter 14

VALENTINE'S DAY

"Where are my glasses? I can't find my glasses. Jason!"

Amita hurried around the kitchen, fussing. She lifted pots, opened drawers and cupboards, and was down on her hands and knees at one point searching beneath the tables.

"Where the bloody hell did I put them?"

"Have you tried on your head, Mum?" asked Radha.

She appeared behind Amita and almost gave her a heart attack. She reached up and was relieved when she felt the rims and lenses of her specs.

"Thank you, darling," she said, getting back up with a creak.

"It's always the last place you look," said Radha.

She had Josh in her arms, the little boy passed out on her shoulder. Amita squeezed his bare foot and he stirred before falling back asleep.

"He always went to sleep on you," said Amita wistfully. "Even when he was a week old he'd only ever go to sleep on you. It used to make me frightfully jealous."

"I know," said Radha. "You've told me a million times before."

"You were the same, of course. You only used to sleep if I settled you. Your dad used to go ballistic at that. I think he saw it as a failure of some kind. And no matter how many times I told him it was what bairns do, he wouldn't listen."

"He could be pretty pig-headed at times," Radha said. "It didn't do him any favours, especially when we were teenagers."

"He did his best," said Amita, turning away to find something to busy herself with. "He was under a lot of pressure. He never asked to inherit your grandfather's business."

"We were his family, Mum. We should have come first."

"You *did* come first, always," Amita said, feeling a lump forming in her throat. "You did, we did. Of course we did. Did we ever make you do anything that wasn't for your own good? Did we not give you everything you ever wanted? You and your siblings were looked after, brought up properly, the way I was. I made sure of it. Your dad's family, god rest them, they were much stricter people."

"I never knew them," said Radha.

"And all the better for it," said Amita. "They used to torment your dad something terrible. He never got over it. I think that's why he lost his faith, lost his belief. I was never that religious, nor were your grandparents. They wanted me to find my own beliefs, and I wanted the same for you, and for the kids now. Your dad's family though, they were more than devout. I got him away from all of that."

"I saw flashes of it, Mum, we all did," Radha said.

"It was just, I don't know, he had a lot on his plate, a lot of fires to put out. Maybe he could have been a bit kinder at times, or softer, or played with you more. But he always provided for the family."

"And in the end all we could do was mourn for him," said Radha with a sigh. "He's dead twenty years this November, Mum. That means next year the scales are tipped, and I'll have been without Dad longer than I had him."

"Yes," Amita agreed. "Time makes fools of us all."

Josh wriggled a little. He rubbed his head on his mother's shoulder and soft snoring started from his running nose. Jason came thumping down the stairs. They creaked under his feet and Radha shot him a dirty look.

"Sorry," he whispered.

"You're not going dressed like that, are you?" asked Amita.

"What?" he said, holding out his arms.

"Seriously?"

Jason looked down at his trainers and wriggled his toes. The shoes were stained a bright green from when he'd last cut the grass. His jeans had faint spots of paint, the stubborn ones that had refused to be washed away. At least his rugby shirt was clean, if faded from years of wear.

"Need I remind you we're going to a vigil, Jason, not bleeding the brakes in the car."

"What's wrong with what I'm wearing?"

"You look like you're going scrumping," she said.

"It's a vigil, Amita, not a funeral. We're only going to be standing around in the dark for twenty minutes, looking and feeling miserable. I hardly need to dig out my morning dress, do I?"

"You've got morning dress?"

A sudden flare of excitement made Amita's eyes burn. Jason quickly extinguished it, dreading what his mother-in-law would have him wear and do, given free rein.

"I'm going like this, Amita," he said firmly. "You'll simply have to be embarrassed."

"You could put a shirt on at least," she said. "Would that kill you?"

"I look fine. Radha, tell her."

"Don't get me involved in any of this," she said, edging past him and heading up the stairs. "You two can fight it out perfectly well on your own. I'm putting our son to bed then coming downstairs and opening a bottle of wine. If you're back in time you can join me. If not, have a good night."

Jason and Amita watched her go. There was a moment of quiet between them. He knew what she was up to. He knew *all* Amita's tricks. This was the old cold shoulder, the quiet tutting and standing around waiting for him to cave. Out of principle, he didn't budge and pulled on his coat.

"At least zip that thing up, Jason," said Amita, defeated at last. "We'll stand away from the streetlights so nobody sees you."

"Ah, lurking in the shadows. How I've missed that."

The weather was miserable. The first hints of winter were already creeping in and everywhere was pitch-black already. The unhealthy glow of the streetlights splintered on the windscreen, everything blurry before being cleared by the wipers. Jason drummed his fingers on the wheel. Amita was silent, staring ahead into space, deep in thought. He reached for the radio.

"Don't even think about it," she said.

"Oh come on, I was going to put Radio Four on for you especially."

"It'll be some game show or panel show or some other rubbish at this time of night. I need to concentrate."

"Concentrate on what?" His hand retreated to the wheel.

"On what happened to poor Madeleine."

"You're not still thinking about that, are you?" he yawned.

"Of course I am, Jason. There could be a murderer out there right now, on the loose. I get the sense that nobody thinks she was killed, except us. It's our civic duty to bring whoever it was to justice. Not to mention the safety of other pensioners in the area."

"You worried he might come after you?"

"Obviously," she snipped. "And who said anything about it being a man?"

Jason blinked. He should have been working on the story – or at least finding out whether it was a story or not. Instead, he'd left it to Amita to turn amateur profiler.

"You think it's a woman?" he sniffed, trying not to let his interest show.

"I think it could be anyone," said Amita. "I'm not going to rule anything or anyone out, especially not because of something as silly as their gender. For all we know, it could be that housekeeper of hers."

"Edna?" he said. "You think she did it?"

"I don't know," she answered him. "Yet."

"Come off it, Amita, it's not Edna."

"So you *do* think there's a murderer."

"I didn't say that. I said I *didn't* think Edna the house-keeper was a murderer. I didn't say there *was* a murderer. The two aren't mutually exclusive, you know. And we've been through this before. The woman has a lot of pressure on her shoulders. She's under a lot of stress. I can't imagine doing away with old Madeleine would alleviate that any."

"What about her next door neighbour then?" she asked.

"Who?"

"That farmer, what's his name?"

"The one Georgie Littlejohn knows?" he asked. "Taylor something," he snapped his fingers. "Mike, Michael Taylor, that's it."

"Yes, him," said Amita. "He could have done it. He comes across as a complete thug."

"He's an old man," said Jason.

"And what do you determine as old these days, Jason?" she twisted in her seat, rain mac squeaking on the vinyl.

"You saw him. He's a dog whose bark is worse than its bite. He wouldn't kill anyone."

"And how do you know that for certain? Eh?" she jabbed a finger at him. "How do you know he's not secretly glad she's dead now that there's more land to build on up at his farm? You saw the state of that place – it's going to be awash with houses in the next few years. How do you know he's not cashing in on Madeleine passing away?"

"Because it's not his land," said Jason with a laugh. "What possible interest could he have in someone else's estate? He's a farmer, he'll know every blade of grass down to the square inch of what he owns. But Madeleine's field and house and all of that isn't his. He's her neighbour, was her neighbour, sure. And that's all. I can't knock through the wall of our house and expect to get a slice of cake, can I?"

"You could be doing with getting your paint brush out, though," she said, folding her arms. "The downstairs bathroom is looking a bit tired."

"It's on my to-do list, Amita, thank you."

"That list is getting longer by the minute."

"That's what it's there for," Jason was starting to get mad.

He took a long, deep breath. Images of Alby frothing at the mouth flashed in his mind. He didn't want to end up at anger management classes with that dinosaur.

"I don't trust him," said Amita.

Jason had to think for a moment. Was she talking about Alby? Had she developed telepathy? He wouldn't put it past her.

"There's something about his face I don't like. Did you hear the way he spoke to you when he came stomping into the site office?" she asked.

"Yes," said Jason with more than a little relief. "Yes I did. Our Mr Taylor's quite an ugly character. Then again, a lifetime of being up at the crack of dawn to shovel horse manure can't be very conducive for a sunny demeanour."

"No, I suppose it can't be, when you put it like that," Amita agreed.

An ocean of red lights lit up in front of them. Jason slowed the car until it was practically at a standstill.

"A traffic jam?" he asked. "At this time of night?"

"Madeleine was very well liked in the community," she said.

"You think this is all for the vigil?"

"I wouldn't be surprised. Georgie has a penchant for rustling up town and country when she puts her mind to it."

The sneer had returned to Amita's face. Jason kept his own smile-free. He quite liked this rivalry the pair kept up. Although at times it felt rather one-sided.

"We're better parking up and walking around to Market Square, it'll be quicker," she said.

"But we're still at least a mile out," Jason moaned.

"It'll be good for you, to get some exercise after you were gattered the other night."

"I wasn't drunk," said Jason, throwing the car around and searching for a space. "I had one or two libations with an old friend."

"The smell of drink would have knocked Ernest Hemingway on his back."

"Yes, well, Papa H didn't have his mother-in-law to thank for getting him up at the crack of dawn the next day, did he? And besides, if I hadn't gone out that night, we wouldn't be on the hunt for this so-called elusive killer, would we?"

Amita reluctantly agreed. Jason parked the car and they got out. The rain was getting heavier, dropping down in heavy sheets that came out of the night sky like runaway trains. Amita pulled her anorak close about her and Jason did the same. They trudged up the street, passing the long line of traffic that snaked its way towards Market Square. Neither of them felt like talking anymore. The sense of occasion was getting to them.

The further on they walked, the busier it became. They marched on in silence, both knowing the other was thinking the same thing – somewhere, in the crowd of mourners braving the rain for Madeleine's vigil, there could be a murderer.

Chapter 15

YOUNG AND KEEN

The bingo club regulars were gathered in a little huddle around the entrance of the hall. Some looked like monks, heads bowed and hooded, standing in quiet contemplation. Others, like Georgie Littlejohn, had deployed their umbrellas, the sodden canvas material scraping against one another as they milled around waiting for the event to start. Georgie's brolly was, of course, that little bit bigger than everyone else's, enforcing a reverential distance around her.

The whole of Market Square was lined with a crowd three deep. Amita and Jason made their way through the people, heading for the bingo hall. A chorus of polite 'excuse me' and 'pardon me' parted the crowd like the Red Sea until they eventually made it to the front.

"Ah, you're here, finally," said Georgie.

Jason pretended to flap away some rainwater from his shoulders. He had to give it to the old snob, she certainly knew how to cut someone down with only a few words.

"Of course," said Amita, matching her venom. "Did you think we would miss it?"

"No, not at all," Georgie retaliated. "It's simply that time is getting on. Everyone's been here for about twenty minutes. We did say it would be starting at seven sharp, and look."

She pointed up at the clock that shone through the rainy darkness.

"It's only ten past, Georgie. Drop it, would you?" said Sandy. "We're all here now. We can get started."

"Thank you, Sandy," said Amita warmly.

The big man gave her a wink and tipped the brow of his flat cap towards her. Georgie tutted loudly and started for the church hall entrance. Her umbrella almost took the vicar's eye out as she went.

"I'll fetch the candles then, shall I?" she asked spitefully.

Nobody answered her. The bingo club regulars all seemed in low spirits. The chat was kept to a bare minimum. Even Ethel was silent, staring blankly ahead at the open square where the mourners had gathered. Jason, relegated to the back of the crowd, tapped Amita on the shoulder.

"Is everything alright here?" he asked.

"Why, what do you mean?"

"I don't know. They all seem a lot sadder than they did at the funeral."

Amita looked about her. She shook her head and whispered quietly, "Funerals are for show, Jason. When you get to this age, it's as much about a day out as anything else. Didn't I tell you that?"

"No, you didn't, far from it, Amita," he said.

"The service, the flowers, how expensive the coffin is, a funeral is a spectator sport. Whereas this, this vigil here, this is more serious stuff. This is a proper chance to mourn who's been lost. And to think about how long you've got until, well, you know."

She turned away from him again. Jason looked out at the gathered crowd. They were all on their best behaviour. Even the young kids who'd been dragged out by their parents and grandparents all stood stiffly to attention. He certainly noted the serious atmosphere. It seemed that everyone had gotten the memo except him. He zipped his jacket all the way up to the top to hide his rugby shirt and was glad it was too dark to see his trainers. He felt the sudden weight of shame hanging over him.

Then he spotted him. A face, white as a sheet, as white as the untidy hair that poked out from beneath his hat. The man who had cornered him in the pub when Laura was at the bar getting the next round. The Ghost. Even in the gloom of the rainy square Jason could see the old man was looking at him. Big sunken eyes burrowing out from his skull, little dog sitting faithfully at his feet.

The encounter in the boozer came flooding back to him. In his hung-over state and the subsequent excitement at Madeleine Frobisher's, he'd forgotten all about The Ghost. He was about to grab his mother-in-law by the arm when a huge box of candles was dumped in his arms.

"Take one and pass them along," said Georgie, out of breath from lugging the heavy box. "Chop chop, Jason. We're already late and bingo is meant to start after the vigil."

He fished out a candle and handed the box to the next person. More boxes spread out into the crowd in the opposite direction. Jason tapped Amita on the shoulder, candle in hand.

"Who's that old man?" he asked her.

"You'll need to be more specific, Jason," she said. "There are rather a lot of old men at this vigil."

"The old boy with the dog. He's standing over . . ."

He trailed off. The Ghost had vanished, and with him his dog.

"Who?" she asked.

"He was there, just a minute ago," he said, pointing across the square. "The old man with the little dog. He was talking to me in the pub the other night. I meant to ask you, I didn't recognise him."

"I think you're seeing things," she said.

"No, it's true. He's old, wears a big, smelly wax jacket and flat cap. Has mad eyes, wild eyes. Looks like he could have been a junkie once. Or maybe he still is. He must be about your age."

"I'm *not* really old, Jason. I'm seventy and like to think of myself as still being spry, thank you."

"That's not what I . . . you know what I mean. He was right over there, in the crowd. Now he's gone."

"I can't very well tell you who someone is if I can't see them, can I?"

"But you know everyone, Amita. I've described him in graphic detail."

"No, I don't know who you're talking about," she said. "You said you met him in the pub?"

"Yes. Like I said, I was in the pub the other night and he came up to me when Laura was at the bar."

"Is this the same night you came home and stunk the whole house out? The same night that you couldn't even manage to get up the stairs without your wife helping you?"

"You *know* it is, Amita, that's not fair."

"What's not fair is waking the whole house up in the middle of the night because you've had one too many libations."

Jason shook his head. He wasn't going to get anywhere, not when she was in this sort of mood. He scanned the opposite side of the square, trying to hunt out The Ghost. There was no sign of him, he was gone.

"Damn," he said.

"Sshh," said Amita. "Father Ford looks like he's about to say something."

The timid vicar stepped out into the middle of the square. His coat was shimmering from the streetlight shining on his sodden shoulders. He pushed back a thick mop of chestnut hair that had been plastered to his forehead by the rain. He blinked as he looked up at the storm.

"Searching for inspiration, perhaps," whispered Jason, watching the pastor.

Amita wasn't the only one who hushed him down this time. Sandy, Georgie, Ethel and a dozen others. Jason didn't argue. He stepped back into the shadows and watched on quietly, well and truly put in his place.

"Erm . . . good evening, ladies and gentlemen and . . . of course . . . children, too," Father Ford started, his voice weak and being drowned out by the slapping rain on the cobbles and pavements. "It's an absolutely horrible night, truly awful. But I can't thank you enough from the bottom of my heart that you've turned out for this special vigil in memory of our dear friend, Madeleine Frobisher. I know she touched the hearts of many of you here, otherwise you wouldn't have braved this awful storm to pay your respects tonight."

"Didn't we hear this speech already at the funeral?" Jason whispered to Amita

"Jason," she hissed back. "Show some respect, would you?"

The usual disapproving glares and tuts from Georgie followed and he focussed on Father Ford in the middle of the square. He was harping on about piety, pity and moving on. It wasn't that Jason was an ardent atheist; he gave organised religion its place, especially if it was helpful and inspirational to the flock that followed. He was simply a bit too sceptical in every part of his life to be able to be swept along with the emotion.

"So can I ask everyone to join me in a simple gesture for Madeleine," said the pastor. "Nothing too complicated or long-winded – the rain is still chucking it down and we have bingo in ten minutes or so."

A few furtive twitches from the regulars, Amita among them.

"If you'd like to light your candles, please, and join me in a rendition of *Onward Christian Soldiers*. We'll have to be a cappella as the organist is visiting family in Carlisle this evening. But I'm sure we'll manage."

The candles slowly sparked into life around the square. Father Ford fished a light out from his pocket. Soon the whole square was lit up by candlelight, everywhere except for the middle of the square where the vicar stood. His wet thumbs slipped and fumbled as he tried to light his own candle. This continued for a moment until a collective cringe went around the mourners when he dropped the lighter into a puddle.

Even Jason decided to look away. The dropped lighter was, however, Georgie's cue.

"Father Ford!" she shouted, pushing her way to the front of the throng. "I can help you, don't worry, dear."

"No, wait, hold on!" cried Amita a split second later.

With the force of a British Lions player, she shouldered her way through the crowd. Jason could only watch as the two pensioners biffed their compatriots out of the way, racing towards the beleaguered Father Ford. When they made it out of the mourners, the foot race was on. Neither Amita nor Georgie was willing to give in. Jason had seen Olympic sprint finals that had been slower. The sight of the two women in mourning gear legging it across the street to help Father Ford was something nobody in Market Square would likely forget in a hurry.

"Here you go, Father," said Georgie.

"No, here you are, Father Ford," panted Amita.

"I insist," Georgie waved a box of matches in the pastor's face.

"Those won't work, they'll be soaked through. Take my lighter," Amita insisted.

"The matches are fine!"

"The lighter is already lit!"

"But I got here first!"

"Did you heck, Georgie. I beat you by a furlong."

"A furlong! You must be joking, Amita. Have you left your spectacles at home?"

"There's nothing wrong with my eyesight. It's yours that needs checked, Georgie."

"Oh, is that so?"

"I wouldn't say it if it wasn't, would I?"

"So you're saying I'm blind?"

"If the boot fits, Littlejohn."

"Ladies! Please!"

Father Ford, much to his surprise, was able to bring the furious row to an end. Georgie and Amita turned to face him, chests heaving as they bottled their anger. Jason, from the safety of the spectators, took in the scene. He'd never been to a vigil before, but he was fairly sure that a fight over lighting a vicar's candle wasn't part of the traditional line-up.

"I can't thank you both enough for your help and your enthusiasm," he said. "But I think it would be in everyone's interest if we got on with the hymn and then called it a day. Don't you?"

Amita didn't answer. She wasn't going to be the first one to concede. The two women simply stood there, getting wet and stewing in their mutual silence.

"I'll take that as agreement, thank you," said Father Ford.

He took Amita's lighter and brought his candle to life. Giving himself a little count in, he started to sing the opening verse of *Onward Christian Soldiers*. Slowly the rest of the gathered crowd joined him. Jason didn't sing. Not for any other reason than he was a terrible singer. He knew his limits.

When the hymn was over, there was a little, muted applause. The candles were all snuffed out and the crowd began to clear from the square. Father Ford led Amita and Georgie back towards the church hall where the others were still lingering. He thanked them both again and went off to open the doors of the hall. With the vigil over, attention was quickly turning to the main highlight of the evening, namely bingo.

An energy seemed to jolt through the regulars as they milled around the front of the hall. And when Father Ford unlocked the doors, the soothing glow from within warmed them all and brought them back to life. Amita, however, wasn't feeling the same energy.

153

"Are you quite finished?" asked Jason.

"That bloody Georgie Littlejohn," she said. "She brings out the very worst in me, Jason. I don't know what it is. She's got some sort of hold on me. I can't shake it off."

"If you want to know what I think, which you probably don't, I thought it was hilarious."

"Hilarious?"

"Oh yes," he smiled. "I mean, what's not to enjoy about two divas arguing over who can set fire to a vicar in the rain? It's the stuff of legend, Amita."

"Oh lord," she groaned. "I'm never going to live this down, am I?"

"Not a chance," he clapped her shoulder. 'Does this make us even for when you had to collect me from the cop shop in my PJs?'

Amita was about to offer a retort, when she stopped. A hunched figure down the narrow lane beside the church hall caught her eye. She peered through the gloom of the thundering rain. As she stepped forward, the figure looked up.

"Sandy?" she asked.

The glow of the hall lights made every line, crease, wrinkle and divot in the old man's face stand out. But it was his eyes that shocked Amita the most. Ringed in red, they were bloodshot with tears. The normally stoic giant of the group was in the alleyway blubbing like a scolded schoolboy.

"Are you alright?" she asked.

Sandy didn't answer her. He erupted in a fit of sobs. She dashed forward and caught him, hugging him close to her. His big arms wrapped around her in a bear hug. Even Jason was a little moved by the scene.

"What the hell has happened Sandy?" she asked.

"It's Madeleine," he said. "I . . . I . . . I loved her."

Chapter 16

SWEET SIXTEEN, NEVER BEEN KISSED

The rain hammered down hard on the roof of the car, giving the three occupants a constant, throbbing drumbeat. Jason half-expected the roof to give in at some point. It had been nothing short of a miracle that his old, bashed-up family motor was still watertight and functioning. Come to think of it, he was a little surprised he was in the same condition.

They sat in silence, listening to the rain. Jason thought about turning on the wipers so they could see the outside world in all its dreariness. Then he thought better. The stillness and quiet seemed to be working – Sandy had stopped crying and was staring aimlessly ahead of him.

He was a big man – huge, in fact. His shoulders were like the deck of an aircraft carrier and poked over the edges of the passenger seat. His long coat was less a jacket and more like a tent. Even his face seemed like a caricature, eyes bulging, nose a little crooked, the hairs poking from each nostril like iron railings.

Yet there was also a tenderness to him. Jason didn't really know Sandy. He'd seen him about town – it was hard to miss him. And his interactions with him when dropping Amita off at bingo had always been polite, if slightly curt. Now the big guy was sitting in his passenger seat, mindlessly glaring at the rain running down the windscreen in huge tributaries.

Sandy was clasping his hands on his lap. They hissed as he rubbed the calluses and dry skin over each other. Jason didn't want to think about what those hands had seen or done. They were fighting hands, made for destruction.

"Are you feeling any better, Sandy?" Amita asked.

She leaned forward from the backseat and let her hand rest on one of Sandy's mighty shoulders. It woke him with a little startle and he quickly remembered where he was.

"Yes, thank you," he said, voice still deep and commanding. "I don't know what came over me back there. I think it was all a bit too much."

"That's perfectly understandable," she assured him. "It's been a hard few days for all of us. If for nothing else, for the shock value. I don't think any of us were expecting what happened. Were we, Jason?"

"What?" he said, distracted by a particularly heavy run of water snaking its way down the side window.

"The shock of what's happened," said Amita angrily.

"Oh, yeah, absolutely. Been a real shock."

"It has been," said Sandy, still looking ahead. "You just don't expect something like this to happen to people you know, people that you care about. Not so suddenly, snuffed out . . ."

"I've been saying the exact same thing, Sandy," she squeezed his shoulder. "Haven't I, Jason?"

"Yes, you have Amita," he quietly agreed. "A real shock for everyone involved."

They sat in silence for a moment. Jason started to get that prickly sensation in the back of his neck. It was a new thing, something he'd started to develop since hanging around with his mother-in-law. Like some sort of sixth sense, it was an anticipation of the awkward or downright blunt. Amita, dutifully, delivered.

"You said you loved her, Sandy," she blurted out. "I had no idea you two were, you know, romantically engaged."

Jason felt his whole body tense up. He wasn't sure why. Maybe it was the sheer size of Sandy – the old man was as big as a mountain. If he wanted to kick off then there would be very little Jason, Amita or anyone else could do about it. And from the demeanour he'd presented before, asking about his love life felt like a very bad idea.

Much to Jason's surprise, and relief, Sandy did nothing. His moustache twitched and moved up and down as he chewed over what he was about to say. Then he raised his eyebrows and dropped his gaze down to his hands.

"No, we weren't," he said with a huge, regretful sigh. "We weren't a couple or anything. And I wasn't some sort of creep who loved her from afar. I was happily married for forty years, Amita. I loved my wife Linda with all of my heart. But I loved Madeleine Frobisher, too."

Sandy took a long, deep breath that seemed to make his huge chest even bigger. He took his time. He was clearly upset and wrestling with something. Amita tried her best to gently coax him.

"You're with friends, Sandy," she said. "You're a proud man, a well-liked man. Nothing you tell us here tonight needs to go anywhere beyond these four, admittedly slightly rusty, walls. I promise you that. *We* promise you, don't we, Jason?"

"Yes, of course," said Jason. "Absolutely. In case you didn't know, Sandy, I'm not quite the epicentre of the gossip circles. Far from it. Nobody wants to hear what I've got to say, not even my employers."

He'd thought a little joke might lighten the mood, but Sandy was stony-faced, his head still bowed.

"I'm not ashamed to say that I loved her," said Sandy. "I'm proud I knew her long enough that I had the opportunity to love her. You see, Madeleine and I go back a long way. She used to be a singer."

"Yes, at the Eurovision, or whatever it's called," said Amita.

This seemed to ignite Sandy into life. He sat upright and twisted in his seat, wet coat and springs all squeaking as he did so.

"How did you know that?" he asked.

"It's not a secret," said Jason, butting in. "You can see all of her performances online."

"How did you know that she was a singer, though?" Sandy pressed. "She never talked about it. She never uttered a word to anyone up here. She kept it quiet, deliberately so. It wasn't something she ever wanted people finding out about. It was a long time ago."

The big man was getting agitated. Jason could hear a note of anger creeping into his deep voice. Amita held up her hands and tried to calm him down.

"Sandy, it's okay, we haven't told anyone else about Madeleine's past life, but we know."

"But how?" he turned around further and the whole car rocked. "How did you know? Madeleine wanted to leave it behind her. She never told another living soul for years, decades even. It was her secret, her burden."

"If she didn't tell anyone, how come you know?" asked Jason.

Sandy's fire was snuffed out instantly. His shoulders dropped and his whole face sagged. He looked like a burst balloon. He sat there in silence.

"We found out through a friend of Jason's," Amita said calmly. "Another reporter, a Eurovision superfan. Jason happened to mention to her that Madeleine had died and she knew Madeleine used to be Maddy Forster the singer instantly. That's how we know, Sandy – nothing sinister or underhanded, it was a little quirk of fate that we found out."

This seemed to appease the hunched figure. He nodded and rubbed his face with his big, calloused hands.

"You didn't answer our question though, Sandy," said Jason, smelling blood. "We've told you how *we* know. Now it's your turn."

Sandy blew the air out of his giant nostrils. He kept nodding, face etched in pain and misery. He gently rapped his knuckles off the dashboard and began to speak slowly. "I used to be a bouncer in the East End in the sixties," he said.

"That's London's East End, right?" said Amita.

"Yes, it is," he continued. "When you watch documentaries on the telly and read books and newspapers about that time, you'd think it was some golden age, some wonderful place where everyone had a great time. Well let me tell you both, it wasn't, especially in my game. I've lost count of the number of friends I lost over the years – stabbings, shootings, drugs, you name it. The Swinging Sixties is a story for tourists. This was real life and it was ugly, believe me. I've got the scars that prove it."

He shifted a little uncomfortably in the passenger seat.

"It must have been around sixty-two or sixty-three when I first met Madeleine. She was like a breath of fresh air, so elegant, so talented. When you worked the doors of the pubs and clubs, you got to know some of the acts. You'd see them two, maybe three times a week depending on where you were working. *Ronnie Scott's* on a Monday, *The Marquee* on Wednesday, *La Chasse* on a Friday night, it could get very tasty. But there was always this sort of kinship between the acts and us in security. Maybe because we all worked the same hours, or that we looked out for each other. A lot of them were a load of rubbish, even by today's standards. Have you heard what's on the radio these days?"

"Awful," said Amita. "All thump, thump, thump, thump. I can't stand it."

"Focus," said Jason.

"Yeah, sorry," Sandy went on. "Madeleine, she arrived in sixty-three I think it was. And she was a star instantly. You could tell right away that she was going to be a big hit. The voice, the way she carried herself on stage, her professionalism. And that face of hers, she was so beautiful, so natural. She was heading straight to the top from the moment she set foot in London.

"I remember that first night I saw her on stage, I can see it, even now, after all of these years. It was some dingy little place in the back end of Soho. The floors were sticky and the smoke was so thick you could barely see the end of your nose. No health and safety back then of course. It was either put up or shut up. Madeleine always put up, because she was a professional. Here she was, barely in the city, I think she'd got the train down from Salford that *day*, in fact. And she was singing in front of a bunch of drunks who didn't know talent from a boil on their backsides. But I tell you both this now, as I sit here, if they didn't know her before they certainly did when she finished her set. She blew the roof off the place. That voice, that stage presence. She had everything.

"When she was finished and we closed up for the night, I went backstage to speak with her. There was the usual rabble of creeps still lingering, looking for a bit of the action. I always remember her standing at the door of the dressing room trying to be polite to those weirdos. They were leering at her, all hands and dirty looks. And Madeleine, the picture of professionalism, was still smiling and being polite. I stepped in and pretended to be her boyfriend. That quickly dissipated the crowd. She thanked me and invited me into the dressing room for a cuppa. I took it. And that's *all* I took, you have to understand. From that moment on Madeleine and I were inseparable, but only as friends. We were the very best of friends. And I had the pleasure of watching her grow from a nobody to one of the faces on the circuit. She even got a record deal from that horrible little club to the Palladium, and beyond. She asked me to be her escort, her bodyguard, and we went everywhere together. Until I met my wife."

"Let me guess," said Jason. "She wasn't happy with you spending all your time with a glamorous, gorgeous pop singer."

"No, it wasn't like that," said Sandy. "Linda knew how close I was to Madeleine. She knew that we were friends and *only* friends. They got on well together, enjoyed each other's company. But the life of a bouncer and bodyguard isn't one that helps make for a safe or sound family life.

And I had the stark choice – family or career. It's not a choice really, it never was in question. We moved up here to be with Linda's family in sixty-nine and I've been here ever since. I left all the violence and late nights behind me. But I also left Madeleine. A year later that bastard Starbuck got his hands on her and I've never, ever forgiven myself for that."

Sandy smashed his fist against the dashboard. It was hard and fast, a little flash of what the old man had once been capable of. There was no damage but he rubbed his knuckles. Jason looked over at his mother-in-law, confused.

"Starbuck?" Amita asked

The old man was sneering and staring out through the rain. He was still rubbing his knuckles when he finally heard Amita.

"Freddie Starbuck," he said with venom

Amita hesitated. She was hoping, praying almost, that Jason would recognise the name. Little did she know that he was doing the same. They both drew a blank.

Sandy sensed their confusion. He looked at them in turn, his face dropping a little.

"Freddie Starbuck," he said again. "You've never heard of Freddie Starbuck? I thought you knew about Madeleine being a singer?"

"We did know," said Jason. "But this Starbuck character, I've never heard of him. Have you, Amita?"

She shook her head.

Sandy let out a long, frustrated groan. He bit his knuckle. "I'm sorry," he said. "Forget I said anything."

He reached for the door. Amita grabbed him.

"No, Sandy, please wait," she said. "We don't know this Freddie Starbuck person but you have to tell us."

"No, I've said too much already, me and my big mouth. I'm sorry," he pushed the door open.

"Sandy!"

It was too late. The old man had surprising speed. He was off and out the door, the rain still lashing down outside.

"Get after him, Jason!" Amita shouted.

"What?"

"Go after him. We have to know who this Starbuck man is. It might be a clue."

"And it might be nothing, Amita. He's been through the ringer. Maybe we should let him go."

"And what if this Freddie Starbuck has something to do with Madeleine's death?"

"And what if he doesn't?" said Jason. "What if we're simply twisting the knife into the back of poor old Sandy who's on the verge of a breakdown?"

"Fine," said Amita, throwing open her passenger door. "If you want something done you need to do it yourself."

"Amita, wait!"

She hurried down the pavement, splashing through the puddles that were slowly turning Penrith's streets into a scene from Venice. Jason gave chase and they caught up with Sandy in the shadow of the bingo hall.

"Sandy, please!" Amita shouted at him.

At first he refused to stop, hands shoved in his pockets, head bowed low, rain running off the rim of his flat cap.

"Please, you have to tell us who this Freddie Starbuck is, it's vital."

"What could possibly be vital about dredging up the past, Amita?" he asked angrily. "Let sleeping dogs lie. What's done is done and you can't change it."

"And what if there was still something that could be done?" she said. "What if Madeleine's death wasn't an accident?"

Sandy stood upright. He towered over Amita and Jason, growing ever taller.

"What did you say?" he asked.

Amita was suddenly bashful. She wiped the rain from her eyes and looked to Jason for inspiration.

"We've been doing a little investigating," she said. "We . . ."

"*You*," said Jason sharply. "I'm still on the fence."

"I think there might be something sinister going on with Madeleine," she said bluntly. "I think she might not have accidentally fallen and broken her neck. I think there might be someone out there, right now, who meant to cause her harm. And I'm not going to stop until I know they've been brought to justice. Now you can help us, Sandy, or you can get in our way. But from what you've told us tonight, I can't imagine you'd want anything awful to have happened to poor Madeleine."

Sandy's eyes began to tear up again. His mouth was trembling, chin puckered as he fought back his sadness.

"Now please," said Amita, taking his hand. "You must tell us who Freddie Starbuck is. You must tell us everything you know."

The doors of the hall opened and they were all bathed in the soft, warm glow from inside. But the session was already over. The bingo club regulars started to pile out, complaining about the rain as soon as they spotted the deluge. Umbrellas were deployed and hoods pulled up with military precision. Some said hello to Amita and Sandy who stood like statues as the crowd washed over them. Then Georgie Littlejohn appeared.

"Oh," she said. "Fancy seeing you two here. Thought you would have been inside for bingo but you clearly had other things on your mind."

Jason felt a sudden anger towards her. Amita and Sandy didn't say a word. They stood there, looking at each other, still holding hands.

"Well, I see you're busy," said Georgie, realising she wasn't getting a response. "I'll see you both in the week then, if you're not too busy. Goodnight."

She walked briskly off into the night and the hall doors closed. Everything went dark in the street again, leaving only Amita, Sandy and Jason.

"I'll tell you everything," said Sandy, his voice hoarse. "But not here, not in the street. There are too many nosy parkers who would relish a slur on Madeleine's good name."

"Where then?" said Amita.

Sandy looked up and down the street. When he was happy there was nobody else around, he said quietly, "Come with me," and made off down the pavement.

Amita followed.

Jason stood watching them. He looked back up the road to his car, then up at the teeming rain. "Great," he said. "I was going to watch the football tonight. Glad I didn't have any plans."

He pulled his coat collar up and broke into a light jog to catch the others up.

Chapter 17

DANCING QUEEN

Sandy's flat was everything Amita had expected from a widower of his age, right down to the wall dedicated to his children and grandchildren graduating from university. She looked at each of the portraits with a smile. It was a little timeline, not only of Sandy's loved ones, but of life itself. From the top left all the way down to the bottom right, the hairstyles, outfits, even the picture quality, changed with the passing of the years. She had a sudden urge to hug Clara and Josh. She would do it as soon as she got home.

"Memories," she said. "Happy memories of a life well lived, that's what I think."

"Nothing unusual about that, is there?" asked Jason, sitting on the sofa closest to the balcony door. "There *are* a lot of pictures in here, right enough."

Amita stepped away from the wall of fame. She rounded past the huge TV set and onto another table dominated by more pictures. She picked up the nearest one. It was Sandy and his wife on a beach somewhere, his broad chest bronzed in the summer sunshine. The happy couple beamed back from the moment captured in time. It was lovely. She smiled again and showed it to Jason.

"He had quite the physique," she said.

"I'll bet you fifty quid he's still as fit as ever," he said. "These old-timers who worked doors in the bad old days, they never lose it. I wouldn't fancy getting him angry, Amita. Whatever you're planning here, take it easy. He won't swing for you, but he could probably still take my head off."

"Don't be ridiculous, Jason," she scolded him. "Sandy isn't going to hurt us. We're his friends. Or I am at least."

"Not going to hurt us? Have you seen the size of his hands? He could crush golf balls with those things."

Amita hesitated. She looked down at the picture of Sandy and his wife. Then she shook her head.

"What?" he asked.

"No, nothing," she said. "Absolutely nothing. Don't worry about it."

"Do you take sugar?" Sandy's voice came booming in from the kitchen.

"None for me, please, thank you," she said.

"Two for me, Sandy," said Jason.

"You're not allowed sugar," she said quietly to him.

"I'm a guest," he replied weakly. "And besides, since when were you so concerned about my diet? You fed me those two breakfasts the other morning."

Sandy came in with a tray. It was odd to see him so domesticated. Amita had only ever known the big man as a taciturn figure. He smiled weakly as he sat down in his armchair, a thick stain from tobacco and smoke high above it on the ceiling. The wallpaper was yellow too from Sandy's smoking and he didn't delay in digging out a roll-up cigarette from the top pocket of his shirt.

"Don't mind if I . . . you know?" he said, waving it at the others. "It's been a long day."

"No, go ahead," said Jason, drinking his sweet tea.

Sandy patted his chest and pockets for his lighter. Amita got to hers first and handed it to him.

"I meant to ask earlier," said Jason, mid-gulp. "Since when did you start carrying around a cigarette lighter?"

"I know it's been a long day for you, Sandy," she said, ignoring him. "But we'd very much like to know who this Freddie Starbuck person is. He seems to have riled you up no end."

Sandy sucked hard on his roll-up. He flashed his teeth and blew the smoke out between the gaps. His knee was bobbing up and down. He picked at the stitching on the arm of his battered old armchair.

"Freddie Starbuck is . . . is one of the worst human beings to ever walk this earth," he said. "The man was a menace to society, a pest, a little gnat that I could have, *should* have, crushed under my boot when I had the chance. I didn't and people paid the consequences, Madeleine most of all."

Sandy stared into the blank screen of his huge TV. He bit down on his lip and kept bobbing his knee up and down, getting faster and faster. The floorboards creaked beneath him as he sat there, in his armchair, like a caged tiger ready to pounce on its handler when the moment came.

"I came up here just before Madeleine appeared on the Eurovision," he continued. "Linda and I got married in winter of sixty-nine and we moved to Brixton. It wasn't very nice, she never liked it there. I was still working for

Madeleine at the time. We would be on the road for weeks on end, up and down the country, over to Ireland, France, Germany, Italy, you name it. The pop stars worked like dogs back then, worked to the bone. But it was always good fun with Madeleine. She looked after everyone on the tour."

"Linda didn't go with you then?" asked Amita.

"No, she stayed in Brixton. She hated it. I couldn't blame her, really. She was on her own in a new part of the city. She didn't know anyone and I was away for weeks at a time. We had a touring break over Christmas and that was when she told me she didn't want me to leave again. So I didn't. Linda had family up here in Carlisle, so we upped sticks and that was that."

"How did Madeleine take that?" asked Jason, draining his mug.

"She was devastated, of course," said Sandy, looking at Jason with a terrible sadness. "I think it broke her heart as much as it did mine. I told you, I loved her and she loved me, too. We were never romantic, never at all. It never crossed either of our minds. We were just friends, good friends, the best of friends. And this was it all coming to an end. She understood, of course she understood, who wouldn't? I did a couple of her dates in and around London at the end of January and then we came up to the Lakes. A few weeks later I hear she's going to be representing the UK in the Eurovision. I was delighted for her, so was Linda. We thought this would be the global stage she'd always deserved. And it was. She was unlucky not to win it. Ireland, back then, they were the ones to beat. But she came bloody close. She came back to London, and that's when the trouble started."

Sandy realised his cigarette had burned down. He crushed it in the ashtray beside his armchair and took a large gulp of tea. Amita edged a little further forward in her seat at the end of the couch.

"Trouble?" she asked. "Freddie Starbuck?"

"Freddie effing Starbuck," said Sandy. "The man was a maniac. How he was allowed to roam the streets I'll never know."

"Who was he?" asked Jason.

"He was a nobody," he said. "At least that's what everyone thought at first. When I left Madeleine, a good mate of mine, Stan Wilton, took over the security detail. I kept in touch with him from time to time, nothing regular. He used to tell me about this bloke who would hang around at the stage door of places Madeleine was performing. Nothing unusual about that, she had lots of fans. Only this geezer was a grown man. Bit odd, I thought, but Stan didn't think there was an issue."

"And this was Starbuck?" asked Jason.

"The very same," said Sandy. "I trusted Stan, he was a good bloke, good honest kind of guy and he could throw a punch or two when it counted. He said he would deal with it, so I assumed he would. I didn't think anything else of it until Madeleine mentions, in a letter, a few odd things around her flat."

Sandy stood up. He went over to the cabinet that supported the huge TV. Pulling out boxes and spare cables, he produced a small tin coated in dust. He opened it and rifled through the crumpled papers inside. He found a handful, checked the tops of them and handed them over to Amita.

"Letters," she said. "I don't have my glasses. Jason, you read them."

She passed them over to her son-in-law. Jason squinted at them, noting the dates, all from the summer of 1970 onwards.

"We used to write to each other," said Sandy. "I never knew where she would be to reach her on the phone, you see. Like I said, a few weeks after Stan's call she starts telling me about strange things going on at her flat. Shadowy figures outside the windows, odd calls in the middle of the night. She even said she came home one night and one of the back windows had been put in."

Jason scanned through the handwritten notes. He watched the dates tick past as he sifted through the letters. The letters were becoming more frequent, sometimes only days between them. The writing was more erratic, too – lots of exclamation marks and underlined words.

"She was scared," said Jason.

"Terrified," Sandy agreed. "I kept trying to call her, but I could never get through. Even Stan was struggling to reach her. She started showing up late to rehearsals and gigs. That wasn't Madeleine, that wasn't her at all. I told you both, she was a wonderful professional. She had been spooked by whatever this was. So I went down to London for the week, hoping to reach her. I spent the night watching in the lane across from her flat. Nobody came or went until she showed up around five in the morning the next day. She was glad to see me."

"I'll bet she was," said Amita. "So this Freddie Starbuck was what? A stalker?"

"We didn't know who it was, not then," said Sandy. "The police weren't any help. Neither was Madeleine's agent or showbiz people. They thought she was imagining it. Nothing could be done until something had happened.

It was a bloody scandal, Amita, I'm telling you. Can you imagine something like all of this – hanging around at stage doors, windows being put in, crank calls in the middle of the night – imagine that happened nowadays to a big celebrity. It was a joke back then."

"But there was nothing you could do," said Amita.

"No," he said sadly. "Nothing. And nothing happened, not for the week I was down there with her, anyway. But I knew something *would* happen. Whoever was trying to frighten her, this mysterious man at the stage doors, he would have seen me in her flat, would know I was about. And he would have, he *did*, think twice about trying anything on when I was about."

"So what did you do?" asked Jason, putting the letters down.

"I had to go home," said Sandy, his voice cracking. "Madeleine said she was going on tour and she'd be fine. She was looking forward to getting out of London, getting away from her flat, from the city. Moving around for a few weeks, it would mean whoever was stalking her wouldn't know where she was. I told her, if there was any trouble, to give me a call. I would drop everything and be with her as soon as possible. I remember standing at the door of her flat that morning. She was so frail-looking, so timid. Everything that had happened had sucked the life from her, drained her of her confidence. It was tragic. I didn't want to go. I shouldn't have gone."

Sandy thumped his fist into his open palm. It cracked with a loud slap that made Jason's ears hurt. He looked at Amita, trying to remind her of their previous conversation. But she ignored him and stayed calm.

"What happened, Sandy?" she asked him.

The big man cursed under his breath. He paced around the living room, big feet thumping with every step. Jason and Amita watched him carefully as his temper rose, face turning scarlet under his snow white moustache and eyebrows.

"I don't remember the exact details," he said. "Which is awful, because it all came out in court. But I think I must have blocked them out or something, just to try and cope."

"What happened?"

"She was supposed to be getting picked up by the record label," he continued. "They were meant to be sending a car to hers to start the tour, but something had happened, a flat tyre, engine trouble, something stupid. Madeleine being Madeleine had volunteered to get a cab to their offices before they joined up with the road crew. When the taxi arrives she got in, not thinking anything of it. Why would you? Only this wasn't a licensed cab. Who's behind the wheel but Freddie Starbuck. The creep had tapped Madeleine's phone, did it the night he broke in. He'd been lying in wait until he could pick her up and take her away. God knows how long he had been waiting, but he had been waiting nonetheless. And, of course, Madeleine had no idea who he was."

"So she was kidnapped?" asked Jason, mouth ajar.

"She was," said Sandy, his eyes watery. "By the time she realised what was going on he had locked the doors. She was helpless, Jason. Completely helpless. That rat had her for three days in his lockup out Orpington way. Three days with that creep. I can't begin to imagine what that was like for her." He sank into his armchair and rubbed his forehead. "She survived though, god knows how. On the third day she managed to get out. He'd left a door unlocked or something, I can't remember. Even without food and being bound by that monster, she managed to get out and flag down help. Starbuck was nicked, of course. It was in the papers the next day. One of *your* lot had seen her being taken into a hospital and pieced it together from a source at the police who told him everything. I was devastated. I'm *still* devastated all these years later. I should never have left her, *never* have let her wait for the lift on her own. It all happened less than an hour after I left. If I'd just stayed there that little bit longer, been with her. After the way she looked at me. I've never forgiven myself, you know. I've carried it with me all these years. Every day I think about that morning. Every single day."

He started to cry. Amita reached over to him and squeezed his hand tightly.

"It wasn't your fault, Sandy," she said softly. "You couldn't have known. This Freddie Starbuck, he was the one to blame, not you. You had a wife to come home to. You were Madeleine's friend, that's why you went down there in the first place. She wouldn't have blamed you."

Sandy shook his head.

"She never did," he said. "Not once in all the time that followed, after everything that happened. She never once blamed me."

"Because it wasn't your fault," Amita said again.

"What happened to Starbuck?" asked Jason. "You said he was arrested."

"Charged and jailed," said Sandy, sniffing. "It was all kept pretty quiet by the record company. They thought something like this would be bad for their image, and for Madeleine. She was at court every day of the trial, had to listen to that worm try and squirm his way out of what he'd done. His lawyers tried to plead insanity, said he was an obsessed fan who didn't know right from wrong because of his illness. But let me tell you both, as I live and breathe, he knew *exactly* what he was doing. I saw it in his eyes. He smirked at me, blew me a kiss, when the judge sent him down. Gave him twenty years for kidnap and assault. It was never enough. Nothing would ever be enough for what he did, the rotten bastard."

Sandy's sadness and fight seemed to leave him then. His shoulders sank and he looked drained.

"What happened to Madeleine?" asked Amita.

"That was the biggest tragedy of all," he said. "She could have been huge, a proper megastar, Hollywood if she had wanted. But the whole ordeal took it out of her. She couldn't bring herself to sing onstage again – she was terrified of who would be in the audience. Starbuck was locked up but she always worried it would happen again with some-body else. And why wouldn't it? If Starbuck could become obsessed, who was to say it couldn't happen again?"

"So she retired?" asked Amita.

"Then and there, the day the trial ended. The label was furious. She was still under contract, of course. It cost her a fortune in legal fees in the end, but she was just glad that nobody could force her to go on tour or to appear in public ever again. She was a private citizen again and it was the happiest I ever saw her. When she stepped off the train at Penrith station, I could have cried. I think I actually did."

"She came up here then? When was that, the mid-seventies?" asked Jason.

"Yes," said Sandy. "After the trial she said she needed to get away for a while, to clear her head, to be alone. I told her it was quiet up here, she could blend in, become part of the scenery after a while. But she didn't want to come up, not at first anyway. She kept saying she wanted to be alone, to go somewhere completely different to pull her life back together. She wouldn't listen to me, not then. But after a few long months I get a phone call. It was a Saturday morning, I remember, I was just heading out the door and the phone rang and it was her. I was so happy to hear her voice. She sounded different, though. There was something about her, something missing. I couldn't work it out. She said, if the offer still stood, she would love to come up to Penrith to be close to at least some people she knew. Of course, I was delighted. I couldn't wait to get her up here. I said I would help her to change her name, give her a clean break and a fresh start among the fresh air. It took a deal of time to arrange, but I helped her sort out the move. She bought that big house out near Ullswater – it was going to be her pet project, restoring it. She never got around to half of it, of course, she was too much of a dreamer."

He laughed at that. Amita smiled with him.

"I think she was happy here," he said. "I think she was happy to be away from London, away from everything that had happened. She could be somebody normal up here. And she knew I was always close by if she ever needed anything. You knew her, Amita. She was always part of the community. I think that's what she loved most about this place. It was her home for longer than anywhere else and she loved the people. And they loved her, even though nobody knew who she was, or what she had been."

"There must have been some fans over the years?" asked Jason. "Surely she couldn't have dropped off the face of the planet without people realising."

"We had the odd person from time to time," said Sandy. "But nothing dangerous, nothing that would cause her any harm. She would always meet them, and invite them in for tea when she knew it was alright. It was like a pilgrimage almost. I think people saw it as some daft quest to go on, to hunt out the legendary Madeleine Forster. You had to be a real fan to have followed her story, her name change – but those kind of fans were usually the sweetest. Over the years they grew less and less, and she was just Madeleine to everyone. It meant the world to her, and to me, to know she'd been able to move on from Starbuck."

"We had no idea," said Amita. "No idea of any of this, Sandy."

"You can't tell anyone, Amita," he said, suddenly desperate. "Please, you have to promise me you won't tell anyone. I couldn't live with myself if I thought all of this was going to come out now she's died. I would be mortified."

"We won't tell a soul, will we, Jason?" she said.

"Nobody, Sandy, you can rely on us."

"Thank you, both," he said, relieved. "I've kept all of this bottled up over the last few weeks. It's been hard, you know, trying to grieve with everyone else, despite us going back all those years. Really hard."

"I'm sure it has, Sandy, but, you know, you don't need to be alone with any of this, not now," she said. "You've always got both of us to talk to. We're here for you."

He clapped his free hand onto hers. He thanked them again. The clock on the mantelpiece began to ring as it struck ten o'clock.

"We should go," said Jason. "It's getting late. Like you say, Sandy, it's been a long day."

He agreed and they said their goodbyes, Sandy leading them to the door. Amita hugged him once more before they headed to the stairwell outside his flat.

"You will keep your word, won't you?" he called after them. "You'll keep this all secret?"

"Our lips are sealed." said Amita

"Thank you for all of your kindness, Amita," he said with a sad smile. "It means a lot."

"I meant to ask earlier," said Jason. "What happened to Starbuck? If he got twenty years, he'd be out by now surely."

A shiver went down Amita's spine as her imagination started to run away from her. The implications were sinister, to say the least.

"He was a troublemaker behind bars," said Sandy. "He kept getting time added on to his sentence. Fighting, setting fire to his cell, the works. I told you, he was a nasty piece of work."

"So he's still in jail?" asked Jason.

"I don't know," Sandy shrugged. "I used to have friends in the prison service but they're either retired or dead or not far from it. I lost touch on what that bastard was up to about twenty years ago. He was alive and well then and still locked up. What happened to him after that is anyone's guess."

"Don't you wonder?" Jason asked.

"I'm an old man, Jason," said Sandy firmly. "Freddie Starbuck took up too much of my time and hurt someone I love. You reach your limit on how much hating you can do in a lifetime. I'm happy to never know what that scum got up to. If he's dead, he's burning in hell, I can promise you that. And if he's not, well, he's got a long time in the furnace waiting for him soon."

Jason thought better than to press. Sandy was tired and drained but he still cut an imposing figure in the doorway of his pensioner flat. Jason nodded and headed down the stairs, Amita close behind him.

When they reached the front door, they found the night still and quiet. The rain had stopped and everywhere shone with a wet, fluorescent glare from the street lights. Jason fastened up his sodden coat and Amita stared at the ground.

"I hope you're not thinking what I'm thinking," he said to her.

"I don't know," she said, still looking at the puddles. "What are you thinking?"

"That Freddie Starbuck had something to do with Madeleine's death."

"Your hopes would be misplaced then, Jason," she said. "Because that's *exactly* what I'm thinking."

"He could be dead, Amita," he said, starting for the car. "And even if he's not, he'd be an old man."

"And you don't think old men are capable of murdering old women? What about Sandy, you don't think he could do a bit of bone-breaking if he turned his mind to it?"

"That's different," said Jason.

"No it's not."

"It is," he said, reaching the car. "Sandy was a professional doorman. This Starbuck bloke sounds like a professional weirdo. They aren't the same thing. And like I said, we don't even know if he's alive or not."

Amita climbed into the car and shut the door with a thump.

"No, we don't," she said. "So we're going to have to find out."

Chapter 18

COMING OF AGE

Amita was never happier than when her family was around her. She had thought about these fleeting moments a lot in the past few days. The idea of Madeleine lying alone in her final moments had made her value having family nearby. She hated to think of anyone being in that position – found in the cold the morning after something dreadful happened. Most of all, she hated the idea that it would end up happening to *her*.

But she remembered something she'd read years ago about families. Love, it had said, is when you stop opening presents on Christmas morning and just listen. While it might not be the festive season yet, Amita knew all too well what that feeling was like. She had it now, here, at breakfast on this gloomy morning. And for a few moments she could forget about Madeleine Frobisher, Georgie Littlejohn, the bingo club and everything else. She could just sit here, with her family, and enjoy breakfast. Everyone was here. Radha, Josh and Clara, all laughing, smiling and joking. Jason was beside them at the opposite end of the table. Even he looked jolly and jovial for this time of the morning. The warmth in the kitchen was infectious. It made Amita feel very content and lucky. But it also made her remember one crucial thing Sandy hadn't mentioned. The thought made her stop mid-chew of her toast. She carefully put it back down on her plate and looked around the kitchen table.

But, before she could follow her thought, her daughter spoke up. "So," Radha was wiping yogurt from Clara's chin. "What's this I hear about you chatting up a policeman's granddaughter, Jason?"

He spat out his corn flakes. Amita's serenity was gone, quick as a flash.

"What?" she asked.

Jason was spluttering. Radha remained perfectly cool, helping Clara down from her chair and sending her off running and screaming to be with her toys.

"My husband, Mum, was apparently chatting up the grand-daughter of a policeman at soft play the other day," she said.

Amita wasn't sure what she was hearing. She didn't see eye-to-eye with Jason, she never had. She freely admitted, and regularly told him, he wasn't what she'd imagined for her daughter. But she still trusted him not to do something like this.

"Is this true?" she asked.

"No it bloody well is not!" he said, choking for breath. "Who told you?"

Radha tapped the side of her nose, a wry smile on her face. Amita started to feel a bit better.

"I always protect my sources, Brazel," she said.

"Rubbish," he said. "That's a load of old cobblers, and you know it."

"I thought that was a fundamental of journalism," she levelled at him. "That it was one of the pillars on which the great and noble Fourth Estate prides itself."

"Firstly, there's no pride in being a journalist," he said sarcastically. "You check that in at the door with your coat, along with any sensibilities, scruples or moral compass you might have had before the job. And secondly, who told you about my soft play liaison? Was it Cheryl in the hairdressers?"

"No, it wasn't Cheryl," said Radha, starting to tidy up the plates. "She's in Benidorm."

"Frank from the supermarket then. He's forever gossiping."

"Nope, not Frank."

"Helen in the library? Another grade-A gossiper."

"No, wrong again, sports fan. Do you want to keep guessing until you've named everyone we know in Cumbria?"

"No," he sulked. "Just tell me because they've clearly gotten the wrong end of the stick, and I'd like to introduce them to a surgical collar."

"It was Georgie Littlejohn."

"What!"

Amita and Jason both shot up from their chairs at exactly the same time. Radha took a step back.

"Sorry, did I say something offensive?" she asked them.

"Georgie?" asked Jason.

"Littlejohn?" asked Amita.

"Yes, Georgie Littlejohn," said Radha. "I ran into her at the petrol station the other night. She recognised me as your wife, Jason, and *your* daughter, Mum. We had a nice little chat and she mentioned that a friend of a friend, or something, had seen Penrith's Casanova here speaking with a very young, very made-up woman before some detective, Alby was it, came storming in and broke up the whole thing."

"Is this true?" asked Amita.

Jason was speechless. He had suspected that Georgie was an old gossip. That she was Amita's rival was purely a bit of fun. However, after Radha's revelations, it was clear he had underestimated her.

"Yes, and no," he said.

"What does that mean?" Amita jabbed.

"It means yes, I was speaking to Stacey."

"Oh, she has a name now," laughed Radha.

"I was speaking to Stacey at the coffee place in the soft play while our kids were, you know, playing. She was telling me she was an Instagrammer. It was all very polite. Then Alby comes bursting in and goes absolutely ape. I thought he was going to swing for me."

"And how do you know Alby, exactly?" asked Amita.

"He's the lead detective on all the stuff being stolen from the *Standard*'s offices. You remember when the police came and hauled me away and you said you'd never live it down?"

"I'm not going to now, am I? Not if Georgie knows."

"Georgie *always* knows," said Jason.

"For the record, I had no intention of putting you on the cross, Jason. You're my husband and I love and trust you," said Radha, rounding the table and leaning in close to her husband. "Because if I thought you were up to no good, I'd take the garden shears to you. Wouldn't I, darling?"

She kissed him on the lips and gave him a big, devilish smile. He swallowed and watched as she switched on the dishwasher and took Josh out into the back garden.

"Bloody hell," said Jason, when his wife was safely out of earshot. "Georgie Littlejohn, she's worse than the Mafia."

"I did warn you," said Amita.

"Maybe she'd be better trying to catch Madeleine's killer," he said.

"Now, now Jason," said Amita. "Georgie might have all her fingers in different pies. But she's thick as mince, as we've already seen. You really should be more careful, though."

"Careful? I didn't do anything!"

"You've got this family's reputation to think of. You shouldn't be going about speaking with strange women."

"It was at the soft play centre! I was hardly in a night-club, up on the bar swirling my shirt about my head, was I?"

"That's an image I could do without," she said curtly.

Jason sighed. He let his head drop back and he stared at the ceiling.

"Unbelievable. Damned if you do and damned if you don't," he said.

"Yes, well, you can weigh up your philosophical para-doxes on your own time, preferably when I'm out for a run or something. We've got more pressing matters to attend to. Namely Freddie Starbuck."

Jason rubbed his face. He turned his attention back to Amita across the table.

"Freddie Starbuck," he said. "The maniacal stalker who Madeleine Frobisher failed to tell anyone about for half a century."

"The one and the same," said Amita. "I need you to do a bit of digging for us. I had a look online last night before I went to sleep. I can't find anything about him on there. The internet is really terrible for keeping old news-papers."

"Funny that," said Jason sarcastically. "Imagine a brand new technology not cooperating with an old one. Never been heard of."

"You can scoff all you want, but we need a definitive answer as to what happened to Starbuck," said Amita. "We need to know if he's still alive. And if so, is he still locked up or has he been released? If he's been released, we'll have to start looking for where he is now and what he was doing the night before Madeleine was found by the postman."

Jason sniffed loudly. "I thought about this too," he said. "If Freddie Starbuck was really a threat, wouldn't the police know about it? I mean, if Madeleine had been through the ringer like Sandy said, surely it's the first thing a good copper would think of."

"Not if they didn't know about it," Amita waved her phone. "I was online for an hour last night, trying to read up about it, and I found next to nothing, just a couple of entries on old music forums that have been archived. Why would the police think anything of it if Madeleine had spent fifty years or more hiding it from the world? And you saw the state of Sandy last night – he's in no shape to inform them, is he?"

"True," agreed Jason.

"But if you want to ask your detective friend for some help, that wouldn't be such a bad thing," said Amita.

"Alby? Absolutely no chance!" Jason shouted. "Alby could be on the surface of Mars and it'd still be too close for comfort. The man is a menace, and a pretty bad cop on top of that. He wouldn't be able to detect his way out of a paper bag let alone help us with Starbuck."

Amita laughed at that.

"Fine," she said. "We need to know all we can about Starbuck, though. If there's a chance he could have gotten to Madeleine then it might be the breakthrough we need."

"It might be the *only* breakthrough, Amita," he said, getting up and stretching.

Amita detected a shift in his tone. She looked up at him, searching his face as he yawned.

"What's that supposed to mean?" she asked.

"It means we've been running all over the countryside looking for something that might not be there," he said. "Madeleine might genuinely have died from a fall and it was a terrible accident. There might not be anything in this. I think we have to entertain the notion that's the case."

"But what about your story?" she asked. "What about getting back into journalism? And, more importantly, what if there *is* a killer on the loose?"

Jason smiled and shook his head. He cracked the knuckles on both of his hands, making his mother-in-law wince.

"You have to ask some questions, Jason, use some of your contacts," she said earnestly. "We must find out what became of Freddie Starbuck."

"Fine," he said. "But not today."

He headed for the door.

"Not today?" Amita blurted, chasing after him. "What do you mean 'not today'?"

"Not today is what I mean," he started up the stairs.

"You have to, Jason. This is important!"

"I know," he said, pulling off his T-Shirt. "But so is getting the car repaired after you almost wrecked it."

Amita wasn't sure if she should be relieved or not.

"I did not almost wreck it," she said. "That lorry crashed into *me*."

"Either way, I have to take the wreckage up to the building site near Madeleine's estate this morning."

"I thought it was going to some garage in Carlisle?" she asked.

"It is. But our good friend and benefactor, Mr Rory Francis, has insisted I meet him there first and deliver the car over, something about one of his transporters or something. So I'm heading up there just now."

"Could I –?"

"No," said Jason flatly. "No, you can't come with me. No, you can't ask questions. And no, you can't drive the car when it comes back all shiny and almost new. You're barred. Take a day off, Amita, please. All this murder and mayhem is turning you paranoid. Just stay here, in the house, with the door locked and your phone off, for one day. You'll feel much better for it."

"But I –"

"No buts!"

Amita took the hint. Jason gave her a reassuring wink and hopped up the last few steps. Maybe she had been overdoing it recently. She slowly turned away from the stairs and headed for the living room. Clara was sitting on the sofa, clapping her hands as she sang along with the colourful animated dog on the TV. Amita sat down beside her. The little girl slid on her backside over to her grandmother and gave her a hug.

"What was that for?" she asked her.

"I love you, Granny, that's all," said Clara.

"I love you too, darling," she kissed the top of the little girl's head. "I love you, too."

They sat happily watching the animated dog bouncing about the screen. It was nice, gentle, almost relaxing and Amita found her eyelids were getting heavy. Just as she was about to let herself doze off, Clara jumped up.

"Bingo!" the little girl shouted.

"What's wrong?" Amita asked.

"It's the name of the dog," Clara clapped her hands and pointed at the screen. "You know the song. *B.I.N.G.O. Bingo was his name-o*. But I don't like this one. The farmer is trying to bully the little dog."

Amita watched the screen as a huge, lumbering badger came waddling on to the screen, flat cap pulled down over his snout and a pitchfork in hand.

"Off my land!" it snarled.

As she watched, Amita couldn't help but feel she hadn't listened to her own words. If your home was meant to be your castle, what happened when you went to war with your neighbours?

Chapter 19

GOODBYE TEENS

The road leading up to the main site office was slick. Jason had to battle to keep the car on a straight path. The storms of the last few days had made the dirt track little more than sloshy, bubbling mud. Eventually he managed to wrestle and slide his way to the main courtyard outside Mike Taylor's farmhouse. He was glad when he switched off the engine and climbed out.

A loud squelch immediately drew a curse from him. He looked down and saw his right foot was ankle deep in a filthy puddle. He could feel the dirty water being soaked up by his sock already. He cursed again, convinced nobody would notice on a building site. He was wrong.

"You should watch where you're going."

He looked up. Mike Taylor was standing by the door of his house, mug of something steaming in his hand. He blew on it, smiling.

"Morning," said Jason weakly.

He stepped out of the puddle and tried not to wince as he hobbled away from the car. He looked around the site. There was no sign of Rory Francis' flash motor. It was all very industrial. Diggers lifted their huge mechanical arms, scraping dirt from one pile to another. A huge truck loaded high with pipes loomed like a colourful giant lying down for a minute to catch its breath. Beyond the site office, houses were starting to sprout up all over the fields that surrounded the farmhouse. Even in the week or so since Jason had last been here the place was unrecognisable. Bare roofs stood like wooden pyramids in a state of undress. Walls were being stuffed with insulation, teams of hard-hat-wearing workers scurrying in and out of empty doorways like ants in a nest. Progress, Jason thought. Of a kind. He wondered how long it would be until there was no countryside left.

"You lost?" Mike Taylor shouted at him.

"What?" he asked, turning around to face the farmer.

"Are you lost, I said."

"No, not lost, just looking."

"Don't know what you're looking at, son. There's nothing here but houses, houses and more houses. Unless that's your thing."

"Different strokes for different folks," Jason said with a laugh.

"You what?"

"Never mind," he thumbed at the site office. "You don't know if Mr Francis is about, do you? Only I was supposed to drop off my car to get repaired."

"Francis? Here? You must be joking, lad," Taylor sipped from his mug. "You won't see that smarmy bugger around these parts until all the houses are finished and they get Princess Anne to come and cut the ribbon."

Jason furrowed his brow. He didn't understand. Francis had messaged him telling him to be there for nine sharp. Everything was going to get sorted, he had nothing to worry about. Francis' words, not his.

"But he was here the other day," said Jason. "He's the boss. Isn't he, you know, meant to be on hand in case something goes wrong?"

"Something did go wrong, didn't it," Taylor laughed, pointing at the car. "You and that woman friend of yours should look where you're going."

"So you do remember us, then," said Jason.

Taylor snorted. He took another sip from his mug and then threw the dregs into the dirt. He pushed himself off the stones, covered in lichens and filth, and picked at his teeth. He looked Jason up and down and then frowned.

"Come on then, I'll make you a coffee," he said, opening the front door.

"I reckon I should probably give Francis a call and –"

"He won't answer," said Taylor. "He's got no interest in this place, and he's sunk millions into it. It's all to keep Daddy happy. What makes you think he's going to answer you about some trivial car that's been smashed up by one of his trucks?"

"But . . . I'm a journalist."

That made Taylor laugh. He threw back his head and clutched his sides. Eventually he started coughing. The fit was so bad he doubled over and had to lean on the doorframe. Jason started for him, going to help.

"Sod off!" came the response from the old farmer. "I don't need your help. I don't need *anybody*'s help."

Jason stopped dead. He was starting to feel altogether very foolish. To say that he had suspected Francis was too good to be true would have been an understatement. Everything about the businessman seemed slick, preened, all for show. Taylor made a good point – why *would* he help Jason and Amita? He had turned on the charm offensive and it had worked.

"Bugger," he said, realising his mistake.

"If you come in, I'll give him a ring" said Taylor, standing up to his full height with a wheeze. "He won't answer his phone to you, but he'll do it for me. I've got him by the short and curlies."

Jason wasn't sure what he was more surprised at – the offer of help from Mike Taylor or the fact he was accepting the offer. He nodded and followed the old farmer into his run-down house.

The smell of damp was so strong he did his very best not to be knocked flat on his back. The farmhouse was a gloomy, dank place that felt like it had never been dry. The walls were bare, no sign of pictures, wallpaper or even paint. The floorboards were uneven and creaked just looking at them. Everything about the place felt like it hadn't changed in the several hundred years the building had been standing. Its lord and master was at its centre, Taylor drifting through the misery like the Grim Reaper.

He led Jason to the back room that at least had some warmth. An electric heater was burning full blast in the corner of what was loosely the kitchen. Its bars burned a demonic red that cast a glow all over the room. Taylor kicked out a chair from the table, the surface of which was covered in an oily sheet, bits of engine, screws, bolts and other mechanical paraphernalia.

"Sugar?" asked the old farmer bluntly.

"No, thank you," said Jason.

"Milk?"

Jason thought about this. The kitchen, the house, indeed Taylor himself – none of it looked fresh. He didn't suppose there were cows left on the estate and he didn't fancy Mike Taylor was very good with use-by dates. So he said no. It would be safer.

Taylor began rummaging through the dirty plates and pots stacked high in the sink. He clattered about, shouting angrily, until he eventually found a cup he thought was acceptable. Wiping it clean with his dirty hands, he darted a cocked eye at Jason.

"Well? Aren't you going to sit down?" he snapped.

Jason did as he was told. He dusted off the knotted chair Taylor had offered him and kept his hands folded on his lap. A loud rattle almost made him jump out of his skin. He thought the house was going to collapse in on itself. Then he spied what was going on.

Taylor was operating a brand new, very expensive, coffee machine. The device was hidden away in the far corner of the worktop that ran along the length of the kitchen. Jason was amazed he hadn't seen it already, the chrome trims so shiny compared to everything else in the place. The device was rattling away and hissing as Taylor fidgeted with the knobs and buttons.

"Is that . . .?" said Jason, stammering. "How do you have a . . . what's that doing?"

"What are you gibbering about, wooden head?" said Taylor, still wrestling with the controls.

"Your coffee machine," he managed. "That looks pretty top spec."

"This," said the farmer, cracking a smile. "This is top of the range, son, the best that money can buy. Had it shipped all the way here from Milan. You won't get a cup of coffee better this side of Windermere. I can guarantee you that."

Jason was genuinely lost for words. Why, while everything else in Mike Taylor's house was rotten, decrepit and antique, did he have a top of the range, Italian imported coffee machine that probably cost more than Jason's car?

"Try that," said Taylor, offering him a steaming cup. "If that's not the best coffee you've ever had, then you're a liar, boy."

Jason took a tentative sip. It was glorious. His tongue was set on fire, not only by the temperature but from the richness and glory of the divine brew he was drinking.

"She's my pride and joy," laughed Taylor, tapping the machine on its lid. "Treated myself to something a bit special when I got my first down-payment for this dump. You've got Rory Francis and his millions to thank for that coffee. I've had quite a few on him, I'll tell you that for nothing."

When the pain had subsided, Jason could actually enjoy his coffee. Taylor made himself one and sat down across the table from him. He let out a loud, satisfied groan and savoured the drink.

"So," he barked. "You're one of these reporters, then?"

"I try to be, yes," said Jason. "When the stars are aligned and it's a full moon."

"Eh?"

"Nothing. It was a vain attempt at humour."

"Well, don't take this the wrong way, son, but stick to the day job and leave the joke-writing to the professionals."

"I'll bear that in mind."

Jason put his mug down. He instantly wished he had more. He wondered how much the machine cost and, more importantly, if he could afford one.

"I saw you, you know," said Taylor, draining his own mug with a growl.

"Pardon me?" said Jason, woken from his criminal daydream.

"Up at the Frobisher place. I saw you and that woman."

"When?"

"The other day there, when you crashed your car. I saw you snooping about the old house, in and around the back."

Jason wasn't sure where this was going. He sat a little stiffer. "And how did you see that? We didn't see you there."

Taylor got up. He walked stiffly over to the window of the ramshackle kitchen and tapped the glass.

"See that forest there?" he said. "When Francis and his boys are finished, that's going to be completely gone. And when it's chopped down and used to make cabinets and drawers, you'll be able to see Madeleine Frobisher's mansion clear as day. The woods are about the only place I can go now where I can't hear drilling or digging."

"So you were spying on us?" asked Jason.

"Spying, don't make me laugh," said Taylor. "I was out for a walk at the border of my land, son. There's no law against that, far from it. And the amount of noise you two were making, I should have called the police on you just for that, let alone the trespassing."

Taylor had him there. He gulped and decided not to press it further.

"I'm wondering, though," said the old farmer. "What were you two doing lurking about at Frobisher's? You know she's dead, right?"

"Yes, we know," he said as neutrally as possible.

"So what were you doing? I watched you go into her garden then come out again. I thought there were rules for journalists against breaking and entering."

"There are," he said. "And we didn't break in anywhere. We were just having a look. I'm writing a story . . . about Cumbrian country houses that have fallen into ruin."

He was grateful this half-baked lie had survived in his memory. Taylor nodded, perhaps not convinced, but appeased for the moment.

"You know she was mad as a box of frogs, that one, don't you?" he said.

"What?"

Taylor put his hands into his pockets. A defensive demeanour fell over him. It was subtle but Jason spotted it. He'd been around enough people who didn't want to talk to him to know when there was a shift in their body language. Taylor seemed more uptight, his eyes narrowing slightly as he spoke.

"Madeleine Frobisher," he said. "She was completely cuckoo by the end."

"Was she?" Jason asked, sitting forward. "From what I've heard from everyone in town, it seems she was a lovely, friendly, kind lady. Nobody has mentioned her being, as you say, cuckoo."

"Oh she was, believe me," said Taylor. "And nasty with it."

"Nasty in what way?"

The old farmer shrugged. "Each to their own, as you said," he growled. "But she was always a bit crackers, if you ask me. She never wanted my help. I offered to look after things with her fields and grounds, years ago. I could see she wasn't keeping on top of it, so thought I'd offer. No skin off my nose. I used to do it for this place, what's another few acres to cut back or mow? But she always bit my head off, told me where to go, the cow."

"I'm sorry, Mr Taylor," said Jason, scepticism clear in his voice. "I might not have known Madeleine, but I know people who *did* know her, my mother-in-law at the top of that list. She's only ever spoken of Madeleine in the highest order, says she was a very friendly and generous woman who gave up a lot for her community."

"Oh aye, I'm sure she did," scoffed the farmer. "But how many of these people, including your mother-in-law, had to live beside her? Eh? How many of these people had to watch offers for the land come and go because she wouldn't sell up and move on? Tell me that."

An intense bitterness was now oozing out of Taylor. His face was turning scarlet, eyes bulging with anger. "Do you know how long I've been trying to sell this place for?" he asked. "Do you?"

"Of course I don't," said Jason.

"Twenty years," said Taylor. "Twenty years of my life spent trying to get somebody to take this dump off my hands. And, every time, that woman managed to scupper the deal for me. Every, single, time."

"I don't understand, Mr Taylor," said Jason. "What's that got to do with her mental health? Or indeed to do with Madeleine Frobisher at all?"

Taylor stormed over to the table. He cleared away all the clutter and picked up a heavy bolt and a thick nut. He plonked them in the middle of the tarpaulin and spread them apart. With a greasy finger, he drew a rough line between them.

"This is my house," said Taylor, pointing at the nut. "And this bolt is Frobisher's mansion. The land is split down the middle. Now, when you look at them as two separate places, it doesn't amount to much. But if they're together, then you've got yourself a big chunk of Cumbrian countryside. And that's what these developers want – space. Space to build their sheds on and call them family developments, or whatever."

Jason looked at the crude display in front of him. He still didn't quite follow.

"But Francis *is* developing on your land," he said. "You *have* managed to sell up."

"Eventually," said Taylor. "And how many times have deals fallen through and I could have been out of here, living in the sunshine instead of up to my neck in the mud and the rain? She cost me, she cost me dearly. Now she's dead, and too bloody late by all accounts. Fat lot of good her estate being sold off now is going to do me."

Jason cringed. "I don't know what you've gone through, Mr Taylor, but I don't think you should be talking about Madeleine that way. People could think you had something to gain from her death."

"Oh? Is that a fact?" said Taylor standing straight. "You're going to tell me you know more about a woman I lived beside, and with, for forty years? You're going to tell me I'm being unreasonable about her stubbornness and arrogance having cost me the better part of my retirement? Forcing me to live in this shack for decades longer than I had to, all because she refused to cooperate? Is that what you're telling me?"

He was standing over Jason now. He might have had several decades on Jason but there was an intimidating aura about Mike Taylor when he wanted there to be. Jason felt his skin crawl. He looked all about the kitchen, anywhere but at the farmer bearing down on him.

"No, that's not what I'm saying," he managed. "But I don't feel comfortable with you bad-mouthing someone who is, first and foremost, dead, and secondly has had the sympathy and mourning of a whole community since she popped her clogs. It doesn't sound like she did anything wrong – other than refuse to sell her home. That's all I'm saying."

"Get out!" Taylor screamed.

His voice was loud enough to reverberate in Jason's chest.

"Go on! Clear off! I'm not listening to this rubbish in my own house!"

"But . . . Rory Francis? You said you were going to call –"

"Get out!"

Flecks of spit were flying from his mouth now. Jason slid out from his chair and started to back away from him.

"Look, I'm not wanting to cause trouble, Mr Taylor," he said, trying to be diplomatic.

"Get out!"

"But I really need to get my car fixed and I can't do that without Francis."

"I said, get out!"

Taylor stopped. He pulled open a cupboard door and began rummaging through it. When he emerged, Jason felt his stomach drop.

Mike Taylor was brandishing a shotgun. He wore a snarl that could have killed all on its own. He stalked forward, both barrels pointing at Jason's forehead.

"Wow!" Jason said. "There's absolutely no need for that now!"

"I said, get out!" Taylor screamed. "Get out of my house!"

"Look, this is really uncalled for!"

"If you don't get out right now, I'm going to blow your head off!"

"You're not serious."

"Oh, I am serious," said Taylor, nodding. "And when I've done that, I'll go and fix that mother-in-law of yours too, unless you get off my property right this second."

"You . . . you can't say that and expect me just to –"

"Get out!"

Jason turned and ran as fast as he could. He almost tripped over the step as he barrelled through the front door, slipping and sliding his way across the muddy court-yard. A few of the site workers nearby looked perplexed. Only when Taylor emerged from his run-down farmhouse did they realise what was going on.

"Gun!" someone shouted.

"Gun!" came somebody else.

"Look out, he's got a shotty!"

"Let's get out of here!"

Mass panic spread like a wild fire across the site. Workers ran and clambered down from scaffolding, dropping everything as they bolted down through the fields and muddy roads. Jason scrambled into the car and swung it around as quickly as he could. He tore down the single road leading away from Taylor's farm, the engine roaring as it battled to go as fast as he wanted it.

"Bloody hell," he said, his breath short. "Bloody hell, bloody hell, bloody hell."

He was panicking, the world racing past him a million miles a minute. He weaved in and out of workers fleeing the site. He looked in his rear-view mirror and spotted Mike Taylor at the top of the road. The old man was still brandishing his shotgun.

"Bloody hell," he said again, pulling onto the main road.

In all his years as a reporter, he'd been threatened only a handful of times. Having a shotgun pointed at his head, however, was the brand new number one on that list.

Chapter 20

ONE SCORE

"He did what?"

Jason rubbed his forehead. He'd already told Amita the story at least four times since he'd come home. The drive was something of a blur now. But he had considered not mentioning the whole incident to her. Then when he stepped through the front door and was the colour of pale custard he knew he wouldn't outlast his mother-in-law's questioning. Plus he'd have to explain why the car wasn't off being repaired.

"He pulled a shotgun on me," he said.

"He pulled a shotgun? On *you*?"

Amita was pacing back and forth across the living room floor. The motion was making Jason feel sick. He just wanted to go to bed. Or, if that wasn't an option, to draw the curtains, lock the door and hide under the kitchen table. Maybe he'd have a little cry. That usually sorted him out.

"He pulled a shotgun on you," said Amita again.

"Yes," said Jason. "He pulled a shotgun on me. I'm not sure if there's a way I can say that to make it any clearer. Mike Taylor pulled a shotgun on me and aimed it at my head."

"This is unbelievable, absolutely unbelievable," said Amita.

It was her turn to rub her forehead. The colour was draining from her face.

"This is bad, Jason, really bad," she said. "Have you phoned the police?"

Jason hadn't even thought about the police. He'd been in such a state of shock and terror that all logical thought had taken a vacation.

"No," he said. "I didn't. I was more concerned about getting out of that house without having my head blown off my shoulders."

"You should call them right away," she sat down beside him. "This is a very serious crime. He threatened you with a shotgun."

"I don't want to, Amita," he groaned, lifting a cushion to his face. "I don't want to think about it, let alone go through a whole rigmarole of filing a police report."

"Didn't you hear what I said?" said Amita, pulling the cushion away. "He *threatened* you. With a *shotgun*."

"I know he did, Amita. I was there, remember? But that doesn't change a thing. I'm not reporting him."

"You *have* to!"

"And what then?" Jason blurted. "What happens when Alby, or one of the other boys in blue, goes around to Taylor and collars him? Is that really the type of person you want holding a grudge against me? He'll get a caution, then he'll be straight round to our door."

She pulled out her phone. Jason watched her for a moment, then panicked.

"What are you doing?" he asked.

"If you're not going to call them, I will."

"What? Didn't you hear what I just said, Amita?"

"I'm phoning the police and getting them around to Mike Taylor's farm straightaway."

"No!"

He lunged and grabbed Amita's phone from her.

"What are you doing? Have you lost your mind?" she asked. "Give me that back!"

"No, I don't want to get the police involved," said Jason.

"You have to, Jason. This is serious."

"I know it's serious, believe me," he said. "I just want to sit here for a minute and try and get my head together."

"You can do that after you've spoken to the police."

"Please, Amita. You don't know the full picture."

"I know enough."

She tried to get her phone but he evaded her. Jamming it under the cushion, he sat on it and folded his arms.

"There," he said. "You're not getting it now."

"Are you really being *this* childish, Jason? You know your son and daughter don't act this petty."

"I know that," he said. "But I'm deadly serious, Amita. I don't want to go to the cops. Not right at this moment."

"Why?"

Jason couldn't hold it in any longer. He had tried his best but she wasn't going to stop, not until he gave her a good reason. "Because if I do, then you're in trouble," he said.

"What? Me?" she asked.

"Yes, you," Jason sighed. "Taylor, when he was trying to get me out of his house he was babbling, shouting at me. But he wasn't just threatening me, he threatened you too."

"What did he say?" she asked.

Jason felt sick. He closed his eyes and could see Taylor in front of him, the gun hovering just inches from his face. He didn't want to tell Amita anything. He didn't even want to think about it. "He said he would blow my head off if I didn't leave. And then he'd come around here and 'fix' you, too," he said. "I can't let that happen, Amita. You have to understand, the man is deranged. And I'm not putting your life at risk for the sake of what happened today. I can live with being threatened; it's happened plenty of times before. What I *can't* live with is something happening to you, or Radha, or the kids. If that means keeping my trap shut then so be it."

"He's clearly unhinged and very, very dangerous and . . ." Amita trailed off.

Jason closed his eyes tightly. He didn't want to think about Mike Taylor. He didn't want to think about shotguns. And he definitely didn't want to think about being shot in the face by one wielding the other. He sat in silence for a moment until he realised that Amita had tailed off.

"Amita?" he asked, opening one eye. "You stopped halfway through a sentence. Nothing less than an earthquake usually stops you."

Amita was over by the living room window. She was staring out at the little front garden she tended in the summer.

"Amita?" he asked again.

"Very dangerous," she said again.

"You've lost me," he said.

"Mike Taylor," she said. "He's unhinged and very dangerous."

"Yes, he is," he said. "That's why I don't want to go to the police. There are plenty of other activities I'd rather do than grass on an old nutter with a firearm. He might be an angry old grouse but I don't really see him snapping Madeleine's neck – he's more bark than bite, I'd say."

"Don't you see, Jason?" she turned back to face him.

"Clearly, I don't," he said. "Otherwise you would have left me alone by now and I'd be at least three bottles of wine worse off."

"Mike Taylor," said Amita. "Unhinged and very dangerous. He threatened you with a shotgun, and for what? Because you challenged him on Madeleine's character? Well, what does that say about him?"

"It says he's the type to bear a grudge," said Jason. "Perhaps against people who report him to the police."

"Jason!" she said loudly. "What have we been doing for the last few weeks?"

He tried to sum up the whys and wherefores of it all. Then decided against it.

"We've been trying to catch Madeleine's killer," she said.

"Mike Taylor could have murdered Madeleine Frobisher," she said.

She shivered. She'd been doing that a lot recently. She hoped it was just the worry and anxiety of everything that was going on.

"No, I'm not having it," said Jason. "Madeleine fell – she wasn't blown to smithereens by some old hunting rifle.'

"Look at the facts," she said, raising a finger. "He's violent, he's angry, he's aggressive and he clearly has no concerns for anyone else's safety. Do those not sound like the makings of a murderer?"

"Plenty of people are like that," said Jason. "In fact, I've seen *you* go through that whole spectrum when you're told there are no fritters left at the chippy."

"Jason, please, I'm being serious," she said. "And what was all this you were saying about not being able to sell his land for years? There's a motive, if I've ever heard one."

Jason mulled it over. The old farmer clearly had a chip on his shoulder about his neighbour. Even if Taylor thought Madeleine wasn't quite the full shilling, there was a bitterness there that ran deep between the two of them.

"He got what he wanted though," he said. "Despite Madeleine's protests, he's sold his land to the developers and been paid well by the sounds of things. I saw the huge coffee maker he has in his kitchen – it came from Milan."

"I'll bet he didn't get anywhere near the amount he wanted though," said Amita. "He had to settle, take the only offer that was on the table. He's a farmer, Jason, he knows business. And that's the sort of bad deal that would drive him up the wall." She tapped her fingers on her chin. "Yes, it's starting to make sense now," she said. "Taylor has been looking to sell for years. He needed Madeleine onboard but she wasn't for moving. And we now know why – her house was her refuge, her lifeboat from the trauma of her past. So they have a war of words that goes on for decades. Until finally, now that he's been forced to sell at a cheaper price for only half of the land, he snaps. He goes around to Madeleine's and they have a screaming match that the housekeeper hears. Only Edna has that awful amnesia from the stress, if she even sees him at all. Taylor loses his temper, breaks poor Madeleine's neck in a fit of rage and fakes the whole window cleaning accident. It's perfect!"

She clapped her hands and looked at Jason expectantly.

He shook his head. "There's only one problem with your perfect murder, Amita," he said.

"What?" she seemed offended.

"A little thing called evidence."

"Evidence?"

"Yes, evidence, you know, proof that everything you've said actually happened and it's not all just a figment of your imagination. Sorry, *warped* imagination."

"He pulled a shotgun on you! Isn't that evidence enough?"

"It's evidence, sure, that he wanted to shoot me for absolutely no reason," said Jason. "It's *not* proof that he throttled his neighbour to death over some decades-long feud about property sales."

The front doorbell rang. Jason was thankful. He could feel his head starting to hurt with everything that was going on. No sooner was he up on his feet than Amita had grabbed back her phone from beneath the cushion.

"Do not call the police," he warned her.

"I'm not," she said. "I'm phoning someone much more useful."

Jason headed for the front door. If he thought his day was going badly, he hadn't really considered the implications of tempting fate quite so bluntly. Things, he found, could *always* get worse. And they did, right on cue, when he opened his front door.

"Brazel!"

Detective Inspector Alby pushed his way into the hallway.

"Yes, come in, why don't you," Jason said. "Pull up a chair, make yourself at home. Would you like a pair of my pyjamas to get more comfortable?"

"Enough!" Alby spun around and pointed an angry finger at him. "E-bloody-nough. I'm sick to the back teeth of hearing your name, Brazel. I'm sick of seeing your face and, most of all, I'm sick of listening to that nasal, whinging voice of yours."

"Takes one to know one, Detective Inspector," he said.

"Don't," said Alby, walking right up to him. "Just don't."

"What's all the shouting about?" Amita poked her head into the hall. When she saw Alby and his uniformed acolytes at the front door, she rolled her eyes. "Oh Jason, what have you done now?"

"Me? I haven't done anything!" he yelped.

"Tell me this," said the angry cop. "Why was it when I heard 'shotgun' and 'harassment' I immediately thought of Jason Brazel?"

"Because you're obsessed, maybe?" said Jason. "Because you have some sort of sick preoccupation with making my life a misery? I should report you to the IOPC."

The mention of the police watchdog seemed to crank Alby's blood pressure up at least ten notches. His already bulging eyes almost popped clean out of his head.

"What were you doing at Mike Taylor's farm this morning?" he snapped.

"Hold on, am I being questioned here?" asked Jason.

"Don't say anything, Jason!" Amita rushed to his side. "I've seen how these things work on TV. Honest victims stitched up by a corrupt police force looking for a quick fix to sweep crime under the rug."

"Who is this woman?" asked Alby, looking to his officers.

"Oi, less of the *this woman* chat," said Amita angrily. "I'm Amita Khatri and I'm Jason's mother-in-law, if you must know."

Alby curled his lip into an even fiercer sneer. He shrugged. "And?"

"And you can't come barging in like this without a warrant."

"Listen, lady."

Jason braced himself. "Big mistake," he said under his breath.

"Lady?" said Amita, stepping forward. "Did you just call me *lady*?"

"Yes I did, and –"

"Who do you think you're talking to?" She was taller than Alby by about an inch and looked down at him. "You can't go about breaking into people's homes and speaking like that. There are manners, you know, and they cost nothing. Now, whatever half-baked crusade you're on, I suggest you stop it immediately, before I do call up your bosses and complain about this unbelievably rude behaviour from one of their officers. I have friends, you know, lots of friends. Many of them know people who know people. And I don't think those people would take too kindly to hearing of your antics, officer . . . officer . . .?"

"Alby," said Jason, wiping his face with his hands. "DI Alby, Amita."

"Alby," she said. "Do I make myself perfectly clear?"

Alby stood in stunned silence. He looked to his officers for support. Both of them whistled and pretended to be watching the street.

Finally he turned to Jason. "Is she serious?" he asked.

"Oh yes, I'm afraid so," said Jason. "And a small word of warning. I wouldn't continue to press her buttons. There's a lot more where that came from. Believe me, I live with her."

Alby puffed out his cheeks. He ran a hand over his comb-over and smiled weakly.

"Well, Ms Khatri, you have me," he said. "In forty years on the force I don't think I've ever been given such a stiff talking to."

"And what does that tell you, Detective Inspector?" she asked.

"It tells me that if you two don't shut up and start answering my questions, I'm going to haul you both down to the station and lock you up for the night for insubordination."

"That's not a crime," said Jason. "And how can we shut up and answer your questions at the same time?"

"Right! That's it!" Alby shouted. "In the car!"

The two officers at the door quickly turned around. Like well-trained attack dogs given their command, they snapped into action, stomping forward.

"What?" said Jason.

"You can't do this," said Amita.

"I can and I am," said Alby, pointing out the door.

The two officers didn't lay a finger on them, but they didn't have to. Their presence was enough and they escorted Jason and Amita from the hallway and out into the front garden.

"Are we under arrest? We have rights, you know!" shouted Jason.

"You can't do this to me!" Amita protested. "I'm going to write to my MP about this. I'm a member of the W.I.!"

None of it made a difference. Alby had spoken and that was all. Jason and Amita were guided to the waiting police van and bundled into the back behind the metal grill. The doors slammed shut with a fierce finality.

Amita looked at her son-in-law. "What are we supposed to do now?" she asked him.

"Don't look at me," he said. "How the hell am I supposed to know?"

"But you deal with this sort of thing all of the time."

"I beg your pardon?" he said, hurt. "I do not, thank you very much."

The two cops climbed into the front of the van and they set off. Jason sat back as they were taken away. For the second time in as many weeks, he found himself being driven away by the police, yet he still wasn't under arrest. That didn't make it any easier to handle. Or, indeed, understand. He wasn't sure if that was a good thing or a bad thing. So instead of thinking harder about it, he sat back and closed his eyes. Police vehicles, it turned out, were actually quite comfortable. When you got used to them.

Chapter 21

KEY TO THE DOOR

Amita was in a state of apoplexy. She couldn't even begin to think of what to worry about first.

"I'm never going to live down the shame, am I?" she kept saying over and over.

"Would you sit down? You're making me seasick," said Jason.

"Sit down? Are you mad? We're in a police station Jason. We're in an interview room, for goodness sake! This is what you see on TV, isn't it? What you read about in books. An angry policeman is going to come through that door any moment now and grill us until we fess up to a crime we haven't committed. I'll be on the front of every parish newspaper. I'll be the talk of the town."

Jason, remarkably, considering the setting and circumstances, felt rather mischievous. He leaned forward, his plastic chair squeaking beneath his weight. "And don't forget Georgie Littlejohn," he said.

If Amita had been pale before, she was now positively monochrome. She stopped her pacing and looked at him.

"Oh god," she said. "I hadn't even *thought* about Georgie. She's going to *love* this. Wait and see. She'll have me hanged at dawn, a Great Train Robber, the Zodiac Killer finally unmasked, the works."

Jason laughed. He folded his arms and sat back again. He was going to put his feet on the table but decided against it. He didn't want to distress Amita any further.

"Would you try to relax, please?" he said. "We're not under arrest."

"Then what are we doing here? How do you know that detective inspector, who seems to hate your very existence, isn't cooking up some phantom crime to have us put away for a very long time?"

"If we were under arrest, Amita, we wouldn't be in the same interrogation room," he said flatly.

She stopped her pacing. He watched as his logic settled in her mind and she worked it out for herself. Something close to a smile crept across her face. "No, you're right," she said. "Yes, that's very true. I hadn't thought about it like that."

"It's Alby," said Jason. "For some bizarre reason, he seems to think that I'm somehow at the centre of every crime and misdemeanour in Cumbria. And he's clearly on the warpath with this Mike Taylor thing."

"You think somebody reported him?" said Amita.

"They must have," Jason shrugged. "The building site was full and everyone scarpered when they saw him chasing after me with his gun."

The door opened. Alby came stomping in, his face an unusually pale shade of scarlet. Jason thought he almost looked normal.

"Right, Tweedledum and Tweedledee, do you want to press charges?" said the cop.

Amita took her seat beside Jason. They both looked at Alby, silent.

"Well?" he asked. "Come on, out with it, I don't have all day. There are about a million other places I'd rather be than in here talking with you two morons."

"Like at the soft play," said Jason.

He couldn't help himself. It had been too easy.

"Very good, Brazel," Alby cracked a grin that somehow made him even uglier. "You're a regular comedian when you want to be. Too bad you're not as good a reporter, otherwise I wouldn't have to write 'unemployed' on your witness statement."

"Ouch," whistled Jason. "That was a low blow and a half, Detective Inspector."

"I can go lower."

"I'm sure you can. And would!"

"We don't follow you," said Amita, cutting in. "Press charges for what, and on whom?"

Alby held his gaze on Jason a little longer than he needed to before turning to Amita. "Mike Taylor, Ms Khatri," he said. "We have reason to believe that Mr Taylor wielded a firearm in the direction of your son-in-law at some point this morning. Another member of the public brought it to our attention. Our investigations have since concluded that, while the weapon wasn't loaded, there was still a degree of panic created. However, without Mr Brazel's cooperation

215

and willingness to press charges, we will be forced to let things drop."

Amita nodded. She looked at Jason.

"Why are we in here?" he asked Alby. "Couldn't you have been this nice at the house? Feels like you're harassing us for no reason, Alby."

Alby puckered his lips. He drummed his fingers on the table between them. Then he sucked in a sharp breath of air. "I can assure you my policing methods are sound," he said. "I, and the rest of the department, have conducted ourselves above and beyond the call of duty in keeping you and your family safe."

It all sounded rehearsed, like he'd been *told* to use those very words.

Jason smelled a rat. "Come on," he said. "What's your *real* reason?"

"Would you like to press charges, or not?" said Alby. "I've got a team ready to go and lift that old bugger, Taylor, and put him away for the rest of his days. But as much as it pains me to say this, Brazel, I need *you* to cooperate."

Jason smiled. He looked at Amita and then back at Alby.

"It's nice to be needed," he said.

"Don't do this to me, Brazel," said the cop. "I'm literally counting the hours until I can call all of this quits forever. I've spent years, decades even, fighting bad guys and keeping the thin blue line alive and well. I've put up with more than my share of arseholes like you in that time. Just tell me what you want to do, and let me ride off into the sunset in peace, would you?"

Jason couldn't lie – he was enjoying every minute of watching Alby squirm. He might not have known the detective inspector very long, but it had been more than enough time to realise they wouldn't ever get along. Fate, it seemed, had destined them to be on opposite sides of a coin. This little reversal of fortune felt more than deserved, and he intended to enjoy it. Only Amita could ruin the moment for him. Which she duly did.

"We think Mike Taylor murdered Madeleine Frobisher."

The bluntness caught Jason short. All of his smugness evaporated in an instant. He sat forward, coughing a little.

"Wow," he said.

"Wow is right," Alby agreed. "Say that again?"

"Mike Taylor, we think he murdered Madeleine Frobisher," said Amita. "We think he went around to her house, had a big argument about selling her land to developers and undermining him, and he throttled her, broke her neck by all accounts. Then he dumped her body in the back garden and tried to make it look like an accident. Which worked as far as your officers go, Detective Inspector, but not with us."

Alby did well not to sit with his mouth agape. Jason wasn't quite so polite.

"Ms Khatri," said the cop. "Do you realise the seriousness of these allegations?"

"She doesn't," said Jason.

"I do," said Amita spitefully.

"No, Amita, you don't, you *really* don't," he grabbed her arm. "Tell the nice police officer that it's nothing more than a joke, a little game we've been playing."

"What? No!" she said, pulling her arm away. "Jason, tell him. You've been there with me. We were talking about it before he arrived. Tell him you think it might be true. Tell him you think there might be something suspicious about Madeleine's death."

Alby raised an eyebrow as he turned to Jason. "Well, Brazel?"

This was awful. Jason felt like he was back in school. He had to choose a side. He had to pick which direction his life was about to go in and live with the consequences. And consequences there would be. Did he back Amita and fess up to his amateur sleuthing, all at the risk of getting the police involved in something that might not be true at all? Or did he side with Alby, dismiss the whole thing and hope the cop would simply think they were an eccentric family with too much time on their hands?

"Eh . . ." he breathed. "Eh . . ."

"Detective Inspector Alby, it's quite simple," said Amita, leaning on the table. "Mike Taylor has sold his farm for some fortune. He told Jason as much. But he could have had *so* much more if Madeleine had made a deal. He told Jason that this goes back years and that there were offers on the table that she passed up, all costing him money. He has a motive. And, as you've seen today, he has more than the temperament to cause trouble if he turns his mind to it."

Alby held up his hands. He waved them in front of Amita, trying to get her to be quiet.

"Enough!" he said. "Enough. I'm not listening to this. I'm too old and too close to retiring to get involved in any of this. It's another department's problem. I'm here to deal with Mike Taylor and his itchy trigger finger. That's all."

"But he could be a murderer!" Amita pleaded.

"I don't care," said Alby, shaking his head. "If he is, then some of the finest policing minds in the next room over will catch him. Not me, love. I'm finished." He narrowed his gaze on Jason. "Are you wanting to press charges, yes or no?" he said. "I need an answer, Brazel, so I can go home to my great grandchildren and read them a bedtime story. Maybe the one about the loony reporter and his wannabe police officer mother-in-law. They've not heard that one before."

Jason cleared his throat. "No, I don't think so," he said, sounding much less confident than he did before. "The gun wasn't loaded, and he was upset. Nobody was hurt. Maybe let sleeping dogs lie."

"Jason!" Amita shouted. "What are you doing? He doesn't mean that, Detective Inspector. He wants to press charges."

"No, I don't."

"Yes, he does."

"No, I don't. I honestly don't."

"Jason!"

He didn't look at her. A terrible guilt was writhing about in the pit of his stomach. He could almost feel it inside him. He wanted only to leave this room, this police station, go home and be alone.

"Is that your final answer?" asked Alby, giving him another chance.

"Yes," he said, head bowed.

"Fine," Alby got up. "Can't say I'm surprised. Once again you've wasted my time, Brazel. Once again I've spent an afternoon running around in your wake and getting absolutely nothing back in return. What a wonderful way to spend my last few days on active service. I can't think of a better end to an illustrious career. If it's not missing photocopiers, it's old men with shotguns wanting to shoot you."

He slammed his hands down on the table and both Jason and Amita jumped. He muttered something under his breath and stormed out of the interrogation room, leaving the door open behind him.

No sooner had he vanished than Amita pounced. "What the heck is wrong with you?" she blurted. "Why aren't you pressing charges? Mike Taylor is a dangerous man, Jason. He needs to be punished."

"Nobody was hurt, Amita," Jason said sluggishly. "Let's just leave it at that."

He made for the door, Amita following him.

"But he might have killed Madeleine! Why didn't you say something?"

They reached the front desk and the officer on duty signed them out, handing them back their belongings. Jason trudged down the street, hands in his pockets, head bowed low.

"Why are you being like this?" she asked him. "We could have gotten some answers back there."

"No, we couldn't have!" he snapped. "We couldn't have, Amita. Don't you see? You can accuse people of whatever you want in the house, in the car, even to the bingo hall cronies. But you can't do that sort of thing to police officers!"

"Why not? It's what we believe!"

"What we believe and what the truth is might not be the same!" he shouted. "Don't you get it? If I had pressed charges there, it would have opened a proper investigation, arrests, court dates, everything. And if you're accusing Mike Taylor of murder, that has to be looked at, too."

"But we *are* accusing him," she said.

"No! We're not. *You* are accusing him, Amita. It's you who is accusing him. What if you're wrong? What if they opened their inquiries and found that Mike Taylor had nothing to do with Madeleine's death? What then? He could sue you for defamation, and would win probably. Who's going to pay the legal bills and the inevitable compensation? *We* are – your family. We're barely making ends meet as it is, Amita. How do you think Radha would take that news? That she would have to defend you in a court over wild accusations that you've got absolutely no proof for?"

He was shaking with anger. He grabbed his mouth, trying to calm himself down.

"She wouldn't be happy," said Amita quietly.

"No, she wouldn't," he said. "She wouldn't be happy at all. She'd be pretty bloody well upset."

They stood in the quiet back street close to the station. Everything was silent, no traffic, no passers-by, not even a bird chirping above them. Jason held out his arms and let them drop against him with a clap.

"Look, I'm sorry, okay," he said. "I don't mean to be cruel, I really don't. This whole thing with Madeleine, it's been crazy. The last few days, weeks even, it's been good fun. I've felt like I've gotten a bit of life back in me and, god knows, I needed that. I don't need to tell you. But it's been a wild goose chase, Amita. Nothing happened to Madeleine. It was an accident. She fell off a set of ladders and broke her neck. Horrible, I know, but that's all it is. I think we need to stop running around the countryside accusing people of serious crimes. Because if we don't stop, if somebody like Alby or his colleagues gets proper wind of it and starts to investigate, the ramifications could cost us all dearly."

Amita's chin was practically buried in her chest. Jason thought he could see tears in her eyes. She nodded and sniffed loudly.

"Yes, you're right," she said sadly. "I hadn't thought about it like that. You're right, Jason. We can't afford to be wrong with this sort of thing. We have no evidence. I shouldn't have said what I did back there. I'll go back and apologise."

"Just leave it, Amita," he said, starting to feel guilty. "Alby doesn't care. He's got bigger fish to fry. Just let it go."

He felt terrible. He hadn't been lying when he said he'd enjoyed his time with Amita. Nobody was more surprised at that than him. In the years they had known each other, they'd never really become close, certainly not as close as they had over the past few weeks. And as much as it pained Jason to admit it, he had been impressed with her determination, not to mention her contact book.

"It's been a good bit of fun though, hasn't it?" he asked her, trying to lighten the tone.

She gave him a surprised, warm smile and nodded again.

"Yes," said Amita. "It has. I think it's probably been the most fun I've ever had with you, Jason. Not that we had much to compare it to, right enough."

"No," he laughed. "That's true. Maybe, then, if nothing else, we've gotten that out of it."

"Yes, I suppose so," she agreed.

An awkwardness descended between them. He couldn't quite place it. He scratched the back of his head and pointed down the street.

"Should we, you know, get the bus home or something?"

"No," she sniffed. "You go ahead. I think I'll go and get some shopping done. I'll surprise Radha, drop in on her at the office and say hello. She'll like that, a little surprise."

Her phone started to buzz. She pulled it from her jacket pocket and arched her eyebrows. She flashed the screen at him. "Georgie Littlejohn," she said. "Word spreads fast in this town, especially if you're at the bingo."

Jason laughed.

"I had better take this," she said, clearing her throat.

"Sure," he said. "I'll see you at home."

"Okay," Amita turned from him and started along the road back towards the police station.

As Jason headed in the opposite direction, he heard his mother-in-law explaining to her nearest, dearest rival what had happened. What he'd said to her had been bothering him – he just hadn't realised how much. He knew he had to say it, though. Making accusations, no matter how vaguely credible, to police officers was a serious business. People's lives were on the line. Things had to be watertight. And they weren't, not by a long shot.

He turned onto the main street and walked towards the nearest bus stop. Taking a seat, he stared off into space. He was right, he kept thinking. He was right to bring it all to a stop right now. Nobody had been hurt and everyone could move on with their lives. Everyone except Madeleine Frobisher, of course. But there was nothing he could do about that. And there never had been.

Amita would get over it. She always did. She might harbour the resentment for a long while. There was nothing new in any of that.

No. He had done the correct thing. He had taken the right course of action in ending their investigations before they got themselves into more trouble. So why did he feel so terrible?

Chapter 22

TWO LITTLE DUCKS

Jason was in a gloomy mood. He stood staring at the bubbling bolognese in the pot in front of him. Staring, however, was a little generous. Mindlessly looking down at the hob was probably more accurate. His head wasn't in it. His head wasn't even in the house.

The front door clicked open. Jason felt the hairs on the back of his neck stand up. He hurried over to the kitchen door and looked down the hallway. Radha came in, arms filled with files, laptop bag slung over her shoulder.

"Oh," he said, forgetting himself.

"Oh?" she shouted back at him. "Oh? Were you expecting someone else? Are you trying to tell me I don't do it for you anymore, Jason?"

"What? No," he said, quickly going to help her. "Don't be ridiculous. You're as beautiful a woman as you were when you left this morning."

"Charming," she said, handing him the files. "With unrestrained romanticism like this, is it any wonder I don't tire of this bohemian lifestyle?"

Jason lumbered into the kitchen with his wife's work. She stopped and said hello to the kids doing their homework in the living room. When she reached the table, Radha collapsed into a chair and kicked off her shoes.

"What a day," she said, rolling her head and shoulders. "Honestly, I think the world is getting worse. I know it was always a bit nuts. But there's something about what people are drinking or smoking that's sending them to cloud cuckoo land on a whole other level."

"Yeah," said Jason, returning to the bolognese.

"I mean we had a woman in the office today who was looking for somebody to represent her over what she claimed was defamation."

"Yeah?" he said.

"Now by her own admission she wasn't a saint," she said, rubbing her aching feet. "She was claiming that because a national news website had covered the court case where she beat up a woman in a nightclub – seven years ago, I should add – she was being unfairly treated."

"Yeah."

"She sent over the link to the story. She failed to mention she put the other woman in the hospital for six weeks with a fractured skull and broken eye socket. Of course, when I read that I started being a lot more polite to her. How do you tell somebody with a bit of a temper that they stand as much chance as a snowball in hell of clearing their name?"

"Yeah."

Radha stopped rubbing her feet. She looked across the kitchen at her husband, mindlessly stirring the dinner. Something was wrong.

"So anyway, that's when she stood up and stripped off all of her clothes," she said. "There she was, stark naked."

"Uh huh," said Jason, not flinching.

"And she started singing *I Shot the Sheriff*, not the Bob Marley version, the Eric Clapton one, you know, that came out not long after the original and the one you always say you hate because it did better in the charts. Anyway, she started doing all the backing vocals too, like one of those Tuvan throat singers. It was actually, probably, the most extraordinary thing I've ever seen in my life."

"Yep."

Radha was getting annoyed now. She decided to drop the charade.

"Jason!" she shouted.

It was loud enough to cause him to drop his wooden spoon. It rattled off the cooker and splattered bolognese all over the kitchen floor.

"What?" he said.

"You weren't listening!"

"What? Yes, of course I was," he said, groaning as he bent down to pick up his spoon. "Of course I was listening. I always listen to you."

"So what was I talking about?" she folded her arms expectantly.

"You were talking about work," he said. "And something about Tuvan throat singing. And Bob Marley. See, I was listening."

"You weren't!"

"I was," he stuck the spoon back in the pot without cleaning it.

"You bloody well were not," she said, nudging him out of the way and removing the spoon. "You were standing there lost in your own little world and not paying attention to your wife who has been out there fighting the good fight all day."

Jason took a step back. He had been caught. There was no use in trying to deny it. Radha had always been the brains of their operation. He was merely a pilot fish swimming in her wake.

"Sorry love," he said. "I'm not feeling myself tonight."

"Are you ill? You don't look ill. You've actually got some colour in your cheeks, for a change."

Radha touched his forehead with the back of her hand. He leaned against the kitchen worktop, shoulders slumped and an aura of misery about him.

"No, I feel fine," he said. "I walked home, picked the kids up on the way. Took us ages, that's why they're only doing their homework now."

"You walked? What's wrong with the car? Is it repaired?"

"No," he said. "There was . . . an issue."

"What now?" she sighed.

"I don't want to talk about it," he said. "It's too complicated. It involves shotguns and the police, and I'm not sure I have the energy to go through the whole thing again."

"Shotguns? Jason, what the hell is going on?" she said. "You can tell me. Come on, out with it."

"It's nothing," he said, fidgeting. He spied a loose thread on the cuff of his jumper. Trying to occupy himself with it, he hoped she would leave him alone.

"Jason," she said.

No such luck.

"It's nothing, honestly," he said. "Mike Taylor, the farmer who owns the land up at that new housing estate, he threatened me with a shotgun."

"He what?" she blurted.

"It wasn't loaded," said Jason. "Then the police came around here and picked me and your mother up for questioning."

"They what?"

"They wanted to press charges, but I didn't want to, not after Amita started accusing Mike Taylor of killing Madeleine Frobisher."

"She did what?"

"Then I had it out with your mum in the street outside the police station," he said, feeling rotten. "I told her I thought the whole Madeleine Frobisher murder thing had run its course, that she couldn't go about accusing people of murder when there was no evidence, especially not to the police. She seemed to take it quite well, only she didn't come with me to get the kids. I think I might have offended her."

Radha stared hard at her husband. The bubbling bolognese finally broke the deadlock.

"I wish I hadn't asked now," she said. "You two running around playing detective was always going to end in tears."

"I know," he sighed.

"She gets too caught up in things like this, Jason, you know she does. She gets obsessive. I blame her not having enough to do since she retired."

"Not enough to do? She's on about a thousand committees and focus groups! If there's a conference or a free lunch to be had, your mother will be front row and centre. She's not called the Sheriff of Penrith for nothing, you know."

"Yes, I know that, Jason," she said. "But this all sounds like it's getting a bit out of control. She's seventy. She's not as young as she used to be."

"Nobody threatened *her* with a shotgun, Radha," he said. "It was me who had to stare down the barrel, quite literally."

Radha pulled the pot from the hob ring.

"Damn," she said. "Blimey, what a day it's been for all of us, eh?"

Jason suddenly felt a little bit better. He stepped over and took his wife's hand. He hugged her close and she did the same. They stood there in the middle of the kitchen for a moment, still and silent.

"I love you," he whispered.

Radha let him go, and smiled at him. "I love you, too," she said. "But you need to be careful, Jason. You can't let her imagination run away with her. It's bloody dangerous."

"I know," he said. "I feel terrible. I shouldn't have led her on for so long. I should have put my foot down and not got caught up in what she was spouting. But she's very convincing when she wants to be. And the chance to get back into work, with what would have been a great story, must have clouded my judgement."

"You don't need to feel bad about wanting to get back into work," she said. "It's been a tough few months for you, for all of us. And you're trying your best, Jason. I know you are. The kids know you are. Even my mother knows you are, and that's saying something."

Jason felt a lump forming in his throat. He tried to swallow away the discomfort.

"And I've never known you to be so close with my mum, either," she laughed. "Normally you two are at each other's throats all day and night, and the rest of us are caught in the crossfire."

"I know, right," he said. "I don't think anyone is as surprised as I am at that. But I can honestly say I've enjoyed being in her company. She is, much to my surprise, actually quite funny when she chooses to be. Not all the time. Certainly not all of the time."

"I'm sure she'll be delighted to hear that," said Radha.

They hugged again and she kissed him on the cheek.

"I love you," she said. "You big idiot. You just have to learn not to get swept up in everything. And that includes my mother."

"I will," he sniffed. "I promise."

Radha lifted the wooden spoon and started stirring the bolognese. She grunted as she tried to free the burned bits from the bottom of the pot.

"This is about ready," she said. "Do you want to get the kids ready before you put the spaghetti on? And give my mum a call down."

Jason nodded. He fetched the pasta from the cupboard and leaned over to the door. He was about to shout the kids when he stopped.

"Wait a minute," he said, confused. "What do you mean, call down your mum?"

"My mum," said Radha, knuckles white as she battled with the burned bolognese. "Give her a shout. She can help with getting the kids ready."

"You mean she's not with you?" he asked.

"No, Jason," she said. "I came straight home from the office. You saw me with all of my case notes and junk when I came in the door."

"But she said she was going to meet you at your office," he said. "She told me she was going to drop in and surprise you, and she'd get a lift home for dinner."

Jason felt something shifting in his stomach. A horrible, gnawing, dawning realisation was beginning to settle in there. And he didn't like it.

"She's upstairs, is she not?" asked Radha.

"No," he said. "She didn't come home with me. She said she was going to surprise you at work."

"Well, she didn't come home with me, either. Where did you last see her?"

"Outside the police station, after we had the big fight," he said. "Well, less of a fight, more of a rant on my part."

"And you've not seen her since?"

"No," he said. "I went to get a bus but thought better of it. I walked from town to get the kids from school and then we came back here. I assumed she would have come home with you, like she said."

"I haven't heard from her."

The panic was infectious. Radha dropped the spoon and grabbed her bag. She pulled out her phone, dialling her mother's number as she went.

"It's ringing out," she said.

She tried again. Jason heard Amita's voice coming from the speaker, the pre-recorded voicemail message.

"Jason, it's ringing out. She never lets it ring out. Where is she?"

"W.I.?" he asked.

"No, that's a Thursday night."

"Aqua aerobics, maybe?"

"No, those classes have stopped after the instructor was found to be peeing in the swimming pool."

"Bloody hell."

"Maybe she's gone to bingo early?" asked Radha.

"That's on Wednesday nights," he said. "Believe me, I know."

"Got it," she said, snapping her fingers. "I'll use the tracking thing on her phone."

Radha began scrolling through her phone. She brought up a map with a tiny little flashing dot.

"There," she said. "Wait a minute, that can't be right. She's halfway to Ullswater? In the middle of the country. How the hell did she get all the way out there on her own?"

A chill ran down Jason's spine like a sluice of ice-cold water. He didn't stop to say anything, grabbed the car keys and raced out the front door.

"Jason!" Radha shouted. "Where are you going?"

"I need to rescue your mother," he said. "She might be in a house with a murderer."

Chapter 23

A DUCK WITH A FLEA

Amita knocked on the door. There was no answer. She looked about the empty yard. The place was dark and desolate. Strange, she thought, how a woman of her age could still be frightened of shadows and strange noises. Generally, she was not a fearful type. That happened when you'd been through most of what life can throw at you. But right now the scaffolding of the houses stood out against the clear night sky like the skeletal remains of some herd of giant elephants. The moon was weak and pale, hanging in the sky like a Christmas ornament. There had been no rain for hours now but still the whole yard, the construction site, was damp and sodden.

Her trainers were caked with mud and felt like they weighed ten tonnes each. The walk from the bus stop had been further than she had thought. And with every step, Amita had been less convinced that this was a good idea.

That thought was never stronger than now. She stood looking at Mike Taylor's front door, almost willing it to stay closed. There were no signs of life from anywhere in the house. All the windows were dark and lifeless. She stood silently, waiting, listening to her own breath. There was a creak from behind her and she snapped her head around to see nothing but the empty yard.

She was about to leave when the front door opened. Amita spun back around, so quickly in fact that she almost tripped over. Mike Taylor's sturdy hand grabbed her by the arm before she landed in the wet mud. She stabilised herself until she was confident enough to speak.

"Thank you," she said.

"Gave you a fright, did I?" he laughed.

Amita noted that he was still holding on to her arm.

"No, I'm quite alright, thanks," she said, gently tugging at her arm.

She tried to contain her panic, no longer sure this was a great idea, thinking of ways she could break free and get out of there. She didn't fancy her odds. They were in the middle of nowhere with no regular transport to flee on. All her self-defence-class knowledge had vanished, just when she actually needed it. There was a brief moment where it felt like Mike Taylor wasn't going to let go. Then she freed herself. It took all of Amita's effort not to slip in the mud with the relief.

"I don't understand," said the old farmer. "You knocked on my door. Why are you here?"

"Yes, sorry about that," she said, walking away slowly. "Don't know what I was thinking. A bit of a mistake, I think, yes, something like that. Well, nice to see you, Mr Taylor. Have a nice night and . . ."

She trailed off as the rain started to fall. Looking up at the large gathering of clouds moving across the path of the pale moonlight, Amita could have cried. It was the last thing she needed. Not that anyone would have seen her tears, the rain now starting to hammer down from the heavens.

"Why don't you come in?" said Taylor from behind her. "I've just put on some grub, if you're interested."

Amita bowed her head. She was stuck. The rain was falling in great sheets. There was no way she'd stay dry out here, in these clothes and in this weather. There was nowhere to shelter and the next bus would be an hour away. Reluctantly, she turned and took up the offer.

Taylor closed the door behind her. The thud made her squirm. Then she thought better of herself. What was it she always said – best to make the most of every situation? As hard as it was going to be, she pushed herself on. She was here now, in the lion's den. She should at least try to make the most of it.

"You're that Brazel lad's mother-in-law, aren't you?" asked Taylor, still lingering at the door.

Amita's confidence was fleeting. She had half-hoped that an element of surprise might bode well. That was gone now. She had to keep going. "Yes," she said. "That's actually what I'm here about."

"I see," said Taylor, his mood souring. "You'll know he was up here this morning, then. We didn't see eye to eye."

"Yes. And no, you didn't," she said, trying to stay confident.

"Right," he nodded. "You better come through."

Taylor locked the front door. He put the key in his pocket and brushed past Amita in the narrow, dingy hallway. She let him walk on for a few paces before following him. This was a nightmare, she thought. An actual, proper nightmare.

She reached into her pocket and felt the familiar shape of her phone. She thought about making a quick call to someone, anyone, just to get out of there. Then Mike Taylor turned around.

"Do you drink coffee?" he asked.

"Tea, if you have any," she said.

"Tea?" Taylor scoffed. "Lady, I've got a coffee maker with more gadgets than a space ship sitting in this kitchen! And you want tea."

"That's very nice for you," said Amita. "But I don't drink the stuff. Caffeine isn't good for you in large doses."

Taylor laughed at that. He started to cough and called her into the kitchen. Amita joined him as he switched on the kettle. The room was warm and comfortable. In the burning glow of the heater in the corner she could survey the damage. In short, she was an absolute state. Mud clung to her whole bottom half and everything was wet. She wriggled her toes, feeling the squelch of her socks. Hardly the best first impression but it would have to do. Thankfully, her surroundings weren't quite what she was used to. And Mike Taylor was clearly no Georgie Littlejohn.

"He told you what I did, then," said Taylor.

"He did," said Amita.

"I wasn't going to shoot him, for god's sake," he said. "The gun wasn't even loaded. It's not worked for years."

"Jason didn't know that," she said firmly. "Or all the people working on the site. For all they knew, you were ready to start shooting up the place like some half-witted cowboy in a Western. They've got families, these people, as does Jason – two young children, my grandchildren. What did you expect him to do?"

236

Taylor put the spoon and mug down with a clatter.

"I'm sorry, alright," he said. "I said I was sorry to the police earlier when they came around. I've said sorry to you. What else do you want from me? Blood?"

Amita noted how angry he was getting. It didn't take much to set him off. Flashes of Madeleine Frobisher darted into her mind. Could this man really have killed her? He didn't seem to be trying to cover up his gun-toting earlier.

"You came here to give me a telling off, then?" he said. "That's why you're here, is it? Your son-in-law sent you to fight his battles for him."

"No," she said, bowing her head. "No, he doesn't know I'm here. Nobody does, actually."

She bit her tongue. Was she trying to make it easy for Taylor? She might as well put the knife in his hand and drive it into her heart and be done with it at this rate.

"I mean, they don't know I'm in here, that is." It was a weak attempt at a backtrack.

"I see," said Taylor offering her a mug. "So, to what do I owe this pleasure?"

Amita thought very carefully about what she was about to say. She'd been thinking about it all afternoon, how she was going to try and catch Taylor out, try to get a confession from him. The idea had come to her as soon as Jason shot her down so brutally and frankly. She couldn't blame her son-in-law for what he had said. He was under a lot of stress. And maybe she had been a little hard on him, too hard on him, about losing his job for all these months.

But that didn't make her any less worried that there was a killer on the loose somewhere in the area; or that Madeleine Frobisher may have died at the hands of another person, for something as trivial as money. Amita needed to know, even if that put her in the eye of the storm.

"Your neighbour, Madeleine Frobisher," she said slowly. "Jason told me you didn't get along with her."

"I'll bet he did," said Taylor, staying near the cupboards and sink. "No, we didn't get along. And I don't make any bones about hiding that fact. You ask anyone around these parts, I didn't like Ms Frobisher. I thought she was stuck up. I thought she was losing her faculties. And, above all else, I thought she was downright bloody stupid not to have sold up a long time ago and let us all move on."

"But you've got what you want now, haven't you?" said Amita. "You've managed to sell up to Rory Francis and his development."

"I have," said the old farmer. "But it's about twenty years too late! Twenty years I've waited for this. Twenty bloody years, toiling away, out there, trying to make ends meet and keep this farm going, the same farm that killed my own dad and his dad before him. Twenty years – it's been a bloody prison sentence."

Taylor was breathing hard now. He had reached down to the edge of the kitchen worktop and was holding on, steadying himself. Amita watched him carefully, her confidence growing.

"Mr Taylor, I'm not going to beat around the bush with you," she said. "What you did to my son-in-law was absolutely abhorrent. And you're lucky that he's not going to be pressing charges. If it was me, I absolutely would be, you can trust me on that one."

"Well, it's not you, is it," he said spitefully.

"No, it's not. And, as I said, that's not why I'm here tonight. I'm here because I wanted to ask you a simple question and one that I know might put me in terrible danger."

Amita could feel her heart thumping in her chest. Her legs were quivering, turning to jelly. Everything was tingling, like a current had been passed through her skin. She stared across at Mike Taylor and prepared to risk it all.

"Did you murder Madeleine Frobisher?"

The question was a simple one, much simpler than she had ever thought it could be to ask. Not that Amita Khatri had ever imagined she would ever have to ask such a question. Five simple words, that's all it took. Five little words and she had played her hand. It was now up to Taylor.

"What?" he croaked, his face slack. "What did you say?"

"I asked you if you murdered Madeleine Frobisher," said Amita, straight. "Did you break her neck and make her death look like an accident for the postman to discover the next morning?"

"What kind of question is that to ask someone?" Taylor coughed. "Are you off your rocker? Did I murder Madeleine Frobisher? Of course I bloody didn't! Why would I do something like that?"

His answer disarmed Amita slightly. She reloaded and prepared to go in again.

"You said it yourself" she continued. "You said she was a stupid woman for not selling up sooner. Jason told me you knew you'd get more if she sold her land to developers at the same time as you. She robbed you of twenty years, if not longer. I'd say that's pretty strong motive to decide to bump somebody off."

239

"What are you talking about, woman? This is *insane*!"

"Is it, Mr Taylor?" she wagged a finger at him. "Is it any more insane for me to accuse you of this dreadful act than it is for you to have carried it out? You've already proven today, this morning even, that you're capable of violent outbursts. You threatened Jason with a shotgun, for goodness sake. All the pieces fit together nicely. And they show a picture with you at the centre of it."

"You're mad!" Taylor shouted. "You're absolutely mad, doolally. How can you say something like this to me? Yes, I admit I didn't like the woman but I never murdered her. Bloody hell, just saying it out loud gives me the chills."

"Oh come off it, Taylor," Amita changed her tactics, boosted by her confidence. "You murdered her, didn't you? You sold up here and went around to gloat. And when she wasn't having any of it, you turned on her, snapped her neck like a twig."

"No! No! Absolutely not!"

"Yes, you did! You're guilty as sin!"

"No! I . . ."

Taylor's legs gave way beneath him. He fell to the floor with a hard crack. The old farmer let out a muffled groan as he started to writhe on the cracked and broken tiles, his body folded up like a pile of crooked golf clubs. Amita stood perfectly still. She didn't know what to do.

"Help . . . help me . . . please!" Taylor reached out to her, his eyes bloodshot, tears running down his face. "Please!"

Amita's paralysis was broken. Her instincts, her desire to help, kicked back into action and she leapt over to him.

"Oh my god," she said. "Are you alright?"

"Pills . . ." he said, speech slurring. "My pills . . ."

His teeth clamped together and he winced in agony. With a heavy, shaking hand he pointed towards the cupboards above. Amita stood up, her knees clicking loudly causing her to let out a little yelp. She began pulling the cupboards open, desperately searching for pills. Finally, she stumbled across Taylor's stash in the last cabinet.

"Blimey," she breathed. "Look at all that medication. It's like a chemist here."

The cupboard was filled, from bottom to top, with boxes of tablets and pills. A flurry of names Amita couldn't pronounce danced in front of her. She didn't know where to begin.

"Which ones?" she asked frantically. "There are too many. I don't know what to give you!"

"No, don't . . . give me anything," Taylor's breathing was getting more laboured. "I've . . . I've had too many . . . brown bottle, in . . . the brown bottle . . . help me . . ."

The tendons in his neck were standing out and he was shuddering with the pain. Amita pushed the boxes out of the way until she found the brown bottle he had described.

"Got them!" she said, holding them up. "Morphine? But there are hardly any in here. How many have you taken?"

"Hurry!" he said, his eyes getting heavy. "Please . . . call an ambulance . . . the pain, it's so bad . . ."

Amita dropped to her knees. She cradled Taylor's head in her lap. His heavy hands reached up to her and he grabbed her arms. She watched the old farmer as he slowly stopped writhing. At first she panicked that he had gone. But Taylor continued to breathe, much to her relief.

He was covered in a sheen of cold sweat, his lips turning purple. His breathing slowly returned to normal, although it sounded like he had a rusty old motor lodged in his chest. Everything was calming down when an almighty clatter came from the hallway beyond the kitchen.

Amita's mind began to function again, the bare-faced panic of the whole encounter easing up a little. It was only then that things started to make a little more sense.

A moment later Jason came thundering in, out of breath and sodden, hair pasted against his forehead. He skidded to a halt when he saw Amita and Taylor on the floor.

"It's okay," she said, before he could ask the inevitable question. "It's alright."

"Are *you* okay?" he gasped.

"I'm fine," she said. "But I think you should probably call for an ambulance, Jason. Mr Taylor isn't well."

"But I . . . I thought you were . . . he could be . . ."

"It's okay," she smiled calmly, her voice almost soothing. "Everything will be alright. You have to stay calm and call for an ambulance. We have to go to the hospital."

It all made sense to her now. She could see Jason trying to work things out. Bless him, he tried, she thought. Only when he wanted to, but at least he tried sometimes. And he'd clearly come here to rescue her.

"I don't get it, Amita. What's going on here?"

"It's fine, Jason," she said again. "Just call for an ambulance. Mr Taylor here needs a doctor."

"But . . . but why?"

She looked down at the old farmer who was breathing more steadily now, still comatose in her lap. Carefully, she tucked her fingers into his hair and pulled. The mop of white hair on Mike Taylor's head came away with ease, revealing he was completely bald underneath.

"Be a dear," she said, looking back up to her son-in-law. "Tell them that he's going to need some extra strong painkillers when he comes in. Mr Taylor, it seems, has cancer. And I think the morphine he's on has caused him to pass out. I came here to find a killer, but this is not the one I expected."

Chapter 24

TWO DOZEN

"I don't think he did it," said Amita.

Jason rubbed his forehead for the millionth time since he'd sat down. He was bent over, elbows resting on his knees. His coat smelled of damp and rotting mud. Beside him he could see Amita's feet tapping. Her trainers were filthy, mud splattered up her trousers.

"What a day," he said, furrowing his brow once more.

"Did you hear what I said?" she leaned forward. "I said I don't think he killed Madeleine."

Jason let out a long, tired sigh. The waiting room in A&E was slowly filling up. They'd been waiting for over an hour already and it was twice as full now. The patients ranged from the obviously hurt to the questionable at best. From bleeding foreheads and limping youngsters with ankles the size of basketballs, to those who clearly simply needed somewhere to sit out of the rain, it was a slice of society that many rarely got to see.

Jason had never before looked properly at A&E. There was usually a very good reason he was here in the first place, and people-watching wouldn't be top of his list of priorities.

He recalled a particularly nasty challenge he'd taken at football one night when he was a student. He'd been rushed into this very waiting room which hadn't changed much since then, except that the TVs were newer, as was the vending machine selection. He'd been screaming in pain, his leg feeling like it was on fire. His embarrassment had no end when the doctors finally diagnosed little more than a sprain that would sort itself out in a few weeks. Jason never went back to football after that.

"I could have been a doctor, you know," he said, sitting back.

"Could you?" asked Amita.

He'd expected something a little more sarcastic from his mother-in-law. But she seemed genuinely intrigued.

"I thought about it, at least," he sniffed. "More than thought about it, actually. I gave it real, proper consideration. Picked my subjects, had a look at universities, local and up in Scotland, too."

"So what stopped you?"

"Not quite sure," he puffed out his cheeks. "It wasn't that I didn't want to study, nothing like that. I guess I just took my eye off the ball, so to speak. There was something about journalism that was a bit more glamorous, if you know what I mean?"

"I'm not sure I do, Jason," she said.

"You see it on TV, don't you, the battle-scarred hack with their hat and the little press card poking out of the rim. There are always foreign correspondents on the front line, dodging bullets and bombs, and getting to the heart of the story nobody else wants to tell."

"Like Kate Adie."

"Exactly, Amita, exactly that. Like Kate Adie. Getting your flak jacket on with 'press' written on the front. Speaking to camera while missiles whistle all about you. Or digging deep into some dodgy politician and bringing down cabinet ministers and the like. There's something quite cool about all of that."

"And saving lives wasn't cool enough for you?" she tutted.

The doors of the waiting room opened with a bang. An ambulance crew pushed a stretcher in as a flurry of medics and nurses huddled around, barking instructions and orders at each other. They disappeared behind the main door of A&E, never to be seen again.

"I didn't, and I don't, have the chops for it," he admitted. "These people are heroes, Amita, real heroes. It's not about glamour with them. I mean, who the hell would want to be elbow deep in blood and vomit if they didn't have a vocation, eh?"

"Very true," she agreed.

"Not that I still think of journalism as being glamorous. Far from it, in fact. There's nothing glamorous about court stories and writing about local parking shortages."

"No, I don't suppose there is."

Jason looked about the waiting room. There was an atmosphere, a charged buzz about this place. It was humanity unfolding right in front of him. No, he couldn't have ever been a doctor. But he appreciated their work beyond words.

"Hold on," he said. "Did you say you *don't* think he murdered Madeleine Frobisher?"

"Yes," said Amita, casually.

"Where did that complete turnaround come from?"

She was about to answer him when a nurse came up to them. She was reading notes, flipping a page over on her clipboard.

"Mr Brazel and Mrs Khatri?" she said. "You're here with Michael Taylor, is that correct?"

"Yes, we are," said Amita. "We came with him in the ambulance. My son-in-law here called the ambulance."

"Okay. And you're not relatives or next of kin of Mr Taylor at all?"

"No" said Jason.

"Just concerned acquaintances."

"And you don't know how to contact Mr Taylor's family?" asked the nurse.

Amita looked at Jason. They both shrugged.

"We don't know if he even *has* any family," Amita said.

"We don't really know him," said Jason.

"Oh, right," the nurse said. "Were you just passing by when he took a turn, then?"

"Not exactly," Jason said.

"Mr Taylor threatened to shoot Jason with a shotgun earlier this morning. And I was questioning him over the suspected murder of his neighbour, Madeleine Frobisher. You might have heard of her, dear?"

Jason put his face in his hands.

"Oh," said the nurse again. "I'll be honest, I've worked in A&E for nearly ten years and I think that's probably the strangest answer I've ever had."

"Try living with her," said Jason.

"Jason!" Amita tutted. "We understand there are confidentiality issues, dear, of course we do. And Jason is right,

247

we don't really know Mr Taylor at all. But we're here to help in any way we can. That's why we've been waiting here all this time."

The nurse smiled warmly. "You're dedicated, I'll give you that," she said. "You're more dedicated to a random stranger than some of the families we get in here, I can tell you. But I'm not sure I can give you any information. The rules are very strict, I'm afraid."

"Please," said Amita. "We just want to know that he's alright, and to speak with him for a moment. It won't take long."

"We've been here for hours," said Jason. "We're not going to cause any trouble."

"Please," said Amita again. "Is he alright? That's the main concern, obviously."

The nurse bit her bottom lip. She looked over at the main desk where her colleagues were processing the sick and needy. Then she clicked her pen. "He's fine," she said. "He's suffered a bit of a shock. We think it's been brought on by stress. The medication he's on for his cancer is strong stuff and he shouldn't be overdoing things, not at his stage of life, or with the illness. But he's upright and awake."

"Thank goodness," said Amita. "Could we see him?"

"I really can't. I shouldn't have told you what I have, and . . ."

"Please, miss," said Amita. "We won't be long. It's important. We have to say sorry to him."

The nurse shook her head. "You think you see and hear everything in this job," she said. "But two folk who've been threatened by a patient, and are accusing him of murder, tops the lot. And now you want to go and see him."

"You couldn't write it, huh?" said Jason.

"No, you couldn't," she tucked her clipboard under her arm. "Right, you'll have to be quick. He's being moved to an overnight ward soon. Five minutes, that's all I can give you."

"Thank you, my dear," said Amita.

Jason was less enthusiastic. The nurse led them into the bowels of the hospital to a waiting ward. She drew back a curtain to reveal Mike Taylor in his bed. He was wearing an oxygen mask, eyes bloodshot and glassy. He turned to look at the pair as they were introduced by the nurse.

"Hi Mike," she said. "You've got some visitors."

Taylor raised his hand towards them, a thick IV line poking out from the top. Amita did her best not to cry. She was dreadful in hospitals, especially at visiting time. Jason was much more stoic.

"You need to be quick," said the nurse. "Five minutes and you're getting kicked out. Is that clear?"

"Thank you," said Amita.

The nurse left the three of them together. Amita and Jason hovered at the edge of Taylor's bed. What did you say to the man you'd accused of murdering his neighbour in cold blood, causing him to collapse?

"You're looking well," said Amita, deciding a lie was probably for the best.

"Go for the jugular, why don't you?" whispered Jason.

"Ha!" Mike coughed, his voice muffled by the oxygen mask. "Don't make me laugh. I look like I've been dragged through a hedge backwards."

"Oh, come on," said Jason. "You looked like that at the best of times."

The old farmer threw him a disgruntled look.

"We're here to apologise, Mr Taylor," said Amita.

"Apologise?" he grunted. "What for?"

"We were wrong. *I* was wrong. I shouldn't have accused you of murdering Madeleine Frobisher. If I hadn't, you wouldn't be in here now. I had no idea you were so ill. You never said anything."

"I never got . . . the chance to," he said. "You came in and started . . . accusing me of these terrible things."

He pulled the oxygen mask off his face. He looked awful, gaunt and old. The man who had threatened them both seemed like a distant memory now. In the hard light of the ward, he was skeletal and weak. Even Jason had pangs of sympathy for him.

"How bad is it?" he asked.

"Jason, please," said Amita.

"No, it's fine," said Taylor. "It's fine. Well, I'm not fine, far bloody from it, in fact. Ten to fourteen months left, that's what I've been told. It's in my lungs, spreading fast by all accounts. Shouldn't have been smoking since I was fourteen, should I?"

"Blimey," said Amita, reaching out and taking his hand. "I'm so sorry, Mr Taylor."

"Why?" he smiled wryly. "It's not your fault I'm riddled with cancer. You didn't force me to start smoking. You didn't force all those fry-ups down my gullet. No, it's all on me, this one. I only wish I could have seen it all out in sunnier climes."

He started to cough. He leaned over the bed and was sick into a bowl. Amita instructed Jason to take the bowl from him. When he did, he saw it was full of blood.

"Bloody hell, Mike," he said.

"That's nothing," Taylor said. "I've been living with this damn disease for seven years. The docs only gave me six months to live, initially. But I've been fighting it, fighting it and fighting it. That's why I wanted to sell up and go. It's been hard and I'm tired. I needed that bloody woman to see some sense."

"Madeleine?" asked Amita.

"Yeah," said the old farmer. "She wouldn't sell up, as you know. And every time she didn't, that was another nail in my coffin, especially in the last few years. That slime-ball, Francis, threw me a lifeline when he handed me the cheque and wasn't bothered about Madeleine's land. I thought I was free. But it was too late. I'm not fit enough to go to Penrith let alone the Costa del Sol or the Bahamas. What use is money if you're too sick to spend it, eh?"

He clapped a hand to his bald head. Swallowing, he winced in pain. Amita watched him, still holding his free hand and rubbing it gently.

"We had no idea," said Amita. "And I'm sorry. I'm sorry for confronting you like that. If I'd kept my bloomin' mouth shut, you wouldn't be in hospital now."

"It's okay," said Taylor, catching his breath. "I don't blame you. I don't blame either of you. The docs, they say I can't get too excited, not with the medication. Well, I've hardly been the nicest host to either of you, have I? And with all the construction and that snake Francis, something like this was bound to happen, wasn't it?"

He looked up at Jason.

"I wanted to say I was sorry, son," he said. "I shouldn't have been such an arse to you this morning. Your mother-in-law here told me that you aren't pressing charges. I appreciate that, I really do. The last thing I need is to see out my final days in a prison cell. It takes a lot of guts not to hold a petty grudge. I'd know, I've got plenty of them. And you could have easily put me deep into it. I am truly grateful."

Out of the corner of his eye, Jason could see Amita beaming. She was like a proud parent at school prize-giving, ready to take a picture. The old farmer freed his hand from Amita and offered it to him. Jason took it, feeling every bone as he squeezed.

"I'm sorry, too," he said with a sigh. "I'm just glad I arrived when I did. Otherwise this could have ended a lot worse for everyone."

"Absolutely," said Amita. "Is there anyone we can call for you? Anything we can get you?"

"You saved my life," he said. "You both did. If you hadn't called the ambulance I'd be dead by now. So I'm grateful to you both."

"The nurse was talking about family. Is there anyone we can reach for you?" asked Jason.

"No chance," he laughed. "They all lost patience with me a *long* time ago. No, I'll be fine. They'll have me out of here in a day or two."

The nurse stuck her head around the entrance of the cubicle.

"That's your five minutes," she said. "You two really need to go before my bosses come in here and start asking questions."

"Okay, thank you," said Jason. "Come on, Amita, we've caused enough bother for one day, I reckon."

"Yes, I think you're right," she agreed.

"There is one thing you could do," said Taylor, replacing his oxygen mask.

"Anything," said Amita. "Just let us know."

"Tell Francis I'm in the hospital," the old farmer started to laugh. "He still needs me to sign over the last of the land for this great social project of his. If he thinks there's a chance of me croaking it before then, he'll be all over me like a rash. I won't have to lift a finger."

"Alright," Amita smiled. "We'll tell him straightaway. You can rely on us, Mr Taylor."

"Please," he said, taking her hand. "Call me Mike."

She nodded and squeezed his hand.

"Amita," said Jason quietly. "We need to go."

She let the old farmer go and they left the examination booth. Thanking the nurse for her help, Jason and Amita made their way out of the ward and through the waiting room. They walked in silence to the car park where their beaten-up motor was waiting for them.

When they reached it, Amita stopped. She looked across the roof of the car and winced. "I'm sorry to you, too, Jason," she said.

"What for?" he laughed.

"I shouldn't have gone to Mike Taylor's farm tonight, not alone, anyway. I was running a terrible risk."

"You were," he said. "You didn't know what you were walking into. And that's before you consider you thought he had murdered Madeleine."

"I know," she said regretfully. "I think I was upset from earlier today. Upset by what you said."

"Amita, I . . ."

"No, please, let me finish," she said. "You were right, of course you were. We've been like headless chickens these past few weeks, chasing nothing more than a theory. I shouldn't have spoken to that DI Alby the way I did,

253

and I certainly shouldn't have gone to the building site on my own. I had to know, that was all. I had to rule him in or out. But what's it achieved? We're no closer to finding out who killed Madeleine Frobisher. Or, indeed, if there ever *was* a killer. Seeing Mike Taylor like that, facing death, made me realise it's coming for us all in the end. And most of the time, there's nothing unnatural about it. I'm sorry, Jason. I'm sorry for worrying you and I'm sorry for bringing you into this. You were only giving me a lift to the bingo."

He was touched. The sting behind his nose and the lump in his throat were back. Amita didn't have to speak like this. She never had before. That she would take the time now was something rather special.

"Why don't we draw a line under it?" he said. "Maybe I could have been a bit nicer earlier today, too. Maybe my tone isn't always the most polite, either. You should know how much I value you and your opinion, Amita. You're my family and I wouldn't have you any other way. So maybe we should let bygones be bygones and head home. It's been a very, very long day."

"That", she said, opening the passenger door with a creak, "Is the best idea I think you've ever had, Jason Brazel."

Chapter 25

DUCK AND DIVE

There was a renewed calm about Amita and Jason as they drove into town. Wednesday night, bingo night. After everything that had unfolded over the past few weeks, they both seemed glad to have some sort of normality. The weather, at least, had cleared up, Jason glad to be able to see where he was going when he drove.

"Did you remember your glasses?" he asked Amita.

"They're on my head," said his mother-in-law, reaching for her spectacles.

"What about your pens?"

"In here," she said, tapping her handbag.

"You're all sorted, then. Not the usual last minute panic."

"No, quite sorted," she smiled. "Makes a pleasant change. We should do this every week."

"We both might live longer."

Jason couldn't help but feel a bit worried. Things weren't normally this smooth. A fortnight had passed since the whole Mike Taylor affair. The old farmer was back at home and Amita had even gone to visit him a few times, taking him soup and things to read. Their car had been fixed, Rory Francis more than happy to help after his favourite landowner had put in a call. The engine was purring, the bodywork good as new. Even the inside had been given a good clean, five years' worth of crisp packets and crumbs all sucked out and disposed of.

Then there was the job front. If the affair with Madeleine Frobisher had taught him anything, it was that life was short. He couldn't spend another minute at home farting around watching daytime television. He'd rebooted his job-hunting in earnest and had an interview. It wasn't a reporter job but it would do for now. Any and every penny coming into the house had to help.

Jason didn't want to jinx his happiness. It was, after all, fleeting at the best of times. Instead he continued driving, a comfortable smile on his lips.

"Did you put your suit into the dry cleaners?" asked Amita, as if reading his mind. "For your interview?"

"Radha picked it up yesterday."

"Good. Are you prepared?"

"Yes, I think so," he said. "It'll be nice, if I get it, to be able to go to work and not worry about contempt and having angry people calling you up moaning about a story you did on them. I don't imagine you get a lot of that in a call centre for a bank."

"No, I don't suppose you do."

"And it's local," he added. "Which is great. Yeah, feeling very positive about it."

"I'm glad to hear that, Jason," she said. "I think, with everything we've just been through, staying positive is what will get us through it."

Jason pulled the car up right outside the front door of the church hall. Father Ford was standing welcoming the regulars in as they arrived. A few were still milling around at the bottom of the steps, pulling the last drags from their cigarettes. Sandy was among them, a towering figure, his face beneath the rim of his cap lit up by the glow at the end of his smoke.

"I see old Sandy is back," said Jason.

"So he is," said Amita. "I didn't come last week. I wonder if he's feeling any better about everything."

"Hard to tell with him, I imagine. He's not the most talkative in big groups, is he?"

"No," she said.

"You okay?" he asked. "Going back into the vipers' nest?"

"Yes, of course I am," said Amita. "There are only friends in there, Jason."

"Even Georgie Littlejohn?"

"*Especially* Georgie Littlejohn," she said firmly. "Believe me, if I can't handle her barbs and jibes, then I'm not worth my salt."

"True, but you know what she's like," he said. "Especially when she's holding court, as I'm sure she will be in there."

Amita looked up the steps towards the entrance. She would have been lying if she said she wasn't a little apprehensive. She didn't doubt for a moment that everyone inside would know about her being hauled into the police station, and everything that had happened with Mike Taylor. That's why she'd taken a week off from the Wednesday night thrills.

"I'll be fine," she said. "Sometimes you've got to be a pilgrim in an unholy land."

"Very prophetic," he said. "Pick you up at ten?"

"I'll be here waiting for you."

She climbed out of the passenger seat. Jason pulled off and she did something she had never done before – she waved after him.

"I must be getting soft," she said to herself as she headed up the steps.

Father Ford was standing chatting to a man in a thick coat and baseball cap. They were blocking the way into the hall so she stood patiently.

"Oh, hello Amita," said Father Ford. "How lovely to see you again. We were all worried about you last week."

"You were?" she said, a little surprised.

"Oh yes, we were wondering where you were. Georgie Littlejohn in particular was concerned."

"I'll bet she was."

"What's that?" he asked with a meek smile.

"Nothing," she smiled back. "Nice to be missed and all of that. Thought I would take a little break for a week, spend it with my family."

"Ah, how lovely. Are they keeping well?"

"Yes, they are, thank you, Father. All very well. Jason has a job interview with a bank next week. He's very excited."

"Wonderful. He will have my prayers. You can tell him that from me."

"Very kind of you."

"I'm going to go," said the man in the baseball cap.

Amita still couldn't make him out, his face covered in shadow. He shook Father Ford's hand and stepped down past Amita without saying hello. She watched him go, then turned back to the pastor.

"Was it something I said?" she asked, stepping up to the door.

"Not at all," said the vicar. "Poor Mr Billings. He's not been the same since that awful discovery."

Amita shuddered. "That was Geoff Billings? The postman?" she said. "I didn't recognise him at all. He was all covered up."

"Yes, I'm afraid he's gone a little off the rails, Amita," said Father Ford. "He was just stopping by to thank me for the shopping I dropped off at his flat the other day. He's become very despondent since the grim discovery he made. I imagine he'll take early retirement after all this. I can't imagine what it must have been like for him to find poor Madeleine in such a state. I don't mind telling you that I'm worried about him."

Amita watched the postie as he walked up the street. He kept his head bowed, watching his feet. Anyone who came close to him immediately moved out of the way, probably frightened of being knocked over by him as he charged along the pavement.

"What a shame," she said. "He must be taking it pretty hard."

"I've encouraged him to get some professional help, to see a doctor, but it doesn't seem to be making a difference," said Father Ford. "We can only keep plugging away and let him know he's not on his own."

"Yes," said Amita.

"Crumbs, look at the time. We should probably get started," said the vicar.

He ushered Amita into the hall as the last of the stragglers came in behind them. Amita looked about at the long tables arranged into their usual rows, hoping to find a seat on her own so she wouldn't have to deal with anyone.

Unfortunately for her, a hand was waving wildly in the far corner of the hall.

"Yoohoo! Amita!"

Georgie Littlejohn's voice was like a foghorn. Even over the hubbub of the seventy-something pensioners gathered in the hall, she was loud and clear.

Amita gave a small wave back. As much as she had given out to Jason about facing off with Georgie, she still would have preferred *not* to have to deal with her. Everything was still a bit raw on that front. A peaceful night where she could concentrate on her numbers would be much more preferable. Instead, as she made her way towards the far table, she was walking into the lion's den.

"Amita, so good to see you, my darling," Georgie offered her arms for a hug. "We were all worried sick about you last week."

"Thank you, Georgie," she said, taking the kiss on each cheek with good humour. "I was with the family last week. It was lovely."

"Sounds it. Come on, sit down next to me. I've saved you a space."

She was being overly nice. Amita smelled a rat. She sat down and got her materials out as Georgie passed her a game-book. Sandy came thumping in and sat down across from her. They exchanged a pleasant smile as Ethel bobbed her head in approval.

Amita pulled her pens out of her bag and cleaned her glasses. She felt a tap on her shoulder as Georgie leaned in close to her.

"I'm glad you're okay, Amita," she said, her voice hushed. "I heard about your little brush with the law. And that awful business with Mike Taylor."

Amita bit her tongue. She hated when she was right.

"I just want you to know that I think you've done a wonderful job these past few weeks under difficult circumstances."

"Difficult circumstances?" she asked. "What do you mean?"

"Well, I don't like to gossip, as you know," said Georgie. "But a lot of people have noticed how you've been getting into – what shall we call it? – *trouble* with that son-in-law of yours."

Amita felt her blood boiling. No matter what her relationship with Jason had been like before, she always defended her family in public.

"It can't have been easy, given all this business with the police," Georgie went on, her voice hushed and low.

"Jason has been helping the police, Georgie," lied Amita. "They've been asking him questions and getting information on a couple of things that have happened recently, that's all."

"Still," Georgie sniffed. "Can't be very nice being carted away by policemen from your front door. Mrs McCarthy – you know, the retired schoolteacher? – she lives at the end of your street. She told me she saw the van and the car outside the other day. I haven't told a soul, Amita. I know how that sort of thing spreads."

"Appreciated, Georgie," Amita feigned a smile.

"And then all that nasty business with Mike Taylor and his gun, pretending to shoot people. Rupert told me all about it. The poor little cock was shocked to the core. He said he'd never seen anything like it."

"No, I don't imagine any grandson of yours would have."

"I just thought I'd let you know that I'm here for you, as always," she squeezed Amita's shoulder. "We've all got to stick together now, don't we? Especially after Madeleine died in such a horrible way. We have to watch each other's backs, fronts and everything else."

"Good evening, ladies and gentlemen. Shall we begin?" Father Ford announced from the stage as he fired up his electronic number machine.

Georgie placed her glasses on the end of her nose, the gold chain attached to their legs rattling against her drooping earrings.

"Oh, and before I forget," she said to a fuming Amita. "Remind me to speak to you at the end of the night about what we'll get that poor postman with the collection money. We raised over five hundred pounds at the vigil. I'm thinking about a nice commemorative silver jug. Or maybe something he could use at his desk."

"Do postmen have desks?" asked Amita.

"Oh yes, I'm sure he does," she sniffed arrogantly. "We'll have to be quick. The money is resting in my account. Don't want anyone thinking I've stolen it. Wouldn't want you and Jason to start investigating me, or anything."

She laughed and elbowed Amita in the ribs.

"No, we wouldn't want that," said Amita through gritted teeth.

She started dotting off numbers on her game card without listening to Father Ford. She was far too angry for bingo now. It was a shame, really – she had been quite looking forward to the game. Typically, Georgie Littlejohn had other ideas and she had put Amita in the most foul of moods.

"Downing Street, number ten," said Father Ford.

Amita noticed she had clenched her fist so hard that she was hurting her knuckles. She took a long breath and tried to calm down.

"Tweak of the thumb, fifty-one."

The idea of Georgie giving *her* help, after everything she and Jason had been through, was the very worst part. That somehow Georgie was still the great philanthropist who could do no wrong.

"Top of the shop, number ninety."

"House!"

Georgie sprang up from her chair and waved her book around. Subdued applause went around the hall. It took all of Amita's effort to clap both of her hands together once, let alone join in the chorus.

"What a stroke of luck," said Georgie, sitting back down. "I wasn't even going to bother coming tonight. Glad I did now."

"Yes, me too," said Amita through gritted teeth.

What had started as a lovely evening had quickly soured. This was going to be a long one.

Chapter 26

PICK 'N' MIX

"Can you believe the nerve of her! Honestly, how can anyone be so bloomin' conceited? Can't she hear herself when she opens that big gob of hers?"

"I think that's the point," said Jason. "Georgie Littlejohn is one of life's great blowhards, Amita. And in my experience, people like that usually like the sound of their own voices more than anything else in the world."

"That's true. Can you imagine the nerve of her, though?" said Amita.

She was still angry from bingo, even though they'd been on the road for fifteen minutes.

"To talk about you that way, to talk about us! And then the little joke about not wanting to be investigated by us."

Jason laughed at that bit.

"What's so funny?" she asked.

"Seriously? You don't think that's a little bit hilarious?"

"No, I don't," said Amita firmly. "I find it rude and completely overblown. We were doing valuable work, work that might have been incredibly important to Madeleine's legacy and the safety of the community. A community of elderly residents that includes her, I should add."

"I thought you had prepared yourself for the onslaught?" he asked. "I thought you said you could take it."

"I know," Amita calmed down a little. "I thought I could. But it's very difficult when you're in the presence of the Gorgon not to get carried away with all of her rubbish. And another thing, she says it all with such authority, nobody would dare stand in her way or stand up to her."

"Like you, you mean?"

"Yes, exactly."

"So what did you do?"

"What?"

"What did you do when she was speaking to you like that?" asked Jason. "What did you do about it?"

"Well, nothing," Amita conceded. "What was I supposed to do? Box her ears? I'd end up back in the cells with that awful DI Alby all over me. Georgie would love that, too. No thank you. She's not worth that."

"No, she's not," said Jason, pulling the car into the driveway in front of their house. "And she's not worth you getting your blood pressure up for either, Amita. If we take anything from the strangeness of the last couple of weeks, it should be that life is too short to spend on bitterness."

"True," she said.

Jason got out of the car. Amita gathered her things and followed him.

"I meant to say to you," she called after him.

"Sshh," he hushed her down. "The kids will be asleep." He pointed up to the dark window high above them.

Amita winced. "Sorry," she said. "But I meant to tell you when you picked me up. I saw Geoff Billings just before we all went into the hall. He looks dreadful and he's not holding up very well."

"He's the postman, isn't he?" asked Jason, unlocking the door.

"Yes. Father Ford says he's become really down since it all happened with Madeleine. He went around to Geoff's flat to drop off shopping. That's not a good sign, not if he lives on his own."

"Is he getting any help?"

"Father Ford said he was trying. Maybe I should pay him a visit."

Jason laughed as he took off his coat and headed into the living room.

"What's so funny about that?" Amita asked, following him in.

He sat down on the sofa with a thump and gathered up a stack of papers from the floor. He started to leaf through them, details of his job interview and the role highlighted with bright yellow circles.

"You're visiting everyone and their grandmother at the moment, Amita. Mike Taylor, Sandy, now this chap. You're visiting more houses than the postman."

"I'm just trying to be thorough, Jason," she said. "If the police have washed their hands of all of this, then it's up to us, Madeleine's friends, to do it."

"I see."

"But if it makes you feel any better, I've taken on board what you said the other day."

"You have?" he asked.

"Yes," she said. "I'm not going to go about accusing anyone of murder in a hurry. At least, not until I have some firm evidence."

Amita dumped her bag beside the chair and kicked off her shoes. Reclining, she stared up at the ceiling. The ancient artex looked back at her, the swirls like waves cresting in the ocean. Up there, beyond the plaster and the floorboards, her two grandchildren were fast asleep. She was under the same roof as them, lived with them, got to watch them grow up in front of her eyes. It was a luxury that not many could boast. She knew she shouldn't take any of that for granted. Madeleine should still be enjoying nights like this. And whether it was a nasty fall or something worse, Amita owed it to her and her friends to find out.

The living room door opened. Radha came in, rubbing her eyes and yawning.

"I thought I heard the front door," she said. "I must have fallen asleep when I was reading to the kids."

"You used to be the same," said Amita with a kind smile. "You wouldn't fall asleep unless you knew me or your father were in the bed with you. Many a time I'd fall asleep beside you, only to wake up at two in the morning, all the house lights on, the TV blaring, no dishes washed."

"Those were the days," Radha smiled.

She sat down on the arm of the sofa and rubbed Jason's shoulder.

"You all set for tomorrow?" she asked.

"Yes, I think so. Just a bit of last minute swotting," he said, raising the papers.

"Good. I've ironed you a shirt and your laptop is charging in the kitchen. Be yourself and you'll be fine."

"I want to get the job, Radha – the last thing I want to be is myself."

He neatly stacked the papers together and yawned.

"Have you thought anymore about what you'll say you've been doing for the last few months?" asked Radha.

"I'll say job-hunting," he said glumly. "Easiest thing in the world is to simply tell the truth."

"You could tell them all about your amateur detective work with Mum," she said. "You two made a good team."

Amita and Jason scoffed. They batted her away, neither looking at the other.

"No, I'm serious," she said. "You were a great team. Jason, you had all your knowledge of the legal system and what happens in situations like murder and assault and so on. And Mum, you had the energy and the enthusiasm."

"Not to mention a contact book as big as Cumbria itself," Jason smiled.

"Oh, stop it, you two," Amita blushed.

"And you both know how much closer you've gotten," Radha went on. "I've seen it in both of you. You've been a lot happier, had more zest and life about you both. It's a shame that nothing came of it in the end. Well, I say a shame, it's probably for the best, isn't it? What happened to that woman was bad enough. Murder on our doorstep would have been even worse."

Radha ruffled Jason's hair. He didn't say a word. And neither did Amita. They sat in silence, letting what she said sink in.

"Anyway, I'm going back to bed," Radha said. "Make sure everything is locked up, would you? Don't want burglars getting in and nicking all the wonderful kids' toys and the ten-year-old telly, do we?"

She wandered out of the room, the others still silent. She stopped at the door. "One more thing I've been meaning to ask these last few weeks,"

"Yes, love?" asked Jason.

"Whatever happened to the stalker? You know, the guy that was banged up for the assault and kidnap of Madeleine in the seventies?"

"We drew a blank," said Amita.

"I couldn't find anything more online," said Jason. "It was so long ago, and Madeleine had been out of the lime-light for so long, nobody had thought to archive it on the web. Which is incredible really, to think you can't find out about it online. One of those little quirks – too old and not enough people cared."

"Kind of sad," said Amita.

"Yeah, it is," Radha agreed. "Oh well, it is what it is. I just thought you guys might have found out what happened to him. What was his name again?"

"Starbuck," they both said together.

"That's him. Suppose it doesn't matter now. Case is closed now Jason's had to hang up his amateur detective hat. Night."

She closed the living room door behind her and climbed the stairs. Jason and Amita were silent, listening to her footsteps until she got into bed.

Neither of them wanted to say what they were thinking. But somehow they already knew. Jason drummed his hands on his knees. Amita's foot was tapping up and down. They didn't look at each other. They both knew what was coming.

"So . . ."

"Don't," said Jason, holding up a finger.

"What?" Amita pleaded.

"Amita, don't even think about it."

"I have no idea what you're talking about."

"You absolutely *do* know what I'm talking about. And it's a no. A strong no. As strong as a no can be."

She sat upright in the armchair and looked across at her son-in-law.

"Don't look at me like that, Amita," he said, getting to his feet. "I'm not going down this road with you. It's over. I'm done with it. No."

"Please, Jason. It's important."

"No! It's not," he smiled a frustrated grin. "What's important is accepting the fact that, if the police don't think there's a case to answer, we'd be best off believing them. We've been through all this. It's finished. You heard what Radha said, the case is closed."

He clapped his hands together. She got up to face him.

"I know, I know," she said. "But what if we missed something really important? We got distracted by Mike Taylor when we should have been looking for Starbuck all along. What if he managed to find her again?"

"Amita," he droned.

"Come on, Jason. One last push. It might all come to nothing. If he's long dead, or still safely locked up, that would mean we *definitely* had closure and it would all be over. I would drop it then. But what if that's *not* the case? What if there's an outside chance he *is* alive and he *is* free and he *did* find Madeleine after fifty years and caused her harm? Surely that outside chance makes it worth seeing through to the very end?"

Jason shook his head. "This is bordering on obsession now, Amita. It's a slippery slope, and I don't want you making yourself ill over it."

"I'm fine!" she exclaimed. "I'm fit as a fiddle, never been better."

"Please," he said. "I'm begging you. We're in a nice place at the moment, you and me. We've had a fortnight of calm, relaxing, proper time together without shotguns and DI Alby, and even the gossip from bingo has died down. And besides, where the hell would we find that information? Starbuck has no online presence."

"What did people like you do before the internet?" asked Amita.

"What do you mean, people like me?"

"Journalists? Reporters? What did you do before you had a computer on your phone?"

He sighed loudly. "We used an archive system. Libraries. Good old-fashioned shoe leather, going to places and asking questions."

"So there's an archive at your old office?"

"Yes. No. I don't know, Amita. The workmen are clearing the place out," he said. "And it doesn't matter anyway. Firstly, I'm not a journalist anymore. And secondly, I'm going to bed as I have a job interview in the morning. I need my beauty sleep."

He left Amita in the living room. His head was thumping, a large slab of pain resting square on his forehead. This was the last thing he needed. He crept around the landing, avoiding the floorboards he knew were squeakier than others, until he reached his bedroom.

Radha was sound asleep. He slipped into his pyjamas and climbed into bed beside her. Closing his eyes, he was convinced he had pushed all thoughts of Madeleine Frobisher, Freddie Starbuck and, most of all, Amita his mother-in-law, out of his head. He needed some rest. He needed to be on top form in the morning for his interview. This was his chance to get back on his feet, to feel valued and a member of society once again. He couldn't blow it. Not now.

So why was he still awake at two in the morning putting together a list of ways to check up on Starbuck? He had to hand it to Amita – when she wanted to, she could still bait a hook.

Chapter 27

STAIRWAY TO HEAVEN

Amita watched the car pull out of the driveway. She waited until it had disappeared around the corner at the end of the road before sparking her roll-up. There was a cold draught this morning, a wind blowing through the attic vent carrying with it a hard edge she wasn't used to.

She took a long drag from her cigarette, held the smoke in her lungs and then released it. Her mind flashed back to the hospital and Mike Taylor lying stricken. She knew this smoking wasn't good for her; especially when she could see the direct results lying in front of her. She thought about crushing her roll-up out there and then. But she paused.

A thought had popped into her head. This was why she was here, wasn't it? A little illicit time on her own to think things through, to concentrate. She did, after all, deserve it after everything that had happened. Or not happened. Either way, she was here and the alone time was working.

Mike Taylor hadn't killed Madeleine Frobisher. He was far too weak for anything like that. The man's bark was much worse than any bite he could ever muster. It was a great shame. As awful as his reputation was, he was no killer.

Throughout the course of the investigation, she had come to realise one thing. To be a killer took something above and beyond a run-of-the-mill cruelty. It took a savage sort of courage. To know that you had taken another life and not been punished. To be walking around with that weighing on your mind, on your conscience – it took something different, something warped and distorted. Mike Taylor wasn't a killer and he never would be, no matter how many times he waved a shotgun at Jason.

She took another drag. Breathing the smoke out, she watched it dance in long, wispy curls as the hard wind blew in through the vent. The rain was light, for the moment. Gentle drips from the guttering above her were like the ticking hands of a clock – drip, drop, drip, drop, a natural metronome for her to think by.

That there was a killer, she had no doubt. She might not dare admit that to Jason – she didn't want to scare him off. But Amita wasn't vain or selfish enough not to know when she was being overtaken by her imagination. There was a killer out there, she knew it. She could *feel* it.

Jason had been right. Things had spiralled out of control all too quickly. She had been wrong to bring the police in so early. And thankfully they hadn't acted on her accusations. Otherwise Mike Taylor might have been finished off. She might have had another funeral to go to, instead of quiet afternoons in his kitchen drinking expensive coffee. She would go up there later this afternoon to check on him. Maybe take him some soup to make sure he was eating. It was her penance for bringing on his bad turn in the first place.

That wouldn't catch the killer though. There was no way she could do that on her own. She had to think. Who could it be? Who would have the most to gain from Madeleine being dead? Who would even *want* her dead?

Her phone vibrated on the bare floorboards beside her feet. She reached down with a groan and picked it up. It was a message from Jason. She opened it and was met with a picture of him, all smiles, giving a thumbs up in the passenger seat of the car.

"I hope you straighten your tie before you go in," she read her own reply aloud. "They won't give you the job if you look like you've been dragged in by the cat."

She sent the message. Then she did something she never did. A strange, all-consuming sense of nostalgia drove through her. She flipped the screen to her pictures and began scrolling backwards. Days turned to weeks and then to months and finally years. She stopped when the calendar flashed 2015. She clicked on the folder and a host of pictures appeared, pictures she hadn't looked at since they were first taken.

The bingo club had arranged a weekend in Blackpool. Travel, accommodation, meals, everything pre-paid. In the end, a dozen had signed up for the trip and they left early on the Friday morning for the drive to the coast. Amita had a terrible feeling as soon as she climbed aboard the minibus. She wasn't really a group trip type of person. She had always preferred everyone in the club on an individual basis. She knew a lot of them, like Georgie and Madeleine, from other groups, too. The thought of being stuck with them for a weekend, however, hadn't much appealed to her.

It had been Radha's idea. Amita hadn't long moved in with her daughter and family. She had believed that Radha simply wanted a weekend to herself without her mother's fussing. So she had reluctantly agreed. Off they went, down the M6, singing songs and trying to be jovial.

The hotel wasn't up to much, nor was the food, she recalled. However, as the weekend wore on, she became much more relaxed and friendly with her fellow bingo hall regulars, especially Madeleine. In the battle for supremacy between Madeleine and Georgie, Amita always had her back. She scrolled to a photo of the group standing on the beach with a donkey in the middle of them. The famous tower loomed in the background, almost totally obscured by the fog and rain.

Amita smiled. Georgie was beside her, nose lifted high into the air, her bouffant hair rigid against the bitterly cold wind blowing in from the Irish Sea. To her left was Madeleine, all smiles and much more welcoming. She always made Amita feel at home – asking questions about Radha and the grand-children, saying how important family was. Sandy stood at the back of the group, the vaguest of grins on his granite face. Amita read more into his expression now she knew the depth of care and friendship behind it. Then there was Ethel beside him, not confined to a wheelchair at that point. A few of the others were gone now, passed away in the interim years. The thought made Amita dreadfully sad and she felt the tears welling up.

"Oh bugger!" she yelped.

Her roll-up had burned all the way down to her fingers. She hopped around, sucking on her finger where the flame had caught her.

"Stupid sentimental old fool," she said when the pain eased.

She reached down to pick up her phone. The pictures were gone and the screen was frozen. She mashed the buttons until something started to work. When it blinked back into life, her web browser appeared first. It was showing an old page she'd been looking at weeks before – a search for Freddie Starbuck.

The sight of his name made her shudder. She clicked on the browser, remembering her attempts to try and find out more about Madeleine's stalker. She gave a quick scroll down the search results – there weren't many. Like Jason had said, it must be a strange mixture of age and lack of interest. Fleeting mentions of Starbuck on forums, but nothing substantive. There wasn't even a photo of him, something Amita couldn't get her head around.

"I don't understand," she said, locking her phone. "No picture, no details, nothing. It doesn't make any sense."

She leaned against the wall and peered out of the vent. The day was brightening, and so was Amita's mood. She headed back down from the attic, being careful to cover her tracks as usual. She closed the hatch and dusted off her hands, then headed downstairs to fetch her coat and bag.

She made sure everything was locked up before leaving. The air was damp and cold and she thought about returning for a scarf. But there was no time. She had the bit between her teeth now. Only she couldn't do it on her own. Amita pulled out her phone and dialled a familiar number.

"Hello?" came a hoarse voice from the other end of the line.

"I didn't waken you, did I, Sandy?" she asked.

"No, no, not at all. I was . . . I was just . . ."

She heard a rustle of papers in the background.

"Everything alright, Amita?" he asked, pulling himself together.

"Yes, everything's fine," she said. "Listen, I need a bit of a favour from you."

"Oh crikey," he said. "That's never a good sign. I'm not dressing up as the Easter Bunny again for a charity collection, if that's what you're after. Or Santa Claus – those kids ate me alive last year."

"No, nothing like that," she said. "It's a bit funny actually, and you've got every right to tell me to get stuffed. But I wouldn't ask and put you in this position if I didn't think it was important enough to warrant the risk."

Sandy was silent. She heard him breathing heavily down the line as she walked towards the bus stop.

"Sandy?" she said.

"Yes, I'm here," he said, his tone more serious. "What do you need from me, Amita? You and Jason have been good to your word. I'll help you with anything you want, if I can."

Amita smiled. There was that sting of tears again.

"Meet me at the old *Penrith Standard* offices in half an hour. There should be a side door to the building. The removal people are in at the moment, so try to keep a low profile."

"Roger Wilco," said Sandy and hung up.

Amita arrived at the bus stop just as one was approaching. As she climbed onboard, she checked her own sanity once more to make sure it was still intact. This was the right thing to do. Wasn't it?

Chapter 28

IN A STATE

Jason smiled and gave a thumbs up. He sent the picture to his mother-in-law and then put his phone back in the pocket of his suit jacket.

"She'll appreciate that," said Radha, sitting in the driver's seat. "I meant what I said last night, Jason. You two have been getting on like a house on fire recently. It's been really lovely to see."

"Oh stop it," he batted her away.

"No, I'm serious," she continued. "Not only lovely and nice for me, but for the kids, too. They're getting older and they can pick up on a lot of things that washed over their heads before. The constant bickering, the one-upmanship, it's draining, you know? It's been such a lovely atmosphere in the house. I know it's been hard these last few months with you being out of work."

"Hard?" he said. "It's been bloody awful."

"I know that," she said, taking his hand. "But I want you to know, as I've told you time and time again, that

I love you and I'm proud of you. And if this new career path is meant to be then that's what's meant to be. I know you've always been a journalist and I know it's what you wanted to continue doing. So this sacrifice for the family, and for your own sanity, is very much appreciated, Jason."

"I know that," he said, still smiling. "I'm sick of sitting around the house getting older and poorer by the day. If there's no work in what I've done before, then I guess I need to do something else. I'm not the first hack who's jumped ship, and I won't be the last, judging by the way the industry is going."

"You're right," she said. "I love you, Jason Brazel. Always have and always will."

She kissed him on the cheek and he squeezed her hand.

"Wish me luck," he said.

"You don't need luck. You're going to smash it. Like you always do."

He climbed out of the car and crossed his fingers, waving back to her. Radha smiled before driving off, leaving him on the pavement outside the huge industrial estate. The close din of the motorway made everything sound like he was inside a washing machine. Everywhere he looked, it appeared nature was fighting back against the big, ugly buildings and seventies office blocks that had sprung up like Brutalist Lego.

"Industrial chic," he said. "Nice."

He walked into the industrial park. The building he'd been directed to was directly ahead. One of the older ones on the already decrepit-looking industrial estate, it didn't fill him with great confidence or inspiration. The beige cladding was stained and filthy, covered in decades' worth of soot and smog from the nearby motorway. The tinted brown windows stared down at him as he approached, giving the whole place the look of a box of chocolates with all the sweets taken out.

The truth was, Jason's confidence was beginning to sag. And it had been since he got up that morning. Three hours sleep could do that to a man, especially when he's been thinking about the possible murder of Madeleine Frobisher.

He opened the door and tried to get himself geed up for the interview. This was the first new job he'd gone for in twenty years. He should be more excited than this.

There was a reception desk in the lobby but nobody behind it. A list of the businesses in the building stood behind it and he found where he was going.

"Top floor," he said. "Nice views, I'll bet. Maybe I'll get a corner office, rooftop bar and pool. Perfect."

He went to the lifts but they were broken, a haphazard sign hanging over the button. He started up the stairs and that's when he noticed it. There were no people around. The place was completely deserted. Jason's imagination started running wild. Had this been a set-up? Was there some awful enemy he'd made as a reporter waiting on the top floor for him, ready to throw him out of a window? What if it was Madeleine Frobisher's murderer, unhappy that he and Amita had been snooping around trying to untangle the web of deceit and murder?

At last he reached the top floor. A grey door met him and he rang the buzzer. The door clicked open and all Jason's fears of being alone were put to rest. Inside was the call centre – row after row of narrow cubicles, bobbing heads appearing and disappearing behind the partitions. Voices rose up from each of the booths as a thousand different conversations were had all at once.

"You Brazel?"

Jason dragged himself away from the human battery cages. A short man with a dirty blonde beard and curly hair came waddling up to him. He offered a clammy, outstretched hand.

"Yes," said Jason. "Marcus, is it?"

"Aye, that's right," said Marcus, a hint of a Scottish accent. "The agency said you were coming over. You want to step into my office and we can get things started."

Marcus turned quickly and waddled away from the battery. Jason noticed the large sweat stain that had formed between his shoulder blades, his pale blue shirt stuck to his skin, beads running down the folds of the back of his neck.

If Jason's confidence was waning before, now it was skating on wafer-thin ice. He took a few tentative steps behind Marcus and thought about bolting for the door. Only his desire not to leave empty-handed kept him in the call centre. Maybe it would be better in the office.

"Here's my office," said Marcus.

It clearly wasn't going to be better in his office, not that it could be called that. Marcus pulled out a chair from a large, round table in what was loosely a communal kitchen area. In the far corner a tall, slender woman was hanging around a kettle, waiting for it to boil. She stood looking into space. Marcus didn't even acknowledge her. He swept his arm across the table surface, clearing away loose crumbs. He sat down and loosened his tie so it hung like a noose around his neck. He mopped his brow, dragging his hand down his face, stretching his skin like rubber.

"Sorry about the heat in here," he apologised. "We've got the men coming next week. Reckon I'll need to take my shirt off at this rate. Might bring out a calendar."

He laughed raucously, slapping his hands on the table. Jason managed a polite chuckle, but it was clear he was falling short.

"Go on then, take a seat," said Marcus. "I want you to tell me why you want to join our merry little band of mischief makers."

"Mischief makers?" asked Jason.

"It's just a bit of a laugh. That's what I call us, isn't it, Jess?"

"Piss off, Marcus," said the woman loitering around the kettle.

She sneered as she walked past the table before disappearing into the battery.

"Just her little joke," Marcus winked. "She can't keep her hands off me normally, that one."

"I'll bet," said Jason.

"So, John, tell me why you're here?"

"Jason."

"Eh?"

"Jason, it's Jason Brazel," he said.

"Oh aye, sorry. I'm terrible with names," said Marcus. "Forget my head if it wasn't screwed on, I would."

That drew another laugh at his own joke. Jason didn't bother being polite this time. He sat with his hands on his lap, afraid to touch any surface in this place for fear of what he might catch.

"You used to be a reporter then, did I read that right?" asked Marcus.

"I did."

"You ever interview anyone famous?"

"No."

"You ever take pictures of anyone getting in and out of a taxi then?" he winked and puckered his lips. "You know what I mean?"

"No, Marcus, I don't know what you mean."

"Yes, you do," he flashed a sleazy smile. "I know what you journalists are like. Sex-mad, you are. Me, I don't like that sort of thing. I used to buy *FHM* and *Nuts* every week. But since they stopped I don't touch the stuff."

"The stuff?" asked Jason.

"Yeah, newspapers and that."

"But . . . *FHM* and *Nuts*, they weren't newspapers."

"Aye, I know that," he sounded almost offended. "But it's all the same, ain't it?"

"What's all the same?" Jason could feel his heckles getting up. "The media?"

"Aye, the media. It's always lying to you and that."

"Marcus," Jason said, being very careful how he worded what he was about to say. "There's a *very* big difference between a lads' mag and a newspaper. There are whole worlds of differences between the different kinds of newspapers you can buy – tabloid, broadsheet, a Sunday edition, for example. I don't think it's fair to tar them all with the same brush."

"Aye, but they all make up stories, don't they?" he laughed. "They are all out there trying to make a quid."

"They're businesses," Jason said. "And, for what it's worth, I've never met or known a journalist who made up stories. It's hard enough trying to get work without jeopardising your career with a load of lies."

Jason got to his feet. He was angry now. Marcus cowered in his chair, its legs squeaking beneath his weight.

"And another thing," Jason went on. "What gives you the right to sit there and criticise another man's, or woman's, work like that? Do you think running a place like this makes you immune to criticism? You've got two hundred people back there packed into this god-forsaken throwback to 1976, all boiling away like they're hens laying eggs. If you want to talk about professional standards, start with your own front step, mate."

He turned quickly and headed for the door. Nostrils flaring, he could feel the adrenaline pumping through his legs as he went.

"Wait!" Marcus called after him. "Don't you want to talk about the job?"

Jason reached the door. The hubbub had stopped, every worker now standing up and looking to see what all the fuss was about.

"Take your job and shove it up your arse, Marcus!" Jason shouted back at him. "I'm a journalist, and I'm proud of it. And the only mistake I made was thinking that ship had sailed. I've got stories to find."

He shouldered the door open and slammed it closed behind him. There was a brief pause before a roar of applause and cheering went up from the call centre. Only Jason was too mad to acknowledge or enjoy the victory. He stormed down the stairs, pulling off his tie, and stomped out into the cold air.

The freshness brought him to his senses. He took a few large gulps of air and looked up at the sky. The clouds were swirling, ready to burst. He turned to look at the seventies monstrosity, half-expecting a mass exodus of disenchanted call centre employees to have followed him out. Nobody was there.

It didn't matter, though. He had seen and done enough in the ten minutes he had been a part of that world. And he didn't want to go back. A little gnat of imagination, of doubt and curiosity, had grown and grown since the night before. Maybe even long before that, since the night he had met Laura in the pub and they'd first talked about Madeleine Frobisher's untimely death.

Jason started walking off the industrial estate, hoping there would be some way to get back into Penrith. He pulled his phone out of his pocket and saw a message from Amita.

"I hope you straighten your tie before you go in," he read the message out. "They won't give you the job if you look like you've been dragged in by the cat."

Jason laughed. He immediately dialled his mother-in-law's number. It rang once before she answered.

"Amita, it's Jason," he said.

"Yes, I know, Jason. I have caller identification, like the rest of the planet," she said.

"Yeah, sorry," he scratched the back of his head. "Listen, I'm going to be straight with you. The interview didn't go very well. In fact it didn't go at all."

"What?"

"Yeah, I don't think the job was right for me. I don't think the career move was right for me at all. I'm a journalist, a reporter, that's what I'm good at. And I was thinking about what you were saying last night, about Madeleine and Freddie Starbuck. I think we should get to the bottom of this, once and for all. Get it done. See it through to the end, no matter what that end is. If we're wrong, we're wrong and . . ." He trailed off. "What's that noise in the background?" he asked. "Are you out?"

"Yes," said Amita. "I'm on my way into town. I'm meeting Sandy. We're . . . erm . . . doing some research."

"Research?" he wrinkled his nose. "Research into what? And where?"

"The old *Penrith Standard* offices?" she said, like a question.

"What? What on earth for? Amita, please tell me you're not going to do anything rash. The offices are closed, remember? They've shut up shop."

"I know that, Jason. Where do you think I've been for the last six months? Mars?"

"Please tell me you're not going to do anything stupid."

"Okay, I won't tell you, then," she said.

"Amita?"

"Jason."

"Do not do anything until I get to you, do you hear me? Please. Alby is looking for thieves who broke in there and lifted a whole load of equipment. He won't think twice about throwing the book at you if you wind up doing something utterly idiotic."

There was silence from the other end of the phone. Jason started to panic. "Amita? What have you done?"

"Too late."

"Too late for what?"

"Doing something stupid," she said.

Then the phone went dead.

"Amita? Amita!" Jason shouted.

He looked at the phone. The screen was blank. A little empty battery logo appeared, showing he was out of power.

"No!" he shouted, voice drowned out by the nearby motorway. "Amita! Wait until I get my hands on you!"

He started running along the pavement. He had no idea which way he was going but that didn't matter. He had to get back into town and to his old workplace as quickly as possible. This was turning into *another* one of those days.

Still, at least he didn't have to work with Marcus.

Chapter 29

RISE AND SHINE

"Are you sure this is a good idea, Amita?"

Sandy had stopped himself before he stepped across that line between legal and illegal. His huge hands were gripped around the handle of a fire escape. Legs spread, he had squared his shoulders, ready to try with all his might to break his way in. It was an old trick he'd learned many moons ago, and one he had hoped would still work with modern fire escapes. Not that there was anything modern about the *Standard*'s building. It looked like it was on its last legs, and that was only from the outside.

If she had told the truth, Amita wasn't sure if this was a good idea or not. Usually, in her experience, if it wasn't clear that an idea was a good one, it meant that it was probably bad. And this was as good proof as any of that working theory.

"How confident are you that you can get us in here?" she asked him.

Sandy bobbed his head from side to side. "I haven't had to break into many buildings for a very long time, Amita, you have to understand that," he said pragmatically. "But a door is a door and a lock is a lock. I reckon if I give it a good go, this thing will pop open no bother. It's on the other side that worries me. If those renovators out the front have turned off the alarm, then we're laughing."

"And if they haven't?" she gulped.

"You better get ready to run," he smiled. "Last chance to say no."

Amita thought about it. She thought about what they were doing but, more importantly, why. She nodded to Sandy. "Do it," she said.

Sandy nodded back. He tightened his grip on the handle. With his feet fixed and standing straight, Amita had never seen him look so powerful. His broad shoulders were perfectly square, his long coat flowing down from them like a superhero's cape. He gave a low, rumbling grunt and began to shake.

"Sandy," she said. "Are you alright?"

His face had turned scarlet and was verging on purple. The door was beginning to rattle on its hinges. There was a creak and a scrape, then he fell backwards, and the door came with him.

"Sandy!" Amita shouted as they landed on the ground.

"I'm fine," he said, pushing the flimsy metal door off his giant frame, normal colour returning to his face. "No alarm?"

Amita looked back at the empty space where the door used to be. There was no sound coming from inside the building. She looked up and down the alleyway that ran along the side of the old newspaper offices. Again, nothing.

Traffic was passing by as it always did at either end of the lane. Nobody, it seemed, had noticed or cared that Sandy had just pulled a fire escape door off its hinges and was now lying on his back with Amita fussing over him.

"I think we've gotten away with it," she said.

"Good," breathed Sandy, getting to his feet.

He dusted off his big coat and adjusted his flat cap. He stepped back to the doorway and peered inside.

"Just a stairwell," he said. "I imagine the offices are up a few flights. We'll need to be careful not to run into the builders. We don't have any excuse to be here, Amita. This is breaking and entering, pure and simple."

"I know, Sandy, and I'm sorry that I've got you involved in all this," she said. "But if anyone stops us, we're simply a pair of old-timers who've gone the wrong way."

"The wrong way through a locked door?"

"I take your point, but I have to know. I have to be sure that whatever happened to Madeleine was purely an accident. That there's no chance of anything sinister having happened, or that Freddie Starbuck was involved in some way."

"I know, Amita," he clapped her shoulder. "You were a good friend to Madeleine. She always spoke very highly of you when you weren't around. And I know she would have appreciated what you're doing."

"You, too," she said.

"Oh, I don't know about that," he said wistfully. "I wasn't there for her when that Starbuck rat struck. And I could have been."

"You weren't there, Sandy, that's true," she said. "But nobody knew what was about to happen to her. And you're here now, helping me break into a building to make sure justice is served, if it needs to be."

"Thank you," he said quietly.

"Stop!" Jason's voice echoed down the alleyway and startled both pensioners. "For god's sake, stop! Don't do another thing!"

He came charging down the lane and skidded to a stop beside Amita and Sandy. His face was flushed and he doubled over on himself, gulping at the air to get enough of it back into his lungs.

"Are you alright, son?" asked the big man.

"I . . . I . . . I got here . . . as quickly as I could," Jason said, straightening up. "Stop whatever it is you're doing or planning on doing. Please."

His head was throbbing. He'd run from the high street, six blocks, at full speed in his dress shoes and best suit. His shirt was sticking to him with sweat and a stitch in his side was making breathing pretty unbearable. When he'd finally managed to catch a bus from the industrial estate it had taken the strangest route back into the centre of town. The whole journey he had spent biting his nails, nervous as to what his mother-in-law was planning. Now he was here he could barely stand up. He wished he was fitter, wished he hadn't eaten so much at breakfast. Wished he was somebody else.

"What the hell happened to that door?" he asked, pointing at the gap in the wall.

"Jason, we're going into the offices," said Amita. "We're only going in for a quick look around the archives to see what we can learn about Freddie Starbuck, and that's all."

"You can't," Jason said. "It's a closed building. The renovators are in. You're breaking the law, and there's already a police investigation ongoing around stuff going missing from here! What do you think Alby will say if he finds out we're involved in all of this? Our feet won't touch the ground!"

"Jason, we have to," she said. "We have to know. You said so yourself."

"I know I did," he sighed. "But this isn't the way to do it. We have to go through correct channels. There are procedures. We can make requests to offices who hold whatever we want and –"

"There's no time!" Amita shouted.

Jason was startled by how loud she yelled.

"There's no time, Jason," she said again. "For all we know Freddie Starbuck is loose and he could be anywhere by now. We need to know once and for all that he had nothing, or something, to do with Madeleine dying. You're absolutely right about everything you've said. And I don't condone what we're doing. But desperate times call for desperate measures."

Amita's face was all determination. Jason knew that look all too well. It was the look that told him there was no movement here. This was what she had her mind set on and that's all there was to it. Whether it was breaking and entering, or what they were having for Sunday lunch – Amita had made up her mind.

"Jesus H Christ on a pogo stick," he said. "You two are off the map, do you know that? I mean I half expect it from her, but you, Sandy? I thought you were a respectable member of the community."

"This respectable member of the elderly community just pulled that door off its hinges," said the big man. "Imagine what I'd do to your arms if I got the chance."

"Touché," said Jason. "Right, this is what you want, then? Once we go in there, there's no going back."

"We've crossed that threshold already, Jason," she said.

"I know, but I thought I'd say it anyway. It made me feel a bit better, at least."

"Yes," said Sandy. "We have to know."

"We have to know," Amita agreed.

"Alright then," Jason said, taking a deep breath. "Once more into the breach we go."

This was a bad idea, he knew it. Jason had spent his career avoiding bad ideas like this. But that might be why he'd just stormed out of a job interview after calling the manager a moron. What a morning.

He stepped into the dark stairwell of the fire escape. Amita was beside him, peering up the steps. Sandy moved to join them, but Jason stopped him.

"Hold up there, big chap," he said.

"What?"

"We need a lookout man," Jason said. "In case somebody comes down the alley and sees your handiwork."

He pointed down at the door.

"But Sandy has as much right to know about Starbuck as us," said Amita.

"And we'll tell him everything we find out," assured Jason. "But, if we're going to break into private property, I'd like to stand at least half a chance of getting away. No, Sandy, you stay here and guard the door. If you see anything suspicious, give us a call."

Amita couldn't argue with the logic. "He's right, Sandy," she said. "Best to get a heads up before anything untoward happens, eh?"

Sandy hesitated for a moment. He looked like he was ready to argue. But he took a step back and adjusted the cuffs of his coat.

"Doorman duties," he said with a wry smile. "I know how to do that. Used to be the best, back in the day." He dipped his head to Amita and then to Jason. "Have a good night, folks. Don't do anything I wouldn't do."

Chapter 30

BURLINGTON BERTIE

The building was stuffy and close. Most of the windows they passed had been boarded up. Thin beams of light from the outside world shone through the gaps between the wooden placards and the edges of the windows themselves. Large dust particles swam in the air, making everything feel used and worn.

It was the smell that was different for Jason. He'd been coming to this building for the better part of his adult life. He hadn't set foot in it for over six months but already it felt like a strange, new place. A newsroom, he had always agreed, needed people. The people were the lifeblood of any paper. Talking, laughing, shouting, and sometimes crying. The very best and the dreadfully worst of human life unfolded on the floor of a newspaper office. Without the people, it was nothing more than an empty room.

As he stood looking out across the huge, open-planned office, he felt his heart sink. The place had been gutted already. All the desks were gone. All that was left were their vague outlines on the floor where the carpets had been worn down around them. Whether removed by the renovators or thieves, there was nothing left here. Years of memories gone forever. And with it, the people who made those moments.

"You okay?" Amita whispered.

"What? Yes, of course," he said. "Why?"

"You've been standing here for about five minutes just staring blankly at the emptiness and not saying anything," she said. "I would have said something sooner but I wasn't sure if you were having a moment or something."

"Having a moment, please," he said, dismissing her. "What do you take me for?"

"Well, it's been such a long time since you've been in here, I thought you might be, you know, a little nostalgic or something."

She stepped forward and something hissed beneath her feet. She stooped down and picked up a ragged page of newspaper that had avoided the cull. She handed it to Jason.

"Recognise this?"

He took it from her. The paper was grubby and torn, the page yellow and stained. He made out the familiar *Standard* masthead and the date.

"It's from ten years ago," he said. "I don't remember the story. But then again, how many times did temporary traffic lights in Market Square make the front page? Classic local news."

"Where was your desk?" she asked him.

"My desk?"

"Yes," said Amita. "You never invited any of us in to see you at work."

"You wouldn't have liked it in here," he said. "Not with deadlines looming and frazzled reporters scrambling around to find stories. It could get pretty intense."

"I'm sure it did. But one trip would have been nice. I know the children would have liked to have seen where their daddy worked. Not to mention Radha and me too for that matter."

"I never thought," he said. "*I* barely wanted to see where I worked. Why would anyone else?"

"So this is your chance."

Jason got his bearings. He peered down and pointed towards the far end of the newsroom.

"See that huge stain on the floor, the one that looks like a Persian rug?"

"No," Amita squinted.

"There," he said. "That stain was from one of our work experience kids who came in one afternoon with their lunch, a pot of soup. Only it had a crack in the bottom and she'd walked through the whole building leaving a trail of minestrone in her wake. When the editor clocked it, he went berserk, something about the carpets only having just been cleaned, which was a load of rubbish. These carpets haven't been cleaned since the Ark was launched. Anyway, in her panic and sheer fright at having the editor screaming in her face, she dropped what was left of the pot onto the carpet and tried to rub it in with her shoe. Hence there used to be a giant soup-stained patch of floor beside where my desk sat. Again, classic local news."

A loud bang from beyond the windows made them both jump. There was another, and then a third. The distant sound of laughing filled Jason with dread. He hurried over to the windows that lined the far wall of the old newsroom. Peering through the gap between the wood and the sill, he could see the street outside. A team of workmen were climbing out of a van. They were laughing and fooling around, dumping their rubbish in the huge skip that was filled with the last remnants from the office. Break clearly over, they made their way into the building, their voices echoing up the stairwells at either end of the newsroom.

"Quick," he said. "We need to go."

"But we haven't found the archives yet."

"We don't even know if the archives are still here. They could have been cleared out."

"Then we have to hurry. Which way?"

Jason peeled himself away from the window. He headed back the way they had come from the fire exit. They climbed the stairs to the top floor. He tried the door and to his surprise it opened without resistance. Inside was a small lobby. Voices echoed up from far below. He pulled Amita inside and closed the door until it was only open a crack. Holding his breath, he saw the shadows of the workers on the walls of the stairwell.

They were shouting and laughing at some awful joke. Thumping up the stairs, every step brought them closer to catching Jason and Amita. Until mercifully they stopped with a few storeys to go. The voices faded and Jason began to breathe again.

"Blimey," he said. "They must be working on another part of the building."

"Look!" said Amita.

She had slid back a wide wooden door at the other side of the small lobby. Beyond it were rows and rows of files and folders. A small army of cabinets bookended the high shelves that housed the archive department of the old *Penrith Standard*.

"They're all still here," she said, heading inside. "We've struck gold, Jason."

"We'll see," he said. "We still don't know if what we're looking for is here."

Amita walked slowly up the nearest aisle between two of the high shelves. She let her hand dance carelessly over the folders and stacks of files that were piled up collecting dust. It was incredible, she thought, that all this history, all of these clippings and notes, pictures and negatives, were simply left here to rot. The digital age had some answering to do.

"Amazing," she said. "Absolutely amazing. Have you ever been here before, Jason?"

"Not in a long time," he said. "I thought everything was digitised. Come on, we won't have long. We need to get moving before we're caught and thrown in prison for real this time, not just at the behest of DI Alby."

Amita clapped her hands. "Okay," she said. "Where do we start?"

Jason looked about. A small desk and an ancient computer were tucked away in the corner close to the wall. There were no windows in the archive, the lights flickering into life when they detected a human soul passing beneath them. He slid into the chair and pressed the "on" button. The computer whirred and bleeped before a very basic screen appeared, with a bright green cursor blinking at them.

"Bloody hell," he said. "The eighties called – it wants its PC back."

"What does that mean?" asked Amita.

"Don't . . . it doesn't matter."

"Ask it about Freddie Starbuck."

"Ask it? Amita, what do you think this is? *Star Trek*? It's a forty-year-old computer left to rot in the archive of a regional newspaper. It's not got voice recognition. We'll be lucky if its ancient brain is still working."

"What do you propose we do, then?"

Jason cracked his knuckles and flexed his fingers.

"Good, old-fashioned BASIC coding," he said. "Hours and hours of taxpayer's money on my school education was clearly not a waste. I might be terrified of technology, Amita, but this is different. So long as the computers aren't connected together so you could tell someone on the other side of the world what you had for breakfast, I'm a natural."

He began rattling out commands on the computer, the keys tapping and stuttering like a machine gun. Despite his confidence, Jason was as surprised as his mother-in-law when the screen changed. A list of file numbers appeared.

"What's that?" she asked.

"It's what we came for. It's a list of everything in the archive that features the terms Freddie Starbuck and Maddy Forster. See? There are five entries into the paper's archive system that feature them both. Five articles or clippings, and that's your lot."

"Okay," she said, getting excited. "Let's get them."

Jason took three codes and Amita the other two. They split up and started hunting the files they were after. Before long they reconvened at the computer desk, folders in hand, the spoils of their searches.

"Right, makes sense" said Jason, opening one of his folders.

"What makes sense?" Amita asked.

"These files we've pulled, they're all marked under 'national interest'," he said, pointing to a handwritten note on the top right of the folders. "It means that they're not necessarily from the local area, but maybe something in them related to Penrith and the editors would have asked the archive to store them."

"I see. Did that happen often?"

"Not really," Jason shrugged. "The archive folk used to hate when it did. They'd have to catalogue the whole document, for thoroughness, even though the local angle might only be a few dozen words. Sometimes it was more, of course; 'local outrage that goes all the way to the Prime Minister', that sort of thing. You never knew what little local stories would be picked up by the nationals. And it never hurt to have more info in the archive, I suppose. We should be thankful we have something. Knowledge is power and all that. Let's see what we've got."

He opened the first folder. The smell hit them both.

"Blimey," said Jason, coughing. "That's pungent."

The files were old. The paper was yellow and brown, held in place by ties to the cardboard of the folder. Jason examined the date.

"January 1971," he said. "That's after the attack. Look here, it's a breakdown of the court case."

The article went into the details Sandy had shared with them. It concluded with Starbuck's sentencing.

"Still no picture of him," she said. "Next one."

She peeled the report away. The next file was a few more ancient pages underneath. They scanned the archived paper until Jason spotted Madeleine's stage name.

"This is from 1975," he said.

"Read it aloud," said Amita. "I don't have my specs on me. I left the house in such a hurry."

"'Notorious stalker Freddie Starbuck has had his sentence extended by another three years by a local magistrate. Starbuck was jailed in 1971 for the kidnap and assault of pop singer Maddy Forster. Maddy, who competed for the UK in the Eurovision Song Contest, was snatched from her front door by Starbuck and subjected to days of mistreatment and abuse. The monster was jailed for twenty years but has now been given extra time at HMP Belmarsh for assaulting another inmate and a warden during a riot in the infamous jail.'"

"That's it?" she asked.

"That's it," said Jason.

"And still no picture of him?"

Jason flipped the clipping over.

"No, not that I can see."

"Okay, we should crack on."

The third file was much bigger than the others. It was made up of an actual newspaper dated March 1986. Jason peeled the pages over and over until he came to the centre spread. It was a feature on notorious criminals from around the UK, a map with arrows and boxes pointing to their locations. The one next to Cumbria had Starbuck's name.

"Freddie Starbuck, currently serving time for the assault and kidnap of local pop star, Madeleine Frobisher, in 1970. Originally sentenced in 1971, he's still behind bars for continued assaults and general trouble. One parole board expert described Starbuck as being 'much cleverer than he looked' and 'a menace to society'."

"Painting a picture we already knew," said Amita with a sigh.

"True," said Jason. "This is like a trip through time, though."

"I'd love to continue this little history lesson on another day, Jason, but we are up against it," she said.

"Yes, sorry."

He closed the cardboard file and picked up one that Amita had delivered. Another small clipping was located inside, neatly filed, this time in a plastic covering.

"Okay, what have we got here?" he said, holding it up to the light. "'Starbuck appeal denied'."

"Appeal?" Amita blurted. "When is that from?"

"It says 1991. Here we go. 'Freddie Starbuck, the notorious criminal and lag, has had his appeal heard for his sentence to be quashed after spending twenty years behind bars. His lawyers had claimed that the time spent in prison had changed their client and that he was no longer of sound mind to be incarcerated with some of the country's most notorious villains. Starbuck, now forty-seven, has had at least a decade added to his original sentence due to bad behaviour inside. However, his appeal was rejected by a panel of senior judges who still deemed him to be too much of a risk to society. They have referred him to a Crown psychiatrist for reports.'"

"So he was still in prison thirty years ago?" asked Amita. "That would make him, what, in his seventies now?"

"Almost eighties, which makes sense. Madeleine was a little older than you, wasn't she?"

"Not by much," said Amita. "And still no picture of him? That's odd, isn't it?"

"Not really," said Jason. "These aren't big stories, you have to remember. We're lucky they even covered this sort of thing so long after he was convicted. And there was a feature in there, too. It's not unheard of, especially when resources in print were so limited throughout this period."

Amita looked down at the last file. She wasn't sure what she was hoping to find. She picked it up slowly, like it weighed more than anything else in the world. She handed it to Jason.

"Last chance," he said.

"I know," she said. "Maybe I should do the honours. Seeing as it's me who has brought all kinds of trouble to our doorstep, if this turns out to be a wild goose chase."

Jason handed her back the folder. She took it in both her hands and stared at it. It was a bottle green colour and in much better shape than the others. She took another deep breath of the stale, acrid air. Then she opened it.

Silence followed. Not just silence for the sake of it. A prolonged, almost agonising silence as Amita stood stony-faced, staring down at the contents of the folder.

"Amita?" asked Jason. "Are you alright?"

He wasn't sure if her reaction was a good or a bad thing. Amita being quiet was normally something to be alarmed about. And his mother-in-law was still quiet. She hadn't spoken. She hadn't even moved.

"Amita?"

She turned from him quickly and was sick on the floor.

"Bloody hell, what's wrong?" he asked, reaching out to her.

She batted him away, pointing at the folder. He took it from her as she coughed and spluttered.

"What the hell is wrong? What's in here . . .?"

Jason trailed off as he opened the folder. Inside was a full newspaper. Its front page story was a black and white photograph of a man. His forehead was wrinkled, a look of malice in his eyes. He wore a sneer that made his razor-thin lips curl at the ends. But there was something else, something wholly familiar about this man. His face, the look, the eyes, the forehead, the ears, even the crooked nose. Jason recognised it, recognised it immediately as someone he had seen before.

"What . . . what is . . .?" he stammered.

The headline above the picture was simple.

"'Monster dead'," he read aloud. "'Freddie Starbuck, 1945 to 2003'. He's dead, Amita, he's dead. But I don't understand. I've seen this man before. I've seen him . . ."

Amita rounded, tears in her eyes. She wiped her mouth and nose on her sleeve. She took the paper from the file and held it up to her son-in-law.

"Billings," she said. "Geoff Billings. The postman who found Madeleine. It's him. This picture is the spitting image of Geoff Billings."

Chapter 31

GET UP AND RUN

There was a shout from outside the archives.

"Oi! The lights are on up there. Isn't that meant to be closed off?"

"Nobody's working up there, are they?"

"Maybe it's faulty?"

"Go up and take a look, Ted."

"You go, you fat sod. I've climbed enough stairs in this place."

"We'll all go."

The argument went on for a few precious seconds. Jason grabbed Amita by the hand and they raced through the archives. He ran as fast as he could, feeling his mother-in-law flailing behind him. The voices were getting closer. And as they slipped into the stairwell at the opposite end of the archive room, Jason saw the workmen coming through the door.

"What was that?"

"Someone's up here!"

"Hey! Come back here!"

Jason didn't look back again. He bounded down the steps, taking them two and three at a time. Amita followed as best she could. They hit the bottom floor with a thud.

"Quickly!" he shouted at her.

"I can't go on," Amita wheezed. "I'm not used to assault courses."

"Come on, through here."

He barrelled through a door. What used to be the old canteen opened up in front of them. Only now it was covered in dust and crumbling masonry. The walls had been stripped of their wiring, the floor chipped and broken and littered with plaster. There was no sign that it had ever been where Jason spent most of his lunchtimes. But there was no time for nostalgia. They had to get out of there, and quickly.

"We're almost there, Amita, just hold it together," he tried to assure her.

She was getting harder to pull behind him.

"Come on! I thought you went running, you should be beating me to the finish line!"

"Power walking, Jason," she gasped. "This *isn't* power walking."

They reached the other side of the building. They ducked into the fire escape, and the open doorway loomed ahead of them like some great pearly gate. When he heard them coming, Sandy stuck his head through the open gap.

"Sandy!" Amita shouted, relieved to be with him. "We were right. We were right all along. Madeleine, she was . . ."

"Calm down," Sandy said, grabbing her and stopping her from falling. "Calm down, Amita, you're going to give yourself a funny turn."

"We need to go, guys, right now," said Jason, bundling them out into the alleyway.

"What's happened?" asked the big man.

Amita clutched her chest. She was pale and looked ill. Jason hopped up and down on his aching feet.

"We found him," she said. "We found Starbuck. He's dead. He died in 2003. Here."

She handed Sandy the paper. He took it and his face dropped.

"It's him," he said.

"It's Starbuck," said Jason. "You knew him, Sandy. Is that an accurate picture?"

"No, that's not what I mean," Sandy said. "It's him. It's the postman."

"Guys, we need to go," said Jason. "Those workmen are right behind us. They'll call the police if they catch us."

"Billings, the postman!" said Sandy again. He dropped the paper in shock. Stepping away from the door, he lumbered about the alleyway, numbly staring into space.

"It's not your fault," said Amita. "Penrith may be a small place, but he probably did all he could to stay clear of you."

"How could I have been so blind?" he asked her. "After all these years? That face, Starbuck's face. I still see it at night when I close my eyes. That bloody postman was at the funeral, wasn't he? They're identical. How didn't I see him? I've failed her, again. I've failed Madeleine *again*, Amita!"

In a fit of rage, he punched the brick wall of the *Standard* building. He didn't even flinch as he turned away, tears rolling down his cheeks. Jason was torn. The man was clearly distraught – who wouldn't be in his position? But they were dangerously close to getting caught.

"Sandy, please, we need to get out of here," he said. "Amita, tell him."

She nodded at her son-in-law. Moving over to Sandy, she rubbed his back as he sobbed. "Sandy, I know this is hard," she said. "I'm as shocked as you are. Believe me, I wasn't expecting this when we went in there. This isn't your fault, though. You couldn't have protected Madeleine from someone you didn't know existed. But Jason is right. We have to move. We have to get out of here and catch Billings before he disappears. He's got to be related to Starbuck in some way. We need to find out what he did to poor Madeleine, and bring this all to an end."

"Down there!" shouted one of the workmen. "The fire exit is open."

"That's our cue," said Jason, starting down the alley. "Come on, we have to go."

Sandy wiped the tears from his eyes. He reached out and touched Amita on the cheek with his big, swollen hand.

"Go," he said to her.

"What?"

"Get going, go on," he said, heading for the door. "You and Jason, get out of here, while you still can. I'll stall them, hold them up and take the fall."

"Sandy, you can't do that –"

"Go," he shouted. "Get out of here. Leave this lot and the police to me. But you have to promise me something, Amita. You have to promise me you'll get that bastard. Whatever he is, whoever he is, and whatever he did to Madeleine. You have to promise me you'll get him."

She nodded. Sandy smiled, his eyes bloodshot and raw. He pushed her away and walked over to the fire exit. Standing as broad and tall as he could, he stepped inside.

"Hello there, boys," he said, then the sound of something being slapped.

Amita turned and ran as fast as her legs would carry her. Jason was at the end of the alleyway already. She reached him and they hurried down the street, trying to look as innocent as possible.

"Don't look back," Jason said under his breath. "Whatever you do, don't look back."

"We can't just leave him, Jason," she said. "He'll take the fall for us all. They'll throw him in jail."

"They're not going to jail a pensioner for standing in the wrong doorway," he said.

They cleared the end of the block. When they were around the corner, he began to slow down.

"I have to sit down," Amita said. "I need a cup of tea or something, Jason. I feel faint. I might pass out."

The good people of Penrith were going about their daily business quite unaware of Jason and Amita. None of them seemed to care. Why would they? They didn't know what was going on. And if they did, they would most probably wish they didn't. Amita envied them. She watched the faces walking past her. Innocent, oblivious, men, women, children, everyone. In the distance, they heard police sirens.

"I think I'm going to be sick," she said. "Or I'm going to pass out. One or the other. I'm not sure which is worse."

"Okay, okay," said Jason.

He was pale, paler than usual.

"Where are we?" He looked about to get his bearings. He quickly found them and was warmed by a wonderful thought. "Around the corner, come on," he said.

"Where are we going now?" said Amita, eyes closed.

"*Murphy's.*"

Amita opened her eyes. She could have cried at the mere mention of the cafe's name. It was their sanctum, their safe place, somewhere that the terrible deeds of the world and the people who did them couldn't go. It was consecrated ground, a refuge. If there was anywhere in the world she wished she was right now, it was *Murphy's*.

Chapter 32

BUCKLE MY SHOE

Jason picked the booth in the far corner of the cafe. An alcove surrounded seating with battered old cushions on two sides. A tall partition topped with a long, brass pole kept the next booth at a respectful distance. It was far enough away from the door that the whole cafe could be seen from this vantage point. Generals, emperors, kings and the greatest military minds of a thousand generations would all agree that this was the best seat in *Murphy's*. Jason was relieved to be there.

He turned the salt cellar round and round in his hands. Staring out of the booth and towards the door, he couldn't concentrate on anything. His mind was going a hundred miles a minute. Nothing was settling, everything was a blur – Freddie Starbuck, Geoff Billings, Madeleine Frobisher, Sandy, everything.

Amita sat across from him. Her phone was on the table between them and it hadn't stopped buzzing since they sat down. Message after message, alert after alert, the bingo club network was clearly learning about what had happened to Sandy. Someone must have heard the sirens, seen Sandy. The gossip merchants would feast on this forever, Jason thought. All the while poor Sandy was probably having the third degree from Alby.

Amita had her head back, resting on the booth's cushions. She was holding a hand across her eyes like some renaissance model. Jason was utterly drained and didn't know the first thing about what to do next. Thankfully, Amita had a plan.

"We have to go to the police," she eventually said. "We have to tell them what we've found out. This is it, Jason. This is what we've been looking for all these weeks."

"We haven't found anything," he said, still turning the salt cellar over and over.

"What do you mean we haven't found anything? Geoff Billings!"

She shouted the postman's name. Jason looked around. Nobody even raised an eyebrow.

"Keep it down, Amita," he said. "What I mean is we still don't have any evidence. All we have is that Billings looks a bit like Freddie Starbuck."

"A bit? A *bit*? Are you joking, Jason? Look!"

She pulled out the crumpled newspaper she had taken from the archives. Laying it flat on the table, she pointed angrily at it, trying to keep her voice down. "Billings is the spitting image of Starbuck, it's uncanny. You would think they were separated at birth."

"It doesn't make sense," said Jason, the salt cellar now turning around quicker in his hands. "How can they be linked? Billings is what, in his fifties? Starbuck has been dead for twenty years or more. How can they be the same person? Starbuck was in jail for the majority of his life."

"Look at him, Jason," she said. "He looks exactly like Billings. There's more than a passing resemblance. You saw it, and so did Sandy, for goodness sake. And he *knew* Starbuck."

"So why didn't he twig with the postie?" asked Jason. "Why didn't Sandy, of all people, see that resemblance?"

"He told you, he didn't know him. Geoff wasn't Sandy's postman. He was on a different route." said Amita.

"What about the funeral?" asked Jason. "He must have seen him there."

"Not necessarily," she said. "They were sitting in different parts of the church. Sandy would maybe have seen the back of Geoff's head. And besides, none of us were exactly on top of our game, Jason. It was a funeral, after all."

Jason nodded in agreement.

"You saw how distraught he was when he *did* find out," Amita went on. "He was devastated, the poor man. He's carried that guilt with him for all these years and now there's more to pile on top of it. You're right, we don't know the connection. He could be a brother, a cousin, a son even. It could be anything. But I don't believe in coincidences and I know you don't, either. Madeleine Frobisher, the woman Freddie Starbuck did those terrible things to, is found dead by a postman who looks almost exactly like him. Come on, it's all there."

"It's *not* all there, Amita. We've been through this already," Jason said, getting angry. "We can't go to the police accusing people of heinous murders when we don't have a single shred of evidence. That's how we end up banged up with Sandy – for wasting police time and defamation."

"We have to do something."

"We can't!" Jason slammed the salt shaker down on the table, as a waitress arrived with their pots of tea. She was young, in her late teens. She gave a wide-eyed look to Jason, and then to Amita, unsure what to do.

"Sorry," he said. "It's been a long day."

The waitress nervously delivered their pots and cups from the tray, desperate to get away. When she was gone, Jason let out a long sigh and rubbed his eyes. He opened them again and saw Amita on her phone.

"What are you doing?" he asked, a terrible feeling brewing like the tea in his pot.

"I'm doing something," she said. "Seeing as you're so hell-bent on doing absolutely nothing, I'm taking the bit between my teeth and being proactive."

"Amita," he said. "You know you make me nervous when you're proactive. What are you doing? Who are you texting?"

He went to snatch the phone but his mother-in-law was much too quick. She slid out of the booth, eyes locked on the screen as her fingers furiously typed away.

"Amita, give me the phone," he said. "You can't do this, you can't get us into trouble."

"Madeleine Frobisher was killed," she said flatly, looking down at him in the booth. "Geoff Billings had something to do with it, and I'm going to find out what that was, by hook or by crook. There's absolutely nothing you can do to stop me, Jason. So I suggest you either rethink your tactics or get onboard with the winning team, I believe the parlance is."

Amita's phone pinged. She smiled. That grin made Jason's chest tight.

"What?" he asked. "That look, I know that look, Amita."

"What look?"

"*The* look. The look that's only missing a five-pointed star badge, a Stetson and a horse."

"Pardon me?"

"The Sheriff of Penrith rides again."

She handed her phone over to her son-in-law. Jason took it and looked at the message on the screen.

"It's an address," he said. "From Georgie Littlejohn."

"Geoff Billings' address," Amita confirmed. "Her gardener's daughter plays badminton at the leisure centre on a Thursday night. Apparently Billings is also there at the same time as part of some squash club or something. Anyway, the gardener's daughter was once asked out by Billings, but nothing serious ever came of it. Hence, now we have his address. Connections, Jason, connections."

"Connections," he snorted. "Couldn't you have simply asked Father Ford? I thought he dropped off shopping to Billings' place the other day."

"You don't get any gossip from Father Ford," said Amita dryly. "Come on," motioning to the door.

"Lord," said Jason. "No, Amita, please. It's been a long day. We're in way over our heads here. This has *bad idea* written all over it, and I don't want to have a shotgun pointed at my face again."

"Jason," she said sternly. "I told you, I'm going whether you like it or not, whether you come with me or not. I'm going to Geoff Billings' house and I'm going to confront him. Now, if you can live with having your septuagenarian mother-in-law walking straight into the lair of a pensioner-killer on your conscience, then you stay sitting there on your bum drinking tea and spilling salt all over the place. But I think you're better than that. And I also think, given you clearly didn't get the job this morning, you could be onto the scoop of the year."

"The job," said Jason wistfully. "I forgot all about that."

"Then come on," she said. "And to think we made a collection for that man . . ."

She turned and walked smartly out of the cafe. Jason sat still for a moment, sensing this was the calm before the storm. Life, it seemed, came flying at him fast, and he had no time to think, to act, to try and anticipate the next move. He was always being dragged along in the wash, left to flap and sputter in Amita's wake. Still, he couldn't fault her energy. He hoped he had even a fraction of that when he reached her age. *If* he reached her age.

Jason couldn't be sure why it happened, but in that moment an image of Marcus in the call centre came flooding back into his mind. He remembered what Laura had said in the pub – what felt like a hundred years ago now – about Madeleine Frobisher's death. Should it be suspicious, it would be a story every newspaper in the land would be after. And he had a chance to uncover the scoop, right here, right now, if he walked out of that door. In twenty years of being a journalist, he had never been anywhere *near* something as dangerous or as exhilarating as this.

"You're a bloody fool, Jason Brazel," he said as he got to his feet. "A bloody fool for waiting so long."

He weaved between the tables and chased after Amita. He was just about at the door when something trundled under his feet. He wobbled as a little yelp went up from underneath him. Jason staggered, bashing his thighs against the corner of a table, the cutlery and glasses on top rattling in unison.

A little dog stared up at him, eyes pathetic in an adorable sort of way. When the pain cleared, Jason recognised it and its owner sitting at the table he'd walloped himself on.

"You," he said.

The Ghost smiled at him and touched the brim of his cap.

"Nice to see you and your mother-in-law in these parts again," said the old man.

"Look, I don't have time for this right now," said Jason, hobbling towards the door. "I don't know who you are – I'm not even sure you're real and this isn't all some massive hallucination as the result of a complete breakdown – but I'm in a hurry."

"Give my regards to Amita," said The Ghost with a wink.

Jason ignored him and hurried out, the door of *Murphy's* cafe slamming closed behind him.

At the counter, where the waitresses and manager were gathered, they watched him go. Then, after a second's thought, they all realised the same thing at the same time.

"Oi!" they called after Jason. "You haven't paid!"

Chapter 33

ALL THE THREES

Jason didn't like this. It felt like the universe was conspiring against them. Every mile they covered, every second that ticked past, he was getting more and more anxious about what they were planning on doing. When he thought about it, he wasn't sure he even *knew* what they were planning on doing.

"I don't like this," he said, shaking his head as he watched the road. "I don't like this one bit, Amita. This stinks, this whole situation stinks. We're being set up for a disaster here."

"I don't know what any of that means, Jason. Try to make more sense in the future, please and thank you," she said curtly.

"*This*, this whole situation." He stirred his hand like it was in a huge pot of soup. "*This*, what we're doing, where we're going, who we're going to see. That address, it's in Bowscar. That's in the middle of nowhere. And look, it's starting to get dark already."

"Well, you insisted on going home first to get the car."

"I know I did," he said, worried. "I wanted to make sure we have our own method of transport in the event things get, you know, hairy."

"They won't get hairy," she said, looking out of the window. "They can't. We have him caught bang to rights. And besides, there are two of us and only one of him. How hard can it be?"

Jason didn't reply. He didn't have to. He knew that Amita was more than aware of his general cowardice. He'd been in three fights in his whole life and two of those came when he was in primary school. The third was with Mike Taylor when he'd threatened to blow his head off with a shotgun.

They drove on. Bowscar was a tiny village, a speck really, on the immaculate Cumbrian countryside that surrounded Penrith. Jason only knew it from a story he had covered years ago when the local residents had complained about drivers speeding through too quickly. Calls for a camera on the main road had been rebuffed. They weren't happy. He doubted any of them would remember him.

The village was only a few miles from the centre of Penrith, but Jason was feeling *very* isolated. What little light left in the day was fading fast and the hedgerows and meadows were taking on a distinctly sinister appearance. He knew it was only his imagination, but it was difficult to ignore. Everything was screaming at him to stop the car and turn around. Go home, lock the door and let somebody else worry about what they had discovered. Only it was never that simple.

"Here," said Amita, pointing at a fork in the road. "In on the left, that's it in there."

Jason pulled off the main road. A small cul-de-sac faced them, two rows of small terraced houses on either side of the pot-holed street. The whole place was dark, a weak glow from a pair of streetlights providing little illumination. Beyond the cul-de-sac was an open view of the countryside and, in the distance, Penrith. Jason had never longed for home quite so much in his life.

"Number two," said Amita.

He stopped the car outside the first terrace on the right. It was a dismal-looking building, hard grey stone cladding covered in cracks that had been badly and quickly repaired. A chimney stack looked about ready to collapse if the wrong breeze came along. And the windows were dark, curtains drawn.

"Do you think he's in?" she whispered.

"Why are you whispering? It's only you and me in the car," he said.

"I don't know," she said. "Maybe I'm nervous."

"Well, you're making *me* nervous."

"Sorry," she said. "Do you think he's home?"

Jason peered through the car window. The house was dark. There was no sign of life.

"I'm not sure," he said. "In my experience of knocking on doors, you can never tell until somebody actually opens up and either says hello or punches you in the face."

"Charming," she said. "Come on then, we better go and take a look."

"Amita . . . wait, hold on . . ."

She was out of the car before he could stop her. She hurried around the bonnet and made her way up the path to the front door. Jason raced after her.

"If you're going to do something as dramatic as that, can you give me a warning first?" he whispered.

She knocked on the door.

"Amita! We haven't even discussed what we're going to say to Billings. We can't go charging in all guns blazing. This needs tact."

Amita knocked again, a little harder this time. The hinges of the door creaked as it opened a little. Jason and Amita looked at each other. She prodded the door a little and it opened fully. The house inside was dark and still.

"Hello?" she shouted.

There was no answer from inside. She licked her lips, throat dry.

"I think we should go in," she said.

"Amita," said Jason. "That's trespassing, and you know it."

"He might be in trouble," she said. "Door hanging off the lock, nobody answering our calls. For all we know, he's lying in the bathroom dying from a heart attack and we have the chance to save him."

"Have we come to accuse this man or save him? Amita, don't," he said.

"Don't what? Help another human being? We don't know what his involvement is, Jason, but he's still a person."

She stepped through the door and into the darkness.

They crept along the hallway. A small living room peeled off to their left and up ahead they could see the kitchen. A narrow staircase led to the second floor, no lights or sign of life from up there.

"Hello?" Amita shouted. "Geoff? Are you home? Can you hear us?"

Jason spotted a door at the end of the hall. He knocked on it, then pulled it open.

"Just the toilet," he said.

"I wonder if he's upstairs?" asked Amita. "We should probably go and check."

"I don't know," said Jason with a shiver. "I don't like this. There's something properly creepy about this place, and we really shouldn't be here."

"And what if he's –?"

"Dying behind the door, I know. It's a wafer-thin defence at very best, Amita, but you're right."

She gestured for him to go up first. Jason reluctantly obliged. The stairs creaked loudly under their feet as they made their way up to the second floor. Everything was cramped up here and a potent smell of damp clung to the walls and carpets. There were three doors off the small landing. Jason peered into the first one, another bathroom inside.

Amita checked out the other, a bedroom containing a single bed with bare mattress and pillows. They reconvened at the final door and opened it tentatively.

"Geoff, hello?" she called. "Are you in here? We're just making sure everything is okay? And we'd like to talk to you about . . ."

She trailed off as she stepped in. The room was in total darkness. The window had been covered up with something they couldn't make out. Jason felt the hairs on the back of his neck stand on end. There was an atmosphere to this place, a feeling of dread.

"What's that on the walls?" asked Amita, peering through the gloom.

"I don't know. Hold on."

He felt blindly at the wall beside the door. When he found the light switch, he flipped it and immediately wished he hadn't.

All around them, on every wall of the dingy back room, were pictures of Madeleine Frobisher. Old press clippings from her prime in the sixties all the way up to what appeared to be photos taken shortly before her death. Amita and Jason walked around the room, unsure what to make of what they were seeing. There were newspaper and magazine articles, savagely cut and torn out and stuck in great montages all over the windows. In the far corner was a small desk with a computer and laptop sitting beside it. Camera equipment was stuffed down between the desk and the wall. Jason walked over and picked up a long lens.

"I take it all back, Amita," he said. "I don't think our postman friend uses this stuff to win the *Countryfile* calendar competition."

"I can't believe it," she said, trying to take everything in. "This is terrifying. Utterly terrifying. He's obsessed with her."

She stopped at one cluster of photos near the door. Peering closer, she pulled one picture down, disturbing the others so they fell like leaves from a tree in autumn.

"What's that?" asked Jason.

"This picture," she said, getting out her phone. "I was looking at this only today. It's of our trip to Blackpool a few years ago."

She dug out the picture and held it beside the hard copy in her hand. It was of the bingo club on Blackpool Beach.

"He's searching through our social media?" she asked. "This was put on the bingo club's social media after we came back. Georgie thought it would be a good idea to have something like that for new members. It didn't last."

"He's thorough," said Jason.

"But it's from years ago."

"You said it yourself. He's obsessed. This isn't healthy, all of this. He's clearly deranged. And I think we need to get out of here while we can."

"I'm not going empty-handed," she said, throwing the picture down angrily. "We're leaving here and heading straight to the police station. But not before I've taken pictures of all this."

She started snapping away with her phone. She covered every inch of the room, making sure that all the obsessive pictures, clippings and history were documented. When she was finished, she took a deep breath.

"You okay?" asked Jason.

"Yes, yes I'm fine," she lied. "It's all been a bit of a shock. I always thought there was something going on, something sinister, as you know. But you don't actually expect it to be *this* bad. It's like something you read in those detective novels, isn't it? The country house, the shrine to a victim. All we need is for Billings to come through the door in a mask and wielding a chainsaw."

They both silently looked at the door. There was nothing.

"I think that's our cue to get out of here, Amita," said Jason. "I don't want to ride our luck any further by ending up in a horror movie."

"Agreed," she said.

Jason made for the door. Amita paused and took one last look around the haunting room. There was still nothing to link Billings to any wrongdoing, only that he had an unnatural obsession with Madeleine. But it was all adding up, the evidence mounting against him. She knew she had been right all along. And now this whole mess might be drawing to a close for good.

"You know, I should really thank you, Jason," she said, following him through the door. "If it hadn't been for you, we wouldn't have –"

Something moved in the darkness. It was too fast to react to in time. There was a hard clank and Jason went tumbling forward, hitting the ground like a bag of cement. Amita stopped dead. She recoiled, heading back into the room with all the photographs.

Geoff Billings came stalking in after her, slowly, menacing, a shovel hanging loosely in his hands. Amita gulped, terrified, unsure what to say, what to do. She was paralysed with fear. Billings smiled, sensing it.

"I don't have many guests," he said. "I hope you like what I've done with the place."

Chapter 34

ASK FOR MORE

"Okay, just . . . just take it easy, Geoff," said Amita, her hands held up in front of her. "This isn't what it looks like. You have to stay calm and let me make sure my son-in-law is okay."

Billings lifted the shovel's blade up to the light and examined it. Flicking crusted dirt off the edges, he cocked an eyebrow and looked about the room.

"You've stumbled across my little tribute to Madeleine, I see," he said.

"Yes, yep, I certainly have done," said Amita nodding. "It's . . . it's quite something."

"I bet I know what you're thinking."

"I . . . I highly doubt you know what I'm thinking, Geoff. And it's probably too rude to say aloud, anyway."

"I bet you're thinking this is all a bit strange, aren't you?" he smiled. "This is all a bit on the odd side, a bit doolally? That's what you're thinking, isn't it?"

He stepped forward, his grip on the shovel tightening. He raised it like an axe. Amita recoiled, her backside bumping into the computer desk.

"Oh god, please, don't do anything you might regret," she said.

Billings stopped dead. He let the shovel drop a little, a look of confusion on his flat, meaty face.

"Regret?" he asked. "Why would you say that?"

"What?"

"Regret. Why would you say I might do something I *regret*? Why? Answer me!"

His moods were shifting quickly, almost as quickly as Amita's terror was rising. She remembered reading somewhere about people on the edge, how quickly they could turn from placid to manic almost in the blink of an eye. She was certain Billings had some deep-seated psychological damage – how else could you explain this room, and what he'd just done to Jason?

At that moment, it became clear to her. A sudden confidence filled her up from her toes to her head. She tingled as she stepped a little forward. She thought she might know what to do.

"I meant if you hurt me," she said. "If you hurt me you might regret it. That's all I said, Geoff, that's all."

She was calm and collected. It was taking all of her effort and she could taste the sweat on her top lip. Every few seconds, she cast a look towards the door. She had to get out of this room and collect Jason to make sure he was okay. But first she had to deal with the maniacal postman.

"*Regret* though, why would you say that?" he said, a terrible sneer on his face. "Why regret? Don't you think I regret what I did? Is that what you're saying?"

Amita's ears pricked up. "Hold on," she said. "Regret what you *did*? What did you do, Geoff? You can tell me, it's okay, it's only the two of us here."

Billings circled the room. He looked up at the light, teeth clenched, tendons standing out in his neck. He looked like he was in pain. He scrunched his free hand into a ball and beat it against his temple.

"I didn't mean to do it!" he screamed, tears starting to roll down his cheeks. "I didn't mean to do any of this. I only wanted her to love me!"

Amita's legs turned to jelly. She steadied herself on the wall, her hand crumpling a picture of Madeleine that looked recent. She peeled it off and held it up to Billings.

"Madeleine," she said to him. "Did you do something to Madeleine, Geoff? Was there an accident, an incident?"

He spun away from her. Stomping around the room, he started tearing at the pictures on the walls, ripping and clawing at everything he had put up there. Amita huddled away in the corner. She thought about making a run for it, but she needed answers, she needed to know the truth.

After a furious moment, Billings calmed down. He slumped down onto his knees, the shovel acting as a makeshift crutch. He looked up to Amita, red eyes bulging, face bright as a tomato.

"She was my mother," he said to her. "And I killed her."

Amita's blood ran like ice. She could only stand there, watching Billings bawl and sob, surrounded by the ruins of his shrine to Madeleine.

"Your mother?" she asked him, voice barely louder than a whisper. "Madeleine? Madeleine Frobisher?"

"Yes!" he rasped. "Yes! Yes! Yes! She was my mother!"

"But you . . . but you look so much like . . ."

"Freddie Starbuck," Billings said. He snorted loudly, and wiped away drool and snot with his sleeve.

"My father," he said. "The monster."

"I don't understand, Geoff," said Amita. "I don't understand any of this. Freddie Starbuck spent his whole life in jail – he wasn't running around fathering children."

Billings stormed over to Amita and pushed her out of the way. Opening his laptop, he pulled up a picture and showed it to her.

"My birth certificate," he said. "Look at it."

"Geoff, I . . ."

"Look at it!" he screamed.

Amita flinched. She leaned down and looked at the screen. The scanned image of a birth certificate was staring back at her. In the bottom where it said "parents", Madeleine Forster's name appeared. The official date was July first, 1971. "Father unknown" it said next to it. Not that there was any doubt when she looked at the resemblance between father and son. But Madeleine must have wanted to get her revenge on Starbuck, and keep his name away from hers.

"See?" he said. "You didn't believe me. Nobody ever believes me. I've never been believed my whole life. Even Madeleine, my own mother, didn't believe me at first. She didn't *want* to believe me."

He stepped away from the computer.

"She wasn't expecting me to turn up," he said. "She didn't want anything to do with me. And I don't blame her, I didn't blame her, I should say."

"How did you find her?" Amita asked. "She disappeared off the public stage fifty years ago. It can't have been easy."

"It wasn't," he laughed. "It's taken me a lifetime to get to this stage. I was put up for adoption when I was born.

That birth certificate you see there, that's the only piece of documentation that proves who I am, in this whole entire world. Can you imagine that? Can you imagine what her fans would think if I was to release that on the internet?"

"I don't care what the fans would think, Geoff. I want to know what happened to Madeleine," she said.

"I was put up for adoption as soon as I was born," he said. "I learned later that Madeleine had me in secret, away from everyone she used to hang around with in London. That was before she moved up here. She mustn't have been able to bear the thought that I was the proof of what my father had done to her. But she did the best she could by me. I had a happy childhood, a warm and safe one at that. My parents, my adopted parents, they looked after me. We didn't have much growing up. We moved to Southampton when I was a teenager. Then, on my eighteenth birthday, I was told that I had been adopted. Can you believe that? 'Happy birthday son, you're a man now, we're not your parents'."

"That must have been hard," said Amita, a pang of sympathy making her heart hurt.

"Hard?" he laughed again. "It's devastating. To know your parents didn't want you, or couldn't care for you – to not know why, it sent me reeling."

"What did you do?" she asked.

"That's the thing about losing your past; it blows away your future, too. I ran away. I joined the Navy, saw a bit of action, too, as it happens. The ship I was on was sent to the Gulf. Five years fighting the bad guys and seeing the world, only to come back here into the sodding rain and still not know who you are. That's the thing about the military, it gives you a sense of pride and belonging. But when you're done with it, you're out on your arse."

"That's not true, Geoff," said Amita. "There are plenty of charities that help veterans. The W.I. does fundraising for them every year –"

"You don't know what it's like!" he shouted. "You don't know what it's like to have to rely on hand-outs and freebies. To have nothing of your own, to not even have a roof over your head at night. When you've dossed in every major city in this country, you quickly learn that the only person looking out for you is you. Nobody is going to help you. And that's when I started thinking."

"About Madeleine?" asked Amita.

Billings nodded. "I went back to Southampton to my adoptive parents. My dad had died a few years before. I had it out with Mum. I asked her, demanded that she told me where I came from, where they adopted me. She gave me all the paperwork she still had. That's when I started to trace things back from the moment they adopted me to the moment I was born, and before."

"And you found out about Starbuck."

"Yeah, I found out," he smirked. "Despite the name not being registered, I saw the stories in the press. The dates told me all I needed to know. I found out what a total bastard he was and what he did to Madeleine. I even visited him in prison. This must have been about two or three years before he died. The smug git was pleased to see me, said he'd always thought he'd have a kid out there in the big bad world, somebody to carry on his 'legacy', as he called it. Said I was no mistake, said I was the product of two people who were destined to be together, no matter the odds."

"He was ill," said Amita. "He wasn't a well man, Geoff. There were psychiatric reports that should have raised concerns about him long before he took Madeleine."

"Yeah, maybe," he sniffed. "Only it didn't matter, not back then, and not now. That one meeting, that's all I had with him, and he sat there, smug, arrogant. He looked about the visiting room and declared to everyone else that I was his son. I was so embarrassed, but he seemed to enjoy the fact I was squirming in front of him. I was a fully grown man and I felt like a frightened little boy all over again. I don't know how he did that, how he could control my feelings so well. He was a monster, a total monster. I hated him. I hated him when I found out what he did to Madeleine. The idea that his blood ran in my veins made me want to be sick. It still does. I hated him. I *hate* him."

"And what about Madeleine?" Amita asked. "How did she take the news about you?"

"I tried to find her," he said. "I tried everywhere, I tried everything. There was no trace of her anywhere. It was like she'd fallen off the planet."

"She had good friends," said Amita. "She had help to make sure something terrible never happened to her again, and Starbuck would never be able to find her if he ever was released."

"And he didn't," said Billings. "But I did. I did eventually. When you're in the military, they teach you to think on your feet, to never rule anything out. Nothing is impossible. If you need to solve a problem, go for the easiest option, it's usually the simplest. So I did. I became a postman. I joined the postal service and suddenly I had access to millions of names, millions of billing addresses, everything I could have ever wished for. When I found her records, her new name, it all made sense. She came up here to the Lake District to get away from everything. I asked about, dug deep, found a few old faces from the sixties who she used to hang around with. And that old bouncer – Sandy – his name kept coming up. So I followed him, followed the paper trail, started piecing it together based on when I was born, where she could have gone from there. I knew they were close and it made sense she would stick with him. The census records gave me all the information I needed. It was a start, enough for me to get my feet on the ground and start putting faces to names. Even the changed ones. Of course she would come to a place like this. Of course she would get as far away from Starbuck as she could."

"So you transferred," said Amita. "You started on this beat up here so you could get close to her. Only it took you a long while. Somebody said you've been here for years?"

Billings nodded. He bowed his head, almost ashamed of what he was about to say.

"I was frightened," he said.

"Frightened?" Amita blurted. "Frightened of what?"

"Frightened of what she would think of me, what she might say," he said. "I remember the first time I saw her, in real life I mean, not in a magazine or online. She was the most beautiful, glamorous person I ever laid eyes on. She was in a supermarket, shopping. She moved with such grace and elegance. She was like a ray of sunshine, a beaming beacon. She oozed charm and charisma. She was destined to be on the stage, and that bastard Starbuck ruined all that for her. And for me."

Amita rubbed her forehead. Jason hadn't moved or made a noise in a very long time. He needed an ambulance. She had to find a way to get out to him.

"So what happened then?" she asked. "The day you 'found' her in the back garden. That story was all a load of rubbish, I take it?"

"I wrote to her," said Billings. "I told her who I was and that I wanted to meet her. I even delivered the letters myself. I never let her see me – she had that fancy letterbox on the main road. She would recognise me, I knew. She *did* recognise me when I finally plucked up the courage to confront her."

"She never wrote back?"

"Never," he said. "Not once. And I'd had enough. I'm fifty. I've spent my life living in the shadows, being a nobody – I'd had enough. I needed to speak to her. So I went to her home. I knocked on the door and her housekeeper let me in."

"Edna," said Amita. "We met her, questioned her. We thought she might have had something to do with Madeleine's death."

"Don't be ridiculous!" Billings scoffed. "That old bat had nothing to do with it except that she let me into the house. But I'll tell you something for nothing – she used to tell me stories about Madeleine when I gave her a lift into town. She was trying to talk Madeleine into signing over the house. She wasn't supposed to be there that day. Madeleine had given her the afternoon off. She was only back to feed that mangy cat."

"What happened?" Amita asked, her heart beating faster.

Billings came closer. "I told Madeleine who I was. Just like that. Years, decades of hiding in fear, all over in a matter of seconds," he said. "I told her and she believed me. She told me she had always known this day was coming, that she would have to face her past and that she had hoped, almost wished and prayed, that she would die before it ever happened. She was tortured, you see. It ate her up inside."

"What did?" asked Amita.

"The fact that she had a child, her own flesh and blood, a son that she so desperately wanted to love, to adore, but she couldn't. She couldn't because everything about that child, about me, would remind her of that monster Starbuck and what he had done to her. She told me this, she told me how much it had haunted her all these years. And I told her I loved her, that I had always loved her and that I had forgiven her for everything she had done. For a moment, I thought it was everything I'd ever wanted. But it wasn't enough for her, even the forgiveness of her own son, wasn't enough . . ."

He trailed off. He was standing right in front of Amita now, but he wasn't looking at her. He was fixated on a picture on the wall, one that had survived his rampage. It was of Madeleine, smiling, as she greeted the Queen and the Duke of Edinburgh at some black-tie event.

"What happened, Geoff?" said Amita, her voice barely louder than a whisper. "What happened to Madeleine?"

"I saw the housekeeper leaving," he said. "I watched her go. When she was safely gone, I told Madeleine, my mother, that I wanted to be a part of her life. But she said it was too late. She wanted me to leave her alone and live out my own life without her. She was crying, I remember that. I begged her. I threatened to go to the newspapers, to expose the whole affair, to show the world that I was the secret child of a famous singer and a monster. She said she didn't care about the newspapers. She said she didn't care about anything. She said Freddy had done that to her. She even said we had that in common – two lives ruined by my father. I thought that meant there was hope, that she understood me.

"Then the housekeeper came back. She was moaning about something or other, saying she had to feed the cat. But I managed to stop her before she found my mother all distraught. A quick hit to the back of the head, that's what they taught us in the service. It was a quick blow – just enough to put her out cold for a little bit. No lasting damage. But my mother saw. Said it confirmed everything she feared – if I'd done that to Edna, maybe there was more of my father than of her in me. She called the ambulance. The old dragon was fine, but Madeleine said that was it, there was no hope for a relationship between us if I could do that to a defenceless old lady. She was so sad, so old-looking, devastated that I had turned up, that I had brought all of those memories back to her after such a long time. And at that moment I knew what I had to do. I had to free her, to put her out of the misery of a lifetime of bad memories and trauma. So I did."

"What did you do?" asked Amita.

"I hugged her," he said, a single tear rolling down his cheek. "And then I threw her down the stairs. It was so simple. She didn't even scream. I was too quick for her, too strong. I must have stood there looking at her body for about an hour, maybe longer. I don't know if I wanted her to be okay or not. That sounds strange, doesn't it, thinking that about your own mother, your own flesh and blood? But I knew she had suffered for so long at the hands of my father. I knew deep down that this was the best thing for her."

Amita's hands were shaking, her whole body quivering. She didn't dare take her eyes off Billings as he loomed over her.

"And then, because I knew it would be the last time, the only time, I lay down next to her. Held her hand. I don't know how long I stayed like that. I came to my senses about two in the morning," he said. "The cat, of all things, woke me up when it walked across my neck."

"Tumnus," Amita whispered.

"I knew I had to do something. I knew it would be too dangerous to leave her there. So I lifted her and carried her into the back yard. Then I propped a ladder and bucket beside her to make it look like she'd had an accident. And it worked too. I went to work as normal the next day. Did my route, and phoned the police when I got to Madeleine's place. They took one look and assumed the obvious. I've spent the past few months waiting on that door going and the police coming to lift me. That's why I'm leaving, tonight – hence the shovel." He lifted it up. "Had a bit of digging to do in the back garden, fastest way to dispose of all this equipment. Can't have a paper trail. I'm leaving and I'm not coming back."

"Gotcha."

Amita and Billings both snapped their heads around towards the door. Jason was standing against the wall, a trickle of blood smeared across his cheek. He was holding his phone up towards them.

"Jason!" Amita shouted. "Please tell me you got all of that."

"Every rotten word," he said, blinking and trying to stay conscious. "Well done, Amita. The Sheriff of Penrith rides again."

"No!" said Billings. "It wasn't meant to happen like this . . ."

Blue lights started flashing outside the house. They lit up the horrible shrine in great waves.

"It's over," said Jason. "Give it up, Billings, and come quietly."

"No!" said the postman, getting angrier. "No, no, no, no!"

"It's finished Geoff, please," said Amita.

"No!"

"Come quietly and they'll understand," said Jason.

"No!"

Billings grabbed Amita by the wrist. He turned and launched the shovel at the window. The glass shattered and he started climbing out, pulling Amita like a rag doll behind him.

"No!" he screamed as they scrambled onto the roof.

Chapter 35

JUMP AND JIVE

The old roof slates were slick from the rain that lashed down in sheets. Amita's trainers slipped as Billings edged up towards the apex. The whole cul-de-sac was awash with police cars and vans. The blue lights flashed and brought much needed illumination to the street.

"Move!" he demanded.

"What good is this going to do you, Geoff?" she asked. "You're only making it worse for yourself."

"Shut up and move!"

They reached the peak of the roof. Billings wobbled a little, unsteady on his own feet. He waddled along the cracked and damaged slates until he reached the precarious chimney stack at the end of the terrace. Amita was in tow, doing her very best not to trip and tumble away.

"Let the woman go, Billings!" came a hard, metallic voice from down on the street. "We have you surrounded. There's nowhere for you to go. Come down and there won't be any trouble."

Amita pushed the wet hair from her face. A policeman in a white cap was shouting up at them through a megaphone. A small army of officers surrounded him, all standing by their cars and vans. In the darkness, she spotted other police too, these ones armed.

"Don't do anything stupid now, mate," said the cop in charge. "Come down and we can keep this civil."

"Civil!" Billings laughed maniacally. "What's so civil about what I've done, eh? And civil isn't sending an armed unit to try and shoot me, either."

He spun Amita around and pulled her close to him. His arm was jammed under her chin as he used her as a shield.

"There, you can't shoot me now, can you?" he laughed again. "You're not going to shoot an innocent old lady just to get to me."

The unmistakable whoop of helicopter blades interrupted him. They both looked up into the rain as a bright, white light drenched them. The police helicopter was hovering above, doing circles around the cul-de-sac, as the whole county turned out in force for the siege.

"This is exciting, isn't it!" he said. "I bet we're on the news tonight."

"You can't be serious, Geoff," said Amita. "You're trying to tell me you're doing all this for *publicity* now? What would your mother think?"

"Who cares what she would think," he tightened his grip around her neck. "She didn't care for me, she didn't want me."

"And you think this is how you should be getting your own back? A standoff with the police? This is the *police*, Geoff, they're not the Boy Scouts. They will shoot you if they think you're a threat to them or me."

"That's a risk I'm willing to take," he said.

Billings squinted up at the helicopter light still hanging over them. He started to wave, a crazed smile on his face.

"Call the media!" he shouted at the chopper. "Get the news down here, I want to make a statement."

Amita was starting to panic. She could feel the adrenaline ramping up as it coursed through her body. She was shivering, with fear and cold, as the rain continued to plummet down. She didn't know how much longer she could keep upright. The roof was getting slippier, and Billings more unstable, as the seconds ticked over.

She spotted movement down near the window they had climbed out of. Police were starting to make their way onto the roof now, creeping as stealthily as they could. This wasn't going to end well.

"Geoff, listen to me," she said. "This is going to get worse before it gets better, for both of us. You need to be sensible."

Billings stopped waving at the helicopter. He looked down across the roof and spotted the armed officers climbing out of the window.

"Stop! Stop right there! I see you!" he screamed. "One more move and I'll throw her off the roof. So help me god, I've done it before and I'll do it again!"

The cops looked at each other and stopped. They were still a good distance away. Amita didn't reckon any of them could reach her in time if Billings decided he had had enough of her.

"Stay back! I'm serious! I'll kill her!" he shouted again.

"Geoff, please," she said. "You're making me nervous. And if I'm getting nervous then so are those police officers."

"Tell them to stay back, then!" he shouted in her ear. "You tell them."

"I think you should stay back," said Amita nervously. "I have good reason to believe that Mr Billings here will be more than willing to act on his threats."

The cops remained silent. They were perched and ready, guns trained on both of them. Amita could hear Billings' breaths behind her getting shorter and quicker. He was getting nervous and that made him even more dangerous than he already was. With the police still too far away, she reasoned that the only person getting her out of this jam would be herself.

"What do you want from all of this, Geoff?" she asked.

"What?"

"All of this, the standoff, up here on the roof, what are you trying to achieve?"

"I don't know," he said. "I can't think. My head is messed up, I can't think straight. I haven't been able to think straight since I killed her. I can't think, I can't focus. I can't do anything. No! I want everyone to know, that's what I want."

"Everyone to know what?"

"That I was her son!" he laughed. "I want the world to know who she was, who she became and that she rejected me – her own son, her own flesh and blood!"

"That won't matter if you're dead," she said.

"It will to me!" he rasped. "The world will know, the press, the media, your son-in-law. He'll write about it, everyone will write about it, about how I'm Maddy Forster's son."

"It doesn't have to be like this," she pleaded. "Let these people help you, Geoff. Let me go and we can all go back downstairs and sort out this whole mess. Wouldn't that be nice? Certainly nicer than being up here in the pouring rain."

Billings hesitated. Amita thought she felt his grip loosen a little under her neck. Then it tightened again.

"No, you're trying to trick me," he said. "You're working for them, aren't you? That's how you found me, that's how you found my room with my pictures and my computer. That's how you knew about Madeleine."

"I'm not working for the police, Geoff," said Amita.

"Then how did you find me?"

Amita pondered that question for a moment. How had she found him? To explain to him everything that had gone on over the past few weeks would be far too long-winded. How did she explain to a man on the edge that it had all been down to the members of the Penrith bingo club – whether that was Sandy's secret history, or Father Ford's throwaway remarks about Geoff's troubled state. That might tip him over the edge completely. Or worse still, *she* might be for the tipping.

"It doesn't matter now," she said diplomatically. "It's all over, Geoff. You've got nowhere to run and nowhere to hide. These police officers, they're trained professionals. And they can wait you out longer than you can hold out."

Billings was silent. Amita sensed she might have his attention.

"Look at them, down there," she said. "There must be two dozen, maybe more of them. They've turned out in force, Geoff. This is only going to end one way, and it's not with you being allowed to get to your car and drive off into the sunset. Everything you choose to do now is only going to go against you when it gets to court. You're not your father, Geoff, you have to remember that."

His grip loosened around her. Amita sensed her opportunity and risked a step forward. There was no resistance from Billings. She saw the police starting to move but she batted them away. Turning to face the postman, she silently admitted she had great pity for him in that all too brief moment.

"You aren't Freddie Starbuck," she said to him again. "What you've done is unforgivable, Geoff – Madeleine didn't deserve to die – but let them see you're sorry, that the madness ends here. You'll have to face the consequences, but this standoff isn't going to help you."

Billings was crying now. The bright, white light floodlight shone down on him, sending dark, long shadows over his eyes and beneath his nose. He wiped away the rain water, shoulders slumped, defeated.

"I'm sorry," he said. "I'm so, so sorry. I only wanted her to love me, like I loved her."

"I know, Geoff," said Amita, her own heart breaking. "It was just one of those things. As I always tell my son-in-law, Jason, some things are not meant to be. And there's nothing we can do about it, I'm afraid. We can't control others' feelings – only our own actions."

Billings nodded in agreement. The anger was gone from him now. He looked empty. He looked like a man who had spent his life running marathons in treacle. Now it looked like she might be getting down from here in one piece, Amita couldn't help but have great pity for everything that had happened to him. That didn't excuse what he did to Madeleine. But then again, after everything she learned, Amita wasn't so sure that her friend had acted in the best possible way.

"I'm sorry," he said to her again. "You're right."

"About what?" she asked.

"About everything. This mess, everything. I'm not my father. I'm my own man. And I've spent all of my life thinking otherwise. I need to face the consequences, no matter what they are. I shouldn't have done what I did. And I am truly sorry. I'm tired now, so very, very tired. I need to rest."

He took a step backwards, and leaned back to rest on the shaky chimney stack. It began to wobble.

Amita reached out for him. "Geoff!" she screamed.

His weight was too much for the damaged bricks and mortar. The chimney stack fell away behind him like a crumbling meringue. As he fell, he caught Amita's eye and seemed to linger there for an eternity. Then, with little more than a whimper, he disappeared over the lip of the roof. A second passed and there was a thud as the remnants of the ancient chimney stack cracked and toppled on top of his lifeless body two floors down.

"Oh god," said Amita, her hand to her mouth.

The police were all around her now. She was helped down from the roof before she even knew what was going on. A thick, woollen blanket wrapped around her shoulders, she was led through the house and out into the cul-de-sac where an ambulance crew were waiting for her.

It had all happened so quickly, she didn't quite know where to begin. One moment she had been standing facing Geoff Billings, the next she was in a speeding ambulance being treated by paramedics. All she could do was sit there and let everything happen in front of her.

One thing she did know, however, was that it was over.

Chapter 36

THREE DOZEN

The house felt cold and unloved. The hallway was dark, the kitchen beyond it, so normally full of life, desolate. Even the living room felt like a wasteland, the television having a well-deserved few hours off. Not that any of it mattered to Amita. She was simply glad to be out of the hospital and back in her familiar surroundings.

She flipped the switch and the hall lights came on. In an instant, the whole place changed. The house she had left what felt like an eternity ago was back. The familiar wallpaper, the pictures of the kids on the walls. Even the little mark on the carpet, the one that looked suspiciously like a cigarette burn, the one nobody could remember how it got there. She was home.

"Can you believe that?" said Jason, bundling in behind her, shopping bags making his hands burn. "Forty quid for a taxi. We only travelled five miles. Somebody do the maths, work out how much that is per mile."

"You don't know what forty divided by five is?" asked Radha, coming up behind.

"Eight!" shouted Josh.

"Eight!" agreed Clara.

The front door was closed behind them and Amita breathed a sigh of relief. There was a finality about that familiar sound. It meant they were safe. After an overnight stay in the hospital she longed for her own bed, her own surroundings, her own family. If the past few weeks had taught her anything it was that those she held most dear were worth treasuring. Madeleine and Geoff had never had that luxury.

"You okay, Mum?" asked Radha.

"Yes darling, I'm fine," she said. "Really glad to be back home is all. Having a bit of a moment."

"Should I get some paper towels?" asked Jason.

"Jason!" Radha chastised him. "Why don't you go and sit down in the living room, Mum? We'll get all this stuff sorted out. You've had a time of it."

"Hey!" Jason shouted. "I've had a time of it too, you know. Have you felt the top of my head? It's like I've got a golf ball – actually, scrap that – a *baseball* growing out of my crown."

"You're a fit and healthy man," said Radha. "And Mum is –"

"Choose your next words very carefully, my darling," Amita smiled.

"Mum isn't," Radha said with a grin. "Go in, we can tidy up here. You put your feet up and rest. That's what the doctors said, wasn't it?"

Amita nodded. She took her daughter's advice and headed into the living room. She slipped into her chair and closed her eyes. The sound of the family home coming alive made her drowsy. The voices, the footsteps, the comfort. It was everything she had wanted and longed for. Never again, she vowed, would she ever take this for granted.

The doorbell rang. Nobody seemed to notice. It rang again. Amita opened her eyes. She could hear Jason and Radha in the kitchen, unpacking the groceries. The children had vanished upstairs. There was nothing else for it. Pushing herself up from the chair, she limped and hobbled, stiff from her excursion onto the roof of Billings' house.

The doorbell rang for a third time and she shouted, "We're here! Just coming, just coming."

She opened the door and the strange sight of Detective Inspector Alby *smiling* met her. It made her recoil. Then she remembered her manners. "DI Alby," she said. "What a surprise."

"Mrs Khatri," said the old cop. "The pleasure is all mine."

"I didn't say it was a pleasure," she said.

"No, you didn't," his face still stretched into a forced smile. "But that's what people say to each other when they're trying to get along, isn't it?"

"Yes, it is. Not that you would know anything about that."

"Who are you talking to out here?" asked Jason, coming into the hall from the kitchen. "Oh. Alby. What a surprise."

"Yes I was just saying to your mother-in-law that the pleasure is . . . oh stuff it, I can't keep up the pretence any longer. Can I come in?"

He pushed the door open and barged past Amita.

"This the living room?" he pointed and stomped inside.

Amita and Jason looked at each other. They followed him after a moment and found him lounging on the couch.

"To what do we owe this unpleasantness?" asked Jason. "I see you don't have your enforcers with you, so can we assume we're not getting dragged down to the station this evening?"

"No, that won't be necessary," said the cop.

"Oh, what a shame," said Jason. "I was just saying to my mother-in-law how the ideal first evening home, after everything we've been through, would have been to see the delightfully bland interior of Penrith Police Station. It would have been just the sweet treat after our recent trauma."

"Yes, very good, Brazel," Alby dropped his smile. "You still haven't been asked on tour with Michael McIntyre yet?"

"Would you two stop it, please?" said Amita. "Detective Inspector, I assume this isn't a social call."

"No, it's not," said Alby. "You don't really get social calls in my line of work, Mrs Khatri." He took a quick glance at his watch. Cocking his eyebrow, he turned his attention back to them. "I'm here, firstly, to offer the sincerest thanks from Cumbria Police for your recent efforts. We, of course, appreciate any and all help from the public in investigations. However, I have to informally warn you both that your actions cannot be repeated in any shape or form, as police work should be left to the professionals. Is that understood?"

"Wait a minute," said Jason, waving his hands. "You're thanking us on one hand and chastising us with the other? We caught a murderer for you guys. In fact, if it hadn't been for Amita and me, you wouldn't have even *known* it was a murder at all!"

"Correct," said Alby, a smug smile on his face. "And for the record, it's Cumbria Police speaking, not me. I can't stand the sight of either of you, especially you, Brazel. So I am little more than a messenger, if you can believe that. A lifetime dedicated to law enforcement and my last duty is to deliver a grovelling apology. Where's the justice?"

"There wouldn't have been any justice if it had been left to your lot," said Jason spitefully. "It took a siege with helicopters and armed police, only after a worn-down hack and his do-gooder mother-in-law had cracked the case. Your lot didn't even realise there *was* a case. What does that say about your law enforcement, Alby?"

Alby said nothing. He sat smiling, hands clasped over his chest. He occasionally glanced at his watch, as casual and calm as either of them had ever seen him.

"That's enough, Jason," said Amita. "We appreciate your delivery of the message, Detective Inspector. We appreciate your effort and concern, too."

Jason knew when to keep his mouth shut. He also knew when he was being told to do so by Amita. He stood there and cursed silently.

"What's all the shouting going on in here?" asked Radha. "Oh, I didn't realise we had company."

Alby got up. He offered his hand to her and she took it, looking to her mother and husband for guidance.

"Don't worry about me," he said. "I was just leaving."

"Oh, okay, that's not strange at all."

"Strange," Alby laughed. "Lady, you lot have got strange down to a whole new level."

He shuffled out of the living room door.

Radha was confused. She looked to Amita and Jason. "Okay, I know you two have been up to some really odd things in the past few weeks. But do you want to tell me who the heck that was?"

"Alby," said Jason. "DI Alby, the one who thought I'd stolen . . . the . . . wait!"

He hurried out of the living room and raced to the front door. Alby was at the front gate and heading for his car. Jason chased after him, the wet and cold creeping up his socks.

"Alby!" he shouted. "Alby, hold on!"

"Look, Brazel, I don't do goodbye kisses, that's not my style, okay?" he cackled, getting into his car.

"No, wait," said Jason, banging on the window. "The photocopiers and printers from the *Standard*. Whatever happened with that?"

Alby turned on the car engine. He looked down at his watch and snorted. Rolling the window down, he looked up at Jason.

"You were right," he said.

"I was?" Jason asked. "That doesn't sound like me."

"You were right," Alby said again. "It *wasn't* you who nicked all those photocopiers and the other paraphernalia from the offices."

"I did tell you."

"You did," said Alby. "It seems that some of the renovators were getting sticky-fingered and a little too deep in debt outside of work to resist the temptation. They work for Rory Francis – you'd have thought they'd be coining it in, the number of new builds and renovations he has on the go. But it turns out they were after a little extra on the side. It only came to light when they were questioned over an assault that took place at the offices."

"Assault?" asked Jason.

"Yeah. Some old boy took three of them on. Gave them quite a thrashing, by all accounts."

Jason gulped.

"When they wanted to press charges, we started looking into their history and there were a few red marks that the computer system didn't like." He checked his watch again. "That's that, then," he said, tapping the face.

"What's what, then?" asked Jason.

"It's six o'clock, end of the shift. My last shift. I am now, officially, no longer a police officer. Just like that, the tick of a hand and it's all gone."

He revved the engine and Jason stood back.

"See you around, Brazel," he said with a wicked smile. "Or better yet, never see you again."

"You're not a cop anymore, then?" asked Jason.

"Didn't you hear what I just said, you moron?"

"So that means you're just another citizen, like me?"

"Your detective skills know no limit, Brazel. Have you ever thought about becoming a police officer?"

"So I can say what I like to you?"

"I guess, if I cared enough to listen," said the now retired DI Alby. "But as it happens, I don't. I've got a great granddaughter to care for and her mother who likes to put up videos on the internet of live police incidents involving murderers and local do-gooders fighting it out on rooftops."

"Stacey?" Jason gulped. "She did what?"

"She was driving home from some party and sees flashing blue lights in the distance, didn't she," Alby gritted his teeth. "I tell you, that girl has either the best or the worst luck in the world. She's always in the thick of the bloody action – like a magnet to trouble."

"You mean the siege with Billings?" Jason could hardly believe it.

"The very same. Worse yet, she got her bloody phone and started recording the whole thing on the internet. You should have seen the stick I got for that when my bosses put two and two together and realised it was Stacey. It's gone viral, or whatever they call it. She says she's never had more business. She's some sort of minor celebrity now, thanks to you."

For the briefest moment, Jason felt like he had something in common with the retired detective. He was about to tell him so when Alby tipped him a wink. The former DI pulled off in a puff of burning rubber and squealing wheel-spin. He raced up the road and into the night. Jason watched him go before turning back up the path and heading to the door.

He closed it behind him and stood there for a moment. He squelched his feet on the mat and tutted loudly. As he bent down to pull his socks off, the doorbell went again.

"You've got to be kidding me," he said, straightening up with a crack. "What's wrong, Alby, changed your mind on that goodbye kiss?"

He opened the door and gaped. The Ghost stood on the threshold, his little dog sitting obediently at his feet. Only he was nothing like The Ghost Jason had seen before. This was a whole new Ghost. Gone was the heavy raincoat, the cap and the scraggly beard. Instead, the old man with the sunken eyes was clean shaven, his white hair combed across his head. He wore an ill-fitting suede tuxedo and he was holding a bunch of flowers up like a shield.

"Good evening," he said, clearing his throat. "Is Mrs Amita Khatri in, by any chance?"

"Pardon me?"

"Mrs Amita Khatri. Is she home, at all?"

"What's going on out here?"

Radha and Amita came out of the living room. They were almost as shocked as Jason when they saw The Ghost standing in the doorway with his flowers and dog.

"Oh my," said Amita.

"Now, who is this?" asked Radha.

"Mrs Khatri, my name is Irvine Carruthers and I have admired you from afar for a very long time," he gave a little bow.

"This is the guy, Amita!" Jason shouted. "This is the guy I said was at the vigil. And he cornered me in the pub that night. He told me I should pay attention to you, that you were right."

"He did?" asked Amita.

"I did," said Carruthers. "You all don't realise how wonderful, intelligent and beautiful a woman you have in your family. You probably don't realise that, while I sit quietly at bingo with the other gentlemen on the corner table, I hear everything. I know who's looking out for others and who's only in it for themselves. And I knew that you'd do right by Madeleine, Mrs Khatri. While everyone else was drinking tea and crying, only you saw the truth. Well, maybe you and Ethel. You've got a sharp mind, Mrs K, and it's high time I told you of my esteem."

"Aw, how sweet," said Radha.

"Pass me a bucket," said Jason. "I feel a bit ill."

"That's very kind of you, Mr Carruthers," said Amita. "But I'm afraid I'll have to be perfectly honest and say that I don't recall us ever having spoken."

"That's quite alright, Mrs Khatri," he said. "I can completely understand. I have been something of a waif for a very long time. I've always been better with numbers than words. Part of the reason I like bingo, the numbers – well that and the good Digestives. But since I first set eyes on you at bingo I have been something of a fan. Who else stands up to Mrs Littlejohn? Your recent antics in bringing that swine Billings to justice got me thinking. Life is far too short to spend not telling the ones you love that you do, in fact, admire them. That's why I'm here tonight, to act on my own advice. Your son-in-law was kind enough to entertain me these past few weeks with my questions here and there. And therefore I wondered if you would answer me one last question?"

Carruthers went to bend down but got stuck halfway. His little dog started yapping excitedly. In what was possibly the world's slowest bow, he straightened up again and fought off a grimace as he looked Amita straight in the eye.

"Would you do me the honour, Mrs K, of joining me for an evening of dinner and bingo? Not locally, mind. I thought perhaps somewhere a bit more glamorous – Carlisle. They have jackpots there of a million pounds."

Jason's jaw dropped. Radha was silent. The only one who still had any control of her senses was Amita. She tilted her head to one side and smiled warmly at Carruthers.

"Oh you dear, sweet man," she said. "I think you should come in for a cup of tea and a sit down. I'll get the biscuits."

Carruthers tried to step forward but he couldn't, his back locked. Amita and Radha rushed to help him inside as Jason watched on. The past few weeks had been strange, but this was a whole new level.

"That's it," he said. "I'm off to write up my article."

Chapter 37

MORE THAN ELEVEN

"I thought we had been through this already, Jason? We're not Starsky and Hutch, would you *please* slow down!"

Some things never changed. Amita was still moaning about Jason's driving. They would still be going to bingo every Wednesday night week in, week out, the same old routine. But that was okay. This was their first journey there since it all happened, and they were back in their happy place, though neither had to say that out loud to the other.

Much to his surprise, Jason found himself easing off the accelerator. The routine might be the same but he clearly wasn't. His new-found fame from having bylines in all the major newspapers around the country must be going to his head. He smiled at the thought.

"Do you have your glasses?" he asked Amita, sat beside him.

"Yes," she said. "And my pens and my phone and something to eat at half time."

"Don't you normally get a cup of tea and a scone or something?"

"I'm on a diet," she said.

Jason laughed. His mother-in-law didn't.

"Are you serious?" he asked.

"Of course I'm serious. Why wouldn't I be?"

"A diet? You? What for?"

Amita unzipped her handbag. She rummaged around for a moment before producing a pair of rice cakes wrapped in cling-film.

"What are those?" he asked, switching between her snack and the road. "They look like they're made of polystyrene."

"If there's one thing I learned from being dragged onto a slippery roof by a murderer, it's that I could stand to improve my fitness, Jason," she said.

"Amita, I can guarantee you that you are much fitter than most women your age. Probably most people *any* age."

"That's very kind of you," she said, returning the rice cakes to her bag. "But it gave me a bit of a fright, you know, all of that."

He felt bad for mocking her. The full impact of what they had been through hadn't really settled in yet. In the month since that fateful night in Bowscar when Geoff Billings had died everything had passed like a blur. The police had offered them both counselling for the trauma, but neither had taken up the offer. For Amita, she had just wanted to be at home with her family. For Jason, he was on the clock to write and submit his story that detailed everything in its entirety. He had been busier in the past four weeks than he had in his last five years of local journalism. Not that he was complaining.

"I know it did," he said solemnly. "It gave me a fright, too. More than a fright, actually."

"I don't know why. You were knocked out for most of it."

"I beg your pardon. It was me who called the cops, remember. And I was . . ."

He trailed off when he saw that his mother-in-law was sniggering.

"Oh ha ha, very funny," he said. "Yes, yes, lap it up. Make fun of the cavalry that saved the day. You didn't have to sit in A&E for three hours with a lump the size of a tennis ball sticking out the top of your head."

"No, you're right," she said. "That was very brave of you and I'm very proud of you. You know that already, Jason."

"Thank you," he said.

They pulled up a little way from the church hall. Amita got her things together and took a deep breath.

"You okay?" he asked.

"Yes, just trying to get myself into the zone for tonight," she said. "I haven't been back since all this terrible business unfolded. And I bet Georgie Littlejohn will have plenty to say."

"Yeah, she's a piece of work, isn't she."

"She is," Amita smiled. "Still, we shouldn't be too bitter towards her. She did help out by giving us Billings' address in the end. Without that, we wouldn't have caught him before he left and we might never have got to the bottom of it all."

"Hm, 'help' is a bit strong," he said. "Did I mention the lump on the top of my head? *That's* helping. Not sending an address from your network of spies."

"Jason," she said in her usual tone. "Now, now."

He stared out of the windscreen. It was a lovely, clear night. He could see straight down the main road, the warm glow of the church hall spilling out onto the pavement. The usual lingering smokers were hanging around, their Lowry-like figures moving and shuffling close to the steps.

Then he did something he hadn't expected he would ever do.

"Would you like me to come in with you?" he asked.

Amita, it seemed, was just as shocked as he was.

"What?" she gulped.

"Do you want me to come to the bingo with you tonight? Save you facing the music on your own."

"Sure, yes, of course," she said. "I would be delighted. Gosh, Jason, I'm not sure I know what to say."

"Oh, stop it," he said, opening the door. "You'll need to keep me right with all the rules. I reckon I'll be pretty hopeless at it."

Amita got out of the car and joined him. A beaming pride, a burning happiness, filled her chest. It had been a very long time since she had felt something as strong, as potent, as that. If it hadn't been so public, she might even have given him a hug.

They reached the steps as Sandy was crushing out his cigarette. When he saw Amita, his face lit up. He, it turned out, had no problems with hugging in public.

"Amita!" he bellowed, scooping her up in his big arms. "It's so good to see you back here."

"And you, too, Sandy," she said, catching her breath. "I'm so glad you're okay. We heard that you were arrested."

"Oh, nothing to worry about," he said. "A slap on the wrist for fighting, and being told I should know better at my age. Most exciting thing that's happened to me in years. And Jason, how lovely to see you, son. I read your story. It was very touching, very thorough."

He offered Jason his big paw. He almost crushed his hand and pulled his arm out of its socket. When he released his grip, Jason was grateful.

"A pleasure, Sandy, an absolute pleasure," he said. "And I'm glad you thought it was fair. You knew Madeleine better than any of us."

"I think a part of her would have been proud to be back in the headlines," he said. "Of course, it would have been much nicer if she was there for her singing and not for her demise. But the truth had to be told – it had to be out there in one form or another. And you did that. So I'm grateful, really very grateful."

"Thank you," Jason said.

The three companions headed up the stairs to where Father Ford was standing by the door. He smiled and opened his arms wide when he saw them coming.

"No," said Amita curtly. "No more hugging, thank you Father. I've had quite enough of that for one night, thank you very much."

"Oh," said the pastor, a little deflated. "Not to be, then. Wonderful to see you though, Amita. We've all been missing you greatly since the unpleasantness in Bowscar. In the case of Geoff Billings, it seems one can never truly know somebody until it is too late."

"He had his own issues, Father Ford, as you hinted at," said Amita. "But he's at peace now. Or at least some sort of peace. I'll leave the theology of what happens after you die to you, if you don't mind."

He bowed and turned to Jason. "And here we have the man of the moment, our resident celebrity journalist," he said. "I thoroughly enjoyed your interview on the radio the other day, Jason. I thought to myself – he has such a lovely speaking voice, I wonder if he would like to do a reading at one of my services."

"No!" Jason shouted, then remembered himself. "Thank you, Father Ford. It's very kind of you to say so, but I won't be doing that. I prefer it when I can hide behind my laptop."

"Humble too, it would seem," said the pastor. "God opposes the proud but shows favour to the humble."

"Something like that," said Jason. "Shall we?"

Father Ford dropped out of his little biblical daydream and stepped inside. The church hall was warm and welcoming. The place looked almost full. Amita had lost track of time; they were late. That meant she wouldn't be able to pick a seat. Left to the fates once more, she and Jason took tentative steps towards the long tables.

The hubbub stopped instantly. All the chat, all the laughing, all the bickering and the gossip came to a halt. Every set of bespectacled eyes turned to Amita and Jason.

Then there was a clap from the corner. It was Sandy, standing tall, a big smile on his broad face. He clapped again. And again. With every clap of his big hands, somebody else joined him. A few stood up, then a few more. A whole table all at once and then some of the outliers. Soon, the whole hall was on its feet, clapping, whooping, whistling and cheering Amita and Jason.

Amita took Jason's hand. She squeezed it tightly and he squeezed back. She started to cry and was instantly embarrassed by the whole thing. Jason put a comforting arm around her shoulders as the applause continued.

"Did you know anything about this?" she asked him, over the din.

"No, not at all," he said. "And, if it helps, I'm as red-faced as you are."

She clapped him on the chest. They stood and enjoyed their moment a while longer before Father Ford took to the stage and warmed up his bingo balls. Slowly, everyone settled back down into their seats. Everyone, but Georgie Littlejohn. She stood waving from her usual spot in the corner.

"Coo-eee!" she shouted. "I've saved you a seat, Amita. Here, between me and Mr Carruthers."

"Great," Amita said under her breath. "I think I preferred it when she didn't like me."

"Now, now, Amita," said Jason, walking by her side. "What is it you always say to me? Play nicely."

"Touché," she said.

They sat down beside Georgie who cleared away the bags, coats, umbrellas and every other item of paraphernalia she had used to secure the end of the table. On pain of death, should somebody sit down before her chosen one.

"It's so lovely to see you. To see you *both*," Georgie said. "And Amita, look who's joining us."

"Yes," said Amita, feeling utterly awkward. "Nice to see you, too."

Irvine nodded and smiled warmly back at her. Bingo in Carlisle was still a week away. And Amita didn't want to get too familiar before she was treated to a whole evening of Irvine Carruthers' company.

"Okay, ladies and gentlemen, eyes down please for a full house," said Father Ford.

Mercifully, Georgie Littlejohn wouldn't dare speak over the first game. Amita had never been more relieved.

"Remind me to catch up with you at half time," she whispered to Amita. "I've got an idea of how to spend the vigil money."

"Vigil money?" asked Amita, missing the first number.

"Yes, the vigil money. I've got it sitting in my bank account. It's not going to that Billings now, rest his cursed soul. But I've got a rather nice idea about how we could spend it instead."

She tapped the end of her nose and went back to her game. Amita said nothing. She felt a nudge on her side as Father Ford began.

"Queen Bee, seventy-three. Top of the shop, number ninety. Half a century, fifty. Oh, what do we have here, it's legs eleven."

The bingo club wolf-whistled in unison.

Amita turned and saw Jason leaning in close to her.

"What's a house?" he asked.

"Ssshhh" hissed the table.

Amita was back in the heart of the bingo club. And it was like she had never been away.

Chapter 38

CHRISTMAS CAKE

Ullswater was perfectly still. The lake shimmered like a polished mirror, the reflection of the great hills and mountains that cradled it perfectly rendered on its surface. The whole place was tranquil and serene, the weak mid-morning sun looking down with an approving glow.

Into this serenity rolled a minibus filled with pensioners. The Penrith bingo club had booked their place on one of the famous steamers for the day. No sooner had the wheels come to a halt and the parking gear been pulled than they were breaking nature's silence like a flock of gabbing geese.

"Oh, this is simply wonderful," said Georgie Littlejohn, stepping off first, the group's unelected tour guide. "You know, you live on the doorstep of somewhere as amazing as this and you never come to see it. It's a bloody shame."

"Aye," said Sandy, stepping down behind her. "A shame we're all shouting and bawling and scaring away the fish."

"Fish? I'll take salt and vinegar and mushy peas!" Ethel cried from the back of the minibus, as the driver let her down gently in her wheelchair.

Amita stepped off and took a large gulp of the fresh morning air. She spotted their transport for the day sitting at the end of the jetty. A splendid-looking vessel, her bright red funnel standing tall and proud against the backdrop of the lake. She had been sceptical at first when Georgie had revealed her plans for the money collected at Madeleine's vigil. The thought of spending any extended time with her rival didn't fill Amita with great hope.

Now that she was here, however, it felt like a wonderful idea. The open water, glorious surroundings, and a chance to reflect and relax, seemed like just the ticket.

"It's claimed this boat we're going on is one of the, if not *the*, oldest working passenger ferries in the world."

Amita closed her eyes. Just once, only once, she would like to have enjoyed the moment.

"Doesn't fill you with a great deal of confidence, does it?"

"Thank you Jason," she said. "That's just what I wanted to hear."

"It says so in this leaflet here."

She looked down at the pamphlet in his hands.

He pointed at the information box on the back and shrugged. "You would think that they'd get something a bit more modern, wouldn't you? I mean, from a health and safety point of view alone."

"Can't you simply enjoy it for what it is?" she asked. "A lovely day out in one of the most beautiful parts of the country. If not the world. Don't you think the fact the ship is *still* sailing is testimony to just how valued and cherished the elderly should be?"

Jason shot her a sceptical look.

"And besides, I don't know how you managed to wangle your way onto this trip," she said sniffily. "I thought this was for members of the club only."

"Oh, it's like that, is it?" he said, raising his nose. "I beat you once at your own game and suddenly it becomes too good for riff-raff like me."

"You won one house, Jason, that doesn't make you champion of the world."

"One more house than you won, that's for certain."

They both laughed at that. Georgie was gathering the dozen or so members of the club who had ventured out on the day trip. Corralling them like a sheep dog, she stood at the head of the procession just short of the entrance to the jetty.

"Oh lord," said Jason under his breath. "The holiday camp commandant wants to address us before we all have a good time."

"Jason," Amita hushed him down.

"Hello, ladies and gents," said Georgie. "We've made it. And isn't it stunning here? Absolutely wonderful. It looks like we'll have a nice day for it, too. So fingers crossed. I'm about to go and speak to the captain and hopefully we'll be on our way very soon. But I thought I'd say a few words before we go."

"Great," said Jason. "I thought she might."

"Sshh," Amita said.

"We all miss Madeleine greatly," said Georgie, taking off her sunglasses. "What happened to her is something none of us are likely to forget. Especially two of our members,

Amita and her son-in-law Jason. Without their efforts and dedication to our friend, things might have turned out very differently. Poor Madeleine may never have had the justice she deserved, and a killer might still be delivering our catalogues and Christmas cards. So we thank Amita and Jason, and I know that they appreciate our gratitude."

A muted round of applause went around the group. Sandy patted Jason on the shoulder and Amita looked humble.

"There's a new sheriff in town!" Ethel shouted before cackling.

"Thank you, Ethel," said Georgie, not breaking her stride. "Which brings me neatly on to why we're here. Madeleine was a great lover of Ullswater. She lived just up the road, as you all know. And, with no family left, at first I didn't know what we should do with the money collected in her memory. Then I remembered what she said to me once – friends are the family you choose. So that's why we're here. To enjoy a day on the water and remember our dear friend. I'm sure we'll have a wonderful day and talk about all the good times we shared with Madeleine. And I'm certain that it's what she would have wanted."

Georgie looked up at the clear blue sky, eyes a little glassy.

"This is for you," she said.

The bingo club voiced their agreement and clapped. The group headed on to the jetty and towards the huge steamer waiting to take them across Ullswater. Amita and Jason lingered at the back of the crowd. When they were clear from them, they stopped and looked out at the lake and mountains.

"I think we did a good job," said Amita.

"What?" Jason asked.

"For Madeleine," she said. "I think we did a good job. We saw it through to the end and, like Georgie said, we did her justice."

"Absolutely," said Jason. "I only wish it hadn't been so bloody dangerous. Still, it all worked out in the end. We've lived to tell the tale, and that's all you can ask for in my profession."

"But I'm not a journalist," said Amita.

"No," said Jason, smiling at her. "You're the Sheriff of Penrith. And that's *much* more dangerous."

He put his arm around her shoulder and hugged her. Amita didn't resist, enjoying the moment instead. They set off down the jetty arm-in-arm as Georgie Littlejohn called for them.

"Eyes down . . ."

UK EUROVISION LEGEND'S SECRET SON FACED THE MUSIC FOR HER MURDER

Dateline: Penrith, Cumbria,
UK – By Jason Brazel

UK Eurovision Song Contest legend Maddy Forster was murdered by her estranged son in an act police have called a 'double tragedy'. The pensioner, 70, was discovered in the back courtyard of her property near Ullswater, Cumbria, last month. Initially police considered the death to be an accident, ruling that she had fallen. However, following a standoff with officers in Bowscar last week, it has emerged that she was the victim of a brutal murder at the hands of her estranged son, Geoff Billings.

Detectives initially ruled out foul play in the death, believing that the former singer, more recently known as Madeleine Frobisher, who represented the UK at the 1968 Eurovision, had died following a tragic fall.

The killer had been working in the Penrith area as a postman for the past five years and claimed to have discovered Madeleine's body. After reporting the grim discovery to Cumbria Police, Billings was consoled by the local community and even appeared at Madeleine's funeral in the town.

Madeleine shot to fame in the 1960s before representing her country on the global stage at the competition. She narrowly missed out on victory. Later that year she was the victim of a high-profile kidnapping at the hands of warped serial criminal

Freddie Starbuck. The fiend held and assaulted her for days before she was finally able to make her escape. Starbuck was arrested, charged and jailed. He remained behind bars for the rest of his life due to bad behaviour before finally dying in 2002.

Salford native Madeleine retired to Cumbria where she lived out of the limelight. It has been revealed that she had fallen pregnant with Starbuck's child as a result of his horrific attack on her. The baby was given up for adoption shortly after his birth. The child, Geoff Billings, sought her out in what's been dubbed by one source as 'a lifetime crusade' to find his birth mother. It's understood that Billings confronted Madeleine on the afternoon of her death when he attacked and killed her. He then moved her body into the courtyard to make his discovery appear accidental.

Police were called to Billings' address in Bowscar last week after worried locals reported shouting and screams from his property. Around thirty officers, including an armed response unit, were deployed to the residential street. The incident was filmed and shared on social media, racking up thousands of views in just a few hours. Officers tried to negotiate with Billings before he fell off the roof of the building. He was pronounced dead at the scene. Two members of the public, who didn't wish to be named, have been helping police with their subsequent investigations. Detectives confirmed Madeleine's death had, in fact, been murder and the main suspect was Geoff Billings. The case is now considered closed.

Lawyers representing Madeleine's estate did not wish to make a statement. Donations in memory of Ms Frobisher are being accepted by the Tumnus Foundation, the animal charity due to take over her Ullswater property.

Acknowledgements

When it comes to writing a crime novel, there are invariably too many people to thank all at once. It comes with the territory when you're cooking up horrible things to do to lovely people. I'd be rambling on forever if I were to list every single person who has given me their time, their opinion and advice in the compositing of this book. And I'm eternally grateful for all of the help. But there are a few I'd like to single out for special thanks - it'll be my good deed done for this century.

Firstly - Marion Todd and Emma Christie. The writing of The Bingo Hall Detectives coincided almost exactly with the formation of the Caledonia Crime Collective. As a group of writers, we've supported each other through thick and thin and I'm so thankful for EVERYONE'S help. A special thanks to both Marion and Emma though, who have been invaluable, kind and above all else patient with my various questions and quizzes.

Thank you as always to my agent, Hannah, who continues to champion me, my work and keep me on the straight and narrow, even when I wobble.

I also want to thank Genevieve Pegg and Alice Murphy-Pyle at HarperNorth. They've paid me so many compliments around this book and its weird and wonderful characters that my head can barely get through doors. They have both worked tirelessly to support me and my writing and without them, you wouldn't be anywhere near holding this book in your hands right now. For that, for being great fun and for so many other things, I am forever beholden.

And no acknowledgements section would be complete without a big thank you to my family. To Anne-Marie for her kindness, her patience, her enthusiasm and her love. And to Henry, for being the best listener who lets his daddy play with imaginary people.